TWO

THE LAW IN COTTONWOOD

"Now, boys," the marshal reasoned, "you know one man can't shoot it out with fifteen. I don't want to quarrel with you. There's a reason the town don't want men with guns in it. The guns get used. Usually it's some cowboy that gets shot."

Nobody answered. He said, "The town's waiting for you. The girls. The saloons. The poker game. You'll be treated fairly and you won't need guns."

"What if we don't give up our guns?" one of them snarled.

Marshal Gaunt felt himself go tense. That tenseness and reckless disregard for danger were in his voice when he replied. "Why, then, I guess we'll have to shoot it out right here. You'll get me, boys, but I'll get three of you before you do!"

PRODIGAL GUNFIGHTER

Johnny Yoder stopped pacing and glared at the sheriff. "I'm sick of Slade Teplin," he said fiercely. "The son of a bitch hasn't been here an hour and I'm sick of him. Why the hell can't we just tell him to move on—get out of town. Other towns do and they get away with it."

"This one's different," the sheriff said. "Because this is his home. Ease off, Johnny. He'd kill you. You'd just be committing suicide. And he'd still be alive.

Johnny went to the window and stared out angrily. It seemed as though a cloud had drifted across the face of the sun. The town was in shadow since Slade Teplin had come home. And the shadow wouldn't be gone until Slade was gone—or until he was dead.

LEWIS B. PATTEN

THE LAW IN COTTONWOOD/ PRODIGAL GUNFIGHTER

LEISURE BOOKS **NEW YORK CITY**

A LEISURE BOOK®

November 1994

Published by special arrangement with Golden West Literary
Agency.

Dorchester Publishing Co., Inc.
276 Fifth Avenue
New York, NY 10001

THE LAW IN COTTONWOOD Copyright © MCMLXXVIII by
Lewis B. Patten

PRODIGAL GUNFIGHTER Copyright © MCMLXVI by Lewis
B. Patten

Printed in the United States of America.

THE LAW IN COTTONWOOD

CHAPTER 1

Morgan Gaunt awoke at dawn. For half a minute he lay still, listening. A rooster crowed faintly someplace uptown. Birds chirped in the big cottonwood outside the window of his room on the second floor of the Drovers Hotel. The town water wagon creaked past in the street below, sprinkling dusty Kansas Street in preparation for another day.

He swung his legs over the side of the bed and sat up. He wore only his underwear. His shoulders were broad and muscular, his chest deep, his belly flat.

He stood up and crossed the room to the washstand. He poured water into the basin and washed. Then he shaved and combed his dark, straight hair. He stroked his wide, full mustache a couple of times to make it lie in place, then put on a clean white shirt and his black string tie. His pants came next, then his boots and then his worn brown vest. He picked up the massive gold watch from the dresser and put it into the lower right-hand pocket of the vest. The chain looped across the front, anchored by a gold penknife in the opposite pocket of the vest.

His holstered revolver on its cartridge belt came last. He buckled it around his waist and it settled snugly against his right hip where his pants were worn shiny by its movement as he walked.

He took his wide-brimmed black hat from the coat tree beside the door and settled it on his head. He went out, then closed and locked the door and pocketed the key. He descended the stairs and crossed the deserted lobby with only a quick glance at the sleeping clerk be-

1

hind the desk. He stepped out onto the long veranda into the yellow glow of the rising sun. Its rays struck the gleaming six-pointed marshal's star pinned to the upper left-hand pocket of his vest.

He stood at the edge of the veranda and let his glance run up and down the street. Nothing moved except for the water wagon, now returning from the depot at the lower end of town. From his shirt pocket, Gaunt took a Bull Durham sack, separated a wheat-straw paper from the pack and shook some flakes of tobacco into it. He rolled the smoke, licked it, then twisted the ends and stuck it into his mouth. He scratched a match alight on one of the round white posts that supported the veranda roof, in a place scarred by hundreds of other similar scratches, and touched it to the cigarette. He drew smoke into his lungs, stepped down into the street and started diagonally across heading toward the livery barn three blocks down.

The smell of dampened dust was strong in the air, mingling with the elusive fragrance of lilacs and of fresh-cut grass hay from beyond the upper edge of town. The early air was warm. Another hot one, he thought.

A block from the hotel, the water wagon passed. Luke Matty, driving, raised a hand and spoke respectfully, his soft words indistinguishable because of the clatter and squeak of the wagon wheels. Gaunt returned the greeting and continued toward the livery barn.

It was deserted. Elwood Hooker, the stableman, did not come to work until seven. Gaunt walked back to his horse's stall and led the tall chestnut out. He saddled him, mounted and rode down the inclined wooden ramp into the street.

Now he was complete, a big man on a big horse, the law in Cottonwood. He headed down toward the depot and the cattle pens beyond, beginning his morning rounds.

His horse's hoofs were muffled in the deep, damp dust of the street, but they clattered as the horse stepped up onto the station platform and went past the station to the telegrapher's cubbyhole at its farthest end. The telegrapher, Jim Sutton, glanced up at the familiar sound and raised a hand in greeting as Gaunt went by.

A sign on the depot, facing east, proclaimed that this was Cottonwood, Kansas, Population 412. Adjacent to the station were the cattle pens, stretching away for nearly half a mile. In another day or two they'd be full of bawling, dusty cattle, waiting their turn at the loading chutes. Out on the prairie to the east and west and south would be tens of thousands more, bunched and held and waiting too.

And instead of 412 persons, Cottonwood would hold a thousand or more, the increase composed of wild and lean and sun-baked Texas cowboys who had brought the great herds up the trail. They were one reason the town needed Morgan Gaunt. They were one reason the town paid him a hundred and fifty dollars a month, winter and summer, even though he was needed less than half that time.

The cowboys drew another element; gamblers, saloonkeepers, prostitutes and thieves. They were an added reason the town needed Morgan Gaunt.

He rode at a steady walk down the center alley between the cattle pens and beyond, into the tree-and-brush-grown bed of Cottonwood Creek. He followed its course along the eastern edge of town.

At the upper town limits, he climbed his horse out of the creek bed where Elwood Hooker's hayfields lay bare and freshly cut in the growing heat of the morning sun. A buck rake stood at the edge of one field, along with a rusty dump rake and a wagon with a hayrack on it.

He skirted Hooker's fields, which were fenced with barbed Glidden wire, then entered town again at its upper end on Kansas Street. He could see Matty's water wagon still creaking along the dusty street, but nothing else moved yet.

Up here were the tall, white, coolly shaded homes of the town's wealthy and prominent citizens—Lester Ives, who owned the bank, Sam Kohn, who owned the Cottonwood Mercantile and Kurt Vossler, who owned five of the town's eleven saloons.

Smaller and less-imposing homes stretched along Kansas Street farther down, and on Maple and Oak, which paralleled Kansas Street on either side.

Pacing his horse slowly, he rode along through two blocks of comfortable residences, all of which had both chicken houses and stables at the rear, most of which had vegetable gardens and berry bushes someplace on their premises. The smell of lilacs was stronger here, and the tall bushes, heavy with blossom clusters, were present in nearly every yard.

A couple of dogs walked out and barked at him, wagging their tails as they did. It was a ritual with the two dogs, both of which he knew by name. A good-natured greeting they gave him every day. He spoke to them and they stopped barking, followed him a hundred yards or so, still lazily wagging their tails, then halted, sat down and scratched.

A couple of more blocks between Second Street and Main contained even more modest homes, some of these needing repair. Then the town's business section began with the huge, hundred-room Cattlemen's Hotel at the corner of Kansas Street and Main and the Cottonwood Bank across the street. Next to it on the south was the Cottonwood Mercantile, a store that handled everything from lumber to dry goods, from groceries to guns. Other smaller stores lined Kansas Street between Main and Texas streets, and on the northwest corner of Texas and Kansas stood the Drovers Hotel where Gaunt had his room.

Texas Street was the deadline above which the cowboys were forbidden to come. Most of them didn't want to come north of Texas Street, but every year there were a few who had to challenge anything that restricted them. Gaunt handled them swiftly and efficiently, and they usually wound up in jail unhurt but chastened and willing in the future to abide by the rule.

Gaunt understood Texans, perhaps better than they understood themselves. They weren't mean, only exuberant and fiercely independent. He gave them the respect they felt they were entitled to, and in return most of them avoided breaking any of the rules laid down by the town council and enforced by Gaunt.

A Negro in a white coat was sweeping the veranda of the Cattlemen's Hotel. He spoke to Gaunt, and the marshal returned the greeting. Along this block the businesses stood locked and empty at this early hour. Gaunt rode up on the board sidewalk a couple of times to try a door without getting off his horse. He could smell coffee brewing as he passed the Drovers Hotel.

Nine of the town's eleven saloons were in the next block lining both sides of the street. Largest and most imposing was the Alamo, which had leaded, stained-glass windows depicting a herd of cattle on one side of the doors, a bucking horse and rider on the other. Heavy outer doors were padlocked over the inner swinging doors, and Gaunt's glance automatically checked the padlock before he went on. The town's remaining two saloons were on Goliad, along with dingy shops that catered to the cowboys and drovers. Beyond Goliad, on Kansas, Maple and Oak were the brothels, mostly run-down, tarpaper shacks with bare, unkempt yards, in each of which one or two girls worked.

Two weeks ago, this area had been nearly deserted. Gaunt didn't know where the girls came from or where they worked during the winter. But they always came back a couple of weeks before the arrival of the first cattle herd.

All eleven of the saloons were open for business now, every day. All that was needed was the first cattle herd to get things rolling for another year.

Gaunt finished his patrol at the stone jail next to the

livery barn. He dismounted and tied his horse in the shade of a box elder tree at the north side of the jail. He unlocked the door and went inside.

He knew his job was dangerous. Every year he laid his life on the line at least a dozen times, to say nothing of the minor skirmishes, any one of which could become deadly suddenly and unexpectedly.

He accepted the danger along with the hundred and fifty dollars a month. He was fatalistic, and because he was it was said of him that he knew no fear.

That wasn't so. Every time he walked into a darkened alley to disarm a drunken cowboy who was threatening to kill him, he felt fear as a high tension in his chest, an emptiness in his belly, invisible but very real tremors in his hands and knees.

But there was a fine, high exhilaration in those deadly moments, a stimulus he never felt at any other time. This kept him on the job, a job that often angered and sometimes disgusted him.

He crossed the room to his desk in the center of it, sat down and lifted his booted feet to the desk. The clock on the wall said twenty minutes after six.

The hotel dining room would open at seven. Until then he had nothing to do.

He thought about Buck Robineau. Sometime in the next few days Robineau would be bringing another herd up the trail. Before his crew loaded him on a wagon for the long trip south last year, Robineau had sworn to return this year and kill Morgan Gaunt.

He raised his head at the sound of a horse galloping up the street from the direction of the railroad tracks. He got up, crossed to the door and opened it.

The heat in the street was already considerable, at least ten degrees hotter than the inside of the jail. He stepped outside.

The rider was a tow-headed boy of about thirteen, riding a barebacked horse. He saw the marshal and yelled, "Marshal! They're here! The first herd is here!"

The boy was Leon Satterfield, whose father had a

small farm a dozen miles south of town. He pulled his horse to a plunging halt and slid off his back.

Morgan took half a dollar from his pocket and tossed it to Leon. He could see that Leon was waiting for him to ask who the trail boss was and suppressed a smile. Finally Leon said excitedly, "It ain't Buck Robineau. It's somebody I ain't never seen before."

Gaunt nodded. "Thanks, Leon. You must've left before it got light."

"I did. I left as soon as I got up. They're camped about a mile west of our place. They pulled in last night. I rode over there and talked to 'em. I knew you'd want to know who it was."

Gaunt nodded. Leon hesitated several moments, then glanced uptown toward the Kansas Mercantile. The fifty cents was burning a hole in his pocket, Gaunt thought. He'd probably take home a quarter and tell his pa that was all he'd got. He'd spend the other quarter on candy at the store.

Finally Leon asked, "You goin' out there today?"

"Likely will, after breakfast. You want to ride with me?"

"Sure, Mr. Gaunt. I'll meet you in front of the hotel." He went on up the street, and stopped in front of the Kansas Mercantile. He tied his horse, then sat down on the steps to wait.

Gaunt stood motionless on the boardwalk in front of the jail. People were beginning to come into the street, children to play or run errands for their folks, adults to open the various stores on Kansas Street.

Gaunt waited idly for a while, watching the town stir and come to life. Finally, judging it was near seven, he turned and locked the jail door, then walked slowly up the street toward the Drovers Hotel.

He could smell coffee again before he reached the door. He climbed the steps and went in. The desk clerk was awake. Gaunt turned and crossed the white-tile floor to the dining room. He took his accustomed table at the window. Sunlight flooded in, not yet hot enough to be uncomfortable.

A pretty young Mexican girl brought him coffee. "Good morning, Marshal Gaunt."

"Good morning, Josephina. I'll have a steak. And about three eggs."

"Yes, sir." She hesitated, and he knew she had seen Leon sitting on the steps across the street and had guessed why he was in town. Finally she asked, "Is the first herd here?"

He nodded. "Got in last night, according to Leon."

She nodded and went away. Gaunt sipped the hot black coffee as he waited for her to return with his meal.

He was glad the first herd was here. He was glad that he would now have something to do and could earn his pay. He didn't like the idle winter months of sitting in his office at the jail or in one of the saloons.

But there was a complication this year that had not been the case last year. The town council had passed an ordinance forbidding firearms inside the town limits. Signs had been posted on all roads leading into town, and it was to advise the newly arrived drovers of this new ordinance that Gaunt intended to ride out to the herd south of town today.

It would make trouble, that was sure. For some reason a Texas cowboy didn't feel dressed without his gun. Gaunt had opposed the ordinance, but he had been overruled.

Josephina brought him a steak, three eggs and a generous helping of fried potatoes, as well as biscuits, butter and jam. She refilled his coffee cup and he began to eat.

CHAPTER 2

At eight, Gaunt rode out of town on his tall chestnut, accompanied by Leon Satterfield. The boy looked a little sick and Gaunt knew he had stuffed himself with candy from the store. In a way the boy was like the Texas drovers who, when they hit town after three hard months on the trail, couldn't seem to fill themselves with liquor fast enough. They always ended up sick, too, but they never learned. Next time it was the same story all over again.

They clattered over the bridge at the lower end of town and rode out onto the rolling grassland, following the narrow, dusty road that petered out into a trail about ten miles south of town.

Leon watched Gaunt surreptitiously for a while, but finally he blurted out, "What you reckon them cowboys will do when you tell 'em they can't wear guns to town?"

Gaunt smiled faintly. "They'll bluster and raise hell and swear no cow-town marshal is going to tell them what to do, but in the end they'll come to town without their guns."

"What if they don't?"

"Then I'll have to take their guns away from them."

Gaunt knew that the success of the ordinance against guns would depend largely on what happened today. If he enforced it with these first arrivals, those from the herds that followed would accept it more easily. Even so, there would be plenty of die-hards who had to be convinced.

He let the chestnut lope for several miles until the

animal's hide gleamed with sweat. Then he drew back on the reins and afterward held the horse to a steady, mile-eating trot. The chestnut didn't get much exercise so when he did get out of town, Gaunt usually let him run off his head of steam.

It was nearly ten when he sighted the cloud of dust ahead. Ten minutes later he sighted the point rider, with the herd leaders immediately behind. He turned his horse and rode off to the windward side for several hundred yards. Waiting, he fished out his Bull Durham sack and rolled himself a smoke.

Point rider and herd leaders passed, followed by the strung-out herd. The cattle were trail-wise now, after three months, and they plodded along patiently with a minimum of jostling. Three men detached themselves from the flank and approached.

The first thing their eyes caught was the star on Morgan Gaunt's vest. The man in the lead was spare and stringy, maybe five-feet-ten. His hair was gray and his week's growth of whiskers also had a liberal sprinkling of gray. His hat was dusty, shapeless, with a wide, stained band around the crown where sweat had soaked clear through. His eyes were gray, emotionless and direct. His mouth was a thin line untouched by any smile. Gaunt said, "I'm the marshal of Cottonwood."

"Heard of you." The man's voice was hoarse and unemotional.

Gaunt said, "Welcome to Cottonwood. Yours is the first herd to arrive, so you'll get first crack at the pens. There's a hundred and fifty cars or thereabouts on a siding east of town."

The man nodded.

Gaunt said, "I didn't get your name."

"Wedemeier. Nick Wedemeier. This is a pool herd. Six hundred head. Two hundred of 'em are mine."

Gaunt said, "Your boys are welcome in town. We'll try to show 'em a good time. But there's a new ordinance. No guns in town. It'll be enforced."

Wedemeier scowled and seemed about to argue the point. He changed his mind. "I'll tell 'em," was all he said.

He and the two men with him reined their horses around and trotted back toward the herd.

Leon said; "Not very friendly, is he?"

"He's been three months on the trail. He's likely had nothing but trouble all the way. Now I'm bringing him some more. You can't expect him to like it much."

"You think his cowboys will come to town without their guns?"

"No. They'll come in *with* their guns. It will be a test to see if I can make the gun ban stick." He had hoped it would be different. He had hoped the first trail boss would be a more reasonable kind of man. This Wedemeier would simply tell his cowboys about the ordinance and let it go at that. He wouldn't order them to comply.

Leon looked as if he'd like to accompany the marshal back to town. He knew he couldn't, though, so he said good-bye and turned his horse toward home.

Gaunt urged the chestnut to a trot and headed back toward town. He passed the slowly moving herd and arrived in town before noon.

The streets were crowded now. Once more he tied the chestnut in the shade of the box elder tree beside the jail and walked uptown to the Alamo Saloon.

The town council had offered to hire two deputy marshals at the time they passed the ordinance banning guns. Gaunt had refused. Deputies would only get themselves killed trying to enforce such an ordinance. Gaunt could do it but only because he was known to the Texas cattlemen and their friends. He was known to be tough and uncompromising and was believed to be fearless. He was also conceded to be fair. It added up to "presence," although Gaunt had never thought about it just that way. He personified the law, and the law was only as strong as the man enforcing it.

The saloon was crowded for this time of day. Men

made way for him, and he slowly worked his way through them to the bar. He ordered beer and the brimming mug came sliding down the bar to stop exactly in front of him. He laid down a nickel and picked up the beer.

He felt the soft touch of a woman's hand on his arm and turned his head to see Rose Navarro standing at his side. "Hello, Morgan."

"Hello, Rose." The smile that touched his wide and normally somber mouth held genuine warmth.

"I hear the first herd is here." She was a small, dark-haired woman with ample breasts, a slender waist and full, rounded hips. She was Morgan Gaunt's girl, and because she was other men left her alone. Which suited her. She owned a one-fourth share in the Alamo.

"Uh-huh. They'll be in town tonight."

She knew about the weapons ordinance, but she didn't mention it. She said, "Things will be quiet this afternoon. Come up and visit for a while." Her eyes were warm and personal.

He understood what the invitation included and nodded. He had known her three years, ever since he had come to Cottonwood and taken the marshal's job. He'd never talked with her about his past, and she had never discussed hers with him. She knew he was courting Maggie Conover and knew there could be no future in her own relationship with him. She doubted if Maggie Conover knew about her. She also doubted if Maggie would continue seeing him if she did.

With just a trace of weariness in her voice she said, "Another year."

"You could sell out and do something else. Your share of this place will never be worth more than it is right now."

"And what would I do?"

"How about nothing?" He grinned. "How about keeping house?"

Her smile matched his. "For you?"

His own grin faded, and she was sorry she had embarrassed him. She squeezed his arm. "See you this afternoon."

"Sure."

Morgan went out into the sun-washed street. The heat was building up. Dust rose now in spite of the street's two earlier sprinklings.

It was past noon and time to eat. He headed for Maggie Conover's restaurant, thinking of her and smiling at his thoughts.

He saw nothing inconsistent in his relationships with Maggie and with Rose, although he knew Maggie would not be tolerant if she knew. He was a mature man, and his periodic need for a woman was real and undeniable. Maggie, although she had been married before, was firm in her conviction that intimacy with a man must be preceded by marriage. He had been trying to get her to marry him, but she would not do so until her husband had been dead a year.

Her restaurant was sandwiched in-between the bank and the Cottonwood Mercantile. Already it was nearly filled with customers. There was a vacant stool at the end of the counter near the swinging door that led to the kitchen, and he sat down on it. As he did, Maggie came through the door, carrying four plates with practiced dexterity. She saw him and the way her face lighted made him feel good. She said, "Morgan! I'll be right back."

He smiled, one of his rare, complete smiles, and its warmth made her already flushed face flush more. She went on past and carried the plates to a table by the window occupied by four of the town's businessmen.

Morgan turned his head to watch her. He liked the way she walked, her back straight, her head high, her hips moving naturally but very beautifully. Turning, she caught his glance and a faint smile touched her mouth.

She was taller than Rose, with smaller breasts and a more slender figure, probably from the hard work involved in running the restaurant. Her hair was dark, done up in a bun at the nape of her neck, with wisps of it escaping the restraint and lying now damp on her forehead and neck.

She stopped beside him, laid a hand on his arm and asked, "What will you have, Morgan?"

"Wasn't that chicken and dumplings you just carried by?"

She nodded.

"Then I'll have some of that."

She said, "I can't talk now. Too busy. But stay awhile. This will clear out in a little while."

He nodded and she disappeared into the kitchen. On her next trip out she brought him a cup of coffee and half a dozen trips later brought him a steaming plate of chicken and dumplings and refilled his coffee cup.

He ate, frowning slightly, thinking about Nick Wedemeier and about Wedemeier's crew. He hoped he wouldn't have to start off the year by throwing anyone in jail or by being forced to draw his gun.

Wedemeier would hold his herd a mile or two from town tonight. He'd come in to talk to the cattle buyers and, if they reached a satisfactory agreement, would make arrangements for cattle cars tomorrow. He'd accept an advance from whoever bought his cattle, and would give his cowboys at least a part of their pay. The cowboys themselves would hit town around dark, and Morgan Gaunt would begin to earn his pay again.

Gradually the restaurant emptied until, at a little after one, Gaunt was the only one who remained. Maggie brought a cup of coffee and sat down limply on the stool next to him. Her forehead was damp and wisps of her dark hair clung to it.

Her face was lovely, he thought, as he looked at her. Her forehead was high and smooth, her eyes large and dark and widely spaced. Her cheekbones were high, her mouth full and her chin strong. She said, "I like to have you look at me like that."

"Then I'll do it more."

Her smile faded. "I hear the first herd is here."

He nodded.

"Will they obey the order not to bring guns to town?"

"Maybe."

"And if they don't?" She knew the answer to that, but she wanted to be reassured that he could handle it.

"I'll have to change their minds."

She was silent for several moments, her eyes studying his face. Finally she asked, "You'll be careful, won't you Morgan?"

"Yes." He was always careful, never reckless. He never did anything impulsively, but he could act, when it was necessary, with cold ruthlessness that had gained him the respect, if not the liking, of all the Texans who had happened to cross paths with him.

The cloud remained on her face as she sipped her coffee. He reached out and covered her hand, lying on the counter, with his own. She looked up, met his glance and asked, "Will Buck Robineau be coming back this year?"

"He said he would." Morgan's clash with Robineau last year had been over the jailing of one of the members of Robineau's crew. Robineau had come to the jail with a dozen members of his crew to get the man out. Morgan hadn't had any choice. It was give up the cowboy and lose all the control he had in Cottonwood, or duel it out with Robineau. He'd chosen the latter course and had severely wounded Robineau, who had lain in a room at the Cattlemen's Hotel five weeks before he was sufficiently recovered to make the trip back to Texas in a spring wagon bed.

Before he left, he confronted the marshal with the promise that he would return this year and kill Morgan any way he could. Which meant, since his right shoulder had been smashed by Morgan's bullet, that he'd probably not do it in a man-to-man, face-to-face gun duel.

Maggie asked, "Why don't you quit this job?

Before . . ." She didn't finish but he knew what she had been going to say.

He thought about it a moment before he answered her. He knew it was only a matter of time before one of the bullets fired at him from out of the darkness found its mark. Or before he miscalculated about whether some drunken cowboy would draw his gun and paid for his miscalculation with his life.

Besides, he knew the life of Cottonwood as a cattle town was limited. The herds would stop coming here just as they had stopped coming to Baxter Springs, Ellsworth, Newton and Wichita. And a sleepy farm town would have neither need for his talents nor the funds to pay for them.

He thought about the alternatives, about the jobs he might get, and he rejected all of them. The only thing that might satisfy him would be owning his own ranch, and he knew even that would be pretty dull by comparison. But Maggie was waiting for his answer and he said, "I've always been a lawman. Ever since the war. What would I do?"

He could see that she was thinking too. Of him behind the counter of this restaurant. Or running a store, selling dress goods and hardware and groceries. He didn't fit the mold, and a fleeting smile at the incongruity of it touched her mouth. She said, "There are things. You could start a freight line. Or drive a stagecoach. Or buy a cattle ranch."

He said, "I'll think about it."

There was something speculative in her expression. She was probably considering making his changing jobs a condition of their marrying. But she had the good sense not to issue any ultimatums or impose any conditions. He was not a man to be coerced.

She nodded. "All right." But there was a cloud in her eyes, a worry that, even if she did persuade him to quit after the Texas cowboys had all gone home and the town was quiet again, it might not be soon enough.

He was faced with enforcing the gun ban, not only

against the cowboys from the herd that would arrive later today, but against all those who would come afterward. He was faced with enforcing the two-o'clock curfew when not one of the saloonkeepers approved of it. He was faced with the threat made by Buck Robineau to return this year and kill him by whatever means were necessary. He might not live to quit even if he agreed to do so at the end of the year.

But she could not change this man. He was committed to serving out this year at least. Nothing would make him quit.

Besides, she thought as she looked at his strong and flat-planed face, he didn't really want to quit. He liked the job. He liked the excitement of risking his life every day and every night.

She wondered bleakly if women ever completely understood their men. She doubted if they did.

CHAPTER 3

Morgan Gaunt walked into the Alamo at two-thirty. He drank a beer at the bar, then crossed the room, in which there were now only half a dozen men, and climbed the stairs.

There was a balcony up here, with doors leading to the various rooms where the saloon girls took their customers. Rose Navarro's room was down at the end.

Morgan knocked and when Rose's voice called, "Come in, Morgan," he entered, struck as he always was by the frilly femininity of this room.

She was dressed in something gauzey that gave him just a hint of white skin underneath. He felt his blood stir and his heart begin to pound. She got up and poured him a drink from the bottle on the table. He took it from her and sipped. He said, "You're a damned beautiful woman, Rose."

She wanted to ask him if she was more beautiful than Maggie Conover, but she had the good sense to keep still. She poured herself a drink and extended it far enough toward him to touch his glass. Afterward she drank about half of it.

How long would she have him? she wondered to herself. Would he really marry Maggie when her year of mourning was up, or would he shy away? He had apparently shied away before because he was past thirty and as far as she knew had never been married.

Or had he? That was something she simply didn't know because neither of them had ever discussed the past. It occurred to her that if she arranged to let Maggie find out about their relationship, she might end his

18

relationship with Maggie Conover. But she immediately discarded that idea. Rose had spent all her adult life in saloons, but she had a rigid honesty that wouldn't permit her to stoop to such tactics even to get Morgan, who she wanted more than she had ever wanted anything or anyone.

She finished her drink and Morgan finished his. He got up and came to her, and took her in his arms. He was very direct as he always was, but there was a tenderness in him too that moved her today just as it always had in the past.

Yet throughout, she had the feeling that a part of him was someplace else, and she supposed he was thinking of the herd out on the prairie south of town and of the gun ban he would have to enforce tonight. He was wondering, also, if he would have to kill a man, and maybe he ·was wondering if he would be killed himself, although she doubted that.

He stayed with her for about an hour, then got up and dressed himself and belted on his gun. With his hat in his hand, he bent and kissed her lightly on the mouth. She was so touched by this gentle kiss that said so much that for a moment tears glistened in her eyes. Then he was gone and she could hear the beat of his booted heels on the balcony and later on the stairs.

She supposed she should be grateful for having had as much of him as she had, yet womanlike, she wanted more. She wanted to have all of him, forever, the way Maggie Conover would when she married him.

But Rose was a realist. She had given up all chance for marriage and children and the permanence both bring a woman when she went to work in her first saloon. She had been sixteen at the time although she had looked older, and she hadn't made a conscious decision to give up one thing for another or even known what she might be giving up. Her decision had been dictated by circumstances. Her parents had been killed in a stagecoach wreck. She hadn't been able to find a job to support herself. A saloon had been the only alternative.

Slowly she dressed for the evening, taking her time, occasionally smiling faintly as her thoughts dwelt on Morgan Gaunt. Finished, she descended the stairs, ready for another night.

Here in the Alamo she would soon know whether Morgan had successfully enforced the new gun ban. And she would be among the first to know if anything went wrong.

Kurt Vossler was a huge, grossly fat man in his early fifties. He wore a neatly trimmed Van Dyke beard and mustache. His eyes were close-set, baby-blue in color and nearly lost in the folds of fat surrounding them. They were as hard and dangerous as the eyes of a full-grown boar.

Vossler owned five of the town's eleven saloons and one of the three imposing mansions at the upper end of town. Vossler's saloons were the sleaziest of the eleven. They were also places where anything went, and because they were, they always had a crowd.

Vossler hated Gaunt more than he had ever hated anyone. He blamed Gaunt for the two-o'clock closing ordinance. Gaunt was always there when two o'clock rolled around, ordering Vossler's bartenders to close, and the marshal was always trying to get Vossler on some trumped-up charge, although so far all he had succeeded in getting against Vossler had been misdemeanors that resulted in fines.

He kept on trying though, trying to prove that Vossler knew about the cowboy drunks that went off with Vossler's girls and ended up in the alley with their pockets turned inside out and, often as not, bad lumps on their heads. A few had even died as a result of their injuries, and Gaunt had told Vossler straight out that he knew he was behind the killings and that, sooner or later, he was going to prove it and see that Vossler hanged.

Vossler's direct mind saw only one solution to the problem posed by Morgan Gaunt. The marshal had to go. Sometime this year maybe he would find a man willing to kill Gaunt, someone who had a grievance of his own strong enough to make him forget the risk. When he did, Morgan Gaunt would be gone for good. The gun ban and the closing ordinance would be forgotten and Vossler would start running his saloons the way he wanted to. Hell, this cattle boom wasn't going to last more than another couple of years. The other hell-raising cow towns east of here were dying on the vine. Herds no longer came to them. They had to depend on farmers to keep them alive.

Vossler meant to get all he could before that happened in Cottonwood. And he wasn't doing bad. He had his house at the upper end of town. He had five saloons. He had a sizable amount of money in the bank.

But when this town died, the saloons wouldn't be worth the powder to blow them to hell. The house wouldn't be worth much more. He'd made a few investments, but he wanted more. The next two years ought to put him on easy street. Provided Gaunt didn't spoil everything.

Today, Vossler left home at noon. He drove his buggy down Kansas Street to the first of his saloons— the Red Dog on the corner of Kansas and Goliad. The bartender, a hard-faced man named Sully, came out and helped him alight. He went inside and Sully followed him. Sully said, "The first herd's here, Mr. Vossler. Things ought to pick up tonight."

"Who's the trail boss, Sully? Do you know?"

Sully shook his head. "No, sir."

"Then it probably isn't Robineau, or you'd have heard."

"Yes, sir. I suppose I would."

Vossler sat down at one of the tables and Sully brought him one of his private bottles and a glass. Vossler decided he'd have to wait until Robineau came. Maybe Robineau would get rid of Gaunt and save him the trouble and the risk. If he didn't . . . well, there would be time enough then to hire somebody to do the job.

Or it might get done without him having to take any action at all. It might happen tonight when Gaunt tried enforcing the gun ban on the cowhands who had just arrived.

The thing to do was to relax. Things have a way of taking care of themselves.

After leaving Maggie Conover's restaurant Gaunt had made his rounds for the second time today. The midday inspection was the one he enjoyed the most. A lot of people were on the street and he stopped often to talk with someone for a few minutes, about the weather or the number of cattle likely to be shipped east out of Cottonwood this year or something else of little consequence.

He saw Vossler's buggy in front of the Red Dog, but he did not go in. When he left Rose at the Alamo at three-thirty and saw Vossler's buggy still in the same place, he turned in through the Red Dog's swinging doors.

Vossler's five saloons caused him more trouble than all the others combined. Vossler hired only crooked gamblers, and since the house shared in every game, this increased his take. Gaunt knew in his own mind that Vossler encouraged his girls to roll drunken cowboys every chance they got, and he was sure Vossler got his share of whatever they took from their victims.

Cheating and robbing the Texans was bad enough. But what really angered Gaunt was the fact that all too often the blow intended to render the victim unconscious killed him instead. It had happened three times last year. Gaunt meant to see that it didn't happen at all this year.

Vossler was sitting at a table, a bottle of his special whiskey in front of him. Sully, a hard case Gaunt never turned his back to if he could help it, was behind the bar.

Gaunt stood over Vossler, ignoring Vossler's invitation to sit down.

He said, "The first herd is here, Mr. Vossler."

Vossler nodded. "I heard." He studied Gaunt's face as if trying to read Gaunt's thoughts.

Gaunt said, "Clean up your places, Mr. Vossler, or I'll close them. A violation of the law in one, and I'll close all five."

Vossler's fat face flushed darkly and his tiny eyes glittered. He said softly, "You son-of-a-bitch, try closing me and you'll be dead before the night's over."

Gaunt's expression didn't change. He couldn't arrest Vossler for calling him a son-of-a-bitch, and if he arrested him for the threat, he'd never make it stick. Not with Sully the only witness to the threat. Besides, arresting Vossler on a minor charge would only lay him open to an accusation of harassment later on when he got something serious on the man.

He stared at Vossler, his face composed but with a dark anger in the depths of his eyes. Vossler opened his mouth to curse Gaunt again. Something he saw in Gaunt's eyes changed his mind. Gaunt said, "Remember it. One crooked game, one drunk rolled, and you're closed for ten days. All five."

"By God I'll see the town council about that!"

"See them." Gaunt turned his back and went to the door. He knew either Sully or Vossler was capable of shooting him in the back. But not like this. Not when there was no one else to blame it on.

He stepped out on the boardwalk. The heat was heavy and oppressive now. The sprinkling wagon was wetting down Kansas Street for the third time today.

Gaunt saw the trail boss, Nick Wedemeier, on the veranda of the Cattlemen's Hotel with a cattle buyer named Bart Chapman, the banker, Lester Ives, and Dave Ryan, who worked for the AT&SF railroad. As he watched, the quartet stepped down off the hotel veranda, crossed the street and entered the Cottonwood Bank.

Wedemeier had made his deal, thought Gaunt. He'd be returning to his herd with an advance, and his cowboys would hit town less than an hour afterward.

He meant to meet them at the edge of town. He figured he'd have his best chance before any of them had gotten anything to drink. They'd be anxious to hit the saloons and they'd be thinking about the girls. They'd be less likely to make an issue of their guns than they would later on.

Wedemeier came out of the bank, now accompanied only by the buyer, Chapman, and the railroad man, Ryan. He stood talking with them on the walk in front of the bank for several minutes. Then he untied his horse, mounted and came down the street.

Gaunt mounted his own horse and when Wedemeier came abreast, fell in beside him. "Make a deal for your herd, Mr. Wedemeier?"

Wedemeier looked pleased. He nodded.

"When will you load?"

"Day after tomorrow I don't figure my men will be much good tomorrow."

Gaunt grinned faintly. "You're likely right."

Wedemeier didn't seem to have anything else to say. Gaunt sensed a hidden hostility in the man, and since Wedemeier didn't know him he supposed Wedemeier had heard about him from others who did. He said, "Your boys will be treated fairly, Mr. Wedemeier. You have my word for that."

Wedemeier looked at him but still he didn't speak. He nodded to signify that he accepted Gaunt's statement as the truth, at least until further events proved otherwise.

"You'll save everybody a lot of trouble if you send 'em to town without their guns."

Wedemeier glanced at him, an unsuccessfully hidden mockery in his eyes. "Afraid of them, Mr. Gaunt?"

Gaunt said, "You've heard about me, Mr. Wedemeier. Did you hear that I was afraid?"

Wedemeier reluctantly shook his head. But the stubborn look remained. "I can't send them in without their guns. How the hell are they going to protect themselves?"

"I'm here to protect them, Mr. Wedemeier."

Wedemeier shook his head. "You'll have to get their guns the best way you can. If I send them in unarmed and one of them gets killed . . ." He left the sentence dangling.

Gaunt saw that he had lost. He shrugged, drew in his horse's reins and stopped. He watched Wedemeier cross the railroad tracks and take the narrow road leading south.

He hadn't really expected the trail boss to send his men in without their guns. But he'd had to try.

He rode back to the jail. He took the bit out of his horse's mouth and tied up the reins. He released the horse beneath the box elder tree to graze. There was a vacant lot between the jail and Sandoval's Saddle Shop. It was ankle high with dry native grass.

He brought a straight-backed chair from inside the jail and placed it on the walk. He sat down and tilted it back against the wall. The sinking sun beat hot against him and he tilted his hat forward to keep it out of his eyes. He began to sweat from the heat, but he didn't move.

Glancing up the street now, he could see that he wasn't the only one who had seen Wedemeier leave town. Girls appeared in the windows and on the porches of the tarpaper brothels, painted and provocatively dressed. Gamblers in cutaway coats and black hats drifted from the two hotels into the various saloons. Bartenders and swampers came to work.

Kurt Vossler came out of the Red Dog and waddled out of sight on Goliad, no doubt visiting the remaining four of his five saloons. He reappeared about twenty minutes later, climbed heavily into his buggy and drove away toward home, throwing only a hasty glance toward the marshal sitting in front of the jail.

Gaunt thought idly that he had better be more careful than usual this year. Vossler wanted him out of the way, and while he probably didn't have the guts to try killing him himself, he could have it done.

The sun settled toward the horizon. An hour after Wedemeier had ridden out of town, Gaunt walked to where his horse was cropping grass. He put the bit back into the horse's mouth, mounted and rode down Kansas Street.

He watered his horse in Cottonwood Creek, then took up a position south of the bridge to wait.

CHAPTER 4

Waiting, he thought of Maggie Conover, and then about Rose. He couldn't help feeling guilty about seeing Rose and courting Maggie at the same time, and he felt sure that if Maggie knew about Rose she would break off with him at once.

But he wasn't a priest, and he couldn't be celibate. There were needs a man had that could not be denied. He had urged Maggie to marry him months ago, but she had steadfastly refused, saying she had to wait until a year after her husband's death. Nor would she consider the intimacies of marriage until after the ceremony.

Morgan Gaunt was a bit puzzled as to why one or another of his enemies, of which he had several, had not spilled the beans to Maggie a long time ago. Maybe, in their way, they had their own code of honor. Or maybe they had kept still because they wanted Morgan to keep still. About their own secrets, which Morgan knew.

There was little, actually, that Morgan did not know about the people of Cottonwood. He patrolled the streets at night. Not for long could a husband visit a woman other than his wife without Morgan knowing it. Nor could a wife slip out to visit another man without Morgan eventually seeing her.

But he kept their secrets and never mentioned his knowledge to any of them. Unless what they did was against the law.

It was dusk when he heard the faint, wild beat of galloping horses, first as a vibration in the ground, then

27

as a growing sound in the hot evening air. He straightened and positioned himself squarely in the middle of the road. His hand touched the grips of his holstered Colt's 45, loosened it slightly and let it drop back into place.

It was a nervous gesture that made him smile faintly to himself. He admitted he was nervous. A lot depended on what happened here in the next few minutes. But he also felt that high exhilaration that always came when he faced a showdown.

He liked his job. He liked the risk of it, the danger he had to face every day. Now he wondered fleetingly how he would take to a job driving a stagecoach, or a freight wagon, or punching cows out in the lonesome emptiness of the prairie. He shook his head. He didn't know. But he was going to have to find out because this job wouldn't last more than a couple of years at most. Then he'd either have to do something else or move on, to another trail town farther west, and to another after that until finally they all had changed or disappeared.

The thunder of galloping hoofs grew louder. He was briefly grateful that enough light remained for them to see. In complete darkness he'd be overrun before they had a chance to halt.

They saw him, but they came on, maintaining their hard gallop, trying to make him get out of the road. They didn't know him, but they knew who he was because Wedemeier had told them about him.

He neither flinched nor budged. He sat there like a rock, by his own will holding his horse absolutely still. There were at least fifteen riders, too many to count in the poor light and in the dust that rose from their horses' hoofs.

It appeared they were really going to run him down, but at the last instant those in front hauled their horses to sudden, crow-hopping stops, and those behind, of necessity, followed suit.

Gaunt didn't say anything until the horses had partially quieted. Then he said calmly, "Good evening, boys."

None of them seemed to know how to reply. Morgan said, "It's getting dark so you likely didn't see the sign. It says guns are not allowed in Cottonwood. You'll have to check them with me. You can pick them up at the jail on your way out of town."

One man blurted, "Like hell! You ain't gettin' my gun away from me."

Another echoed, "Mine neither, by God!" and a third man echoed that.

They spread, now, so that they sat their horses side by side, for the width of the road and for a dozen feet on either side of it. Gaunt knew if he drew his gun they'd riddle him before he got off much more than a couple of shots.

Besides, he didn't want a shoot-out with these men. They weren't criminals and they hadn't broken any law. He said calmly, "Now, boys, you know one man can't shoot it out with fifteen, no matter how good he is. Besides, I don't want to quarrel with you. There's a reason the town don't want men with guns in it. The guns get used. Usually it's some cowboy that gets shot."

Nobody answered him. He said, "The town's waiting for you. The girls. The saloons. The poker games. You'll be treated fairly, and you won't need guns."

"How do we know we'll be treated fairly? That ain't what I heard."

"Then you heard about some other town. You'll get a fair shake here. If you don't, you come to me and I'll personally take care of it." He felt briefly ashamed promising fair treatment when he knew he couldn't guarantee that was what they'd get. Not in Kurt Vossler's five saloons.

"What if we don't give up our guns?"

Gaunt felt himself go very tense. That tenseness and a reckless disregard of danger both were in his voice when he replied. "Why then I guess we'll just have to shoot it out right here. You'll get me, boys, but I'll get three of you before you do."

He waited, while that sank in. Suddenly the four who faced him abreast in the road began to have second thoughts. A minute passed, then two. Gaunt's arm was tense, so tense it ached, and his hand wasn't more than a couple of inches from the grip of his gun.

Right now it could go either way. Some hothead's nerve might break, and he might yank out his gun. If that happened, nothing could stop it from continuing to its grisly conclusion. Gaunt would be dead, lying in the middle of the road. At least two of the cowboys would be dead, maybe more. And the only thing that would have been settled would be that the drovers could keep their guns in town.

Gaunt's chest began to ache. It was nearly dark now, but there was still enough gray in the sky to clearly see each form. How very much is risked, thought Gaunt, for each small principle. And yet if the risk is not taken, then no principle is upheld.

The tension broke suddenly. One of the four facing Gaunt in the middle of the road said, "Oh hell, boys, we'll get our guns when we leave town. Besides, if it turns out we need 'em, we can always go to the jail and get 'em back."

The dangerous moment was past. Their horses moved, unchecked by the riders. Gaunt's horse began to dance nervously now that the iron hand on the reins had relaxed. He said, "Just buckle the belts again after you take 'em off so I can hang 'em over my saddle horn."

A belt and holstered gun was thrust into his hand, and another, and another after that. The saddle horn wouldn't hold them all so he hung the rest over his head. When he had them all he said, "Go on, boys. You don't need to wait for me. I'm going to be pretty slow with all this hardware hanging around my neck."

That got a nervous laugh out of some of them. They

dug spurs into their horses' sides and thundered away over the bridge and into town.

He had won another victory. But it gave him no feeling of triumph. He had promised them they would be safe. It was up to him now to see that they were. If one got hit on the head and rolled, and died because of it, he would have a hard time living with himself afterward or explaining it.

But maybe, he thought, his warning to Vossler earlier would have its effect. Vossler would likely hold back, keeping his places orderly for several days. In a week most of this bunch would be gone. Others would have taken their place.

He rode slowly over the bridge and across the railroad tracks. So heavy were the belts and revolvers that he could hardly dismount in front of the jail. He unlocked the door and went inside. In darkness he removed the belts and holstered revolvers from around his neck. He hung them from the coat tree, just inside the door. He went back out and removed the others from his saddle and carried them inside.

It was time for his evening rounds, after which he would have his supper at Maggie Conover's restaurant.

He locked the jail, mounted his horse and rode slowly up Kansas Street. The names of the saloons were familiar to him, Alamo, Texas, Drovers, Red Dog, Pink Lady, Kansas Pride, Longhorn, Mustang, Bijou, Gold Coin and Overman's. Vossler owned the Red Dog, the Pink Lady, Bijou, Gold Coin and Mustang.

There was a routine to the way Gaunt made his rounds, a routine he knew was dangerous. Except for his early morning rounds, he always started at the same place, took the same route and ended up at the same starting point. He was predictable, but there was something about a regular routine that he liked, even if it was dangerous.

He had told himself often enough that he ought to vary it. Regular rounds made it possible for his enemies to ambush him. But varying his routine was, in his mind, a confession of weakness, an admission of fear. And he'd give nobody the satisfaction of knowing he was afraid.

Already he could hear the high yells of the cowboys coming through the open doors of the saloons. He could hear the tinkle of pianos, the shrill laughter of the saloon girls and, closer, the voices of prostitutes calling out to a couple of the cowboys who were more interested in them than they were in the saloons.

There also was, in Gaunt himself, a fine feeling of tension he always had when the drovers were in town. He grinned wryly to himself, then dismounted at the first saloon he reached, the Pink Lady on the near corner of Kansas and Goliad.

He went inside. This place had attracted most of the cowboys for the simple reason that it was the first one they reached. They lined the bar, each with a girl beside him, each with a bottle in front of him. At tables against the wall, the gamblers waited, idly shuffling cards or playing solitaire.

Gaunt stood inside the door. He had warned Vossler but it wouldn't hurt to warn the gamblers in Vossler's saloons as well. He crossed to the gambling tables and positioned himself with his back to the bar, facing the three gamblers. He said, "Honest games, boys. Three complaints of cheating and out of town you go. Kill anyone, and it will be murder because none of the drovers have got guns."

The three stared at him with sullen anger. None replied. He knew only one of them and had arbitrated two cheating complaints against the man last year. He looked straight and hard at this one. "*One* complaint against you, Moss, and out *you* go. Remember it."

He turned his back and heard Moss muttering as he did. He knew the epithet Moss was calling him, but he'd been called that before, and besides, he knew that if he turned and demanded that Moss repeat it, the man would refuse.

He stepped outside, picked up his horse's reins, mounted and went on to the next saloon. Fewer of the Texans were in this one, still fewer in the next. Those after that were empty, waiting for the Texans who would eventually hit every saloon in town.

Satisfied, finally, that everything was quiet and orderly, he rode his horse up Kansas Street. Now he put the animal up onto the boardwalk and leaned down to try each door. Having done that on one side of the street he crossed over and did the other one. This way he eventually reached the bank.

Main Street marked the end of the business section of town. He rode east to the alley behind the bank, turned into it and began checking the rear door of each establishment.

It was pitch black here. His horse picked his way daintily through refuse and piled-up tin cans. Gaunt's senses were now sharper and more alert because he knew that if and when he was attacked it would probably be in a place like this.

He tried each door all the way down to Alamo Street, then rode along Alamo to the alley between Maple and Kansas Street. He repeated his routine of trying doors all the way to Main and afterward rode back to Kansas Street and along it to its upper end.

Here he turned east, skirted Hooker's hayfields and took the creek bed back to the cattle pens at the lower end of town. He rode through the cattle pens to the railroad depot, rode across the wooden platform and then crossed the tracks and entered Kansas Street again at its lower end.

The entire rounds had taken about forty-five minutes. He continued up Kansas Street, remembering as he crossed Texas Street that he hadn't informed the newly arrived drovers that it was the deadline which they were not to cross. He'd been so busy enforcing the gun ban that he hadn't thought of it.

He reached Maggie Conover's restaurant, dismounted and tied his horse. He went inside.

Most of her customers had already eaten their supper and left. There were only two men sitting at a corner table. Gaunt spoke to them, calling them both by name. Then he sat down at the corner of the counter with a smile at Maggie who had just come through the kitchen door. "Evening, Maggie."

There was a light frown on her forehead. She nodded to him and stood behind the counter facing him. Before he could speak again she said, "Another year." She hesitated and then said, "I worry so. I wish I could stop."

"Nothing to worry about," he said soothingly.

"No? What about that confrontation you had with those cowboys at the edge of town?"

He smiled. "You heard about that?"

"Everybody knows about it. Somebody must have been watching you."

"More than one, I expect."

"You haven't answered me."

"All right. The council passed a ban against guns in town. I had to enforce it. It wasn't hard. I asked them to give me their guns and they did."

"Just like that."

"Just like that."

She put her hands on her hips and looked at him with exasperation. "Morgan Gaunt, you know there was more to it than that!"

"A little," he conceded. "They didn't want to give up their guns. But the next bunch will be easier, and the next still easier. By the end of the season I won't even have to meet them at the edge of town. They'll come to the jail and give up their guns of their own free will."

She was shaking her head now, knowing it was no use arguing the point with him. "What do you want to eat?"

"Surprise me. I like everything you cook."

That brought a faint smile to her mouth. But her

eyes were still sparkling, and she was as pretty as he had ever seen her look. She turned and disappeared.

One of the men at the table asked, "Have any trouble getting the guns from those cowboys, Mr. Gaunt?"

Gaunt swung around on the stool. The man who had spoken was Harvey Clay, who owned a hardware store and who was a member of the town council. Gaunt shook his head. "They didn't want a fight. All they wanted was to get to the saloons."

Clay grinned. "You make it sound easy."

"It was."

"You can still have two deputies if you want them."

Gaunt shook his head. "I can handle it."

And he could. Until Vossler hired someone to ambush him in the dark. Until some drunken cowboy challenged him from the middle of the street and began shooting with a gun he'd either hidden or had obtained from someone in town. Until some gambler he had ordered out of town for cheating shot him in the back.

Maggie brought him a plate of roast beef and noodles in gravy and followed that with a steaming cup of black coffee. Hungrily he began to eat.

CHAPTER 5

While he ate, Maggie hurried back and forth between the table and the kitchen at the rear. Whenever she passed, Morgan's glance would raise and touch her. Sometimes she caught his glance and smiled, but once, when she saw a cloud of something that might have been uncertainty in his eyes, she could not force herself to smile.

Morgan was, to her, like a wild thing that has not and cannot be tamed. Like a horse that has run free all of its life and has never known the hand of man.

Could she tame him? She didn't know. Nor was she altogether sure she wanted to. Yet how could she accept life on Morgan's terms? How could she live out each day and night in fear that someone would come knocking on her door to tell her he was dead?

Maybe Morgan could not be tamed. Maybe his destiny was to live violently and die the same way. Maybe she would make a disastrous mistake if she married him.

She caught herself avoiding his glance. Realizing that she was, she stopped directly in front of him and asked, "Do you have everything you need?"

He nodded, his mouth full. Smiling a forced smile, she turned and re-entered the kitchen.

She could not drive away the dark feeling of foreboding that troubled her. It was as if she knew, for certain, that Morgan was going to be killed. She probably shouldn't have been so inflexible about observing a year of mourning before marrying him. She should have agreed when he first asked. If she had, they'd have been married for more than three months by now. She'd have had that much.

But she knew that would not have been enough. Not for her. She wanted a lifetime when she married again. She'd lost one husband and she doubted if she could stand to lose another one.

The two men at the table left and only Morgan Gaunt remained. Maggie cleaned up the dining room, then went into the kitchen and began to wash the stack of dishes piled beside the sink.

Morgan came back, carrying his plate and cup. He slid them into the dishwater, picked up a flour-sack dishtowel and began to dry. She smiled at this unaccustomed touch of domesticity he had assumed, but she could not forget the look of uncertainty she had earlier surprised in his eyes. Was he as unsure as she? Troubled and upset, she finished washing dishes, took off her apron and blew out the lamp.

Morgan followed her out and waited while she locked the door. He untied his horse and walked beside her, leading the animal. Maggie took his arm.

Neither seemed to have much to say, and what they did say came out awkward and strained. At her door, Morgan bent and kissed her on the mouth, holding her briefly but strongly in his arms. He said calmly, "Good night, Maggie," in a voice that, she thought, could as easily say good-bye.

For an instant she clung to him desperately. When she released him he said with surprise, "Well! What was all that about?"

She laughed nervously. "I guess I just can't help being afraid for you."

"No need. I can handle it." His voice held an almost defensive quality.

She knew she should not pursue it, but she couldn't help herself. "Do you intend to continue as marshal, after this year?"

He was silent for a moment. There was a kind of

helplessness in his voice when he did reply. "Maggie, I don't know anything else. Except soldiering."

This was not a new subject for discussion between them and Maggie knew she could say nothing she hadn't said before, yet something seemed to be driving her. "Would driving a stagecoach be so dull? Or running a cattle ranch? These Texans don't seem to think it's dull."

His voice was just a little stiff. "We've talked about it, Maggie, and I've said I'll think on it."

"Yes, we have, haven't we?" Her own voice now was cold.

Again Morgan said in his deep, calm voice, "Good night, Maggie."

"Good night." She hated herself for speaking to him in so cold a voice. She hated herself for letting him walk away, a lonely man facing unknown dangers alone, without even letting him know he had her support.

But the sad truth was, she thought as she turned and went into the house, he did not have her support. She hated the job he held. And, she told herself, she wasn't going to marry him unless he agreed to give it up.

As troubled as Maggie, Morgan Gaunt mounted his horse, which he had earlier tied to Maggie's fence, and rode slowly down the middle of the street toward the center of the town.

He had not missed the coldness in Maggie's voice. He was sure now that Maggie was going to make his quitting the marshal's job a condition of her marrying him.

Could he accept such a condition? No, he could not. Not and remain the man he was.

On the other hand, he would have to quit eventually. The life of Cottonwood was limited, probably to no more than another year or two. Whatever trail towns sprang up west of here would also die in time. Which meant he would have to go somewhere else, to another lawman's job that might be as dull as driving stage or running a cattle ranch. So why confront Maggie over this job which he knew he'd have to give up anyway?

He smiled faintly to himself. It was a principle, he supposed. He couldn't let her issue ultimatums to him. He couldn't let her dictate his way of life, at least not that way.

He felt an overpowering sense of loss, as if Maggie already had gone out of his life. He shook himself physically, to throw that feeling off.

It was dark on First Street between Maple and Kansas streets. Dark enough to warn him that preoccupation could, in his line of work, be the death of him. He put Maggie determinedly out of his mind and forced himself to realize where he was, what the situation was in Cottonwood, and what the dangers were. He reached Kansas Street and turned south toward the huge Cattlemen's Hotel.

There were a hundred rooms in the Cattlemen's. At the height of the season, most of them would be occupied because Cottonwood would be full of cattle buyers, railroad men, trail bosses and their *segundos*, who were permitted north of Texas Street, gamblers and maybe a few female singers, who performed in the better saloons, and their managers. There were usually a number of eastern tourists as well, come to see the "wild, wild West."

Gaunt rode down Kansas in the exact center of the street. He stared straight ahead, unwilling to let a constantly roving glance indicate nervousness or fear. Yet his eyes missed nothing on either side of the street and his ears caught every sound.

The bar at the Cattlemen's Hotel and that at the Drovers were both well patronized by men of the town, probably discussing the arrival of the first herd and the confrontation Gaunt had had earlier with the drovers from that herd. He smiled faintly to himself and continued down the street all the way to the jail. This time, anticipating a possible sudden need for the animal, he tied his horse to the cast-iron hitching post in front.

He unlocked the jail door, but he did not light a lamp. Instead, he picked up the straight-backed chair, carried it out and put it down with its back to the front wall of the jail. He sat down and tilted it back against the wall.

For a while, he sat still, letting the sounds of the town be absorbed through his ears, sorting out each sound and identifying it.

So faint was one of those that he could almost have believed he had imagined it. Yet he knew that he had not and he was moving before it had died away. He hit his horse's back and was off at a gallop in the direction from which it had come. He judged that to be a block off Kansas Street and maybe a couple of blocks uptown.

The sound had been that of a woman's scream, made very faint by distance and by the overriding interference of other sounds. But it had been unmistakable nevertheless to Gaunt's trained ear.

He turned the corner of Kansas and Goliad at a hard gallop, the hoofs of his horse drowning out all other sounds. He whirled onto Oak and now caught a blur of figures up on the corner of Oak and Texas Street. It was so dark he could not distinguish them, but knowing from the scream that a woman was in trouble, he yanked his revolver from its holster and fired twice into the air. On the heels of the second shot's echo, he released a harsh and wordless shout.

He reached the corner, tense and alert, knowing this could be a trap someone had set for him. He left his horse, running, and now, close up, heard the sounds of struggle, a muffled cry, and headed for those sounds.

While he was still twenty or thirty feet away, the woman's attacker broke off and ran. With his hand removed from her mouth, the woman began to weep hysterically. Gaunt reached her and said in his deep, reassuring voice, "It's all right now. He's gone."

She clung to him, slight and small and obviously very young and he stared in the direction her attacker had gone. Voices called questions from the darkness and Gaunt bawled, "Somebody bring a lantern!"

But already he knew the identity of the girl in his arms. Josephina Chavez, waitress at the Drovers Hotel dining room. She lived half a block north of the intersection on Oak. She had been going home.

Men came running, one with a lantern. Josephina's clothing was torn and . there was a bruise on her cheekbone, but otherwise she seemed to be all right. Her father, Heraldo, came running and she left Gaunt and ran to his arms.

Someone said, "Those goddamn Texans!"

Gaunt said, "Whoa. She didn't say it was one of them."

"Who else?"

"There's lots of riffraff in town." He touched Josephina's slender shoulder. "Could you tell who it was? A cowboy? Somebody else?"

She was still trembling violently and tried twice before she could speak. She shook her head as she said, "Not a cowboy. Someone whose hands were smooth."

Gaunt was a little surprised that she would have thought of that. To Chavez he said, "She shouldn't come home alone. You should walk with her."

Heraldo's voice was defensive. "And you should keep the streets safe. That's what we pay you for."

Gaunt ignored the criticism. He knew how upset Josephina's father was. They moved away and the crowd dispersed, talking excitedly among themselves. Gaunt mounted his horse and rode back to the jail.

This was one of the prices they had to pay when they tried to run a wide-open town for the Texans. But he was glad Josephina had not been seriously hurt.

He pulled his horse's reins through the ring on the hitching post without tying them so that he could free them easily and resumed his seat in front of the jail. He fished the Bull Durham sack from his pocket and rolled himself a smoke, noting with mild surprise that his fingers were trembling. Not enough to interfere with what he was doing, but trembling.

He was that conscious, then, of danger to himself. Even while he'd been galloping toward the scream, he had believed in his heart that it was a trap. He struck a match and lighted his cigarette, blowing the match out quickly and dropping it to the walk.

He tilted his chair back comfortably against the wall. His thoughts turned idle as he listened again to the muted sounds of the town, the muffled shouts of revelry, the women's laughter, the tinkle of a piano and, up in the Alamo a woman's voice singing "Oralee."

For the time being he had nothing to do but listen and remain ready in case trouble broke out. His thoughts turned to Maggie and a strange sense of depression came over him.

It was a sense of loss and yet, he told himself, he had not lost her. She would marry him. What if he did have to give up his marshal's job? He was going to quit it anyway, if not this year or next then the year after that.

By insisting on his quitting it, she might, in fact, be saving his life. He smiled ruefully to himself. He was rationalizing, defending her, trying to talk himself into doing something he could not do. He could not permit her to issue an ultimatum to him, even before he married her. Not if their marriage was to succeed.

He thought of Rose with a twinge of guilt. Rose was in love with him. And he was unable to return her love, at least in the way she deserved.

An hour passed. Uptown, all lights except those in the Cattlemen's Hotel and the Drovers, had gone out. The lights in the Alamo cast a soft glow on the walk and out into the street. Men moved back and forth between the various saloons, some walking briskly, some staggering.

Somewhere along Goliad a fight broke out and men's voices shouted angrily. Gaunt rose to his feet and stood there, hesitating. There were no shots and the shouting voices died away. He settled back comfortably in his chair and tilted it once more against the wall.

For a while it was quiet. He thought how unfair it was to disarm the drovers and let saloonkeepers and gamblers keep their guns. At least, though, with the cowboys unarmed there would be little chance either saloonkeeper or gambler would have need to use their guns.

Another hour passed. He came to his feet a second time as a woman's shrilly screeching voice berated some cowboy for something he had or had not done. Again he settled back when the voice had died away.

More herds would probably arrive tomorrow, he thought. Maybe among them that of Buck Robineau. A week from now, Cottonwood would be jam-packed with cowboys and the cattle pens would be full of cattle waiting their turn at the cars.

All through the season new drovers would come, and those whose money was gone would depart. Cottonwood's function was to relieve them all of their money as rapidly and completely as possible.

Gaunt's function was simply to see that the process was orderly.

CHAPTER 6

As the evening wore on, Gaunt occasionally struck a match and glanced at his watch. It still lacked half an hour of being midnight when he finally got to his feet and mounted his horse.

Never before had he begun his midnight rounds so soon, and he wondered why he was doing it tonight. There could be only one reason, but he didn't like to acknowledge it. He was nervous even if he was not afraid. Nervous because of Vossler's threat. Nervous because of the attack on Josephina. Nervous because of the gambler, Moss, in the Pink Lady Saloon, who was perfectly capable of shooting him in the back.

He rode his horse up onto the walk and, leaning down, peered into the Pink Lady Saloon. Moss was sitting at a back corner table, facing toward the door. Gaunt caught the man's eye, his own gaze watchful. Moss's eyes were virulent. Gaunt went on, his horse's hoofs reverberating hollowly.

He crossed the intersection of Kansas and Goliad diagonally, and looked in the door at Overman's, the only saloon west of Kansas Street. Jake Overman was behind the bar. His head was totally bald, his face rough-hewn and coarse. Jake Overman was a hard case, but he'd never given Gaunt any trouble and he didn't keep a gun in the place, saying he was capable of handling anything that happened there. He was, too, thought Gaunt. Overman saw him and raised a hand briefly in greeting. Gaunt acknowledged it, then turned his horse and rode back toward Kansas Street.

He crossed Kansas and rode halfway down the block

on Goliad to the Longhorn. Not a single cowboy was in the Longhorn and the bartender was standing in front, smoking a cigar. Gaunt spoke and the bartender acknowledged the greeting with friendliness. Again Gaunt turned his horse and rode back to Kansas Street.

It occurred to him that maybe he'd started his rounds earlier tonight because of the fact that he'd have to return the Texans' guns at two. That might have had something to do with it, of course, but that wasn't all of it. Still, varying the times he made his rounds was smart, and he should have been doing it all along. No use making it any easier for his enemies than it already was.

On Kansas Street he rode up close to the open doors of each saloon and peered inside. He tried the doors of the closed shops and, where there was a padlock, tugged on it to make sure it had been locked properly.

He did not go around into the alleys to try the doors back there. He would do that on his final rounds after he returned the cowboys' guns to them at two. He always liked to check the alleys after the saloons had closed, so he could look for drunken cowboys who might have passed out or for those who might have been slugged and robbed.

That would be the most dangerous time for him and that was the time he feared the most.

His horse's hoofs made a hollow-sounding, comfortable rhythm as he rode slowly along the boardwalk, first on one side of the street then on the other, checking doors. The town council had been talking about putting in concrete sidewalks, but so far they hadn't been able to agree on it.

Maggie's restaurant made him think of her, and he shook off the preoccupation caused by his thoughts. Once more alert, he checked the doors of the bank and then, moving out into the center of the street, headed uptown into the residential section.

Only one light was visible along the length of the

street. It was in the parlor window of Bart Chapman's
house midway between Second and Third on the west
side of Kansas Street. It went out while Gaunt was still
a hundred feet away but not before he saw the
shadowy figure of a woman slip out the front door. She
saw him and ducked behind a huge lilac bush in Chapman's yard.

Morgan Gaunt didn't stop nor did he give any indi-
cation that he had seen. But he had seen the woman,
and had recognized her too. She was Bessie Overman,
wife of Jake Overman who owned Overman's Saloon
on Goliad.

Gaunt muttered a curse. Bart Chapman ought to
have better sense than to fool around with Bessie Overman. Her husband, Jake, might well be the most dangerous man in town. He'd kill Chapman if he found
out, and he'd probably do it with bare hands.

Bessie Overman was already out the front door
when she saw the dimly looming figure of the marshal
and his horse silhouetted against the saloon and hotel
lights farther down Kansas Street. She ducked behind
the big lilac bush in Chapman's front yard as the lamp
went out and waited for the marshal to pass.

Why was he here so early, she wondered. Never before had he begun his midnight rounds so soon. She
and Bart had often timed his passage by the clock.
Tonight he was half an hour ahead of time.

He went on by, his horse's hoofbeats muffled by the
deep dust in the street. Bessie released a long sigh of
relief. Maybe she had not been seen.

Frightened and nervous, she headed toward home, a
slight, pretty woman who never got over feeling the
guilt of her unfaithfulness. She had been seeing Bart
Chapman for almost a year, although she hadn't seen
him lately because her husband had not been staying
late at the saloon. She tried to justify her unfaithfulness
now, as she always did when guilt assailed her, but she
did not have much success. Jake might not be an ideal

husband and she did not love him; in fact, she never had. But he did support her, he had never struck her despite his violent nature, and when he was not at the saloon he was at home.

Chapman was almost his exact opposite. He was slender and handsome. He had a luxuriant head of hair. He flattered her and made her feel like a desirable woman, something Jake Overman never bothered to do.

But there was no excuse for her infidelity, and she knew that there was not. Yet she also knew she would go on seeing Chapman as long as he wanted her. He knew the risk. He knew how violent her husband was, and he knew Jake could easily break him in two. But he didn't seem to care or else believed they could go on forever without getting caught.

It turned her cold to think that the horseman riding up the street tonight could have been Jake as easily as the marshal. Jake probably would never leave the saloon this early, but he might.

She reached home and with trembling hands unlocked the door. She went inside, almost afraid to light a lamp, almost afraid that when she did she would see Jake standing there, face flushed with rage, eyes accusing her.

Oh God, she thought, I've got to stop. Then she thought of Chapman and of the ecstasy of being in his arms. And she knew she wouldn't stop. She would go on no matter what the consequences might be.

Gaunt rode up the dark street toward Hooker's hayfields at its upper end. Bessie Overman wasn't the only woman in Cottonwood who slipped out at night to visit another man. But Bessie's affair was probably the most explosive because Bessie's husband was so dangerous.

Still, thought Gaunt, there was little he could do about it. All he could do was speak to Chapman and let him know the risk. If Chapman and Bessie then chose to go on, there would be nothing further he could do.

He had always liked Bessie Overman. And he liked Chapman well enough. But he also knew Chapman was a ladies' man who would discard Bessie as soon as another woman caught his eye. Chapman probably deserved what happened to him, if anything did. But Bessie did not. Gaunt smiled at his own inconsistency. His sympathies were with Bessie. Had he been a woman, his sympathies would probably have been with Chapman instead.

The truth was, if his sympathy was anywhere, it ought to be with Overman.

He reached the upper end of town where all the houses were dark, skirted Hooker's fragrant hayfields and then rode his horse down into the bed of the creek. An animal, spooked by the horse, bounded away. A deer. He tensed briefly at the noise and then relaxed. He was jumpy, all right. Too jumpy for this early- in the year.

The ban on guns was partially responsible. So was the confrontation earlier today. But maybe, he thought, he was also getting tired. And weariness was a luxury he could not afford.

It was peaceful riding in the pitch-black bed of the creek and there was little chance anyone would try to ambush him here. Shooting was too risky when there was no light at all.

He climbed his horse out of the creek bed at the lower end of town and picked his way down the alleyway between the cattle pens after first opening a creosoted gate. It was utterly still, and what smell there was consisted mostly of the creosote with which the gates and planks had been treated and the dust-dry manure lying deep inside the pens.

He was loose and relaxed now but he had the feeling that his hearing had never been sharper nor his eyesight more acute. He reached the end of the pens, opened and closed another gate without dismounting from his horse, and headed for the depot, looming darker against the sky.

A single square of light was visible at this end of the depot. Gaunt rode his horse up onto the platform. His hoofbeats sounded thunderously against the thick planks.

Vague uneasiness touched Gaunt as he came into the square of light being thrown through the window and onto the platform. For just an instant he felt like a target. He had to force himself to stop his horse, bend down in his usual leisurely way and tap on the glass as a greeting to Jim Sutton, the telegrapher.

Sutton, who had glanced up as Gaunt's horse stepped onto the platform, returned the greeting and Gaunt went on, letting his breath sigh out inaudibly as he was swallowed by the darkness again.

His own jumpiness bothered him. Was it, he wondered, a hunch or premonition that something was going to happen to him? Or was it simply that he'd been on this job one too many years and should have quit before the cattle shipping season began? He didn't know.

What he did know was that he hadn't quit, and the town couldn't get another marshal this late in the year. He had to stay.

He entered the lower end of Kansas Street and halted at the jail. Without dismounting, he listened for a moment to the jumbled sounds of revelry. Easily then he swung from his horse and passed the ends of the reins through the ring on the hitching post.

His chair still sat on the sidewalk in front of the jail. He sat down, hitched at his gun so that it would be available, then tilted the chair back against the wall.

He fished his sack of makings from his vest pocket and rolled himself a smoke. The match made a glowing spot of light against the pitch-black bulk of the jail.

He felt more relaxed than he had all day. He supposed he had settled his doubts and had fatalistically accepted all the risks a few moments before when he had realized it was too late for the town to get another marshal, that it was therefore impossible for him to quit. And that was a definite relief to him. Now perhaps he could quit worrying and simply do his job.

He finished the cigarette and ground it out beneath his heel. Like a statue he sat, watching, waiting, listening.

Once, nearly an hour after arriving back at the jail, he struck a match and glanced at his watch. It was half past one. In another half hour the saloons would begin to close and shortly after that the cowboys from Wedemeier's herd would come by for their guns. After that he'd make his final rounds, checking to see that all saloons had closed and that all doors to the town's business establishments were secure.

CHAPTER 7

At about a quarter past two, the first of the drovers arrived at the jail to pick up their guns. There were three of them, all drunk enough to stagger. Owlishly they picked through the weapons hung on the coat tree and identified their own. Gaunt passed them out and the cowboys mounted and rode out of town.

Another group arrived, to repeat the procedure, and another after that. Finally, at two-thirty, only three guns remained.

Two more drunken drovers arrived shortly afterward, one of these obviously very angry about something, the other trying to quiet him. Sullenly the pair accepted their guns, mounted and rode south toward the railroad tracks. Which left Gaunt with one gun and cartridge belt. He stared at it for several moments, then went outside and peered into the darkness up Kansas street. No lights visible except for the dim night lights at the Cattlemen's and Drovers hotels.

Gaunt felt a stir of uneasiness. He wondered where the missing cowboy was. He hoped he wasn't lying dead behind one of the saloons, his pockets turned inside out. It was much more likely, of course, that the Texan was either passed out someplace or was spending the night with one of the girls. He'd check that out when he made his rounds.

He waited another ten minutes in the silent darkness. Then he mounted his horse and rode up Kansas Street to begin his final rounds.

At Goliad he turned left and rode as far as Overman's, which was dark and silent. He checked the door and found it locked. Leaving, he thought about Bessie Overman and Bart Chapman, and briefly felt sorry for Jake Overman. He returned along Goliad, checked the Longhorn on the other side of Kansas Street and also found it locked.

He returned to Kansas Street and checked the door of the Pink Lady Saloon where the gambler, Moss, made his headquarters. It was dark inside and the door was locked. That shouldn't have increased his nervousness, but it did.

Now he turned up Kansas Street, checking each saloon he passed. All were dark. All their doors were locked, with one exception. The Red Dog. Sully had apparently taken longer to close than the others had. As Gaunt drew abreast, he stepped from the door, accompanied by another man, then turned and snapped the padlock shut.

Gaunt was about to speak, when a shout came from across the street. "All right, you cheatin' sonsabitches, let's see if you're as tough out here as you are in your goddamn saloon!"

Gaunt froze, himself less than a dozen yards from the pair. There wasn't enough light for accurate shooting, only a small amount from the stars, but the cowboy might possibly score a lucky hit. The chances of either Sully or the man with him hitting the cowboy were slimmer, at least until they had a muzzle flash at which to shoot.

But Gaunt had no intention of letting it go that far. To Sully and the man with him, he said, "If either of you is armed, keep your heads. There's damn little chance he can hit anything with no more light than he's got. I'll take care of it."

Sully said sourly, "Then take care of it."

Gaunt asked, "What's his beef, anyway? You cheat him?"

"No cheating. He lost his money, is all. I never saw a heavy loser yet that didn't claim he was cheated."

Gaunt didn't believe Sully, but this was no time to

argue it. He turned his horse and slowly paced him across the street toward the place from which the cowboy's voice had come. He called, "All right now, son, don't do anything you're going to be sorry for."

The cowboy squawled excitedly, "Marshal, you just stay out of this. That goddamn gambler cheated me and the bartender backed him up. Threw me out of the saloon. Nobody does that to me and gets away with it!"

Gaunt guessed it must have happened while he was at the other end of town making his rounds. The cowboy had probably gone to one of the other saloons, borrowed some money from one of his friends and kept drinking until all the places closed.

It angered him that a thing like this could have happened the first night the cowboys were in town. He'd warned Sully and Vossler, but apparently his warning hadn't done much good.

In a calm and measured voice he said, "Son, I'll see that you get your money back. I don't allow cheating in this town. You should have come to me and let me look into it."

Sully bawled, "Damn you, if you give him his money back it's goin' to be out of your own pocket. He wasn't cheated. He just lost."

Gaunt turned his head and his voice was like a whip. "Shut your mouth, Sully! Don't open it again!"

He was now halfway across the street. He kept trying to see the cowboy, but it was too dark. There was a passageway over there between two buildings maybe a couple of feet wide and Gaunt supposed that was where the cowboy was.

He said softly, "Son, I don't know who you are. You pull back out of that passageway and skedaddle back to your herd and nothing will be done about this. I'll send your gun out with one of the bunch that comes to town tomorrow."

There was no reply. Gaunt said, "Son . . ."

Suddenly a voice from the passageway yelled excitedly, "Marshal, you stay out of this! I got no quarrel with you, only with that cheatin' pair of bastards across the street."

Until now, Gaunt had supposed the cowboy was the one who failed to pick up his gun at the jail. Now he realized this was the angry one who, with his friend, had picked his gun up last. The one who hadn't picked his up was still unaccounted for.

He had stopped his horse, just short of the edge of the boardwalk. He was listening, for a scuffing sound, for the sounds of the cowboy's breathing.

His horse fidgeted. Suddenly the animal looked toward the passageway. His ears pricked forward.

The cowboy was still there. Gaunt said, "Son, I'm coming over there. You got nothing against me, and you don't want to shoot me. You fade back out of that passageway and I'll see that you get your money back tomorrow. You got my word on it."

He touched his horse's sides with his heels and the animal stepped forward. Gaunt meant to ride right to the passageway and block it with his horse's bulk. He didn't think the cowboy would shoot.

But the horse had taken no more than two steps when the cowboy's voice bawled, "Oh no you don't!" Flame blossomed from his extended gun, once, twice.

The first bullet went wild. The second raked a burning gouge along Gaunt's left thigh. And suddenly he was no longer a controlled and thinking man. Instinct took over. His hand went like lightning to his side. His gun came out of its holster in a blur of motion, the hammer back and the gun ready to fire before he ever leveled it.

The cowboy fired again, this bullet going past Gaunt's right ear like an angry bee. After that Gaunt didn't hesitate. He fired, slightly left of the cowboy's muzzle flash and a few inches higher.

Gaunt was diving from his horse before his own muzzle flash had died away. He hit the deep dust of the street on both feet but his left leg folded because of the bullet wound and dumped him in the dirt. The cowboy's gun was silent now.

Cursing soundlessly at the leg that had let him fall, Gaunt struggled to his feet. Gun in hand, he limped painfully toward the passageway.

He was almost sick at his stomach because he knew what he was going to find. He reached the passageway, nearly falling over the yielding, prone body of the cowboy. He knelt, put his hand on the cowboy's chest, then took it away. The man was dead.

For an instant his fury knew no bounds. Sully and his crooked gambler had succeeded in getting him to do their killing for them. He wondered bleakly what else he could have done, and knew he'd had no other alternative. It had been his job to prevent a shoot-out between the cowboy and the two across the street. He had done what he was supposed to do. It just hadn't turned out the way it should.

He knelt there, numb with shock. He'd seen many dead men. He'd killed several men himself. But he never stopped experiencing that strangely bleak sense of loss, of something precious destroyed that can never be replaced.

With forlorn hope, he put his hand on the cowboy's chest again, praying silently to himself there would be movement there that he had missed before. But there was not.

He got slowly to his feet, keeping his weight off his wounded leg which now was burning fiercely with the pain. Blood had soaked his pants; it had run down his leg and into his boot. He could hear voices now, uptown, an indistinct murmuring of question upon question. What's going on, they wanted to know. What's happening?

He turned his head and stared at the dark front of the Red Dog across the street. He could now see the two blurred, indistinct shapes of Sully and his gambler. He would run them out of town, he thought, not doubting for an instant that they had, indeed, cheated the cowboy and then thrown him out of the saloon.

Suddenly, unexpectedly, muzzle flashes blossomed across the street. A bullet took out a window not two feet from Gaunt's head and shards of broken glass showered to the walk. Others thudded into the wooden facades of the two buildings.

Gaunt dived for the passageway, stumbling over the cowboy's body and sprawling full length inside the passageway. He was faced away from his attackers and it was awkward turning around. He did it, though, and then shoved his revolver out in front of him, resting his arm on the body of the dead cowboy.

He understood instantly the way Sully and his gambler friend were thinking. Shots had been fired, supposedly at them, by the cowboy who had challenged them. No one would blame them for shooting back. And if the marshal happened to be in the way, if the marshal happened to get killed . . . Well hell, this end of town would probably want to give them a medal, and the other end of town probably wouldn't object too much. He was necessary as all policemen were, and people acknowledged that. But down deep they didn't really like him or approve of him.

He could have killed Sully and the man with him. He could see both of them dimly against the lighter wall of the saloon. But he held his fire, lying still, knowing that in a few minutes the street would be swarming with townspeople and neither Sully nor the man with him would dare continue shooting at him.

Besides that, he had killed once tonight and he would not kill again. Not so soon. Not if there was any other way.

The voices up the street were coming closer now. There was a lantern, bobbing along, throwing its flickering light on the buildings on both sides of the street.

And from the cribs farther downtown and over on

Maple and Oak came the voices of the girls, asking each other what was going on, and who had fired all the shots.

Gaunt finally got to his feet. Absently he punched the empties out of his gun and replaced them with live ammunition from his belt. His horse, made nervous by the shots, had moved away downstreet and now stood fifty feet away.

The man with the lantern reached Sully and the gambler, standing in front of the Red Dog Saloon. Gaunt knew they couldn't shoot him now. He crossed the street, slowly, limping on his wounded leg.

The man with the lantern asked, "What's going on? What's all the shooting about?"

Gaunt did not reply. He was looking at Sully and the gambler. He swung a hand and the flat of it struck Sully on the cheek with enough force to snap his head aside. The bartender made a move toward his gun, and Gaunt rammed a fist into his belly, a blow that made Sully double and go white with pain.

Gaunt relieved both Sully and the gambler of their guns. He said, "You've got until sundown tomorrow to get out of town. If I see either of you after that, I'll shoot on sight. Is that understood?"

Maybe they had expected him to charge them with trying to kill him a few moments before and had prepared their defenses only for that. Neither man offered any protest or defense.

Only their eyes threatened him. Both men turned and walked away.

By now a crowd of perhaps a dozen men had gathered in front of the Red Dog Saloon. A couple had wandered across the street and were looking down at the still body of the cowboy lying on the walk.

Gaunt said, "Somebody get Ira Blanton down here to pick up the body."

A man hurried away. Gaunt looked up Kansas Street and saw Rose Navarro standing in front of the

Alamo, a wrapper clutched around her, looking worriedly downstreet. Maggie Conover was nowhere in sight.

He walked up the street to where Rose was standing, trying not to limp. She said, "You're hurt," her face white with shock.

"Not much. A crease."

"You could have been killed."

It was true, but he couldn't admit it to himself or to her. He said, "I'll be all right."

"You'll let the doctor look at it?"

"Yes. I'm sorry I worry you."

She forced herself to smile. She knew if he could walk, he was not too badly hurt. She turned and went back into the Alamo and climbed the stairs to her room.

Damn! damn! damn! she thought. Why do I have to fall in love with a man who walks the streets making a target of himself? Why do I have to play second fiddle to a woman who hasn't even the sense to take what is offered to her?

She slammed the door furiously. She felt tears burning behind her eyes. I won't cry, she thought. Damn it, I won't!

But she did. She threw herself on the bed with sobs already wracking her. She wept until she was exhausted and could weep no more.

He was a fool, waiting for Maggie Conover to finish her year of mourning and consent to marry him. He was a fool, letting Maggie Conover dictate to him how he would earn his living and how he would work.

But she was the biggest fool of all. For asking nothing of him. For giving everything she had to give.

She got up and went to the window. She stared down into the street. There were several lanterns down there now. She could see Morgan Gaunt, not bothering now to hide his limp.

She had thought all her tears were gone. But they

were not. They filled her eyes again as she stared down at him.

He had been lucky tonight. But he was doomed. Before the last of the Texas cattle were shipped East, Morgan Gaunt would be dead.

CHAPTER 8

Maggie Conover did hear the shots. Already awake, worrying and wondering what she ought to do, she flinched at the first and flinched again at each succeeding shot. She threw back the covers and sat up on the edge of the bed.

Three shots. She hurried into the parlor and stepped out onto the porch in her nightgown and bare feet. She couldn't see or hear anything.

What did three shots mean? That someone had tried to kill Morgan, certainly. And probably that he had fired back.

Three shots instead of one or two was encouraging, she knew. Morgan Gaunt was probably all right. One shot would almost certainly have meant that he was dead. Suddenly there was another flurry of shots. Again she flinched at each.

She could feel violent tremors beginning in her knees. She sat down like a child on the top porch step and hugged her knees to stop their trembling. She couldn't stand this, she told herself desperately, not any more. She couldn't stand lying awake night after night worrying. She'd tell him tomorrow. She'd tell him that she'd marry him immediately but only if he would give up the marshal's job. She'd tell him that if he didn't, they were through.

There were no more shots. What if he was dead? That second burst of shots had not been reassuring.

She knew she couldn't stand not knowing whether he was all right or not. She wouldn't sleep a wink if she didn't find out for sure. She got up and hurried into the house. She put on slippers and a wrapper, then went out, crossed Maple and hurried along Second to Kansas Street.

Down at its lower end lanterns were moving around like fireflies. The figures of milling men were visible, and she strained her eyes trying to pick out Morgan Gaunt.

She saw his horse. A few moments later she saw a man's figure that must certainly be his. The man was limping painfully.

Her breath sighed out softly with relief. He was alive, then. Only hurt. One of the bullets must have struck him in the leg.

For an instant she felt deep compassion for his wound, his pain. Then she said fiercely to herself, "I'm glad he's hurt! I'm glad! Now maybe he'll be sensible. Maybe he'll give up this job."

A few others had heard the shots and had come into the street or onto their porches to stare downtown. Conscious of their glances, Maggie hurried back toward home. She reached her house, went in and locked the door.

She stumbled back to her bedroom, removed her wrapper and threw herself onto the bed. For several moments she lay there trembling.

The tears came like a flood. She sobbed hysterically for a long, long time. She felt helpless and alone because she didn't think Morgan would do what she wanted him to do, and because she knew she would break off with him if he did not.

It was more than two hours before she finally could sleep.

It must have been nearly half an hour before Ira Blanton's black hearse came down the street drawn by a team of bays. When the hearse was used at funerals it was always drawn by two teams of gleaming blacks, but for picking up a body, a single team was used. Ira made a turn in the middle of the street and pulled to a halt in front of the passageway where the cowboy's body lay.

Gaunt and Ira lifted the body onto a canvas that Ira had laid in the hearse to protect the interior.

Blanton was a short, stubby man who was enormously strong in spite of his rotund appearance. He whistled. "Hell to pay, huh?"

Gaunt said, "I'm afraid so."

"I suppose you want me to wait for word from the trail boss about the funeral."

"That's right. I'll ride out first thing in the morning and tell him."

"Who killed him, Sully or that gambler?"

Gaunt realized he didn't even know the gambler's name. He said, "Neither. I did."

Blanton whistled again. But he didn't comment. He went around and climbed to the driver's seat. He drove away, heading for his furniture store and undertaking establishment on the south side of Main behind the bank.

Gaunt was conscious not only of the pain in his leg but of the blood still flowing from the wound. His foot squished inside his boot with every step he took. He walked to his horse and picked up the reins. To the crowd he said, "That's all. Go home and go to bed."

Still worried about the cowboy who had not picked up his gun, he mounted and rode uptown toward Doc Kelley's house on Third and Oak.

There was a light in the parlor and another in the adjoining room that served as Doc's examining and operating room. The door opened before Gaunt could dismount and Doc stood framed in it, crowned by a halo of bushy white hair. Gaunt limped up the walk and Doc said, "The shots woke me up. I figured someone would need patching up."

He stood aside and Gaunt went in. Gaunt went straight into the examining room. He stuck his left boot into the boot jack on the floor and pulled it off. His face turned white with pain. He left a bloody footprint on the floor when he put down his bootless foot.

Doc said impatiently, "I could have got that off."

"Sure. With a knife. That's a damn good pair of boots." He was already pulling the other off. Sweat stood out in beads on his forehead from the pain.

"Don't want me to cut your pants either, I suppose."

"Why cut them? I can get them off." He already had them off. In his long, bloody underwear he sat down on the table's edge.

Sarcastically Kelley asked, "Is it all right if I cut your underwear?"

Gaunt shrugged. "Go ahead."

Doc Kelley pushed him back and Gaunt was glad to lie full length. His head was reeling and his leg was burning savagely. He felt Doc working at cutting his underwear away from the wound. He closed his eyes.

In a calm and steady voice Doc kept him posted as to what he was doing and what he thought. He said, "Deep. Ragged too. But it didn't get an artery, and it didn't touch a bone. Son, you've lost a hell of a lot of blood. You're going to feel woozy for a day or two. Ought to stay in bed, but I don't suppose it's any use to tell you that."

He poured something on the wound to disinfect it, something that made blackness come down like a curtain over Gaunt's consciousness. Then he laid a thick compress over the wound and began to bandage it. "I'm not going to stitch you up because that will draw the wound together and make it pull. This way it'll leave a bigger scar, but it won't pull and it won't keep you from moving around."

He finished bandaging. By then Gaunt's head was clear again. He sat up and reached for his pants. Doc carried the bloody boot out back to rinse the blood out of it. When he returned he was drying the inside with a towel. He handed it to Gaunt, who put it on.

Gaunt got to his feet. His pants were very tight over the bandage. He asked, "How much, Doc?"

"A dollar."

Gaunt gave him a dollar. "Thanks. I'd better go back to the hotel and change clothes. Then I've got to make my rounds."

"Any chance of you getting shot again? If not, I'll go back to bed."

Gaunt grinned. "No chance. Go back to bed," knowing he lied even as he spoke.

Already he was in trouble with Wedemeier and his drovers over the cowboy's death. If anything had happened to the other missing cowboy there would be hell to pay. In any case, he had to know. He had to find the man.

He went out, limped to his horse and mounted. In front of the Drovers Hotel, he drew his horse to a halt. He swung down, limped to the tie rail and looped his reins around it. He went in, nodded to Hughie Jordan, the night clerk, then crossed the tile-floored lobby to the stairs.

Climbing them hurt, but he did his best not to limp. He reached his room, unlocked the door and went in. Groping, he found the lamp, struck a match and lighted it.

He found clean underwear, pants, socks and shirt, and with a bit of pain in his wounded leg, he changed his clothes. He then belted his revolver around his middle, withdrew the gun and checked the loads. Reloading was automatic with him after he had fired his gun, but he was taking no chances that he might have forgotten it.

He blew out the lamp, went out and locked the door behind him. It wasn't that he had anything he thought might be stolen. He was being careful. He didn't want to walk into a dark room and find someone waiting there for him.

Pain and the loss of so much blood had weakened him. He clumped downstairs, favoring his leg, and went out onto darkened Kansas Street. Mounting his horse, he rode slowly down Kansas to the jail, staying in the middle of the street, his senses painfully alert. He heard no sound, saw nothing move. The brothels all were dark, the girls asleep.

He rode back to Goliad and turned right toward the Longhorn. When he came to the alley, he turned into it, holding his horse to a slow walk. He knew he'd never see the missing cowboy in this complete darkness. He would have to count on his horse to reveal the man's presence, either dead or unconscious but alive.

Now, as sightless as if he were blind, he watched his horse's head and ears. He rode all the way to Texas Street, then turned and retraced his steps, this time trying each rear door as he did. The route was familiar to him; he knew each shed, each sagging fence, each pile of tin cans and trash.

He was still about a hundred feet from the alley mouth when his horse's head turned suddenly to the right. The horse's ears pricked forward nervously.

Gaunt wasted no time. He left the saddle with a single, swift movement, hitting the ground first on his good leg, afterward bracing himself with the wounded one.

Made nervous either by his rider's nervousness or by what he'd seen, the horse danced away. Gaunt's gun was in his hand, the hammer back, while he tried to pierce the darkness and see what his horse had seen.

Nothing moved. No sound broke the silence. The hairs on the back of Gaunt's neck were erect, the flesh crawling underneath.

How long he stood there motionless he didn't know. But when nothing happened, he moved forward, a careful step at a time, as alert and ready as he had ever been in his life.

Three steps. Four. He was out of the alley now, passing a sagging stable at the rear of the Kansas Pride Saloon. Suddenly his boot encountered something soft and yielding and he stopped, knowing what it was, praying silently to himself that the cowboy wasn't dead. He knelt, still alert, still not looking down. This would be the perfect place for Sully and his friend to ambush him, because he would be busy with the prostrate cowboy and not expecting it. But nothing happened. No guns roared. There was no sound.

He put his hand on the cowboy's chest, almost weak with relief when he found it rising and falling regularly. And now the sour smell of whiskey reached his nostrils, the drunken cowboy's breath.

He picked up a stick and threw it against the building wall, knowing this sudden sound would startle anyone who might be waiting in the darkness for a chance to shoot him down. But still no sound came. Still nothing moved.

Satisfied at last, Gaunt lowered the hammer on his gun and shoved it into its holster at his side. He pushed his hands under the cowboy's body and lifted it. He carried it into the alley to his horse.

With a soft grunt, he heaved it up and over the saddle. Then, leading the horse with one hand and steadying the cowboy with the other, he continued north along the alley to Texas Street.

The Drovers Hotel was on the corner of Kansas and Texas streets. He looped his horse's reins around the rail, slid the cowboy's body off the saddle and onto his shoulder, then carried it into the lobby of the hotel.

Hughie was asleep. Gaunt struck the bell and Hughie came awake with a start. Gaunt said, "A room for him."

"Yes, sir!" Hughie grabbed a key and came around. He crossed the lobby, hurrying, with Gaunt right behind.

Climbing the stairs made sweat beads spring out on Gaunt's forehead, but he made it to the top without having his leg give way. He carried the unconscious cowboy along the hall to the door Hughie had unlocked for him. Hughie was inside, lighting the lamp.

Gaunt dumped the cowboy on the bed. Hughie asked in a scared voice, "Is he all right?"

"He will be tomorrow. Except for a headache. Tell

him to stop at the jail for his gun on his way out of town."

Gaunt bent and went through the cowboy's pockets. There was some money, a pocket knife, a few extra cartridges for his gun. Gaunt blew out the lamp. He said, "Leave the key here so he can get out in the morning. But lock the door from the outside."

"Yes, sir." Hughie obeyed, closing and locking the door from the outside with his master key. He followed Gaunt downstairs.

At the desk, Gaunt asked him for an envelope. He counted the money and wrote the amount on the outside of the envelope. He listed the other items below and then put everything inside. He sealed it and handed it to the clerk. "Give it to him when he comes down in the morning."

"Yes, sir." Hughie put the envelope underneath the counter top.

Gaunt went out, conscious of a vast relief. He still had to explain the other cowboy's death, but at least this one was all right.

He untied his horse and mounted to continue his final rounds. His leg was bleeding again; he had opened it carrying the drunken cowboy upstairs. The bandage on it was soaked, and the blood had seeped through and stained his pants.

He wished tonight's rounds were over with. It would feel good to lie down and close his eyes.

CHAPTER 9

Up Kansas Street he rode. He thought about Bessie
Overman when he passed Bart Chapman's house. He
went on, troubled by his thoughts, hoping Bessie would
discontinue her relationship with Chapman before her
husband found out about it. Cottonwood was no different than any small town—its inhabitants liked to gossip. If he knew about Bessie's relationship with
Chapman, it was certain other people also did. And
they would talk.

Farther up the street, where he would normally have
turned to go to Maggie's house, he wondered if she had
heard the shots earlier. When she knew he'd been
wounded tonight she was certain to renew her demands
that he quit the marshal's job. And he didn't know how
to answer her. He didn't want to break off with her.
Just the thought of losing her made the future bleak.

On he went, finally reaching the upper end of town
where Hooker's hayfield was. He skirted it along the
barbed wire fence and, when he reached the brushy
bed of Cottonwood Creek, rode his horse down into it.

It was darker here because of a diminished light
from the stars. It was hard to see anything, even for
Gaunt, whose eyes were accustomed to the dark. But
his horse seemed to have no trouble avoiding obstacles.

He let the reins go slack, contenting himself, in the
absence of vision, with listening. He heard the katy-
dids, the soft murmur of the creek, the scurrying of
field mice and other small rodents. Once he startled
something larger, a deer probably, and the animal
bounded away, crashing through the brush.

He watched his horse's head, knowing if there was a man or men waiting for him to pass, the horse would smell or see them a long time before he did. But the horse plodded along, never raising his head, never pricking his ears.

He reached the lower end of town and climbed his horse out of the creek bottom at the railroad bridge. From here he rode to the cattle pens, still empty, and picked his way along the main alley separating them. Now, even more than before, he kept his glance on his horse's head, sure that the horse would spot anyone a long time before he did.

But nothing happened. He reached the end of the cattle pens, opened the gate and let himself out, closing it behind him, all without leaving his horse. The gate squeaked thunderously as it closed.

That ought to wake them up, he thought, and he could feel himself growing even more tense than he had been before. Only a small distance now separated him from the jail.

He reached the depot. A square of light showed the location of the telegraph office. The sound of his horse's hoofs on the wooden platform as the animal jumped up onto it made Jim Sutton, who had been asleep, raise his head. Gaunt's every nerve was tense as he rode past the window, briefly silhouetted against the square of light.

The report, though expected, startled both Gaunt and his horse. It came crashing out of the darkness, preceded by the barest split second by the muzzle flash. Gaunt's horse jumped a foot into the air and three feet ahead and Gaunt knew he had, at least, been stung by the bullet.

With no urging from his rider, the horse thundered briefly along the wooden station platform, leaving it with a long, running leap. For all of that short distance two guns a dozen yards away flared and racketed, the bullets tearing holes in the frame walls and windows of the station and showering splinters and broken glass onto the platform below.

Gaunt, keeping his seat easily despite the horse's terror-stricken flight, placed the shots before the horse leaped from the platform. There was a pile of ties a dozen yards to the right, and the two gunmen were hidden behind the ties.

Immediately he reined the horse hard to the right. He dug his heels into the already frightened horse's sides, urging him to even greater speed, heading him straight for the pile of ties.

In the dim starlight, he saw two figures materialize from the dark bulk of the ties. They sprinted away toward the cattle pens. Jim Sutton had come out onto the railroad platform and now he yelled querulously into the darkness, "What the hell's going on?"

The frantic speed of the fleeing gunmen was no match for the running speed of Gaunt's horse. The animal overtook the first man and tried to swerve to avoid striking him. Gaunt wouldn't let him swerve. The horse's chest struck the man, knocking him end over end.

The horse tried to slow, now, but Gaunt would not permit it. His heels drummed against the horse's sides and the barrel of his gun flayed the horse's rump.

Seconds after striking the first man, he drew abreast of the second. Half a dozen feet separated them. Gaunt reined the horse aside, forcing him right up against the running man.

His gun barrel descended, striking the man's head with a sodden sound. The man disappeared.

Only now did Gaunt haul the horse to a halt and turn him, once more digging in his heels. The horse leaped forward. Gaunt knew the second man was out of it. He also knew the first could still be dangerous.

And he was right. Flame blossomed ahead of him and a bullet went by a couple of feet away, humming like a bee. The gun's report cut off the sound.

Once more the horse ran straight into the man, who

turned to flee when he saw he was going to be run down again. Too late. The horse struck him and knocked him flying for a second time.

This time Gaunt left the horse in mid-stride. Trained to do so, the horse came to an instant halt when he felt Gaunt leave the saddle. Gaunt's wounded leg collapsed under him as he touched the ground and he fell, rolling in the dust. When he came to hands and knees, the man who had shot at him was less than ten feet away—raising his gun.

Gaunt said sharply, "Don't! Don't or you're dead!" The man dropped his gun.

Gaunt pushed himself to his feet. He was angry now with a cold, harsh anger he seldom felt. He walked to the man and, reaching down, seized his coat collar and yanked him to his feet. The man struggled and cursed and Gaunt, out of patience and hurting now, clipped him on the side of the head with the barrel of his gun. The man sagged and Gaunt let him fall.

Over on the station platform, Jim Sutton called, "Marshal? You all right?"

Gaunt called back, "I'm all right." He went to his horse and took the rope down from its place beside the saddle horn. He made a loop and stooping, put it around the unconscious man beneath his arms. Straightening, he walked to the other man, stooped and dragged him back. He made the loop large enough to go around both men beneath the arms.

Holding the end of the rope, he went to his horse and mounted, trying to favor his wounded leg, which was still bleeding. He looped the rope around the saddle horn.

He drummed on the horse's sides with his heels. The rope came taut and the horse moved away, turning sideways, prancing because of the strange burden dragging along behind. Gaunt's hand on the reins was firm.

The dust was deep and a cloud of it raised behind the two dragging men. One of them came to and yelled with protest but Gaunt neither answered nor stopped.

Across the railroad tracks he went, with the two men bumping over them and on beyond to Kansas Street and from there straight to the jail, a total distance of a block and a half. His horse maintained a steady walk.

He rode beyond the jail so that the pair he was dragging would stop immediately before the door. Then he threw the rope off the saddle horn and dismounted with it in his hand.

One of the men, the conscious one, tried to throw off the loop so that he could rise. Gaunt pulled back. The man failed to get enough slack to free himself.

He reached the pair. Both men were of approximately the same build so he could not distinguish between them. Besides, both were covered thickly with dust.

One was struggling. Before Gaunt realized what he was doing, he yanked a derringer from some hidden place, leveled and fired it.

So angry was the man and so much in a hurry that the bullet went wild. He never got a chance for another shot. Gaunt's foot lashed out, struck his forearm with enough force to make him shout with pain. The derringer dropped into the dust and Gaunt picked it up.

He stooped, his leg afire with pain now. He yanked the men to their feet, one by one. Both were conscious, although one was very unsteady on his feet. Gaunt said harshly, "Into the jail."

They were slow to move so he put a hand on the back of each and gave a shove. Both men staggered toward the door of the jail.

Gaunt followed. The jail door was locked so they could not go in. He said harshly, "Put your hands in the air and keep them there."

They complied. Swiftly Gaunt searched them for hidden weapons, being very meticulous and thorough about it because he knew carelessness could and would cost him his life. Satisfied that neither had another gun, he unlocked the door and pushed them roughly inside.

Both staggered all the way across the room. Gaunt found the lamp and lit it. Now, in the light, he could tell the men apart. Both Sully and the gambler glared at him murderously. He said, "Back to one of the cells. Go on!"

They turned and shuffled into the corridor between the two rows of cells. Gaunt said, "Inside. Move!"

They stepped into one of the cells. Gaunt closed the door behind them and locked it with his key.

He could feel himself go limp now that the danger was past. He looked at the gambler. "What's your name?"

"Jackson."

Gaunt nodded, turned and went back to the office, closing the separating door behind.

He blew out the lamp and went out the door. Mounting, he rode his horse to the livery barn. The animal hadn't worked up a sweat since this morning, so there was no need to rub him down now. Gaunt led him to his stall and got him a measure of oats and a couple of generous forks of hay. He patted the horse's neck, briefly examined the bullet crease on the horse's rump and then went back out into the street.

He returned to the jail, glad his horse hadn't been hurt more seriously. The shallow gouge he had sustained would heal in a week or so.

Inside the jail again, he lighted the lamp. He sat down, tilted his chair back and put his feet up on the desk.

With Sully and Jackson in jail, he knew he didn't dare go to the hotel tonight. But it wouldn't be the first time he had slept on the office cot.

He found the makings in his pocket and rolled himself a smoke. He lighted it, feeling himself relax now that the long day was done.

Tomorrow he had to ride out to Wedemeier's herd and try to explain the cowboy's death to Wedemeier and to his men. He knew what he would say. "He tried to kill me and I had no choice." They'd have to accept it. They had no other choice. But he didn't like the explanation any more than they would. There ought to be a better way to settle things.

His leg ached ferociously. Blood had soaked all the way through the bandage and there was a spot of it on his pants as big as his hand. He eased the leg to the floor, trying to get it into a position where the pain would ease.

But the pain did not diminish no matter how he moved the leg. He'd play hell sleeping tonight, he thought.

Glancing at the clock, he saw that it was already three-thirty in the morning. He opened a desk drawer and took out a bottle and a glass. He dumped the glass half full of whiskey and gulped it down. He poured the glass half full a second time.

His thoughts began to wander now. He thought of Rose, and a small smile touched the corners of his mouth. He thought of Maggie, and the smile disappeared. He thought of Bessie Overman, and a slight frown touched his face.

His thoughts returned to Wedemeier. He hoped the trail boss would be satisfied to let his dead cowboy be buried quietly. But he doubted it. Wedemeier's cold neutrality only masked an underlying hostility. Wedemeier had heard about Marshal Gaunt and had believed everything he'd heard.

And if more herds arrived tomorrow, as was probable, Gaunt's job was going to be complicated even more. He found himself hoping fervently that one herd, at least, would not arrive until all this had quieted. He hoped that Buck Robineau would not arrive for another week.

CHAPTER 10

Gaunt was drowsy now, both from weariness and the whiskey he had consumed. He got up and headed for the office cot. He sat down on it and with difficulty because of his wound, pulled off his boots. He got up and was about to blow out the lamp when he heard a knock on the office door.

Glancing that way, he saw Rose Navarro standing in front of it. He crossed the room, trying not to limp but not succeeding very well, and opened the door.

He stood aside and Rose came in. She threw one hasty glance at his face, which he supposed was pale and drawn with weariness. Then she looked down at his leg, at his blood-soaked pants. She glanced up at his face again.

Her own face was pale, without makeup, and her eyes were filled with compassion for his pain. "Thank God you're alive at least! I heard all those shots, and I had to know!"

She was clad in a nightgown with a wrapper over it. She had slippers on her feet. He said, "Sully and a gambler named Jackson tried to get me down by the depot. I've got them in jail."

There was a touch of exasperation in her expression and he knew what she was thinking. But she didn't voice her thoughts. Instead she asked, "You're not going to bed with that leg bleeding the way it is are you?"

"It'll stop as soon as I quit moving around on it."

"It should be dressed again. That bandage will be stiff as a board by morning when it's dry."

"It'll be all right."

She faced him, hands on hips. "It will not be all right! You just come with me to the doctor's house or else I'll get him to come down here!"

He stared at her pale and angry face. She was not a woman to make demands, but she sure was making one now. And he knew she'd do exactly what she said she would. He shrugged. "All right. It don't look like it's much use arguing with you."

"It's not."

He sat down on the cot again and pulled on his boots. He tried not to show how much it hurt but he could feel the sweat breaking out in beads on his forehead. When he stood, she took his arm, to steady him.

He left the lamp burning, but he locked the door when he went out. Together they walked slowly along the street, Rose trying to support his wounded side but not succeeding very well. He tried not to limp.

Doc's house was nearly seven blocks from the jail. In front of the Alamo, Rose said, "I should have gotten a buggy. Or asked Doc Kelley to come to the jail."

"It's all right," he said, and it was. He liked her close beside him and he liked the faint perfume that rose from her hair. It hurt every time he put his left foot down, but it would have hurt almost as bad lying on the cot at the jail.

Rose said, "You said it happened down by the depot. Were they waiting for you there?"

"Uh-huh. Tried for me as I crossed in front of the telegrapher's window."

"You're lucky."

"I suppose I am."

"What about tomorrow? How are you going to tell that trail boss that you killed one of his men?"

"Show him what his man did to me, I guess."

The town seemed to be asleep. No lamps showed anywhere. Gaunt was drenched with perspiration when they reached Doc Kelley's house. Rose helped him to the door and Gaunt knocked on it.

A lamp was lighted somewhere in the house. It got

brighter as it was carried to the front door. The door opened and Doc asked, a trifle irritably, "You shot again?"

Rose answered for him. "He needs his leg wound dressed, It's been bleeding badly."

Rose stayed in the parlor while Doc took Gaunt into his examining room. Doc closed the door and Gaunt used the boot jack to pull off his boots. He dropped his pants. "There goes another suit of underwear."

Doc was already cutting it away. "Maybe I ought to have sewed that wound up. You've lost a hell of a lot of blood. How much do you think a man can spare?"

"Didn't you sawbones used to bleed a person for just about everything that went wrong with them?"

"*I* didn't!" Doc's face got red, and then he grinned at his own anger. He unwound the bandages as gently as he could. The compress, beneath the bandages, had been stuck to the wound but all the fresh bleeding had loosened it and it came off easily.

Gaunt stared at the raw and ugly wound, even now seeping blood. Doc prepared a fresh compress, saying as he did, "You got to be more careful. Can't you stay off of it?"

Gaunt looked wryly at him. "What do *you* think, Doc? There's one herd here already and a man dead that I've got to explain. There will probably be two or three more herds arriving tomorrow."

"All right. All right. Forget I mentioned it. But you take better care of yourself or you'll be flat on your back and Cottonwood won't have *any* law."

He finished bandaging and Gaunt stood and pulled up his pants. Getting his boots on was no easier than it had been before, but he managed it. He paid Doc and went back into the parlor where Rose was waiting, nervously pacing back and forth. She looked worriedly at Doc. "Is he all right?"

Doc shrugged. "Needs to stay off that leg. But he won't. He as much as told me he wouldn't. Maybe you can get him to use his head."

She smiled faintly. "He's a stubborn man."

All Gaunt wanted now was to get back to the jail and get to sleep. Besides, he was beginning to worry about Sully and Jackson. They undoubtedly had a lot of friends, some of whom might try to break them out of jail if they knew it was unguarded.

He said, "Let's go, Rose." Turning, he looked at Doc. "Thanks. Sorry we woke you up."

"Any time. Don't let it worry you. Nobody ever gets shot in the middle of the day."

He followed Rose out into the street. The lamp went out behind them before they had gone a hundred yards.

Gaunt laid his arm across Rose's shoulders, using her for support. This way, they went over to Kansas Street and along it toward the jail at the lower end of town.

Rose didn't speak and neither did Gaunt. He tried to find a way to put his weight down on the wounded leg that would hurt it least but nothing really seemed to help.

At the Alamo, he stopped. "I'll be all right now. Thanks for—" he hesitated an instant and finally finished—"worrying about me."

"You'll get some sleep now, won't you?"

"Uh-huh."

She stood on tiptoe to kiss him. "Good night."

"Good night, Rose." He waited while she unlocked the door of the Alamo and went inside. He waited until he heard it lock behind her and then hobbled on down the street toward the jail. He knew it must be after four o'clock. He wasn't going to get much sleep, but even a few hours would help.

Limping slowly along the walk, he thought of Rose. It seemed strange to him that it had been Rose, not Maggie, who had worried enough about the shots to come see if he was all right. Strange too that Rose, not Maggie, had worried enough to insist that he go to Doc Kelley's and have his wound freshly dressed.

Always before he had kept the two women in their proper perspective. He loved them both but differently. He needed Rose and she fulfilled his need, giving him, he had often thought with shame, much more than he gave her.

But in his way he needed Maggie too. Not so much for now but for the future. They would raise a family and live and grow old together. Hard as it would be, he would leave Rose forever when he married Maggie, and he knew Rose understood this as well as he.

It would not be easy for her any more than it would for him. He reached the jail, unlocked the door and went inside quietly, not wanting to awaken either Jackson or Sully and have them yelling at him.

He locked the door behind him. He did not light a lamp. He stumbled across the room, found the boot jack by feeling for it with one foot, and pulled off his boots. He stumbled to the cot and laid down on it.

His leg throbbed mercilessly, but the bandage did not feel wet to his touch so he knew that the wound had not bled enough for the blood to soak clear through.

His head whirled. He had the sensation that the cot was turning over. He thought of what faced him tomorrow.

The first thing he'd do would be to release Sully and Jackson. He'd repeat his order and give them until sundown to get out of town.

After that he'd ride out to Wedemeier's herd and tell the boss about the cowboy that he'd killed. He dreaded that. He knew it would be difficult.

He caught himself wondering if the cowboy would still be alive if he'd handled the incident differently. Maybe he shouldn't have tried to put himself and his horse between the cowboy and the two men he was trying to kill. Maybe he should have tried to get Sully and Jackson to retreat back into the saloon and given the cowboy time to reconsider. Maybe if he'd promised the cowboy that he'd not only get his money back but would run Sully and Jackson out of town . . .

He shook his head wearily. Second guessing wasn't going to help. He'd done what he'd thought was best, taking the direct approach that was so characteristic of him. He shouldn't blame himself because the outcome had been tragic and unfortunate.

Determinedly, he tried to sleep but it eluded him. He knew he faced an eventual showdown with Maggie, who had demanded and would continue to demand that he quit the marshal's job. And he couldn't do it. Not in mid-season when the town needed him the most. The only way he could even consider it would be if he was able to find a replacement he thought could handle the job. Which was next to impossible.

He wondered if she would break with him when he refused. She hadn't exactly said she would, but he knew she had come close to it. But maybe when the chips were down she wouldn't break off with him at all.

Then he remembered her face, the firm line of her jaw, her steady eyes. And he felt depressed again.

Finally, as the first faint streak of gray was forming above the eastern horizon, he went to sleep.

Rose Navarro was not so lucky. She lay awake until long after the sky turned light, after the sun came up.

She knew she was a fool, to care so much for him. The trouble was, fool or not, she couldn't help herself.

There was a way, of course, to get him away from Maggie Conover. Let Maggie find out about her and about the relationship she enjoyed with Gaunt. But she couldn't do it. She possessed an extraordinarily strong sense of honor that would not even permit her to consider it.

She buried her face in her pillow and wept. Why, she asked herself, hadn't she met him a long time ago? Why hadn't she been stronger, and found a way to support herself without going into a saloon?

She thought of Maggie Conover. She wanted to hate Maggie, but she could not. The truth was, she both liked and admired Maggie Conover, and she knew

Maggie would be a good wife to him—if he survived this season, which at the moment did not seem too likely.

Tomorrow he would have to ride out and tell that trail boss and his crew that he had shot and killed one of their friends. And even if he survived that all right, there were other herds coming. In two weeks there would be fifty to a hundred thousand cattle waiting their turn at the loading chutes.

And there was Robineau, a bitter man who had been brooding since last year, who had threatened to return this year and kill Gaunt. Robineau couldn't face Gaunt in a fair fight, crippled as he was. So he'd shoot from ambush, use a shotgun, or get Gaunt in a crossfire from which there could be no escape.

It seemed to Rose that Morgan Gaunt was doomed. And when he died, she might as well die too.

CHAPTER 11

It was half past eight before the yelling of Morgan Gaunt's prisoners awakened him. Sunlight was warm in the street outside the jail. He swung his legs over the side of the cot and sat up. His wounded leg still ached, but it was better than it had been last night.

He remembered instantly all that had happened yesterday. He pulled on his boots and stood up. He walked to the door leading to the cells, opened it and asked, "What the hell are you two yelling about?"

Sully asked, "What about some food?"

"I'll get it." He closed the door, ran his fingers through his hair, belted his gun around his waist and settled his hat upon his head. He opened the oustide door, stepped out into the street and, turning, locked the door.

The air was warm but pleasant. There was a slight north wind, and it carried the smell of fresh-cut hay from Hooker's hayfields at the upper end of town. A few people were moving in the street. Gaunt headed for the Drovers Hotel, trying not to limp. He didn't want anybody getting the idea that he wasn't able to carry out his duties as usual.

He climbed the veranda steps and went in. He nodded at the clerk behind the desk, then crossed to the stairs and climbed them to the first floor. He unlocked his room and went inside.

It seemed like days since he had awakened here yesterday. With a spare smile at the thought, he took off his vest and shirt and poured some water into the white china basin. He washed, then lathered his face and, while the lather softened his whiskers, stropped his razor. He began to shave.

Finished, he dried his face and stared at himself in the mirror, looking for some clue as to why he so stubbornly held onto this marshal's job. What he saw was what he had seen every day for as long as he could recall; calm, steady eyes, a mouth that was wide and firm, hollow cheeks and high cheekbones, possibly the heritage of some Indian forbear, and a chin that jutted out.

He put on a clean shirt, shrugged into his vest and settled his hat on his damp, freshly combed hair. He went out, locked the door and descended the stairs.

Josephina Chavez was the only waitress working in the dining room. He ordered breakfast and asked that she prepare two trays for his prisoners. He rolled himself a wheat-straw cigarette and puffed it with enjoyment.

He was not alone in the dining room. Over in the corner was a large table occupied by the mayor, Lester Ives, and several members of the town council. They stared at him and, when he glanced back, looked away almost guiltily. They had obviously been discussing him.

He was sure their discussion had not been critical. But they were worried.

He nodded at Ives, who immediately got up and came to his table. Ives said, "Good morning, Mr. Gaunt."

"Good morning."

"We . . . when you finish your breakfast would you mind coming over? We'd like to talk to you."

"All right."

Ives hesitated a moment and then returned to the others. Josephina brought Gaunt's breakfast. He was hungry and the food made him feel better even if it didn't relieve the aching in his leg. Finished, he got up and strode to the corner table, limping slightly but not too noticeably. He pulled out an empty-chair and sat down, nodding to Sam Kohn, Bart Chapman, Dave Ryan and Harvey Clay. "Good morning, gentlemen."

"Good morning, Mr. Gaunt."

"What can I do for you?"

There was a moment's hesitation as each man looked to the other, not having decided on a spokesman. Finally Lester Ives said, "We're worried, Mr. Gaunt."

Gaunt grinned. "So am I. I've got to ride out to Wedemeier's herd this morning and explain that cowboy's death."

"How's your leg?"

"Sore. But it isn't going to incapacitate me, if that's what you mean."

Ives looked relieved. "We're not being critical, Mr. Gaunt. You had no choice last night when that cowboy shot you. But there's no way we can get another man to take your place. Not this late in the year."

Gaunt grinned faintly. He said, "Maggie?"

Ives smiled nervously. "It's pretty well known that she wants you to quit. And with you wounded, we thought . . ." He stopped.

Gaunt said, "I won't quit you in the middle of the season, gentlemen. Unless I'm killed or incapacitated."

All of the men looked relieved. Ives said, "If there's any way we can help . . . deputies . . . anything."

"Thanks. I can handle it."

The conversation was at an end. Gaunt got up and returned to his table. Ives and the others left. After several minutes, Josephina brought the two trays. Gaunt paid for his own meal, signed the check for the other two and left the dining room with them.

The mayor and the council members were standing on the veranda, lighting up cigars and pipes and talking. Gaunt looked at Chapman. "Mind helping me with these trays, Mr. Chapman?"

Chapman looked surprised, but the others didn't seem to notice it. Gaunt handed one of the covered trays to Chapman and accompanied him off the veranda and across the street. He waited until they were well out of earshot and then he said, "I saw Mrs. Overman leaving your place last night."

Chapman's face darkened. He started to say something, probably that it was none of Gaunt's business, but Gaunt was ahead of him. "It's none of my business, of course. But I know Jake Overman. He's a man of violent temper. He'll kill you if he finds out."

Chapman's face had lost much of its color. Suddenly it was almost gray. Gaunt said, "And he will find out. No matter how careful you are, he will eventually find out."

"You haven't told anyone . . . ?"

"Of course not! And I won't."

Chapman's face mirrored his relief. They reached the jail and Gaunt unlocked the door. He carried in his tray and put it on the desk. He took the other from Chapman's hands, who excused himself hurriedly and left. Gaunt smiled humorlessly, wondering why people always thought they were too clever to get caught. But he had Chapman thinking differently. Chapman knew if Gaunt could catch Bessie leaving his house, her husband could too.

Gaunt carried the trays back and gave them to Sully and Jackson. Both men sat down on their cots and began to eat. Their clothes were still dusty from having been dragged. They were unshaven and dirty, but Gaunt didn't offer them the opportunity to wash. He was going to release them soon and they could get cleaned up then.

He went back out into the street and walked to the stable to get his horse. He saddled and bridled the animal, checked the already healing bullet crease, then rode down the inclined plank ramp to the street. He returned to the jail, dismounted and tied his horse to the hitching post, which was still in the shade. He went inside.

Sully and Jackson had finished eating. Both men stared at him suspiciously as he unlocked their cells. Sully asked, "What the hell are you doing?"

"Turning you loose."

The suspicion in Sully's eyes increased. He said, "Yeah. And you'll shoot us down as we leave and claim we tried to escape."

"You know me better than that." Gaunt's eyes were like ice.

"Then why . . . ?"

"I don't want to fool with you. I haven't got time for two-bit badmen. Get out of here and be out of town by sundown. If I see you after that, I'll shoot on sight. And don't come back. Ever."

Sully said, "Damn you . . ." but he cut what he had been going to say short when his eyes met those of Gaunt. He shuffled along the corridor, through the office and out the front door. On the walk in front of the jail he looked back. Gaunt was bringing the trays out so that he could return them to the hotel. Sully said, "Let's go," and the pair hurried up Kansas Street. They turned on Texas and disappeared.

Gaunt carried the two trays back to the Drovers Hotel. Then he returned, untied his horse, mounted and began his morning rounds.

As he passed Maggie Conover's restaurant, she came to the door and stared at him. He stopped, touched the brim of his hat. "Good morning, Maggie."

Her face was cold. "I heard more shots last night after I went to bed. Were they fired at you?"

He nodded.

"Who? Another of those Texas cowboys?"

He shook his head. "A saloonman and a gambler."

Her face was paler as she said, "And you were lucky again."

He nodded. "I was lucky again." Her coldness bothered him, but he didn't know what to say to change it.

She turned and went back inside the restaurant without speaking to him again. He went on, frowning slightly. It was hard not to compare Maggie's attitude with that of Rose. Rose's worry for his safety took the form of compassion and freely offered help. Maggie's worry only seemed to make her cold and hostile toward him.

He rode up Kansas Street, nodding or speaking frequently to passers-by. The morning air was cool and fresh, and he paused for several moments at the fence that surrounded Hooker's hayfield, breathing in the pleasant fragrance of fresh-cut hay. Hooker had turned a few horses in on the hay stubble and they were grazing quietly in the middle of the field.

Reluctantly, Gaunt went on. He was late making his rounds this morning, and he still had to go out to Wedemeier's herd.

In spite of that, he took his time riding along the bed of Cottonwood Creek, listening to the meadowlarks and wondering what it would be like, owning and operating a ranch. With Maggie. A light frown touched his face. He wondered, in spite of himself, if Maggie would try controlling him in other ways from time to time, wondering too how he would react to her when she did.

Angrily, he put those thoughts out of his head. He touched his horse's sides with his heels and the animal broke into a lope. He felt disloyal and guilty for having had any doubts about Maggie.

The cattle pens were still empty but he knew they wouldn't stay empty long. Already a solitary engine was backing cars along the track to position them in front of the cattle chutes, arranged so that three cars could be loaded at one time.

Wedemeier's herd would have started at daybreak and would be halfway here by now.

His horse stepped up onto the station platform. This morning, Jim Sutton came out onto the platform, blinking against the glare which was not entirely cut by his green eyeshade. He asked, "You all right?"

Gaunt grinned. "Those two are lousy shots."

"I picked up a couple of guns this morning. You want them now?"

"All right."

Sutton went into the telegrapher's office and returned, carrying two guns. He passed them up to Gaunt, who unloaded both into his hand, then passed one of the saddle strings through both trigger guards and tied them on his saddle.

Sutton asked, "What you going to do with those two who shot at you?"

"I turned them loose. Told 'em to be out of town by sundown."

"Think they'll leave?" Sutton was looking at him worriedly.

"They'll leave."

"What if they try killing you again?"

"In daylight? They're not that kind. They'll leave."

He rode to the end of the platform and his horse stepped down into the dust. He crossed the tracks at the intersection, which the puffing engine had now vacated, and rode to the jail. He dismounted, untied the two guns and carried them inside.

One belt and gun still hung from the coat tree. He frowned at it, then took it down and carried it outside. He locked the office door.

He mounted and rode uptown to the Drovers Hotel where he had left the drunken cowboy last night. He went in and left the cowboy's gun at the desk, with instructions to give it to the Texan if he was on his way out of town. He didn't know where the cowboy's horse was, but since he hadn't seen it tied anyplace, he supposed one of the man's friends had stabled it.

He realized he was dreading the confrontation with Wedemeier and had been delaying his departure from town. The realization irritated him enough to make him mount immediately and head out of town at a steady trot. Maybe it *was* time he quit this job. He'd never postponed dangerous or unpleasant things before.

CHAPTER 12

Gaunt held his horse to a steady trot. The animal was fresh and wanted to run, but Gaunt held him in. He didn't want sweat on the horse when he reached Wedemeier's herd. He didn't want them thinking he had come in haste because they were sure to draw conclusions if they did.

Grass lay dry and golden in the morning sun. Meadowlarks trilled their melodious song, but today Gaunt didn't hear. His face wore a frown. However he justified his killing of the cowboy last night to others, he couldn't justify it to himself. He should have been able to stay his hand. He shouldn't have acted automatically, without thought.

Wryly he thought that if he had not acted automatically, he would probably be the dead one this morning instead of the cowboy.

A mile from town, he saw dust on the road ahead and a little later was able to make out the figure of a galloping horseman. Squinting against the morning glare, he finally identified Leon Satterfield.

The boy reached him and pulled his horse to a plunging halt. He was excited as he cried, "Marshal! There's two more herds bedded down south of here. I talked to the men. They said there was another right behind that will get in sometime today. Know whose it is?"

Gaunt smiled grimly. He knew whose herd it was, but he wouldn't deprive Leon of the pleasure of telling him. He asked, "Whose?"

"Buck Robineau's, that's whose! What you going to do about him, Mr. Gaunt?"

"Can't do anything, Leon, until he breaks the law."

"But he swore he'd come back this year and kill you, Mr. Gaunt!"

Gaunt's smile widened. "If he does, *then* he'll have broken the law and I can arrest him."

Leon didn't see the grim humor of that. He said, "Mr. Gaunt, it ain't going to be no fair fight. He'll likely use a shotgun on you."

"Don't worry about it, Leon. A year's a long time. Maybe he's changed his mind." He remembered Robineau now, whip slender and wiry, with a broad, sweeping mustache that dominated his face and eyes above it that were so blue they were the things you remembered about him when all else faded from your mind.

The hell of it was, he'd probably have liked Robineau, even been friends with him had the circumstances been different. Just as he'd probably have liked the cowboy he'd killed last night if he'd had the chance.

Leon was looking at him expectantly. Gaunt fished in his pocket and brought out fifty cents. He tossed it to the boy who caught it expertly. "Thanks, Mr. Gaunt."

Gaunt acknowledged the thanks with a nod. They rode on at a brisk trot for a couple more miles, until they could plainly see the dust of Wedemeier's herd ahead.

By the end of the summer, this lush grassland would look like bare ground, Gaunt thought. The Texas herds that came late would have to bed as much as fifteen miles from town in order to find feed. But the grass always came back no matter how badly it was overgrazed.

He wondered what changes the next five years would bring. The cattle would stop coming, at least to Cottonwood. They'd go someplace else west of here,

maybe to Dodge City when the railroad had reached
that far. This grass would lie golden and unused unless
somebody filed on it and bought cattle to graze on it.

He suddenly looked at the land with different eyes.
He could be one of those who claimed this rich
grassland. He could file on a quarter section, and Maggie could file on another one. That would give them
half a section, and whenever adjoining land was put up
for sale they could buy. Hell, they might wind up with
a damn fine ranch. He grinned faintly to himself. The
excitement of the marshal's job would be missing but
maybe living with Maggie would be excitement enough.
She had a temper and pretty definite ideas about how a
man ought to conduct himself. Life with her sure
wasn't going to be dull.

Wedemeier's herd drew closer until individual animals were visible behind the point rider. Most of the
herd was hidden by a cloud of dust.

Gaunt and Leon left the road and angled to the left.
Point rider and the lead steers plodded past. Gaunt
could see two flank riders and farther back, the re-
muda, being driven by a single man.

Wedemeier must have seen Gaunt through the dust
because he came galloping toward him, accompanied
by two of his men. They hauled their horses to a plunging halt a couple of dozen feet away. Wedemeier's
eyes were red from the irritation of the dust and possibly from sleeplessness. He asked harshly, "Well, what
happened to Jordan and Livingston?"

This was the time Gaunt had dreaded. He said, "I
don't know which is which, but one of them passed out
in an alley and I took him to the Drovers Hotel and
put him to bed. He'll probably be along pretty soon."

"What about the other one?" Wedemeier's eyes were
slitted and suspicious.

"He's dead."

"Dead?" Wedemeier's eyes were accusing even before he heard Gaunt's explanation.

"I killed him." Gaunt moved his horse so that the

trail boss could see the large spot of dried blood on his pants. "He was trying to kill a bartender and a gambler he claimed had cheated him. I tried to calm him down. Promised him his money back. I promised him that if he'd back away, the whole thing would be forgotten. But he must have been too drunk. Shot me and I had no choice."

"You told them they'd be safe without their guns."

Gaunt had been hoping for this remark. "He'd have been safe without his gun. The trouble was, he made out like he was leaving town, and I gave him back his gun. Then he came back."

Wedemeier was scowling angrily and so were the two men with him. Wedemeier asked, "What about the two men that cheated him?"

"I ordered them out of town. They've got until sundown tonight." He didn't mention that Sully and Jackson had tried to kill him last night because he knew if he did Wedemeier would want to know why they weren't dead too. It was a question he didn't want to have to answer, because the answer wouldn't have satisfied even him.

The truth was, they were alive only because their bullets had missed. He hadn't stopped thinking during that attack because he had not been hurt. In the cowboy's case, the wound, its shock and pain, had made his instincts take over from his mind.

Wedemeier said, "By God, we won't give up our guns today."

Gaunt said, "Yes you will. Or you'll tangle with me. I'd advise you, if you want to avoid any more trouble, to tell your men to give up their guns peacefully. Otherwise somebody else is going to get killed."

"Yeah. You."

"Don't count on it. I'm pretty hard to kill."

"Know who's half a day down the trail?"

"I know."

Wedemeier stared at him with grim satisfaction. "Maybe I'll tell my boys to leave you for him."

Gaunt nodded. "That will be fine." He heard hoof-beats on the road behind him and turned his head. The cowboy he had put to bed at the Drovers last night was coming at a lope. Wedemeier said, "That's Livingston. So it's Jordan you killed."

"His body is at the undertaker's. If he didn't have any money left, the county will bury him."

"Like hell. We'll bury him." Without another word, Wedemeier turned and rode back toward the herd. The two cowboys followed him.

Gaunt and Leon rode on, with Leon staying half a length behind. The boy asked, "Lord, Mr. Gaunt, what you gonna do?"

Gaunt looked back at him. "It's all right, Leon. Lots of men say things they don't mean when they're all stirred up."

"Where you goin' now?"

"I'll ride out to those two herds that just arrived and tell 'em no guns are allowed in town. Want to go along and show me where they are?"

"Sure, Mr. Gaunt. I oughta do something to earn that fifty cents."

"All right then. You take the lead."

Leon kicked his horse and moved into the lead. Gaunt was tired from lack of sleep last night. His eye-lids felt heavy. He let his horse plod unguided behind Leon's, the reins slack. He let his head sag onto his chest. He closed his eyes.

He dozed in spite of his worry about how things were going to turn out. He could only do his best, and he was damned if he was going to let worry about various possibilities turn him into a nervous wreck.

Hearing Leon's call he opened his eyes and raised his head. In the distance, he could see the lift of dust. Leon turned his head and said, "There's one of 'em, Mr. Gaunt."

Gaunt nodded. They went on, with the herd and riders gradually materializing out of the dust and dis-tance. To avoid spooking the herd, Gaunt turned off to one side and Leon followed him. The pair sat their horses on a knoll while the herd went slowly past. As the drag drew abreast, a couple of men detached themselves and trotted their horses toward them.

Except for the gun ban there would be no need to meet each newly arrived herd. Yet Gaunt felt no criticism toward the council for having passed the ban. It would save lives in the end if he was successful in enforcing it. It might even save his own life.

In addition, it would mean that bullets would not be continuously flying through the air with the chance that any one of them might find an innocent target, a woman or a child.

This trail boss was burly and grossly fat, seeming too big for the horse he rode. Instead of riding in the stirrups like most men did, this one rode in the saddle, like a lump of clay, sticking to it even while the horse was at a trot as if his pants were glued to it.

Folds of flesh nearly hid his eyes, which reminded Gaunt briefly of the eyes of a huge, fat boar. Gaunt said, "Howdy. I'm Gaunt, marshal of Cottonwood."

The man's expression did not change. The expression of the cowboy behind him was neutral, showing nothing at all. He said, "Heard of you."

"I don't know what you heard, but regardless, you and your men will be treated fairly in Cottonwood. If anybody gets cheated at cards, come to me and I'll take care of it. If anybody gets too drunk and ends up with his pockets turned inside out, come to me and I'll see that he gets his money back."

"Why don't you just clean up your dirty town instead?"

A bit of steel touched Gaunt's narrowed eyes. "Because you boys don't want a clean town. You want women and gambling and all the liquor you can drink. All I can do is straighten things out when they go wrong."

For several moments the two men stared at each other. Finally Gaunt said, "I didn't get your name."

"Rosen. Used to be Rosenstock, but I shortened it."

Gaunt reached out his hand and Rosen took it reluctantly. Gaunt said, "One other thing. The council has passed a ban on guns inside the town. You and your men will check them at the jail as you ride in. It's just beyond the depot on the right hand side."

"Oh no you don't. You'll never get the guns away from my boys!"

Gaunt stared at him a moment. The eyes of the two men locked, and held for what seemed an eternity. Rosen's horse suddenly fidgeted and this gave the man an excuse to let his glance slide away from Gaunt's. Gaunt said, "Your boys are coming in for some fun, not to fight. Tell 'em that. If I see a man wearing a gun in town, it's either give it up or fight."

Rosen studied him for a moment more. Finally he shrugged and turned his horse away. He trotted back toward his herd.

Leon asked excitedly, "What if none of 'em turn in their guns, Mr. Gaunt? What will you do then?"

"They'll turn 'em in. Don't worry about it, Leon."

"But what if they don't?"

"They'll turn 'em in." Gaunt couldn't think beyond that. If one herd got by without turning in their guns, then none of the drovers would. And if none of the drovers did, Gaunt's life wouldn't be worth a dime. The only way he could keep the lid on things was by maintaining strict control.

He had a fleeting doubt that he would be able to keep the lid on things. Wedemeier's crew would be coming in tonight, angered by the death of their friend. Getting them to give up their guns a second time was not going to be an easy thing.

And the men from this herd and the other, farther back . . . they would only surrender their guns if Wedemeier's men already had.

It boiled down to enforcing compliance from the first drovers to hit town. Today, those would be Wedemeier's. He touched his horse's sides with his heels and rode on, with Leon leading the way to the second herd.

He delivered the same message to a trail boss named Harkness, whose reaction was much the same as Rosen's. Then he said good-bye to Leon and headed back toward town.

Half a mile from town, he passed Wedemeier's herd. He went on, knowing he would have to wait to demand the drovers' guns until after they had corraled their herd, loaded the waiting cars, and ridden into town to celebrate the completion of the drive.

CHAPTER 13

When Gaunt reached the depot, he stepped his horse up onto the platform. Jim Sutton had come out of his telegrapher's office and was watching the Wedemeier herd as it moved into the pens. Looking back toward town, Gaunt saw that people were clustered at every vantage point, also watching. The arrival of the first herd of the year was an event. They watched from rooftops, from second-story windows, from the crotches of trees and, if they could find nothing higher, from the beds of wagons and buckboards. A bunch of boys came running and jumped up onto the station platform to watch beside Gaunt's tall horse.

The pens had wide, flaring wings pointing toward the south. Into this opening rode the point rider, followed by the lead steers of the herd. The corral wings were wide enough so that the cattle weren't spooked until they were well inside, and by then it was too late. Inexorable pressure from behind kept them from stopping or turning no matter how frightened they became or how much they wanted to go back.

Wedemeier's cowboys kept pressure against the drag of the herd. Up front, responsibility now belonged to the workers in the cattle pens. Mounted on short, powerful mustangs, they opened and shut gates, expertly filling this pen and then the next, until Wedemeier's herd had disappeared and had become instead of a single herd only groups of bawling steers, confined in the various pens.

It always gave Gaunt pleasure to watch this operation because it was so efficient and precise. Gates opened and cattle streamed into the desired pens. When the gates closed, the stream went on to the next pen and the next. No matter how these wild Texas steers bawled or fought, or tried to run, they were helpless, hemmed in by their own kind and by the stout pens, made to go this way or that by the opening and closing gates and by the yelling men on horseback who moved among them.

On the railroad siding the switch engine puffed and hissed, and the cars waited at the chutes with their doors open.

Where the wide wings of fence that had funneled the herd into the pens narrowed down, men sat on the top rail, with pads of paper and pencils, tallying. When the last animal had entered the pens, they climbed down and walked to windward, where the dust was less, and climbing to the top rail sat side by side and compared their totals. Wedemeier was with them, listening, occasionally commenting.

Wedemeier knew how many cattle he'd had when he left Texas. He knew approximately how many he had lost on the trail. Wedemeier wasn't going to quibble about a few animals. But he wanted the tally to be reasonably correct.

He apparently was satisfied. He accepted a draft from Bart Chapman, climbed down, gathered his cowboys around him and headed toward the foot of Kansas Street.

Gaunt could feel the tension rising inside of him. Now was the time he had to confront Wedemeier and his crew. Now he had to enforce the gun ban again. He smiled grimly. It hadn't been easy last time, and it would now be no easier. One of Wedemeier's crew had been killed. Never mind that he'd had his gun returned and had then gone back into town to use it against the marshal and get himself killed for his pains.

He touched his horse's sides with his heels and the animal stepped down off the platform into the dust. Wedemeier and his men were coming along an alley between the cattle pens. The tension, the strain, the responsibility of the long drive was over and the release was visible in them even at a distance of a hundred yards.

Gaunt's mind was like an animal in a trap, racing back and forth from one possibility to another, frantically seeking some solution, some way out of this that would not result in a shoot-out in front of everyone in town.

He was outnumbered. He could neither outdraw all of Wedemeier's men, nor could he survive if the guns came out. There was a good chance that five minutes from now he'd be lying lifeless in the dust while Wedemeier and his crew rode on, the men to draw their pay at the bank and then go to the saloons for the beginning of a real rip-snorting spree.

He wondered briefly if either Rose or Maggie was watching. He hoped neither was, but that chance was slight. Both were probably watching, wondering how he was going to get out of this alive. They knew he couldn't let Wedemeier and his crew enter town carrying their guns. Nor could they see how he could get the cowboys' guns away from them. Not after one of their number had been killed by him last night.

Gaunt knew suddenly that there was a way. Whether it would work or not, he didn't know.

These Texans were a peculiar breed. Their code of honor was as rigid as any law ever contrived by man, and not a one of them would break it.

If he could turn the confrontation between him and Wedemeier's entire crew into a confrontation between only Wedemeier and himself. . . . That was the one thing that might work. That would keep the others out of it. That would put him on even terms with one man only, and not only give him a chance to stay alive but also give him a chance of getting the cowboys' guns away from them afterward.

With his course decided, he touched his horse's sides with his heels and rode north across the tracks, turning then and positioning himself between Wedemeier's crew and the town of Cottonwood.

Like a rock he sat there, a tall man on a tall horse, letting it be known that they would have to ride over him before they could get into town.

There was the briefest, slightest hesitation in Wedemeier as he saw him take his position there. Then he came on, a little faster and certainly more confident. He had more than fifteen men. Gaunt was alone. As Wedemeier saw it, there could be but one outcome to the confrontation.

Closer and closer they came, and suddenly all sound among the spectators ceased. The only sounds remaining were the muffled shouts of the men loading cattle into the waiting cars and the protesting bawls of the cattle themselves. In town, a whisper could have been heard on Kansas Street.

Fifty feet away, Wedemeier stopped. He called, "Get out of the way, Marshal, or we'll run over you."

Gaunt knew he couldn't deal with Wedemeier at a distance of fifty feet. He put up a hand and cupped it behind his ear. "Too much noise over there in the cattle pens. What did you say?"

Wedemeier came on. Gaunt wanted him less than a dozen feet away.

There seemed to be no fear in the trail boss. Gaunt realized that he liked the man and knew he couldn't kill him unless it was the only way. This time Wedemeier came to within fifteen feet before he stopped again.

Gaunt said, "Gentlemen, you're going to have to give up your guns before you go into town."

A man behind Wedemeier yelled, "Yeah, and get ourselves killed by a bunch of crooked gamblers!"

"No gambler killed that man last night. I killed him. And only because he had a gun. He put a bullet into me first." He waited just a moment and then added, "If he'd been unarmed, he'd still be alive."

Another man yelled, "Like hell! We go in with guns or we don't go at all!"

Gaunt shrugged. "Then don't go at all. The town council passed the no-gun ordinance. All I do is enforce."

This was petty, this bickering. But there was nothing petty about the stakes. He changed his tone. "Go on in, boys. There's girls and liquor and gambling. Just give me your guns as you pass, and there'll be no trouble."

He held his breath for an instant, waiting to see if they would comply. There was some slight hesitation among them, and several looked back and forth from one to another. In the end it was the words of one hothead that decided them. "No, by God! I ain't giving up my gun!"

That brought a grumble of agreement from the others. Gaunt looked at Wedemeier. "Are you the trail boss or is he?"

Slight color touched Wedemeier's weathered face and his eyes narrowed almost imperceptibly. He said, "You know who trail boss is. You don't have to ask."

"Then why's he giving the orders?"

Wedemeier shook his head. "It won't work, Gaunt. You can't divide us that easily."

Gaunt stared straight at Wedemeier. "All right, then. I'm making it personal. Between you and me. Give me *your* gun, right now, before you go into town."

Wedemeier's face was as nearly expressionless as a man's face can be, so it couldn't have been his expression that gave away his dismay. Maybe it was a change in his eyes, the merest flicker of the lids. But Gaunt saw it and knew that this part of his strategy at least had won. He repeated, "Your gun, Mr. Wedemeier. I'll take it now."

Wedemeier shook his head. "Not that way either, Gaunt. Take all our guns or take none of them."

Gaunt's expression was sardonic and his eyes never

left Wedemeier's. "Afraid, Mr. Wedemeier? Afraid without fifteen men to back you up?"

Wedemeier's rage flared like a grass fire. His left hand held his horse utterly motionless, as if it was made of iron. His right was no more than a couple of inches from the grip of his holstered gun.

Now, what Gaunt had known must happen did. The Texan's code would not permit Wedemeier's men to intervene in a private quarrel, no matter what their sympathies. Uneasily, they reined their horses to right and left, getting themselves out of the field of fire.

Gaunt opened his mouth to taunt Wedemeier with the fact that now he was all alone. Instead he relented and said, "It don't have to be this way, Mr. Wedemeier. I can out-draw and out-shoot you, and you know it. I don't want to kill you. All I want is for you to give up your gun."

But it had gone too far and suddenly Gaunt could see it had. Wedemeier had been challenged and his Texas code, as rigid as that of his men, would not permit him to back down. Not and retain his authority over them.

He said, "No, by God! I won't give up my gun. Not unless I'm dead. So get on with it. Draw, damn you! Draw!"

Gaunt shook his head. "I can't do that, Mr. Wedemeier. You're going to have to draw your gun first."

Wedemeier didn't like that; he didn't like the disadvantage it put him at. Not the disadvantage in what now seemed to be an inevitable fight with Gaunt, but a disadvantage so far as his men were concerned.

He said, "No. You want to enforce the gun ban. You draw first."

Gaunt saw no reason to deprive him of his pride. He nodded. "All right. You're sure this is what you want?"

"I'm sure." There was a kind of grayish pallor in Wedemeier's face. It wasn't fear. It was the knowledge that he was going to die. Within minutes. Maybe within seconds.

Gaunt nodded. "All right. Whenever you're ready, Mr. Wedemeier. But I want it understood . . . if you lose, your men will give up their guns. Today and every day as long as they are here."

Wedemeier nodded his head. "That is agreed." He turned his head briefly to look at one of his men. "Rafferty?"

"Yes, sir. That is agreed."

Now was the deadly moment, the two men facing each other on mounts forcibly held still by iron hands on their reins.

Gaunt well knew his own speed. He knew Wedemeier could never match it. The only way he could leave Wedemeier alive was to draw more swiftly than he ever had before, swiftly enough so that Wedemeier would have time to think, to see how badly he had been beaten, and to decide that only certain death awaited if he persisted in trying to withdraw his gun, center it on Gaunt and fire it.

His thoughts as he stared at his adversary were bleak and grim. Suppose Wedemeier's stubbornness was stronger than his good sense? Suppose his reflexes were too slow to let him stop with his gun already halfway up?

But he had to try one last time. He said, "I can beat you. I draw a salary because I'm an expert with my gun. It's no disgrace to change your mind."

Wedemeier stubbornly shook his head. In that instant, Gaunt knew he would have to kill this man. No matter how much he hated it. No matter how much admiration he had for the wiry trail boss. No matter what a waste it was.

Disgust touched him, disgust with a job that forced him repeatedly into situations like this one. He said, "All right. Now!" the last word like the crack of a whip.

His body now took over from his mind. With the restraints imposed on it removed. His right hand moved like the head of a striking rattlesnake. He felt the smooth, worn, cool grips of his gun, felt it withdraw from its holster, felt it rise, so incredibly swift it was doubtful if the human eye could have followed its movements. He felt his thumb on the hammer and felt the hammer come back with a click.

It was in line, cocked and ready to fire before Wedemeier had his gun halfway out of its holster.

Gaunt's heart stopped for a split second. His eyes were glued to Wedemeier's hand still forcing the gun up and out of its holster.

It cleared and he heard the click as the hammer came back. And yet, with his own death staring him in the face, he still delayed. There was a chance Wedemeier would desist, that he would look at certain death in Gaunt's hand and eyes, and let his gun drop from his hand.

It was a deadly risk, but Gaunt took it. He raised his own glance to meet Wedemeier's. He didn't say anything; he didn't have to. Wedemeier knew he was a dead man unless he halted the inexorable rise of his cocked and ready gun.

In Wedemeier's face, suddenly, unexpectedly, Gaunt saw that he had won. Wedemeier was going to give up. He wasn't going to shoot. Gaunt let his glance drop to Wedemeier's gun, cocked but still not level, still not ready for firing.

Wedemeier's hand sagged as though the weight of the gun was too much for it. Then he released the gun, and it fell with a thud into the dust. It could and should have fired, since the hammer was back, but it did not.

Gaunt carefully lowered the hammer of his own gun, spinning the cylinder as he did so that the hammer lowered on an empty chamber. He shoved it into his holster.

There was nothing overbearing, nothing arrogant in his voice as he spoke. It was almost mild, conciliatory. "Let me have your guns, boys, as you ride past. You'll get them back when you leave town."

Wedemeier dismounted, picked up his gun, lowered the hammer and shoved it into its holster. He remounted and was the first to hand over his gun. Sullenly for the most part, his drovers followed suit.

Once more Gaunt hung as many as he could on his saddle horn, the rest around his neck. He sat motionless as the cowboys and Wedemeier headed uptown toward the bank where Wedemeier could cash his draft and pay his cowboys off.

Most of the people watching from their various vantage points had by now disappeared. Gaunt saw neither Maggie nor Rose.

He had won another skirmish, but he hadn't won the war. Two more herds had arrived yesterday and their cowboys would be coming to town today.

And behind those two was Buck Robineau, crippled by Gaunt's bullet, still undoubtedly swearing his determination to kill Gaunt by whatever means were necessary.

Gaunt rode toward the jail. Last year there would have been an almost intoxicating exhilaration at the thought of confronting Robineau. Today there was only weariness. Robineau was just another chore.

CHAPTER 14

Gaunt unlocked the jail door and went inside. His leg was paining him this morning and it was difficult not to limp. He wished he had a cane to take some of the weight off it, but he knew using a cane would be giving notice to everyone that he was too crippled up to do his job properly.

He stayed in the jail only long enough to hang the guns he had taken from Wedemeier's men on the coat tree. Unburdened, he went back outside and mounted his horse. It surprised him how much difference the lessened weight had on the amount of pain in his leg.

He rode uptown at a walk. What he really wanted was a drink of whiskey, or maybe two, but he didn't want anybody saying that he was drinking in the morning because he was coming apart. He dismounted in front of the Drovers Hotel, tied his horse and went into the dining room. When Josephina came, he ordered coffee.

Wryly, as he sipped it, he wondered why he had come here instead of going to Maggie's place. Maybe it was because he suspected she was going to get after him again about quitting the marshal's job. Maybe this morning he'd had enough tension and conflict and didn't want more.

He nodded at several other diners, finished his coffee and got up. He went out, mounted his horse and headed up Kansas Street to begin his morning rounds.

He saw Maggie looking out the window as he passed her restaurant. There wasn't much he could do but stop and talk. He dismounted at the rail and looped his horse's reins around it. He went inside.

She turned from the window as he entered. There was hurt in her eyes. "I saw you go into the hotel. Would you rather have coffee there than here?"

"How'd you know I had coffee?" He felt trapped and didn't like the feeling.

"The place has windows you know."

"All right. I had coffee." He started to excuse himself by saying he'd needed something from his room. Then he changed his mind. He wasn't going to start lying to justify the things he did.

"I don't suppose you want any more."

"I could use a cup. I'm not rushed for time."

She headed for the kitchen, and he eased himself onto one of the counter stools. It sure wasn't hard to get in bad with a woman. And lately it seemed to be extraordinarily easy with Maggie Conover.

She brought him a cup of coffee and one for herself and sat down next to him. "Hattie Budge says she saw you walking up the street last night late. She says you were limping pretty badly and that a woman was helping you. A saloon girl she thought."

Gaunt stared at her, the corners of his mouth beginning to turn up with a grin. "Rose Navarro." He didn't elaborate. Maggie was prying, trying to supplement Hattie Budge's gossip, and Gaunt didn't think she had any right to pry. Hell, they weren't married yet.

"Isn't she the one who has an interest in the Alamo?"

"She is."

"What . . . ?" Maggie had the grace to blush painfully. She said, "I'm sorry. I have no right to ask."

"I had a scuffle with a couple of men down by the depot. Several shots were fired. None of them hit me, but I opened up my leg wound and it was bleeding quite a bit. Rose helped me up to Doc's to have him rebandage it."

"How did she . . . ? I mean, have you known her long?"

"She's a very old friend."

Maggie's face flushed for a second time. Her mouth firmed, and he knew there were more questions she wanted to ask. He also knew she wouldn't, at least not now.

But she'd be asking questions around town. About Rose Navarro. About her relationship with Morgan. And she'd probably find out. He'd never made a secret of his visits to Rose. Probably most of the men in Cottonwood knew about them, and some of them had probably told their wives.

Maggie was slipping away from him. And along with her the dreams he'd had of permanence, of a family, of living without a continuous threat against his life. He said, "Maggie, she heard the shots down by the depot. She came out to see if I had been hurt. I hadn't, but my leg was bleeding and she insisted that I go up to Doc's. It was a long walk, and she just went along to help."

She was mollified, but only slightly. She said, "I heard talk in the restaurant this morning that two more herds had arrived. And that another was close behind. Mr. Robineau's. The one who swore he'd kill you when he came back this year."

Gaunt nodded. "That's right."

"What are you going to do about him? I heard that his arm is crippled from you shooting him last year and that he won't fight fair. One man said he'd probably use a double-barreled shotgun on you."

Gaunt said, "Maggie, a year is a long, long time. A man can't stay mad that long. Robineau's probably forgotten all about saying he was going to kill me this year."

"A man with a crippled arm doesn't forget that fast."

He knew what she said was true, but he wasn't going

to admit it to her. He finished his coffee. "I've got to go. I've got my morning rounds to make."

Her voice was mocking. "To show the town the presence of the law."

He studied her closely. "Something like that."

"Let somebody else do it. Why does it have to be you?"

"Because there's nobody else."

"Then let them do without."

He said, "Without law, the crooked gamblers, the petty thieves, the prostitutes, the murderers would take over in Cottonwood. Not a cowboy would be safe as long as he had a dollar in his pocket. Not a woman would be safe on the streets. Not a business would be safe from robbery. Not a citizen would dare go out after dark. It would be a jungle, Maggie, with the predators in full control."

"And only you can prevent that from happening." There was now an even stronger mockery in her voice.

But Gaunt didn't let it anger him. He said simply, "Only me." Because it was the truth. He might not be the only man capable of doing what he was doing, but he was the only one currently available. If he gave the town council enough time, they could no doubt get someone to replace him who was equally good. But he had to give them time. He couldn't just go to them and say he was going to quit. Today. Or tomorrow. Or even next week.

She was angry now. Her face was flushed and her eyes sparkled. She said, "Morgan Gaunt, I said I would marry you, but I will not marry your job! Either you give it up, or you can give up any idea of marrying me!"

It was finally the ultimatum he had expected and he could see that it had slipped out before she'd had time to adequately consider it. But the stubborn set of her mouth and chin said that she would stand by it now that she had issued it.

He didn't want to quarrel with her. The pain in his

leg had made him edgy, and he knew he might say things he would later regret. He got up off the stool. He didn't make matters worse and insult her by putting a coin on the counter to pay for the coffee. He just turned to leave.

In a shriller voice than he had ever heard her use she cried, "I mean it, Morgan! I mean every word I've said."

He clenched his fists, knowing nothing could be gained and much could be lost if he turned and answered her. He went out and pulled the door closed behind him without turning and looking at her again. As he unlooped his horse's reins, his back still to the restaurant, he could hear her weeping.

The sound almost made him turn around and go back in. He forced himself to mount his horse. If he went back, he'd give in before her tears.

He rode up Kansas Street, scowling to himself. Damn it, the job was hard enough these first few days without having to fight Maggie too.

Deeply troubled and lost in thought, he reached Hooker's hayfield without even remembering getting there. He stopped, dismounted, and leaned on the top wire of the fence with a grass stem in his mouth while his horse reached over the fence for a few clumps of tall grass the mower had missed.

It was dangerous letting himself become preoccupied. Sully and Jackson were still someplace in town and they might try to kill him, perhaps before sundown, or they might hire somebody else to do the job. Wedemeier had been humiliated in front of his crew, and while Gaunt didn't think Wedemeier capable of drygulching him, it was possible the man would get drunk enough to challenge him. Or one of Wedemeier's cowboys might get ideas of taking the trail boss's quarrel upon himself.

And then there were the two newly arrived herds. Men would be coming into town from those herds, later on today. It was even possible that Robineau, being less than a day's ride from Cottonwood, would come in to see if Gaunt was still marshal here and perhaps try killing him.

No. He couldn't afford preoccupation. He mounted his horse, rode along the edge of Hooker's hayfield to the bed of Cottonwood Creek.

The air was already hot. Sweat ran down Gaunt's back and soaked the underarms of his shirt. He let his horse pick his careful way along the bank of the creek while he kept his ears tuned to each small sound and watched his horse's ears, knowing they would prick toward anything unusual long before he was able to detect its presence by himself.

Faintly he could hear shouts down in the cattle pens, and the protesting bawling of the cattle as they were prodded and forced up the wooden ramps and into the cattle cars. Wedemeier's herd would make an entire train. It would probably pull out for Kansas City or Chicago before sundown today.

At the lower end of town, he left the bed of Cottonwood Creek and rode along the main alley that ran between the cattle pens. He stopped once to let some yard workers haze a bunch of cattle across toward the waiting cars. He came out at the depot, climbed his horse onto the platform just as he had a thousand times before. He could hear the telegraph key clacking inside the telegrapher's office. He rode past, stepped his horse down off the wooden platform and rode across the tracks.

Ira Blanton, the undertaker, was waiting in front of the jail. Gaunt dismounted, led his horse over into the shade of the box elder tree at the side of the jail and then returned. "Hello, Ira."

"Hello, Mr. Gaunt." Blanton's expression was worried.

"Something the matter?"

"Well, you might say that. Or something will be. That trail boss, Wedemeier came over to my place a while ago. Gave me a hundred dollars. Said he wanted

a bang-up, rip-snortin' funeral for that cowboy you
. . . I mean who got killed last night."

Gaunt shrugged. "His privilege. A hundred dollars
ought to buy a pretty nice funeral."

"It will. My best casket. The service. The burial.
What bothers me is that he wants a procession down
the entire length of Kansas Street. He's hired the town
band to walk behind the hearse in full uniform playing
the funeral march."

Gaunt grinned faintly. This was Wedemeier's revenge, both for his killing of the cowboy and for his
humiliating the trail boss by outdrawing him and taking
away his gun. It was also a calculated attempt to make
trouble for Gaunt by stirring up the cowboys from the
other herds. He asked, "What time?"

"Late this afternoon. He wants the procession to get
to the cemetery just in time to bury the man before the
sun goes down."

Gaunt's grin faded. Wedemeier's timing would insure
that all the cowboys from the two other herds would be
on hand to witness the entire show. Because that was
what it was going to be—a show.

He said, "All right, Ira. Thanks for telling me."

Blanton walked away uptown. Gaunt hesitated
several moments. His leg hurt. He was hurt inside by
Maggie's angry words to him earlier. He wanted a
drink, and suddenly he didn't give a damn what anybody thought. He could and would handle his job, and
by the time two more days had passed, everybody was
going to know he could.

He walked slowly along the boardwalk as far as the
Alamo. He went inside and walked to the bar. Jim
Boatman was tending bar, a short, rotund man with a
head almost totally bald. He reached for a beer mug
but Gaunt shook his head, and Boatman grabbed a
bottle and a glass. He set them in front of Gaunt.

Gaunt dumped the glass halfway full. He gulped it,
then waited for the pleasant warmth to spread through
his stomach. He asked, "Rose up yet?"

"I haven't seen her. Want me to go up and see?"

Gaunt shook his head. She'd been up as late as he had, helping him.

Boatman said, "I hear Robineau is just south of town."

"That's what I hear. I rode out to talk to the men with the other two herds, but I didn't see Robineau."

"Think he still intends to try killing you?"

"I doubt it. A lot of things cool off in a year's time."

He heard a door close upstairs and turned his head. Rose was standing on the balcony looking down. When she saw him, she came along the balcony and hurried down the stairs. She had fixed her hair but she still wore a wrapper over her nightgown. Rose didn't need to worry about what any man in Cottonwood might say or do in reaction to her appearance in the Alamo. They knew she was Gaunt's woman. They also knew she owned part of the Alamo.

Her face was filled with concern. "Are you all right this morning?"

He nodded.

"Wedemeier's men are in town. Without their guns. I saw some of them from my window. How did you manage that?"

He shrugged. She studied him, a small smile touching the corners of her mouth. "Just like that."

He nodded. She asked, "What about Robineau? Will he reach town today?"

"Probably."

She touched his arm. "I'd say be careful, but it wouldn't change anything. So I'll just wish you luck." Her words were light enough, but there was nothing light or lacking in concern in her eyes. He poured himself another drink and downed that one too.

He bent and kissed Rose on the mouth. "It's going to be all right. The first two or three days of every season are the worst. When they're over, then I hardly earn my pay."

She said simply, "I'm here if there's anything you need."

"Thanks." He smiled at her, then turned and left the Alamo.

CHAPTER 15

Rose Navarro watched him go. She was not a woman given to tears, but suddenly she felt a flood of them gathering behind her eyes. So that no one would see, she hurriedly crossed the room, ran up the stairs and along the hall to her room. She went in, taking time to carefully close the door behind. Then the dam burst and her tears came in a flood. She threw herself face down on the bed and buried her head in her pillow, her body shaking violently as she wept.

She had to be crazy, she told herself. He wasn't even hers and never would be. He would marry Maggie Conover, and she knew she'd never see him after that, except casually.

She shouldn't care this much. But she did care, and she couldn't help herself. She was hopelessly in love with him, as hopelessly as any schoolgirl, and she was terrified that he was going to be killed.

If only he loved her, really loved her. If only there wasn't Maggie Conover. But he didn't love her, at least not the way he loved Maggie. He wouldn't marry her. But that was her fault, not his. She had made her choice when she accepted her first job in a saloon. Oh God, if only she had made a different choice.

But if she had, she told herself, she would never have met Morgan Gaunt. She shouldn't be sorry. Even though she could never have more of him than she'd already had, and even though she would lose that very soon, she'd had him for a while.

And nothing lasts forever. Nothing. Not even Morgan, who seemed so indestructible. He wasn't indestructible. He had been shot last night in the leg and the bullet that hit his leg could just as easily have penetrated his heart.

Her weeping finally stopped. She got up off the bed, went to the window and looked down into the street, wiping away her tears with a scrap of perfumed handkerchief and occasionally sniffling like a little girl. Right now she wasn't Rose Navarro, who owned a part of the Alamo and who knew how to take care of herself. She was just a broken-hearted and very vulnerable woman, who did not know which way to turn.

The truth was, she was completely helpless and there was nothing she could do. Nothing but wait, and hope. That Morgan would survive. So that he could marry Maggie Conover as he planned.

She told herself bleakly that she was even willing to let Maggie have him. If only he did not get killed.

When he left the Alamo, Gaunt began the rounds of the remaining ten of the town's eleven saloons. All of these were below Texas Street. The Red Dog was the first. In Sully's absence, Kurt Vossler was tending bar. Gaunt crossed to the bar, ignoring the scowls he got from the two members of Wedemeier's crew who were in the place. Vossler also scowled at him. "Whadda *you* want?"

Gaunt shook his head. "Nothing to drink. I just wanted to tell you that at least two more crews are going to hit town today. I'll get their guns, but they're sure to hear about the cowboy who got killed last night."

"That's your problem, not mine. You were the one who killed him."

Gaunt said, "Don't get smart with me. He wouldn't have come back to town looking for trouble if Jackson hadn't cheated him. I'm just going to warn you once. Run honest games in all your saloons and see to it that none of your girls empty the pockets of the ones who get too drunk."

"Or what?" Kurt asked insolently.

"Or you'll get what Sully and Jackson got."

"You could've killed them, dragging them to the jail that way."

"Too bad I didn't. If I had, I wouldn't have to worry about them trying to backshoot me today."

Vossler gloated, "You're worried, then. Good. I hope they do get you. Then, by God, we can run this town the way it should be run."

Gaunt didn't reply to that. He turned to leave. "Remember. Cheat one of the drovers, and I'll come down on you. If they don't get to you first."

"What can they do? Without guns?"

"They can get guns. And they can wreck this town, starting with the places that cheated them."

Kurt Vossler didn't reply to that, but his expression said he figured he and his employees could handle any rag-tag bunch of cowboys intent on wrecking the place. Gaunt shrugged slightly and went on out the door.

He visited each of the remaining nine saloons with similar warnings. A few of the saloonkeepers, like Overman, were offended at the suggestion that they would allow cheating in their establishments. To them, Gaunt said, "You can have cheating in your place without being a part of it. All I want you to do is watch extra close. And if any of the cowboys complain, make a fair investigation of their complaints."

He returned to the jail. His leg wound had begun bleeding again from the walking, but riding wouldn't have been easier, getting on and off almost a dozen times. He brought out his straight-backed chair and propped it against the front wall of the jail. He sat down, tilted back and let himself relax.

It was now past noon. He was hungry but he wanted to rest his leg awhile. The newly arrived cowboys could reach town at any time, along with the two trail bosses.

He closed his eyes, realizing how very tired he was. He supposed his weariness was partly caused by the fact that he'd gotten very little sleep last night. Mostly, though, it was because of his wound. The constant pain wore him down, and the loss of blood had weakened him.

Gaunt never before had allowed himself doubts about his ability to handle the marshal's job. Today, a sudden, fleeting thought crossed his mind, "What if one of their bullets does bring me down?"

Angrily, he put that disquieting thought out of his mind. He'd been marshal here two years. This was the third. He'd faced down a good many men who were intent on killing him, or said they were, and who were armed and drunk enough to be dangerous and unpredictable. He'd survived so far. Why should doubt begin troubling him now?

He heard footsteps on the boardwalk and opened his eyes. Sam Kohn and Lester Ives were approaching him. He reached into his shirt pocket for his Bull Durham sack and made himself a cigarette. He licked it, twisted the ends and stuck it into his mouth as they stopped in front of him. Ives said, "You don't look very worried."

"Should I be?" He was worried, but he was glad it didn't show.

"You should. You've ordered Sully and Jackson out of town by sundown, and you ought to know they'll try to kill you rather than leave. After the dragging you gave them last night."

"You don't approve?"

Kohn spoke for the first time. "We neither approve nor disapprove. You're the marshal, and you do what you have to do. But you got out of the shooting last night by pure damn luck. That cowboy's bullet could've gotten you in the chest as easily as in the leg. All we want is for you to stay alive."

Gaunt grinned. "Thanks for your concern, gentlemen."

"Don't be sarcastic. We don't want you killed. We wouldn't want it even if we did not depend on you. We like you. We want you to stay alive."

Gaunt nodded, and this time there was warmth in

his voice. "Thanks. I'll stay alive. Last night I put myself between that cowboy and the two he was trying to kill. I won't be that foolish again."

"What are you going to do about Robineau?"

Gaunt had been trying to decide that himself. Now he answered his own question as well as theirs. "First, I guess I'll find out if he still feels the same way he did last year. If he's intent on killing me, I'm not going to let him roam the streets. I'll throw him in jail, and when he's finished his business I'll put him on the train along with his cattle, tied up if necessary to make sure he don't get off and come back here.

"On the other hand, if he's cooled off since last year and has changed his mind about killing me—well, I guess I'll just let him alone. I feel bad about what I did to him. I didn't have any choice, but I still feel bad."

Ives asked, "Are you having trouble with the gun ban?"

"So far I'm not. I've got the coat tree inside the jail loaded down with guns. That cowboy I shot last night—he came and got his gun and made me think he was leaving town. Then he turned around and came back."

"Maybe men like Sully and Jackson wouldn't be so eager to cheat the drovers if they knew they all had guns."

"Maybe. But the council made the decision and passed an ordinance. It's my job to see that it's enforced. If you're having second thoughts, I'd suggest you have another council meeting and reconsider it."

Kohn peered sharply at him. "What do *you* think of the ban?"

"I think it's a good idea. These cowboys get pretty drunk. And when they get into a drunken argument they use guns if they have them. Thirteen men were killed in Cottonwood last year, eleven of them cowboys. We're doing them a favor by taking away their guns."

He waited a moment and when neither man spoke,

he added, "Besides, the townspeople are safer when there's not so much gunplay in town. It hasn't happened yet, but sooner or later, some innocent bystander, maybe a woman or child, is going to be killed by accident if we allow guns in town. No, gentlemen, I support your gun ban a hundred per cent. Maybe I didn't at first because I could see how much trouble it was going to be for me, but I sure do now."

Both Ives and Kohn nodded. They smiled, and shook hands with him and went on up the street, their expressions revealing that they were still not completely convinced that he could enforce the gun ban, handle Robineau and keep the peace without getting himself killed. He had the wry thought that they probably would begin looking for a replacement immediately so that if he did get killed they'd have somebody on tap to take his place.

He still had not lighted his cigarette. Now he did, and leaned back, enjoying it. A green-bodied fly buzzed around his head and he made a pass at it with his hand.

He was feeling better now, rested. He finished his cigarette and flipped it out into the street. He was hungry and it was past time to eat. He got carefully to his feet, favoring his wounded leg, which had stopped bleeding.

He turned and locked the jail door. Then, walking slowly, again wishing he had a cane, he started up Kansas Street.

He had to decide, now, whether to eat at Maggie's place or whether to eat someplace else. He didn't really want to see Maggie, and that surprised him. He knew if he went to her place, the same tension would be between them and the same argument would probably come up.

On the other hand, if he ate someplace else, she would accuse him of avoiding her, and the ensuing argument would probably be more intense. Finally, shrugging fatalistically, he headed for Maggie's place.

He tried to favor his leg but it didn't do much good. He could feel warmth spreading from it and knew it had begun to bleed again. He cursed softly beneath his breath because he knew he needed to keep his leg quiet to allow it to heal and there was no way he was going to be able to keep it quiet, in the forseeable future at least.

He reached Maggie's restaurant and went inside. He took a table by the window because he didn't want to sit on a stool. He stretched his wounded leg out straight under the table and waited.

The place had practically emptied after the noon hour. Remaining were Bart Chapman and another cattle buyer, sitting at the counter smoking and drinking coffee. Gaunt nodded at the two of them. "When do you think those other two trail bosses are going to hit town?"

"Middle of the afternoon. We're going to ride out in a little while and see where they are."

"Let me know when you get back."

"Sure. Glad to." They finished their coffee, left some money on the counter and went outside. Gaunt was now the only customer in the restaurant.

He made up his mind that he wasn't going to discuss anything more controversial than the weather with Maggie this noon. She'd had her say and he'd had his, and one or the other had to give way before they could get a dialogue going between them again.

She was cool and impersonal when she came to his table, but she did not call him Mr. Gaunt, which would have meant she intended to be completely inflexible. "What will you have, Morgan?"

"What's the best?"

"I've got fried chicken. And roast beef."

"Fried chicken. And coffee."

She went away. He had only briefly glanced at her face and then had glanced away again. Her mouth was firmly set, her eyes without warmth. Her attitude plainly had not changed.

Sitting there waiting, he realized that unless he was willing to give in to her demands, they were not going to get married at all. She certainly did not intend to modify or relinquish any of her demands.

The realization that he was losing her, or had already lost her, was extremely depressing.

She brought his food and put it down in front of him then hastily retreated to the kitchen where she stayed, as if fearing *he* would start the same familiar argument. He ate quickly, anxious to get out.

When he finished, she still had not come from the kitchen. He left payment for his dinner on the table, got up and hobbled from the restaurant.

He supposed she was watching him from the doorway leading to the kitchen, but he did not look back.

CHAPTER 16

There was a deep feeling of depression in Gaunt as he limped back toward the jail. The quarrel with Maggie saddened him, and the trouble was he didn't know what he could do about it.

He simply couldn't see his way clear to doing what it would take to smooth things over with her. He couldn't quit. He couldn't betray the trust of the townspeople who had given him the job. Neither could he let Maggie dictate to him in such an important matter. Not and remain the man she wanted and said she loved.

This was what he didn't understand. She said she had fallen in love with him because of what he was. Now she wanted to change him as a condition of marrying him.

He shook his head helplessly, unable to understand, knowing, furthermore, that he would probably never understand. It was the inconsistency of woman, about which he'd heard so much but hadn't encountered until now. He cursed softly.

He reached the jail. He sat down in his straight-backed chair, tilted it back against the wall, and made himself a smoke. He lighted it, trying to ignore the continuous, throbbing pain in his wounded leg. He fished his watch out of his vast pocket and glanced at it. It was almost two o'clock.

He dozed, but snapped awake frequently at sounds nearby. Finally, at four, he got up, walked around to the side of the jail where his horse was standing in the shade idly switching at flies with his tail.

He mounted and rode out of town at a walk, heading south. He crossed the railroad tracks, glancing as he did toward the cattle pens.

Most of Wedemeier's cattle had already been loaded. Only one pen remained, and it was being loaded now. The engine at the head of the long string of cars was getting up steam, belching a cloud of black smoke. By the time he got back, the train would be gone and another would be backing into position to load tomorrow with cattle from the other two herds that had not yet reached town.

And all season it would be like this, until the hundreds of cars now waiting on several sidings east of town were gone; until all the other cars that would be arriving daily were also gone. Then, finally, the town would quiet down and become once more a sleepy prairie town, dozing through the winter months.

And what would he be doing when that time came? Gaunt asked himself. Would he be dead, only another marker in the graveyard outside of town? Would he be married to Maggie and settled into some less-exciting, less-dangerous job? Or would he be neither, and still the marshal of Cottonwood, waiting out the quiet months until the huge cattle herds arrived next year?

In the distance he saw a lift of dust and knew it was the cowboys from one of the newly arrived herds approaching him. He was still less than a quarter mile from town when he stopped. He could hang the guns from one crew on his saddle horn, but he'd play hell trying to carry all the guns from two.

They saw him waiting in the middle of the road and came on, about a dozen as nearly as he could tell without actually counting them. He felt the old tension come to him and the excitement that a confrontation always brought.

This was in no way similar to the confrontation with Wedemeier's crew yesterday. These men both knew of the no-gun ordinance, but they also knew the marshal would meet them prepared to enforce it no matter what enforcing it entailed.

They drew their horses to a halt when they reached him and looked at him expectantly. They were like all the Texas cowboys who came up the trail to Kansas, he thought. All wore Texas boots, scuffed and worn and run-over at the heels. They wore mostly homespun pants out of which as much dust and grime as possible had been carefully brushed. All but a couple had creased, clean shirts on, shirts that had been carried all the way from Texas in a "possible" bag that each man used for his personal things. Their hair, beneath their sweat-stained hats, was slicked down with water and carefully combed. Gaunt was willing to bet every one of them had bathed, in whatever water was available, and had on clean underwear. Some had whiskey on their minds. Most were thinking of women first, whiskey afterward.

He looked at Rosen, the trail boss. "Howdy. Welcome to Cottonwood."

The man inclined his head. A few of the cowboys replied cautiously.

Speaking to the cowboys Gaunt said, "There's a new ordinance in town. No guns. You're supposed to turn 'em in at the jail when you arrive and pick· 'em up again on your way out."

The trail boss said, "You already told me about it. I also heard one of Wedemeier's men got killed in town last night."

Gaunt nodded. "He picked up his gun and then went back.·Claimed a gambler had cheated him. He was trying to shoot it out with both the gambler and the bartender from the place the gambler worked."

"Who shot him? I heard it was you."

"It was." Gaunt was getting a little angry now.·He said, "I tried to calm him down, but he wouldn't calm. Shot me in the leg, and that didn't leave me any choice."

One of the cowboys muttered, "I ain't giving up *my* gun."

The trail boss turned his head. "Oh yes you are.

You ain't likely to get shot if you haven't got a gun. It's murder if you do." He looked hard at Gaunt. "I figure you'll see that nothing happens to these boys if they do give up their guns."

Gaunt shrugged. "This is a wide-open town. That's the way you boys want it. I can't swear all the gamblers are honest. I can't say all the whiskey is good. I can't say the saloon women or those in the brothels won't rob you if they get a chance. What I can say is that if anything like that happens, you come to me. Don't try to settle it yourself. I'll see that whatever it is gets made right."

The trail boss studied him. Finally he nodded. "Fair enough. Give him your guns, boys."

He handed Gaunt his gun and rode past. His cowboys followed, each pausing and giving Gaunt his gun. He hung the belts over his saddle horn and when that would hold no more, hung the rest around his neck. He watched them. They rode for maybe a hundred yards. Then one let out a whoop and dug spurs into his horse's sides. The animal pounded away, followed by the others, their riders raking their sides with the spurs and whooping excitedly.

Gaunt plodded back toward town in their wake. It had been much easier than he had expected it would be. The drovers from the other herd would probably surrender their guns with no more protest. And that would just leave Buck Robineau.

And Sully and Jackson, both of whom he had ordered to be out of town by the time the sun went down.

They wouldn't go. And neither Robineau nor any of his men would give up their guns.

He rode across the railroad tracks and when he reached the jail, swung wearily from his horse. He carried the guns in. There was no more room on the coat tree, so he laid them down on the cot, doing it carefully because if one of the cowboys had left a shell under the hammer there was a chance a jar might make the gun go off.

He went back outside and sat down. The sun was now low in the west. He tilted his hat forward over his eyes.

He looked idle and half asleep, but beneath the shade his hat provided for his eyes, they were alert and sharp and roving the street ceaselessly. It was getting along toward sundown and he was a stationary target here for any rifleman. Furthermore, if either Sully or Jackson or both of them did manage to kill him, there would be no one capable of bringing them to justice for the crime. Kurt Vossler and his other employees would control the town.

He heard footsteps and glanced up to see Rose coming along the walk. She stopped in front of him, hands on hips, an exasperated look on her face. "Do you have to sit here in the sun like the bull's-eye of a target? Can't you sit inside?"

He grinned. "I could. And that would give them the idea I'm afraid of them."

"You really aren't afraid of them, are you?"

"Of Sully and Jackson? No. Not of *them*."

"I'd think you'd be more afraid of men like them than of someone like Robineau."

He grinned again. "All right. Let's go inside." He followed her inside, leaving the door open. The sun cast a slanting pattern of orange light through window and door onto the floor inside the jail. He held a chair for her and then sat down on the corner of the desk, favoring his wounded leg. "What brings you down here?"

"Ben Murphy has offered to follow you around tonight. Two pairs of eyes are better than one."

He knew who had talked Ben Murphy into it. He also knew that Ben must realize how dangerous it would be. Ben was also a quarter owner of the Alamo and usually tended bar there at night.

He shook his head, and saw the disappointed look

come into her eyes. "Tell him no, but thanks. It's my problem, and I think I can handle it. If I can't, I'll call on him." He had no intention of calling on Ben or anybody else. Neither did he have any intention of letting himself get killed.

She studied him a moment, her fear for him plainly visible in her eyes. Finally she said, "Walk me up to the Alamo. I'll buy you a drink."

Gaunt grinned affectionately at her. This was her way of getting him out of danger, if only temporarily. He could not help comparing it with Maggie's way, and he felt ashamed when Maggie suffered by the comparison. He nodded, still grinning at her. "All right. Best offer I've had all day."

He followed her out, locking the jail door behind. She took his arm, moved in very close to him, and they went up the boardwalk toward the Alamo. Her closeness to him stirred Gaunt even though he knew its purpose, which was to discourage anyone who might shoot at him. She was willing to put herself into the same danger in her effort to protect him. His smile faded, and he looked down at her with more tenderness than he had ever felt before.

They reached the Alamo and went inside. Rose relaxed instantly. She preceded him to a table by the window where they could see out into the street and sat down. Gaunt sat down facing the door with the window on his right and the inside of the saloon on his left. The sun slid behind the building across the street. Not much longer, he thought. The sun would set in another fifteen minutes, and that was the deadline for Sully and Jackson to leave. If he didn't see them leave, he'd have to go looking for them. That would be safer than letting them come looking for him.

Ben Murphy brought them a bottle and two glasses. Gaunt glanced up at him. "I appreciate your offer, Ben. If I should need you, I'll sure call on you."

Ben nodded. He was a heavy man with a noticeable paunch and a shiny bald head above a broad face and

a flattened nose. He returned to the bar, not visibly relieved, and Gaunt knew he'd be a good man if he
needed one.

He poured a drink for Rose and one for himself. She
was trying to smile at him, but she kept looking worriedly out the window. On a sudden impulse he said,
"Let's have supper at the Cattlemen's Hotel."

She glanced at him in surprise. She watched his face
a moment, trying to read his expression without much
success. Finally, with a faint smile, she asked, "You
and Maggie have a spat?"

"Not really. She's after me to quit, and I can't."

"It won't help matters if she sees me with you."

He shrugged.

She thought a moment, then nodded. "All right.
What time?"

"Eight-thirty. All the cowboys that are coming ought
to be in town by then. And I'll have finished my early
rounds."

He finished his drink and got to his feet. "See you
later, Rose."

She nodded, still trying to conceal the worry in her
eyes.

Gaunt went out. There was shade now on the walk
in front of the Alamo, but in places farther down the
street the sun still came over the one-story buildings
and cast its orange light upon the walk.

There was a crowd of mounted cowboys in front of
the jail. He reached them and one man said, "We saw
the signs . . . about no guns in town." There was a
kind of wary hostility in the man. He said, "We'll give
'em up for now. But if there's any trouble . . ." He
didn't finish.

Gaunt took their guns, one by one, and they rode on
up the street, breaking into a wild, whooping gallop before they reached the corner. Gaunt unlocked the jail
and took the guns inside, placing these on the desk. He
made a mental note to get somebody down here tomorrow to put in nails or pegs to hang them on. By the

time the season was in full swing he could be custodian
of a couple of hundred guns every night.

Turning, he relocked the door and headed for the
Red Dog Saloon. Kurt Vossler was still tending bar.
There were half a dozen cowboys in the place and a
poker game going at one of the tables with five players
of which only two were cowboys. Gaunt stopped to
watch a moment, then went to the bar. "Sully and
Jackson here?"

"Here? Why should they be here? You ordered them
to be out of town by sundown."

Gaunt had the feeling both Sully and Jackson *were*
here. In the backroom. But it was not quite sundown,
and he didn't want to press it yet.

He turned and went outside. He could faintly hear a
band playing someplace uptown and remembered that
Wedemeier had ordered an elaborate funeral procession for the cowboy he had killed last night.

The procession was visible at the upper end of Kan-
sas Street. They must have formed on Fifth beside
Hooker's hayfields. The hearse still had not crossed
Fourth.

As the band came closer and its music became
louder, men and women began pouring from saloons
and shops all along Kansas Street until there was a
crowd at the curb as big as any that gathered for the
Fourth of July parade.

Blanton's hearse, drawn by four gleaming blacks,
came first. There was a black surrey immediately behind, containing Wedemeier and a couple of his cowboys, looking uncomfortable in newly bought black
suits with celluloid collars and black ties.

Behind the surrey were Wedemeier's remaining cowboys, mounted, riding in a column of twos. These men
had not bought new clothes, but had spruced up what
they had.

Behind them, whoever wanted to had fallen in afoot.
These included some of the cowboys from the other
herds, a few prostitutes and saloon girls and even a few

barefooted boys, one of whom was yanked unceremoniously out of the procession by an ear as Gaunt watched.

The band, eleven strong, made an ear-splitting racket as it went past in the narrow street. Gaunt received some hard looks from the cowboys. Then the whole thing was gone, leaving only a pall of dust in the street and the diminishing sound of the band.

The crowd began to disperse. The hearse crossed the railroad tracks followed by the surrey and the band, now playing the "Funeral March." The rest of the procession followed, turned left and disappeared.

Gaunt headed for the jail to get his horse. It was time for his evening rounds.

CHAPTER 17

It was a little after sundown when Gaunt mounted his horse to begin his evening rounds. A few high clouds in the west flamed orange, then red, and finally took on shades of lavender before everything turned gray.

He rode up Kansas Street to Goliad, determined tonight to vary the routine of his rounds and so try to throw Sully's and Jackson's timing off. He was certain now in his own mind that they had no intention of leaving town.

He turned right on Goliad before he reached the Red Dog Saloon, peering into the Pike Lady on the corner as he passed. Lamps had been lighted inside, but with the dusk light outside, it was difficult to see anything. He went on, glanced into the Longhorn and then went on to Oak.

Once the sun had disappeared and the clouds had lost their afterglow, darkness settled rapidly over the town of Cottonwood. He rode for a block along Oak, then turned back toward Kansas on Texas Street.

At the alley between Kansas and Oak, Gaunt turned south. The Red Dog was halfway down the block. It was possible he could surprise Sully and Jackson leaving by the rear door and thus get the upper hand. But everything was dark. His horse showed no interest in the area near the back door of the Red Dog. Either Sully and Jackson had already left, or they were waiting until it was even darker than it was now.

He considered waiting a while to see if they would appear but gave the idea up, thinking of the supper he had arranged with Rose and not wanting to keep her waiting.

He returned to Texas Street, rode over to Kansas and beyond, checking the small hotels and shops that lined Texas on the west side of Kansas Street.

He could hear occasional yells from the forty or fifty cowboys who were in town. He could sometimes faintly hear a woman's laughter or the tinkle of a piano. He returned to Kansas and rode up the exact center of the street like a man without a care or an enemy in the world.

Passing the Alamo, he saw Rose standing in the shadows watching him. He pulled aside and halted. She asked, "Do you have to ride in the middle of the street?"

"Always have. It makes things easier for me to see."

She knew what he meant by "things." Drunks with guns who thought they had reason to try killing him. Or sober men, who really did have reason and who, because they were sober, were deadlier.

He said, "Eight-thirty," and she nodded her head at him, her face in shadow so that he could not see what expression it wore. He went on, past the Cottonwood Bank to Maggie Conover's restaurant which was always very busy at this time of night.

He felt guilty when he saw Maggie standing in the doorway watching for him. She would be expecting him for supper when his rounds were finished, and he wouldn't be coming tonight. Moreover, it was possible, even likely, that she would find out he was having supper with Rose instead.

He caught himself regretting the invitation he had issued to Rose on the spur of the moment, and then he felt guilty because of his regret. He made a rueful grimace thinking, "Damn it, you're still a free man. You can do as you please."

He halted his horse. Maggie was hot from the kitchen and there was the shine of perspiration on her smooth forehead. He said, "Evening, Maggie."

Her words rushed out, "I'm sorry, Morgan. I wanted to tell you that. That's why I was waiting here for you."

"It's all right, Maggie. It's all right." But he wasn't sure it was.

She said, so softly he could scarcely hear, "I know tonight will be dangerous for you. I will pray for you."

"Thank you, Maggie." Her words had made him ashamed of the thoughts that had been running through his head. Almost hurriedly, he turned his horse and went on up Kansas Street without looking back.

A dog ran out to bark at him. He spoke to it and the animal stood there watching him, idly wagging his tail. Gaunt felt himself relax. No one would hide in the bushes along Kansas Street. Because of the dogs. Anyone skulking there would be discovered and barked at by the dogs.

His mind went on. Hooker's hayfield? He doubted it. There was little cover at the upper end of town and none north of Hooker's fence because of the fact that the hay had been mowed so recently.

He reached Hooker's fence and turned toward the bed of Cottonwood Creek. He could have turned the other way, but he didn't really want to avoid the ambush he knew Sully and Jackson might have set for him because avoiding it would only postpone the attempt until later on tonight.

Not the bed of Cottonwood Creek, then. It was too completely dark down there. They'd have to shoot at the sounds his horse made moving through the brush and that would not be certain enough to satisfy either one of them.

Where, then, for God's sake? And suddenly he knew. The same place they'd used last night. Neither of them were devious or particularly smart, but it *would* occur to them that the place he'd least expect them to use would be the same place they'd used last night.

Riding along the bed of Cottonwood Creek, he could feel the old, familiar excitement rising in him at the prospect of an encounter with Sully and Jackson in which the stakes would be life itself.

Sourly he thought that it was this kind of excitement in men that made war possible, even inevitable. It was what insured continuous conflict among individual men. Well, whether he liked it or not, he knew now that he couldn't live on this kind of excitement all his life, no matter who he married or did not marry. He would have to find some other way of making a living because this way only had one end. Death.

The phrase that had run through his thoughts, "No matter who he married," came back to him, and he admitted for the first time that he was beginning to have profound doubts about marrying Maggie Conover at all. And for the first time he openly admitted to himself that marriage to Maggie wasn't going to work, no matter how much he loved her, no matter how much she said she loved him.

He felt almost as though she had suddenly been taken away from him. He felt saddened and depressed. He cursed softly to himself and made his mind return to Sully and Jackson, waiting up ahead of him, waiting to shoot him down.

Maggie was right about one thing. It *was* time he quit. It had gotten so he couldn't keep his mind on the job any longer, not to the extent that was necessary to insure survival.

He reached the place in Cottonwood Creek where he always climbed his horse out of it. It was pitch black now, with the only light that small amount coming from the stars. The horse lunged up the steep path made by his own hoofs over the past couple of years. Ahead, Gaunt could see the cattle pens dimly in the darkness. The last train had left, carrying with it the last of Nick Wedemeier's herd. Wedemeier and his men would all be going back to Texas soon, probably in the next two or three days. It didn't take long for the saloonkeepers, gamblers and prostitutes of Cottonwood to relieve the drovers of the wages they'd received for the long drive north. The cowboys would ride south, broke, living off the country as they went, until they reached whatever place they had started from this spring.

He stopped briefly at the edge of the cattle pens, listening. The cowboy mourners had long since returned from the cemetery and were now drowning whatever sorrow they felt over the loss of a comrade in the cheap liquor served in the town's saloons. The hearse had been put away, the band had taken their pay and dispersed.

The faint sounds of revelry from the town's saloons reached him on a light northwest breeze. He touched his horse's sides with his heels and rode on, tense now and ready, as dangerous as a teased rattlesnake. His right hand was never more than two inches from the grips of his holstered gun. His left was high, holding the reins, feeling through them every slight movement of his horse's head. The horse's ears, invisible in this complete darkness, weren't the only things that would warn him of an alien presence. The horse's head would do the same, if Gaunt himself was alert enough.

He rode along the alleyway that separated the scores of individual pens. The smell of manure was fresh and steamy tonight from the cattle that had been shipped out of here today. A new line of boxcars stood opposite the loading chutes, waiting for tomorrow's herd or herds.

Robineau. Gaunt hoped that time had cooled Robineau's hatred, but he doubted it. At least Sully and Jackson would be out of the way by the time Robineau hit town. Unless he came in tonight. Unless he couldn't wait.

Angrily he put that thought out of his mind. He could see the railroad depot ahead now, with the ever-present square of light visible where Jim Sutton's window was. That was where the danger was; that was where they'd hit him. But in spite of that certainty, his alertness did not relax as he approached the end of the alley between the pens.

The gate at the end of the alleyway was closed and he cursed softly to himself. It squeaked when opened or closed and the squeak would warn the two waiting at the depot for him. But there wasn't any help for it because there wasn't any other way of getting out of the cattle pens other than going all the way around, and he was too stubborn to do that.

Without dismounting, he drew back the bar that secured the gate and swung it wide. He turned his horse, closed the gate and secured it again with the bar. As he had expected, the gate squeaked thunderously.

He was now more tense than he could remember being before. One killer after his hide was bad enough. Two was worse.

He reached the depot platform. Now, he told himself, was the time to deviate routine. He damned the pride that wouldn't permit it. He stepped his horse up onto the platform and headed for the square of light that came from the telegrapher's window. He was thinking that he wouldn't give them the satisfaction of making him vary his routine, and then, as quickly as he had that thought he had another, which was that he was being a goddamn fool. Unnecessarily. When your life is at stake, when you are dealing with killers who will shoot you from ambush, there is no shame in trying to protect yourself and stay alive. With death so near, he had a fleeting thought of someone else, and oddly enough, it was of Rose he thought and not of Maggie. He had a supper date with Rose, and no damned foolishness on his part was going to make him fail to keep it.

He was now ten feet from the window, and suddenly his horse's head turned slightly to the right and his ears pricked forward. They were there, all right, just where they had been last night, just where he had expected them to be tonight.

He was less than five feet from the window's near side, almost too late to do anything to protect himself. Almost. He left his horse at the same instant a volley of shots racketed from the darkness on his right less than twenty feet away.

He thought for an instant that he had caught his right boot heel on something as he swung from the saddle, but almost instantly he realized it had not caught at all but had been ripped away by a bullet fired from one of his assailants' guns. His wounded leg hit the station platform and collapsed, just as another two shots racketed, the bullets tearing splinters from the depot walls.

Gaunt's horse let out a snort of surprise and pain, gathered his haunches under him and sprang forward, across the shaft of light sereaming from the telegrapher's window to disappear into the darkness beyond. His passage drew yet a third volley from the darkness, and the gun flashes from this volley registered in Gaunt's mind as he drew his own gun and thumbed the hammer back.

His horse was hurt; he knew that for a certainty. The animal was too steady to spook at simple gunfire unless he had been hurt by it.

The knowledge further angered him. So did the freshly throbbing pain in his wounded leg, which had given way under him. He fired, aiming his first shot a little higher than the gun flash that still seemed seared onto his eyeballs and a little to his right.

It is sometimes possible to hear a rifle bullet hit either a man or an animal, but this range was too short. The revolver's report obscured the sound the bullet made striking flesh.

Yet somehow Gaunt knew his bullet had struck its mark, and he turned his gun on the second ambusher, who obliged him by firing at him again. But so nervous was this ambusher that, instead of hitting Gaunt, he hit the telegrapher's window and the shards of broken glass showered down onto the station platform.

Jim Sutton was probably already flat on the floor, thought Gaunt even as his gun centered on this unexpected new target, pulled right a little and bucked against his palm. This shot was followed, so closely a man might think he had imagined it, by an explosive grunt, as though the bullet's impact had driven a gust of air from the man it struck.

Suddenly all was silent. There was no sound from where all the bullets had been fired. There was no sound from inside the telegrapher's office. The shards of glass had by now all fallen, and Gaunt's horse had crossed the tracks, probably not stopping until he reached the jail.

Gaunt could hear his own breath sighing in and out. He was pretty sure both Sully and Jackson were out of action, but he didn't intend to take any unnecessary chances finding out.

He waited for what seemed an eternity. Then he heard Jim Sutton's shaky voice, "Mr. Gaunt? Are you all right?"

"I'm all right, Jim. You got a lantern in there?"

"Sure, Mr. Gaunt. Want me to bring it out?" He sounded scared and reluctant.

"Yeah. It'll be all right. I'll cover you."

His voice had drawn no shots, further reinforcing his belief that the two were dead. He punched out the empties in his gun by the faint glow of light from the window, then replaced them with fresh cartridges. Sutton appeared at the doorway leading onto the platform from his office, a lighted lantern in one hand.

Gaunt didn't look at him. He was looking out beyond the station, toward the place from which the shots had come. He could now make out two prone bodies, neither of which moved.

Sutton stepped down off the platform, holding the lantern high and squinting, trying to see. Gaunt headed for the two bodies on the ground.

The first thing he did was get their guns. Then he knelt to make sure neither was alive.

Jackson was dead. Sully was breathing, but weakly and raggedly. Gaunt got painfully to his feet. "One of them is dead. The other one likely will be soon, but I suppose I'd better get Doc to look at him."

"Want me to go after Doc?"

"I'd appreciate it. I've got to see how bad my horse is hit."

Sutton hurried away up the street. Gaunt hobbled painfully toward the jail, hampered now not only by his wounded leg but by a missing bootheel on the other foot.

CHAPTER 18

The gunfire down at the depot had brought a crowd out of the saloons at the lower end of town. Cowboys from the three herds that had already arrived began to fill Kansas Street, a few girls, bartenders and gamblers scattered among them. Sutton reached them first and answered their excited questions. He went on through, heading for the doctor's house. Gaunt plodded across the tracks and up the lower end of Kansas Street to the jail. No questions were asked of him as he passed through the dispersing crowd, for which he was grateful. He reached the jail.

His horse stood trembling at the hitching post in front. Gaunt went inside and lighted a lantern. He carried it outside. He held it high while he went over his horse for wounds.

Blood had congealed on the horse's hip. He found a gouge in the horse's rump about two inches long and a quarter of an inch deep. It wasn't a clean wound such as would have been made by a bullet, but ragged and torn. It must have been made by his bootheel, Gaunt thought, after it had been torn off by the bullet. The horse would have a scar, but the wound wasn't serious, not serious enough to require the attention of Lucas Thorne, the veterinarian. He could handle it himself.

Gaunt mounted and rode the still trembling animal up the street to the Drovers Hotel. He tied his horse to the hitching post, went inside and climbed the stairs to his room without glancing at the clerk or at any of the other occupants of the lobby. It was hard to walk with one leg throbbing so painfully and the bootheel gone from the other foot. He was relieved to reach his room.

He got another pair of boots out of the closet. Using the bootjack, he pulled off both boots, then sat down on the edge of the bed and put the others on.

Robineau would be in town by now, he thought—or would be soon. And despite what he had told Rose about Robineau forgetting his grudge, he didn't expect it to happen. When he went out, he'd have Robineau to face, if not right away, then later tonight.

There was a wet spot on Gaunt's trouser leg where blood had seeped through the bandage, but he didn't feel up to changing his pants just now. He blew out the lamp, settled his hat on his head, and went out into the hall.

He was better able to walk now, and managed to make it down the stairs and across the lobby to the outside door without limping too noticeably. Everybody in town knew he had been shot, of course, and expected him to limp. He just didn't want to limp so badly that anyone would get the idea he couldn't do his job.

On the hotel veranda, he encountered Ives and Kohn, both wearing worried expressions. Ives said, "Robineau is here. In town."

Gaunt nodded.

"With about half his crew," said Kohn.

"And they've all got their guns, I suppose."

Both men nodded. "Yes. We think you ought to raise a posse. It's the only way you're going to be able to get their guns away from them."

Gaunt shook his head. "Not the only way."

Kohn looked at him exasperatedly. "You don't have to face every troublemaker one-to-one. He wants to kill you, man!"

"So did Jackson and Sully. So have a lot of others."

"But . . ."

"Gentlemen, I appreciate your concern. And I think I will quit at the end of the year."

"We'll need a police force to take your place!"

Gaunt grinned. "If you'll excuse me, gentlemen, I haven't eaten yet." He went down the veranda steps and headed across the street toward the Alamo.

Rose Navarro, with her ears sharply tuned for the sounds of pistol shots, heard the volleys that sounded like strings of firecrackers down by the depot at the lower end of Kansas Street.

An icy hand seemed to clutch her heart. She waited, heard several more shots, then hurried through the crowd to the door and stepped outside.

She looked down the street in the direction from which the shots had come. She couldn't see anything but a scattered crowd of men and women who had come curiously from the saloons to see what was going on.

She realized that her knees were trembling. She forced herself to go back inside because she knew there was nothing she could do out here. She couldn't help Morgan Gaunt no matter how much she wanted to. She could only wait. And if he survived, she could watch him marry Maggie Conover and turn forever away from her.

Bitterness touched her briefly and then went away. She couldn't blame Morgan for the way things were and she couldn't blame Maggie Conover. The only one she could blame was herself.

But she didn't have to go on this way. She didn't have to stay in the saloon business until she was old and wrinkled and hard. She could get out now and maybe, in time, she could attain some kind of respectability. Even if she could not have Morgan Gaunt.

Ace Kenyon, who owned the other half of the Alamo, was behind the bar tonight. She called to him, "Ace. I want to talk to you." As she led the way to a corner table, she glanced at the big clock behind the bar. It was a little after eight. She was supposed to have supper with Morgan at the Cattlemen's at eight-thirty, and she didn't even know if he was still alive.

Ace held a chair for her and then pulled one out himself. He straddled it, his arms resting on its back. Rose knew Ace liked her and would probably marry her if it wasn't for Morgan Gaunt. And she liked Ace. But not that way.

He asked, "What's on your mind?"

"I want to sell my share in the Alamo."

"Why? It's a good living."

"I want to sell. Do you want it or shall I look for somebody else?"

"I want it. You paid fifteen hundred. I'll give you two thousand."

Rose nodded. "Have the papers drawn up."

He studied her puzzledly. "Mind telling me why? Is it Morgan Gaunt?"

She nodded dumbly, unable to trust herself to speak. She could feel the tears building up like a flood behind her eyes.

"I thought he was going to marry Maggie Conover."

That was exactly what she hadn't needed to hear right now. She got to her feet, tears now spilling out of her eyes. She opened her mouth to tell him that she didn't give a damn what he thought, then closed it without saying anything. She turned and hurried toward the stairs, colliding with several patrons between the table and the foot of the stairs. She went up, ran along the hall to her room, went in, slammed and locked the door.

She was a fool. Morgan might already be dead. Even if he was not, he was not for her. Nor was respectability. Nobody would ever let her forget what she was or what she had been. With tears running silently down her cheeks she went to the window, opened it and stuck her head out so that she could see down toward the lower end of the street.

She felt weak with relief when she saw Morgan on

his big chestnut horse. He sat straight, and seemed to be all right.

Trembling violently, she withdrew from the window and sat down in her chair before her mirror. He would be coming to take her to supper soon. And she wanted to look her best.

Before Morgan Gaunt got to the jail, he met Blanton's hearse going up the street. He stopped, and Blanton stopped. Blanton said, "I thought there was supposed to be two."

Gaunt shook his head. "Only one. The other was still alive."

"Well, Doc didn't find him. He must've crawled away someplace."

Gaunt knew he didn't have much time. But if possible he wanted to know where Sully was and how badly he was hurt. Most of all he wanted to know how much of a threat Sully was.

He rode as far as the jail where he stopped and picked up the lantern. He didn't light it, but mounted and rode to the place where the shooting had taken place. He scouted around in the darkness to make sure Sully wasn't close enough to kill him the minute he struck a match. Then he lighted the lantern, went to where the two had fallen, and by lantern light studied the ground.

The wheel tracks of Blanton's hearse were clearly visible as were the boot tracks of those who had helped load Jackson's body into it. Gaunt paid no attention to these. He was looking for the marks Sully must have made dragging himself away from the scene, and he found them and followed them. They went as far as the loading pen fence. Here, Sully had apparently pulled himself to his feet. His boot tracks led away from here. He had been staggering, but he obviously was a long ways from being dead.

Gaunt went back to his horse, more disturbed than he would have liked to admit. Now he not only had

Robineau and half that man's crew, but he had a wounded and possibly dying Sully, who, if he did not collapse and die between here and town, would also be gunning for him. Sully, if he had as much strength as he appeared to have, would be as dangerous as a wounded grizzly bear, filled with hate and pain, wanting only to satisfy it by killing the man who had hurt him so.

Gaunt blew out the lantern and mounted his horse. The animal seemed to have calmed considerably and was no longer trembling. Gaunt rode back to the Drovers Hotel, where he washed his face and shaved. Now, he took the time and effort to change his pants and shirt and comb his hair. Then he went back down the stairs.

He left his horse tied at the hitch rail in front of the Drovers and walked across the street. The noise from the saloons had picked up as the cowboys began getting drunk. Half a dozen tinny pianos now filled the street with their noise, discordant because not one single tune could be separated from the rest.

Gaunt crossed the street to the Alamo. Ace Kenyon was behind the bar. Gaunt crossed to it and Ace slid him a bottle and a glass. Gaunt poured himself a drink. As he downed it, Ace said, "I'll send for Rose. She's up in her room."

"Thanks." Gaunt wanted another drink but he denied himself. He needed quick reflexes in the night to come.

Ace said, "You're a lucky man."

Gaunt didn't know whether he was referring to Maggie or to Rose. So he didn't say anything.

Ace said, "I'd marry Rose myself if she'd have me."

Still Gaunt didn't say anything. He just looked at Ace, who quickly said, "Ain't none of my business, of course. But she's a fine woman, although I expect you know that without me telling you."

"I do." Something made him turn his head and he saw Rose coming down the stairs.

She was beautiful, dressed in a long, pale lavender gown with a low neckline that showed the creaminess of her throat and upper breasts. He crossed the room to her and she took his arm, trying to smile, trying to blink back the tears that brightened her eyes. She said tremulously, "I thought . . . I heard those shots and . . ."

He said, "It's all right. It's all right."

"Yes." Her smile was brighter now as he walked her out the door into the street. She clung tightly to his arm, keeping her body very close to him as if she knew there was less chance of anyone shooting at him with her so near.

From habit, Gaunt scanned both sides of the street as they walked north toward the Cattlemen's. His glance searched each darkened passageway, each doorway deep enough to hide a man. No drovers were supposed to be above Texas Street, but that didn't mean none of them could be here. Besides, the deadline didn't apply to Sully, who could go anyplace in town he pleased.

The Cattlemen's Hotel was directly across Kansas Street from Maggie Conover's restaurant. Examining his own inner conscience, Gaunt wondered whether he had not had an ulterior motive in asking Rose to supper with him tonight and had picked the Cattlemen's deliberately so that Maggie would see him on the street with Rose.

If he had, he admitted to himself, it was nothing of which he could be proud. If he intended to break with Maggie, he should do it cleanly and face-to-face, not by letting her see him with Rose instead.

But he really hadn't been that devious. The invitation to Rose had been issued spontaneously, with no thought of any possible consequences.

He didn't look in through the windows of Maggie's restaurant as they passed. Neither did Rose. They went on, reached the corner, crossed the street and climbed the steps to the veranda of the Cattlemen's Hotel.

Robineau would probably be staying here, he thought, since it was the best in town and also since the Texas Street deadline did not apply to trail bosses as it did to their men. Trail bosses had to come north of Texas Street to transact their business.

They entered the lobby, in which there were few people tonight. Gaunt was conscious of the stares they drew. Everybody in town knew he was courting Maggie. Everybody also knew he was seeing Rose.

She was watching him, her eyes very steady and calm. She said, "You could have crossed the street. Then Maggie probably wouldn't have seen."

He didn't know what to say to that. But Rose wouldn't let it go. "When are you going to marry her?"

Suddenly, confronted with that question, he finally and squarely faced the truth. "I'm not."

Surprise showed in her face. "But why? I thought . . ."

He said, "It wouldn't work. I thought it would, but I was wrong."

She kept her glance downcast now. Gaunt was already thinking ahead. After supper he'd deposit Rose immediately at the Alamo where she would be safe. He wouldn't subject her to any further dangers by being seen with her on the street. Not until both Sully and Robineau were accounted for.

Rose was afraid to look up at him. Her heart had begun to beat with an almost painful rapidity when he'd said he wasn't going to marry Maggie after all. She was sure he could feel her hand trembling upon his arm.

In her eyes was the old fear for his safety that was always there. But now there was something else, a wild kind of joy. At least, if he survived the night, she was not going to lose him. Anyway not yet.

CHAPTER 19

The Cattlemen's Hotel had been copied after the Stockyards Hotel in Chicago. Its lobby was a hundred feet long and nearly fifty feet wide. It was liberally sprinkled with brown leather-covered sofas and chairs, and against the wall there were many writing desks and chairs. There must have been at least a hundred polished brass spittoons in the lobby, which was floored with white tile and covered with a scattering of large and beautiful Indian rugs. The walls were hung with the stuffed heads of moose, elk, bear, deer and mountain lions along with pictures of Buffalo Bill Cody, Sitting Bull, John Brown, Lincoln and various other well-known figures of the time, alive and dead.

The dining room was even more elegant than the lobby if that was possible. Linen tablecloths covered every table. The walls were of paneled oak and the carpet underfoot was a rich wine color. A candle burned on each table, but the crystal chandeliers, of which there were two, provided most of the light.

They were ushered to their table by a man in a starched white jacket, who held Rose's chair for her while she sat down. Gaunt stretched out his wounded leg as he sat down, then looked at Rose over the candle burning on the table.

She was very lovely by candlelight but then, he thought, she was very lovely in any light. Her life, whatever it had been, had touched her little, and suddenly he knew what he was going to do. But not yet. Not until he had decently broken off with Maggie.

He ordered absently after consulting Rose about

what she wanted to eat. The white-coated Negro waiter brought red wine in a napkin-wrapped bottle and poured it carefully. Rose raised her glass, her face showing no humor and no cynicism but only sober concern. "To tomorrow."

He touched his glass to hers, smiling. "Don't worry so. I told you it was going to be all right."

She sipped her wine, then put the glass down. For an instant she said nothing and it was as though she was gathering her thoughts. Finally she said, "How can you be so sure? Do you know something the rest of us don't?"

"No," he replied soberly. "I just have confidence in myself."

"You were hit in the leg last night, and that wound may kill you yet if you don't take care of it."

"I did something I knew was foolish last night. I won't do that again."

"Why did you do it last night?"

"I miscalculated. I thought the cowboy wouldn't shoot. He didn't have anything against me."

"He was drunk. And drunks don't behave like sober men."

He said, "I'll be careful of drunks tonight."

She stared at him with exasperation. "I don't want to badger you. You get enough of that . . ." She stopped, embarrassed by what she had been about to say. She finished lamely, "Just be careful. Just think before you put yourself into danger."

"All right." He reached across the table and covered her hand with his own. Her glance raised and her eyes met his, holding them almost desperately for a long, long time. Then she looked away and Gaunt removed his hand.

The waiter brought their dinner. Gaunt was preoccupied as he ate, not the cheerful companion he had wanted to be to Rose. She watched him whenever she could without getting caught at it. Her eyes sometimes were bright with tears, sometimes dry and angry, but

always they held her deep concern for his safety
throughout this crucial night.

The supper was finally finished. Gaunt paid the bill
and rose. Rose took his arm leaving the dining room.
Crossing the street she said, "Ace is buying my interest
in the Alamo."

He glanced down at her with surprise, his eyes questioning.

Almost defensively she said, "I'm tired of it."

He opened his mouth to ask her what she would do,
then closed it without saying anything. He was no fool
and he wasn't blind. He knew what Rose wanted to do.
But he wouldn't ask her now, tonight, when there was
a chance he wouldn't live to see the dawn. He had
minimized the danger to him from Robineau, Robineau's crew and the wounded Sully to Rose, but he
couldn't minimize it to himself.

He took her inside the Alamo. She asked, "A
drink?"

He shook his head. "I'll see you later on tonight."

Unexpectedly she stood on tiptoe and, pulling his
head down, kissed him on the mouth. She said something she had never said before, "God go with you and
keep you safe."

Gaunt turned and limped out of the Alamo. Rose
watched him go, as if sure she would never see him
again.

Gaunt stood for a moment on the walk in front of
the Alamo. He glanced uptown and saw Maggie leaving her restaurant. She turned and locked the door. She
glanced down the street, saw him, then deliberately
turned her back and headed up the street toward
home.

She had seen him with Rose, he thought, probably
when they went to supper and also when they returned.
He supposed he ought to catch up and walk her home,
but he didn't move. He had enough on his mind
tonight without doing what he knew had to be done

eventually, breaking off with Maggie. She had, in fact, virtually broken off with him already by issuing the ultimatum that he either quit the marshal's job or they were through.

Standing there, he forced himself to put both Maggie and Rose completely out of his mind. Tonight he needed complete concentration if he expected to see the dawn.

His horse was standing at the hitch rail in front of the Drovers Hotel where he had left him earlier. He crossed the dusty street, avoiding a freight wagon, untied and mounted his horse. This was easier on his leg since he could avoid putting any weight on it except when the horse was trotting. At a walk, his wounded leg could be completely relaxed.

All right. First things first. That meant making the rounds of the saloons and relieving Robineau's men, one by one, of their guns. There was a chance Robineau would be in any saloon he entered, and so he would have to proceed more carefully than he ever had before.

He was counting on the loyalty of Robineau's men to make his relieving them of their guns possible. They knew Robineau wanted the marshal for himself. The crippled trail boss wasn't going to take it kindly if one of his men eliminated the marshal before Robineau had a chance at him.

Kurt Vossler's saloons would be the most dangerous, he thought. So he'd hit them first. Starting with the Red Dog, where Vossler was tending bar. After that, he'd take them one by one as he came to them.

He had a sudden idea and grinned at it. With no little anticipation, now, he headed down Kansas Street toward the Red Dog, just below Texas Street.

There were a few cowboys on the boardwalks. Several girls lounged in the doorways of the cribs across the street, sometimes calling out invitingly to one of the passing cowboys.

Gaunt turned his horse. He rode up on the board-

walk and, bending low as he did, rode his horse
straight into the smoky, noisy saloon.

The noise stopped instantly. Kurt Vossler stared for
an instant in amazement. Then his face got red and he
roared, "What the hell do you think you're doing?"

Gaunt said, "Some of these cowboys still have guns.
I want them. Now."

His horse, used to jumping up onto the station platform every night showed no particular nervousness at
the hollow-sounding wooden floor underneath his
hoofs. But the smoky air and the crowd made him nervous. Gaunt repeated, "Your guns, gentlemen. I want
your guns. You all saw the notices posted outside of
town. You should have stopped and left them at the
jail."

A red-haired, stocky cowboy said, "Wasn't nobody
there."

Gaunt glanced at him. "You one of Robineau's?"

The red-haired man grinned. "Sure am. I'll bet you'd
like to know where he is right now."

"I'll find him."

"You sure as hell will!"

Gaunt said patiently, "Give me your guns. You can
pick them up at the jail when you leave town."

He watched Robineau's three men, the ones with
guns, carefully as they unbuckled their gun belts. He
said, "Rebuckle the belts so I can carry them over my
saddle horn."

The red-haired one said, "To hell with you. Do it
yourself."

Gaunt looked the man squarely in the eyes. He let
his stare hold that of the cowboy for almost a full
minute. When he spoke, his voice was curt. "Buckle
them."

The cowboy looked at his companions, right and
left. For an instant, Gaunt could see he was considering drawing the gun and making a fight of it.

His own hand moved very slightly. When it stopped
it was less than half an inch from the grips of his own

holstered gun. He repeated, "Buckle them." He could have done it himself, of course. But he couldn't let the cowboy get the upper hand.

From behind the bar, Vossler grumbled something and moved, as if to reach under the bar. Instantly Gaunt's gun was in his hand. The hammer made a click as it came back. His voice was like a whip. "Put your hands on the bar."

Vossler did, his forehead shining suddenly with sweat. It was the end of the cowboys' resistance, too. With Gaunt's gun covering them, they now had no choice but to comply. They buckled the three belts and each man handed his belted gun up to Gaunt.

Gaunt hung them on the saddle horn. He backed his horse out of the saloon. The animal jumped nervously when his rump touched the swinging doors but he backed on out, and Gaunt ducked to avoid hitting his head.

He heard the grumbling comments as he turned away toward the next saloon. "Dirty, uppity son-of-a-bitch!" and, "Wait'll he meets up with Buck."

He smiled faintly and without humor as he moved on down the street. He did not minimize the danger he faced tonight. It was greater than any he had ever faced before.

But it would, if he survived it, have its rewards. With Sully and Robineau in jail, keeping order in Cottonwood ought to be easy for the rest of the season. Particularly if he got an opportunity to meet both Robineau and Sully face to face.

A man passed him, hurrying, the red-haired cowboy who had given him an argument back in the Red Dog Saloon. He watched where the man went, able to follow his progress along the darkened street by the light coming from the windows and open doors of the various saloons. The man turned the corner on Goliad, almost running.

Gaunt kicked his horse in the sides and the startled animal leaped ahead, galloping instantly. Gaunt pounded around the corner of Goliad and Kansas, the hoofs of his horse thundering on the hard-packed ground. Dust rose behind him in a cloud.

He saw the red-haired cowboy disappearing into another of Kurt Vossler's saloons, this time the Gold Coin. He saw a man who looked like Moss, the gambler from the Pink Lady running along the street. This man also disappeared into the Gold Coin Saloon.

Gaunt wondered where Sully was. In the Gold Coin too, he supposed. Were they waiting for him there, all of them? Robineau? Sully? Moss? And as many of Robineau's cowboys he had been able to talk into helping him. Three men at least. Six or eight at the most. And one, Robineau, would be armed with a scattergun.

Riding into the Gold Coin would be suicide. Walking in would be equally dangerous. There had to be another way.

Frowning, he slowed his horse, turned him around and went back to the Goliad and Kansas intersection. He rode south to the jail.

He dismounted painfully and carried inside the three guns he had collected. He came back out, locked the door and stood still a moment, frowning and trying to decide what he should do.

The whole town knew how direct and undevious he was. Robineau, Sully, Moss and whoever else was waiting in the Gold Coin for him would expect him to come charging in the front door.

They knew his lightning speed with his gun and his deadly accuracy. Unwilling to trade even one of their lives for his, they'd have it arranged so they could blast him without risk to themselves the instant he burst through the door.

Well, he wouldn't play their game. He'd have to force them to come to him. The only trouble with that was that if Robineau failed to kill him himself, then he'd probably declare an open season on him and would offer a reward to whoever managed to bring him down.

All but three of Robineau's men still had guns. Furthermore, in a town like Cottonwood, guns were always available to anyone who wanted them badly enough.

So he'd have to move fast. Before the number of men who were dedicated to killing him grew any more.

CHAPTER 20

Morgan Gaunt stood there in the darkness in front of the jail for a long time, frowning, trying to work out some strategy that would succeed. He was betting now that all those who wanted to kill him were together in the Gold Coin Saloon. Quite possibly Kurt Vossler was also with them now.

He couldn't go in the front. That would be suicide. And it wouldn't work much better to go in the back. He could wait, of course, doing nothing, and hope they came out after him. But that course was fraught with risk. He wouldn't know where they were. All they'd have to do would be to wait until he appeared and then shoot him down.

Suddenly the worried expression on his face relaxed. There was a way. A way he thought would work.

He unlocked the jail and went in. He did not light the lamp. He took a double-barreled, sawed-off shotgun from the gunrack and, with cartridges from his desk, loaded it. The cartridges were loaded with double-O buckshot. He stuck a handful of them into his pants pocket.

Carrying the gun, he went out into the darkness again and mounted his big chestnut, thinking with considerable regret that he might be sacrificing the animal, of which he was very fond, to save his own life. But there was no help for it.

In almost total darkness, he cut through the vacant lot beside the jail, in case they had a lookout watching for him, and rode up the alley behind it and the Pink Lady on the corner. When he reached Goliad, he could see the lighted, dirty windows of the Gold Coin and through them, the crowd inside.

He stopped, concealed beside the sagging, high board fence behind the Pink Lady. He watched the Gold Coin for almost five minutes. Nobody came or left. Furthermore, little noise poured from the open door, not the usual yells of pure exuberance, not the tinkling sounds of a piano, not the shrill voices of women. They were waiting for him, all right.

He suddenly touched his heels to his horse's sides. The animal started across the street diagonally, straight toward the Gold Coin.

In Gaunt, every muscle, every nerve was tense. His leg ached ferociously from the strain he put on it, bracing it as he did against the stirrup. He kept the horse at a walk halfway across the street, his eyes alternately searching the shadows on both sides of the building and studying his horse's head and ears. He saw nothing and neither, apparently, did his horse. They were all inside, then. They had to be.

Straight for the door he rode, and when he reached the boardwalk, forced the horse up on it, heading straight for the swinging doors. The instant his horse's forefeet came down on the boardwalk with their distinctive sound, he whacked the horse across the rump with the barrel of the shotgun, at the same time leaving the saddle with a single smooth motion that put him on the boardwalk just in time to prevent his slamming against the side of the door.

The horse, lunging because of the surprising and unexpected whack on the rump, could not stop short of the door and went on into the saloon. Gaunt didn't wait to see what would happen then. He was already on his way around to the rear of the building, limping noticeably but now, in the excitement and tension of the moment, completely unaware of the pain.

Inside the saloon, a shotgun roared, its deep-throated sound echoed by several sharper pistol reports. Gaunt heard his horse's shrill nicker of terror.

He heard the thunder of the horse's hoofs against the saloon floor and then he heard the shattering of glass as the horse leaped through one of the big front windows of the saloon. He heard the diminishing sounds of hoofs as the horse galloped down the street in the direction of either the stable or the jail.

Now he would see if his plan paid off. He figured that they'd expect him to be waiting in front of the saloon for them to come out.

If his calculations were right, not one of his intended assassins would go out the front of the saloon. They'd come charging out the back hoping to circle the building and cut him down from the shadows on each side.

He reached the corner of the building and rounded it at a run, revolver still in its holster, shotgun held in both his hands. He tripped on a pile of tin cans and went down with a crash that, he thought, could probably be heard for half a block. The shotgun, held in front of him, dug its muzzle into the ground.

Cursing soundlessly, Gaunt fought to his hands and knees. He supposed the shotgun was useless now. And so, probably, was his plan—unless, by some miraculous chance, the men inside had been making so much noise themselves they hadn't heard the crash he'd made falling over the pile of rusted cans.

As he froze there, listening, everything was silent except for the sound of booted feet on the floor inside the saloon. Gaunt stuck a finger into one bore of the shotgun and then the other one. His finger encountered some loose dirt adhering to the inside walls of the gunbarrel, but no solid plug of earth. He could use the gun, then, without blowing himself up.

The back door of the Gold Coin burst open and a man plunged out. Another came behind him and another still. Gaunt didn't dare wait for any more or these first three would be gone, hidden in the shadows. He roared, "Hold it! Don't take another step!"

A fourth and fifth man burst from the door before the first three could obey his command. Gaunt fired one barrel of the shotgun over their heads and three of the five men stopped. Two kept running and disappeared.

In the small amount of light streaming from the back door, Gaunt had recognized those two. Robineau and Moss. Sully had been the fifth man out. The remaining two looked like cowboys, but they both had guns.

All three men now whirled toward the sound of Gaunt's voice, their guns leveled, the hammers back. Gaunt roared, "Don't!" but he was too late. One of the cowboy's guns fired, the bullet taking out a chunk of board less than three inches from Gaunt's ear, a chunk that tore into his cheek and brought an instant rush of blood.

As always when he was hit, Gaunt's conscious mind ceased functioning. His reflexes took over without direction from his brain. The shotgun leveled and the second barrel roared. Buckshot rattled against the back wall of the Gold Coin Saloon.

One of the cowboys bent and grabbed his thigh, uttering a high cry of surprise and pain. The second doubled, clutching his belly. Sully, the last of the three, caught the bulk of the charge and fell without a sound.

No more men would be coming out the rear door now, Gaunt thought. But there were two, unhurt and deadly, probably less than fifty feet away from him. He broke the shotgun, the smell of powder smoke acrid in his nostrils, ejected the two spent cartridges and shoved two fresh ones in. He ran back to the front corner of the saloon, the shotgun ready in front of him.

Now he could go in, he thought. Robineau and Moss wouldn't do anything until they'd had time to figure out what had happened and what was likely to happen next. The biggest danger he faced inside the saloon would be from Kurt Vossler. The cowboys would most likely meekly surrender their guns, having seen what happened to the pair who had tried to bring the marshal down.

Without a moment's hesitation, Gaunt burst through the swinging door, a corner of his eye noticing the missing window on his left side as he did.

The place was a shambles. His horse, terrified at finding himself inside the noisy saloon, had knocked over half the tables and chairs in the place before he leaped through the big front window. Kurt Vossler was behind the bar, a shotgun lying on it, pointed toward the door.

Gaunt knew the shotgun would cut him in two if he didn't fire first. He leaped to one side, nearly falling because his wounded leg threatened to give way beneath him. The hammers of the shotgun were back.

No time to sweep the saloon with his glance for others who might have guns in their hands. He fired, and Vossler fired almost simultaneously.

Gaunt, his leg finally refusing to support him, fell just as he fired. Vossler's shotgun charge ripped the air over his head, taking out the window on the other side of the door from the one his horse had taken out earlier. Two of Vossler's buckshot, at the outer edge of the pattern, tore into the muscles of Gaunt's shoulder and stayed.

Flat on the floor, rolling, he saw Vossler driven back by the charge of his own gun. Vossler disappeared and Gaunt knew that he was already dead, having taken the full charge of buckshot in the face and chest.

There was broken glass all around him and every time he put a hand down it cut his palm. But he forced himself backward enough to feel the wall beneath the broken window at his back. He swept the shotgun around until it covered the surprised and frightened crowd. He roared angrily, "Anybody that has a gun, shed it. Now!"

In front there was a cowboy with a gun in his hand. There were a couple more with holstered guns at their sides. The three looked into the two gaping bores of the ten gauge and suddenly decided they had enough of their trail boss's fight. The man with the gun in his hand lowered the hammer and tossed it on the floor between him and Gaunt. The other two unbuckled their belts and tossed them after it.

Without lowering the hammer, and using the shotgun as a cane, Gaunt forced himself to his feet. The two pellets in his shoulder burned like fire, but there was little blood from the closely spaced wounds. He was mad now, hair-trigger mad, and the cowboys in the saloon saw his fury and watched him with eyes filled with fear. For all they knew he was still going to blast them with the shotgun at this close range.

He said angrily, "Every damn one of you stay right here! If I see one of you leave, I'll shoot to kill!"

He didn't wait for a reply. He picked up the loose gun and the two holstered ones, turned and went outside, limping but scarcely aware of the pain. He was like a hunted, wounded and beleaguered animal, fighting desperately to survive.

Sully was dead. But there was still Robineau, who also had a shotgun, and Moss, armed with at least one gun and probably two. They were somewhere in the darkness. They might be hunting him separately or they might have joined forces.

More furious than he had ever been before in his life, he tramped along Goliad to Kansas Street and then south to the jail. He unlocked it, opened the door and threw the gun, belts and holsters inside. He locked the door again.

Turning, he saw the crowd that had gathered on the other side of Texas on Kansas Street. They were clustered on both sides, staring south toward the jail. They'd heard the revolver shots and the deep, booming shotgun blasts. He wished they weren't there because of the chance one of them might be hit by a stray bullet, but there was nothing he could do about them now. He had all he could do, keeping himself alive.

He paused for a moment in front of the locked door of the jail. His plan for smoking them out of the Gold Coin Saloon had worked, but he had no other plan.

How do you fight two men hidden by darkness just waiting for you to show yourself?

He supposed both Maggie Conover and Rose were in the crowd staring toward the jail, and he didn't want either of them to see him shot down.

Besides, he was the marshal. He was the law in Cottonwood. Come hell or high water, he wasn't going to skulk in alleys and vacant lots playing Robineau's and Moss's game.

With his mind made up, he turned and walked toward the stable. He went up the inclined ramp from the street, took down the lantern that hung just inside the door, struck a match and lighted it.

His chestnut was standing, trembling, in his stall. Gaunt walked back and led the animal out. Then, carefully, he went over the horse looking for wounds.

There were several glass cuts, all superficial, on the horse's chest. There was the previous wound on his rump. There was a shotgun pellet lodged in his neck, a lump beneath the skin and showing blue, but not serious unless it was pressing on a nerve.

Carefully he examined every square inch of the horse's body. He found no other wounds. The horse was all right. Only scared. Only stung, and skittish from his scare.

Talking soothingly to the horse, he put a boot into the stirrup and swung astride. Damn them, he thought, if they were going to kill him tonight, at least he was going down like a man. He rode down the ramp into the street.

The crowd still stood silently on both walks up on the other side of Texas Street. The pianos in the saloons were still. The shrill voices of the saloon girls and prostitutes were also still. There were no shouts. It was as if the town of Cottonwood was dead, or sound asleep.

Moss would shoot from ambush without warning, Gaunt thought. But Robineau, with his strange sense of pride that allowed him to use a shotgun to compensate for his crippled arm, would not be able to fire without first warning his victim that he intended to.

For a moment Gaunt sat his horse in the middle of Kansas Street, stroking the horse's neck and speaking soothingly to him. He knew the horse was so frightened and nervous that he might bolt at the slightest sound. That might be an advantage and it might not.

He touched the horse with his heels and moved on up the center of the street, starting his late-night rounds even though it was not yet late enough. The only way to smoke them out was to present himself as a target. A show of unconcern on his part could only make them more nervous than they already were.

He crossed Goliad and rode north until he reached the Red Dog Saloon. Nobody seemed to be drinking inside of it. All were clustered at the windows and door, looking out.

A man came running down the street, and intercepted him just short of the Texas Street intersection. He yelled breathlessly, "You damn fool, are you trying to make it easier for him?" It was Lester Ives.

Gaunt said, "It's all right, Mr. Ives."

"What do you mean, it's all right? You're deliberately making a target of yourself!"

"Maybe. But how is it going to look if they make the law in Cottonwood run up and down back alleys like a rat?"

Ives made a disgusted exclamation.

Gaunt went on up Kansas Street, followed by Ives, and when he reached the crowd he said, "Get off the street, folks. There may be gunfire and one of you could be hit."

They began reluctantly to disperse. Gaunt rode on up the street. Rose was standing in the doorway of the Alamo, watching him, and she raised a hand. There was no sign of Maggie at her restaurant and the place was dark, but he had the feeling she was there, watching him, probably weeping and still trying to sort out in her own mind what she ought to do.

He reached Main and went on north, through the residential district of the town. He reached Hooker's hayfields, turned east and then rode south along the pitch-black, brushy bed of the creek.

He climbed out at the south end of town and entered the alleyway that separated the cattle pens. He was halfway when suddenly, directly ahead and in a pen on his right, a fire suddenly bloomed in a loose pile of hay.

It grew swiftly and in less than two seconds illuminated the whole area. So this was to be the place, Gaunt thought.

So rapidly did his mind work that he had no consciousness of trying to figure this thing out. The gist of it was that one of them, probably Moss, had lighted the fire. Both Moss and Robineau were counting on him to whirl his horse and retreat. Or to leave his horse and try to find cover in one of the nearby pens.

If he retreated, he would be silhouetted against the fire as he came in range of Robineau's scattergun. If he went ahead, Moss could cut him down as he passed through the fire's light. If he dismounted and tried to hide, then both of them would hurry to the spot where he'd left his horse and hunt him down.

It looked like a damned good plan. And it might have worked except for the extreme nervousness of Gaunt's chestnut horse. As the fire grew, the horse suddenly and unexpectedly began to buck.

Gaunt could have ridden it out, despite his wounded leg. Instead, he chose to let the horse throw him and lit in the deep, dry manure beside one of the heavy cattle-pen fences. The shotgun roared, triggered by a surprised and already nervous Robineau, and Gaunt immediately fired at the muzzle flash.

Most of the shot rattled against the pen, but one or two brought a grunt from Robineau. Hastily, Gaunt broke the shotgun, shoved in two fresh shells and instantly fired one barrel and then the second, at the same spot. There was one more shot from Robineau, his second barrel, but it was fired at the sky and Gaunt knew he'd gotten a solid hit.

He reloaded the shotgun, got to his feet, and ran as swiftly as he could with his wounded leg, straight toward the fire in the pile of hay. A revolver shot flared across the alleyway, and that was all Gaunt needed. He stopped so quickly he nearly fell, set himself, and fired both shotgun barrels at his hidden ambusher.

Only after he had, did he become aware of a burning sensation along his ribs. And of the warm rush of blood.

He was hit again. But he could see Moss sprawled out on the ground. He opened the gate, went into the pen, and knelt at Moss's side. The man was dead.

Gaunt went back out into the alleyway and walked to where Robineau was. Robineau's chest was a mass of blood.

Gaunt heard the fire engine bell. He started toward his horse, now almost to the depot. Before he could reach the animal, the fire engine, drawn by a team of blacks, came rattling down Kansas Street headed toward the fire in the pens. Men in fire hats clung on behind and a gang of other men came running a couple of hundred yards behind.

Gaunt reached his horse and mounted him. He headed uptown. At the Alamo, Rose stepped out into the street and barred his way. "You get down and come in here. I'll send for the doctor. Let him come to you this time."

There was something authoritative in her voice, but it had a pleading quality as well. Gaunt got off his horse. He was suddenly very tired, and it didn't seem as if there were many places that didn't hurt.

He tied his horse. Rose took his arm and helped him inside. He climbed the stairs with her.

Inside her room, she insisted that he lie down, dirty clothes and all, on her bed. She sat beside him and looked into his face.

Gaunt said, "It will be all right now. For the rest of the year."

Her eyes were large, very serious and questioning. He said, "I'm going to break it off with Maggie."

"Why?"

"I'd like to marry you. If you'll have me."

Tears came like a flood into her eyes. She put her face down against his chest and wept until she heard the doctor coming up the stairs. She raised her head then and in response to his questioning glance, nodded her head vigorously.

He thought that it didn't really matter what he did. If he had Rose, he'd be happy doing anything. He felt guilty about Maggie briefly, and then even that went away.

PRODIGAL
GUNFIGHTER

Chapter 1

At six, Johnny Yoder opened the door of the sheriff's office and stepped out onto the boardwalk. The town of Cottonwood Springs was already stirring under a bright Kansas sun. Shade from giant cottonwoods lining most of its streets threw a dappled pattern of lawns and walks. The sky was a flawless blue. Beyond the town, brown prairie grass rippled in the breeze, looking like a restless sea whenever a gust or whirlwind touched its yielding surface.

The land was almost flat around Cottonwood Springs. Except for the butte half a dozen miles west of town. And except for the bed of Cottonwood Creek which led away to disappear north of the rocky butte.

Yoder stretched, removed his hat and ran a hand through his short-clipped, yellow hair. Scowling he sat down on one of the benches in front of the sheriff's office but there was no relaxation in him. He was tense and jumpy, and there was a smoldering anger in him that would not go away.

He tilted his hat forward against the sun and fished in his pocket for his Bull Durham sack. He rolled a wheatstraw cigarette with strong brown fingers, the backs of which were covered with yellow hair. He licked it and stuck it into his mouth.

With a sudden, angry gesture, he struck a match and touched it to the end of the cigarette. Today was the day. Today, Slade Teplin was coming home.

Slade was already a legend although he was not yet thirty. His name was as well known as that of Wild Bill Hickok, Bat Masterson, Wes Hardin or William Bonney. He had already killed sixteen men. And today he was coming home.

Johnny got up restlessly. He finished his cigarette and tossed it into the street. From a vacant lot next to the jail a shaggy dog approached him, wagging his tail. But this morning Johnny did not reach down to scratch his head as he usually did. He stared up the main street of the town.

A few people were walking along the street. He saw Slade's father, Barney, unlock the door of the bank and go inside just as he had every weekday morning since Johnny first came to Cottonwood Springs three years before. He saw Ern Powers stumble out of the passageway between the Ace-High Saloon and the Emporia. Ern stood blinking against the brilliance of the morning sun before he turned and shuffled unsteadily toward the jail.

Johnny swung his head and glanced down the street. The yellow-framed railroad depot drowsed in the sun, deserted at this hour of the day. Closer, there was Regan's Livery Barn and across from it another, a deserted livery barn that bore across its front the painted legend, "Livery. Est. 1859". Its roofline sagged in the middle, making it look like a swaybacked horse.

Ern Powers reached him. His beard was two days old and his eyes were bloodshot. He looked at Johnny, his glance managing to be both guilty and speculating, then ducked inside. Johnny heard him banging cell doors in the rear as he got the broom and began to sweep.

Johnny turned and walked up the street in the direction of the towering Antlers Hotel. Ern Powers wasn't the only one watching him to see how he was taking the news of Slade Teplin's return. His scowl deepened briefly. What the hell did they expect?

He passed the bank, resisting the impulse to look inside. Barney Teplin probably wasn't looking forward to his son's return any more than Johnny was. Barney had a job as teller in the bank. And John McCracken, the bank president, was almost fanatical on the subject of public confidence.

He went on, somehow not comforted by the knowledge that his own would not be the only life thrown into turmoil by Slade Teplin's return.

He climbed the two steps to the hotel veranda. This early there were none of the loafers on the porch that usually were here. He went into the vast, cool lobby and crossed the white tile floor to the dining room.

The place was deserted except for Sarah Regan, dressed in a fresh, starched, yellow cotton dress. She wore a checked apron, also yellow, and her dark hair shone warmly in the sun coming through the big front window. She smiled and came toward him.

Johnny managed a thin answering smile. "Coffee ready yet?"

She nodded, her eyes resting steadily on his face. Her smile slowly faded and an anger, almost mirroring his own, suddenly appeared in her eyes. She turned and hurried away, returning a few moments later with a cup and saucer which she put in front of him. She hesitated a moment, then sat down determinedly across from him. She studied his face, her anger fading and being replaced by a kind of exasperated sympathy. She asked, "Why's he coming back after all these years? Why?"

"A lot of people are wondering that."

"Is he going to stay? Or is it just a visit?"

He shrugged, not looking at her now but staring steadily at his cup.

"You think it's her, don't you? You think he's coming back for her."

Johnny was silent for a long, long time. His hands, lying on the table top, gripped each other until the knuckles turned white. At last he said in a tight, thin voice, "She's still his wife."

Sarah nodded, her face suddenly drained of color. "That's what you've got to admit to yourself, Johnny Yoder. That she is his wife. She's not yours and she never will be yours."

He glanced up, his eyes steady and cold. "I came in here for coffee, not advice."

"I don't care what you came in here for. It's the truth."

Johnny gulped the rest of his coffee and stood up. Sarah stood up too. There was a faint shine of tears in her eyes as she said, "I'm sorry, Johnny. I didn't mean . . ."

He nodded. "Sure." He dropped a coin onto the table and headed toward the door. He did not look back and so did not see the tears spilling across Sarah's cheeks.

On the hotel veranda he stopped and tried to roll another cigarette. His fingers shook so badly that he spilled tobacco on the steps in a thin brown stream. He gave up and angrily flung the unfinished cigarette away.

Johnny had never seen Slade Teplin. Neither had he ever hated a man before. But he suddenly admitted to himself that he hated Slade. He hated him enough to want him dead. If Slade was dead, then Molly would be free.

He fished his watch from his pocket and looked at it. It was six-thirty now. Slade's train would not arrive until a little after nine.

He stepped off the hotel veranda and strode down the street toward Regan's Livery. Reaching it, he went inside.

Phil Regan was feeding the horses in the stalls. He stopped what he was doing and stood studying Johnny's face. Johnny said, "Get my horse for me, Phil."

"Sure, Johnny." Phil shuffled down the long alleyway toward the open rear doors and the sun-washed corral out back.

Johnny watched him go, wondering how a man like Phil Regan could bring forth a daughter like Sarah. Regan returned, shuffling as he always did, leading Johnny's horse.

Johnny flung the blanket and saddle on while Regan watched. He cinched the saddle down, feeling Regan's steady glance. As he put a foot into the stirrup, Regan said, "They say he's fast, Johnny, faster'n any man alive."

Johnny grunted noncommittally as he hit the saddle.

Regan asked, "Reckon anybody'll try an' take him while he's here?" There was an eager light in his eyes. He licked his lips as though imagining such a fight.

Johnny said sourly, "You'd like it if somebody did, wouldn't you? Even if it cost that man his life."

Regan grinned crookedly. "Why don't you try him, Johnny? You'd come closer'n anybody in town. An' you got reason to want him dead."

Johnny touched spurs to his horse's sides. The

startled animal leaped toward the door and thundered through. Johnny reined him aside and pounded down the street and across the railroad tracks.

His eyes glazed. His mouth was a thin, hard line. He supposed everyone in town was silently thinking what Regan had just said to him. They all knew he had been seeing Molly for almost a year. They knew he wanted to marry her. They also knew she was still Slade Teplin's wife.

There were even those who said Slade was coming home because of Johnny Yoder's attentions to his wife. They said Slade was coming home to kill again.

Johnny raked his horse savagely with the spurs. He thundered along the road that bordered Cottonwood Creek as it wound aimlessly toward the butte.

For a moment he almost hoped Slade was coming home to kill him, even though he knew it wasn't true. Slade had left his wife five years before. He hadn't returned to see her once. He probably didn't even care.

A mile from town there was a small frame house just at the edge of the cottonwoods bordering the creek. There was a tiny patch of lawn in front, a garden in back. Both lawn and garden were watered patiently with pails Molly carried from the creek. Johnny dismounted and tied his horse to the limb of a scrubby cottonwood. He walked toward the door.

Molly taught school in town. But she never left here until seven and it was not yet that late. Johnny knocked and waited impatiently.

The door opened. And suddenly all the anger, all the irritation was gone from Johnny, driven away as dew is driven away by the morning sun.

She stood aside to let him enter, but her welcoming smile was weak and forced. She seemed excessively pale to him. Her eyes revealed the fact that if she had slept at all last night it had been a short and uneasy sleep.

He crossed the kitchen to the table and sat down. Molly Teplin asked, "Are you hungry, Johnny? I can fix something for you in a minute."

He shook his head. "Just coffee, thanks."

He watched her as she got cup and saucer from the cupboard, then crossed to the stove to fill the cup. Her back was slim and straight. Her hair, worn in a demure bun at the nape of her neck, was a burnished copper color that shone almost like metal in the early morning sunlight streaming through the open door.

Her skin was white and there was a bridge of tiny freckles across her nose. Her eyes were sometimes green and sometimes blue, depending upon the light. There was a sudden ache in his chest and he wondered how Slade, or any man, could leave her.

She gave him his coffee and sat down across from him. She picked up her fork and tried to eat but after the first mouthful she gave up. "I can't eat, Johnny. I can't sleep. I can't even think. Why is he coming back now? Why, after almost five years?"

He shook his head miserably. "The important thing is not that he's coming back, but what you're going to do about it. Are you going to let him come back to you?"

He wouldn't look at her as he asked the question, but stared instead at his coffee cup.

She murmured, "I don't know. Oh, Johnny, I don't know!"

He looked up and met her glance steadily with his own. He said, "Molly, I love you. I want to marry you. He deserted you five years ago. A week ago you were going to get a divorce from him and marry me. But since you heard he was coming back . . ."

He watched her, noting the way her glance dropped away from his. He felt a flash of sudden anger, thinking for a fleeting instant that her love for him was too thin and weak a thing to remain steadfast now.

Then, as suddenly as his anger had come, it was gone again. He knew why Molly was considering letting Slade Teplin come back to her. She thought Slade knew Johnny was courting her. She believed Slade had heard she intended divorcing him. She thought Slade was coming back to kill Johnny, and she was willing to become Slade's wife again to save his life.

He got up and went around the table to her. He stood looking down, watching the flush that crept into her neck and face. He said, "Molly, stand up."

She stood up reluctantly, but she would not look up at his face.

Very gently, he put out his hands. He took her shoulders and drew her close. He could feel her body trembling. He could feel, suddenly, his own wild hunger blazing up . . .

His arms tightened savagely, crushing her against his chest. He said in a choking voice, "No! You're not to go back to him! If you do . . . I'll kill him, Molly. I swear to God I will!"

She looked up, tears welling from her eyes and spilling across her cheeks. Her voice was a tortured cry, "Johnny, what am I going to do! What am I going to do?"

"Tell him he can't come back to you. Tell him you're going to marry me."

"He'll— He might— Johnny, you wouldn't have a chance against Slade."

"Let me worry about that. You just let me worry about that."

She drew away. "I've got to go to school. The children . . ."

"Looks like you'd have called off school for today." He tried to make his voice as normal as he could.

"Because Slade is coming home? I can't think of a worse reason for a holiday. They're making a hero out of him as it is."

She began to gather up the dishes. Johnny said, "I'll hitch up your buggy horse."

He went out, crossed the yard to the small stable at the rear of the house and went inside. He harnessed her old, swaybacked buggy horse, led him out and backed him between the buggy shafts. By the time he was finished, Molly was ready, holding several books and a sack lunch in her hands.

Johnny took them from her and put them into the buggy. He helped her up. He got his own horse and led him to the buggy, intending to tie him behind, but Molly stopped him. "No, Johnny. Not this morning. Let me drive in alone today. Enough tongues are wagging as it is."

He stared up at her, hurt and obscurely angry at himself because he was. She made a faint smile that failed to hide the lingering pain in her eyes. She slapped the horse's back with the reins and the horse trotted away toward town.

Johnny stood looking after her for a long, long time. Then he mounted and slowly followed her, a quarter mile behind.

Chapter 2

It was almost seven when Johnny Yoder reached town. He rode up the street to the jail, swung down and tied his horse to the rail out front. Molly's buggy was out of sight, having turned off Main Street at the upper end of town.

He went inside. Ern Powers had finished with the cells and there was an odor of disinfectant in the air. Ern was sweeping the office as Johnny came in. He glanced up.

Johnny grinned humorlessly at him. "Big night last night?"

Ern nodded guiltily. He leaned on the broom, stared at the floor a moment, then glanced up at Johnny again. "I don't know why I do it. I never intend to when I start. I just don't know when to quit."

Johnny sat down at the sheriff's roll-top desk. He stretched his long legs out in front of him.

He heard steps on the boardwalk outside and glanced up. Arch Schilling came in, leaving the door standing open behind him. He looked at Johnny, then at Ern, then crossed the room and hung his hat on the coat tree.

He glanced back at Johnny and said what he'd said each morning for the past three years. "Had breakfast yet?"

"I'll go get some now."

Johnny got to his feet, waited a moment expectantly to see if the sheriff would bring up the subject of Slade Teplin's return. When Arch said nothing, Johnny glanced at him.

He surprised Arch studying him speculatively and grinned. Arch grinned back but did not speak. For an instant there was a closeness between them, an understanding that did not need words.

Arch was a big, rawboned man, sixty on his last birthday. His face was like the map of Kansas, brown and weathered and deeply furrowed by the erosion of the years. His eyes were the blue of a Kansas sky, surrounded by tiny crowfoot wrinkles that deepened when he smiled. His mouth was a slash, hard and tough and uncompromising above a chin equally uncompromising and tough. He had been a cattleman until he was elected sheriff five years ago. He didn't know all there was to know about law enforcement, maybe, but he knew Kansas like he knew the back of his hand. He could trail like an Indian and he wasn't afraid of anything.

Arch said now, gruffly, "Go on and eat. You want to meet the train, don't you?"

Johnny grinned again and went out into the brilliant sun. He hesitated a moment between the hotel dining room and Ho's Restaurant, not wanting to listen to another lecture from Sarah, but in the end he chose the hotel. He'd just as well eat where he usually did. If he didn't, people would say he was trying to hide.

He walked up the street toward the hotel. There were more people on the walks now. Some of them nodded or spoke to Johnny and he returned their greetings as normally as he could. He could feel them all watching him, and occasionally he would catch that speculating look in someone's eyes.

He wondered if there would be any pressure on

Arch to put Slade on as a deputy. Cottonwood Springs was a flyspeck on the Kansas map. Half the people in Kansas didn't even know that it existed. It hadn't been too prosperous since the trail drives stopped coming up from Texas several years before. It was a town that was slowly dying on the vine.

Slade Teplin could change all that. If he was a sheriff's deputy he would give Cottonwood Springs a kind of fame. People would come here just to see him.

Some of the merchants wouldn't want prosperity if its price was bullets in the streets. But there were probably others who wouldn't care.

He reached the hotel. There were half a dozen loafers on the veranda now. One called, "Going to meet the train, Johnny?"

He glanced at the man and nodded. He forced himself to grin. "Everybody else will be meeting it so I guess I'd just as well." His words brought an uneasy laugh from the group on the sunny porch.

He went into the hotel and across the lobby to the dining room. He sat down at his accustomed table next to one of the windows from which he could look into the street.

Mostly, the sheriff's job in Cottonwood County was a tame one nowadays. Arch Schilling and Johnny Yoder served papers. They jailed a few drunks on Saturday night. They mediated a midnight quarrel between a husband and wife. They caught a kid who had broken a store window with a rock.

These were the everyday things. Occasionally they were called upon to handle something more serious. But Johnny could number the serious crimes that had occurred here in the past three years on the fingers of one hand.

The peaceful quality of Cottonwood Springs would change with Slade Teplin's arrival home. He would draw men from everywhere. Just his presence here would accomplish that. They'd come to look at him and talk to him. Or they'd come to try him out—to see if he was really as good as he was supposed to be. Whoever managed to kill Slade Teplin would thereby gain instant fame for himself. And there were plenty of men who wanted that kind of fame.

Sarah Regan came and stood beside his table. There was no longer anger in her face. It was pale and drawn. She said, "I'm sorry, Johnny. I had no right to say the things I said to you a while ago."

He didn't feel like smiling but he did. He reached out, took her hand and squeezed it lightly. "Forget it, Sarah. I'm sorry too."

Her face flushed with pleasure and he released her hand. He said, "I'll have a steak. And some eggs."

Sarah turned hurriedly and walked away toward the kitchen. Johnny let his glance wander over those in the dining room. Most of the people looked away, avoiding his glance. Others nodded or spoke to him almost with embarrassment.

They knew about Molly. Half of them or more probably figured there would be a gunfight down at the railroad station the minute Slade Teplin stepped off the train.

Johnny turned his head and stared out the window. What if they were right? What if Slade had heard about him and Molly and was coming back to kill?

He was surprised when Sarah set his breakfast in

front of him. He hadn't realized that so much time
had passed. He pulled out his watch and glanced
at it. It was almost eight o'clock.

Sarah hurried away, flustered and embarrassed
now. Johnny watched her go, wondering why he'd
had to fall in love with a married woman instead
of with Sarah. He scowled at his food, eating dog-
gedly, forcing himself even though he didn't feel
like eating anything. All he had to do was leave his
food untouched and within half an hour everybody
in town would be saying he was scared half out of
his wits.

He grinned wryly to himself. If he had any sense,
maybe he would be scared. He didn't know Slade
Teplin, except by reputation. He had no idea how
deep Slade Teplin's pride was. The man might even
care for his wife in spite of the five years he had
been away from her.

He finished his breakfast and laid a quarter beside his plate. He rolled a cigarette, surprised that
his fingers were steady now. He lighted it and rose.

He walked out, crammed on his hat and stepped
onto the veranda. He glanced up and down the
street, then headed for the jail.

Another hour, he thought. Another hour to wait.

Damn Teplin anyway! He had the whole town in
a state of nerves. He had accomplished that simply
by telegraphing his father that he was coming
home.

Arch Schilling was sitting on one of the benches
in front of the jail when he reached the place. He
was staring downstreet at the railroad depot, at the
people already beginning to gather there. Johnny
sat down beside him. "What's he like?" he asked.

"Slade? I don't know what he's like now. But
I remember him as a boy." Arch's forehead creased

into a light frown. He was silent for several moments, then he said, "His mother died when he was twelve—same age as Tommy, my grandson. Barney went to pieces when she died. He didn't come out of the house for damn near two weeks. I guess he hardly ate. Slade stayed with the neighbors and with the Newcombs over at the parsonage. Barney began to drink."

He was silent long enough to pack his pipe and light it. "Barney got pretty bad. He lost the house or sold it or something. I don't know. He used to sleep in that old livery barn across from Regan's place. Or he'd sleep wherever it was that he passed out."

"What about Slade? What did he do?"

"He worked for his keep, one place or another. He was a sour-faced, sullen kid. He did his work but it was like he hated the town and everyone in it. I used to come in to town once a week in those days for supplies. He was working at Zachary's Mercantile at the time. He'd help me load up and I tried a time or two to be nice to him. He'd just look at me and then turn and walk away. Like he hated me too and, hell, he didn't hardly know me."

Johnny rolled a cigarette and lighted it. There was a sizable crowd, now, down at the railroad station. Most of them were just standing around, but a few of the men had gathered into a group and were talking heatedly. Johnny said, "If he hated the town I wonder why he's coming back."

"He might be coming back for you, Johnny. Have you thought of that?"

"Yeah. I've thought of it, but I don't believe it. He hasn't seen her for five years. Why the hell should he care?"

"Pride. He doesn't want her, but he's damned if

anyone else is going to have her either. Not in front of everybody in this town anyway."

Johnny didn't speak. He shrugged, and at last he said, "Well, if he feels that way, I guess I'll be number seventeen on his list. Unless I just happen to be lucky today."

"Leave your gun here when you go down to the station."

"What good would that do? I can't leave it off forever."

Arch pulled thoughtfully on his pipe. After a while Johnny asked, "How'd he get started—with his gun I mean?"

"I think he was about eighteen or nineteen. He'd been packing a gun for a couple of years, practicing with it all the time. I think that gun was his way of showing the town that he was someone. Anyway, some drifter began funnin' him about it. First thing you know, Slade yanked it out. He gave that drifter the damndest cussin' I ever heard." Arch shrugged lightly. "It ended like you'd expect. The drifter yanked his own gun out and ended up dead in the street right in front of the Emporia."

"Was that when Slade went away?"

"No. There was a trial. The jury acquitted him in spite of the fact that he drew first. I guess they figured the drifter started it. And I guess they felt sorry for Slade. Barney never took a drink afterward, though. He straightened up and rented a house for the two of them, but I guess it was just too late. Slade left town a few months later and didn't come back until about six years ago. He married Molly and they stayed here for a while. Nobody would give Slade a job, and finally he took her away. She came back alone and she's been here ever since."

Johnny looked at his watch. It was almost nine o'clock. He stood up and surprised himself by nervously straightening his gun belt. He grinned self-consciously at Arch.

Arch said, "Leave it here. You don't know . . ."

Johnny shook his head stubbornly. "If I leave my gun here I'll be letting him know—well hell, more than just that I'm afraid of him. I'll be telling him that I'm ashamed—of what's between Molly and me. I'll be telling the whole town the same thing. And I'm not ashamed. Not one damn bit."

"All right, Johnny. Have it your own way." Arch's voice plainly said that he disapproved, but there was something else in it as well, something that was not disapproval at all.

Distantly, Johnny heard the mournful whistle of the train. He said, "Here it comes."

Arch Schilling got ponderously to his feet. "Let's go."

Side by side they paced down the walk toward the railroad station. Johnny grinned to himself. Everyone waiting on the station platform was turned their way, watching them.

Johnny heard steps on the boardwalk behind him and turned his head. Barney Teplin was walking along about a quarter block behind. His face was white and strained and he looked fifteen years older than he had looked yesterday.

Johnny suddenly felt sorry for him. He knew how he'd feel if he lost Molly—as if nothing in the world mattered anymore. He could understand how Barney had felt when he lost his wife.

But Barney had lost a lot more than his wife. He had lost his son as well. And now the ghost of what had once been his son was coming back—to taunt him before the whole town of Cottonwood Springs.

Johnny didn't believe that Slade was after him. But he was sure of one thing. Before Slade left town he would kill again.

Chapter 3

Johnny Yoder could see the train as soon as he stepped onto the station platform. It was about half a mile away, pouring smoke from its stack, coming on fast.

He felt his irritability rise because no one was watching the train. Everybody on the station platform was watching him.

He turned his head and glanced uptown, thinking of Molly and knowing how she would be feeling as she listened to the train's long, mournful whistle. She probably had her hands full keeping order in the school. The kids must be even more excited over Slade's coming than their parents were.

The engine slowed for the station, then came puffing past the platform to stop just beyond it. There were two coaches and a caboose.

Johnny resisted the impulse to loosen his gun in its holster. His palms felt clammy and he wiped them surreptitiously on the sides of his pants legs. He felt his anger rise, but now it was anger at himself. He wasn't afraid of Slade. In spite of Slade's reputation, he wasn't afraid to face the man. Then why this nervousness?

It had nothing to do with physical fear, he realized. But it was fear just the same. Fear that Slade Teplin would take Molly away from him. Fear that

Slade would force her to come back to him by threatening Johnny's life.

A man got off the first coach, a fat man carrying a valise. A woman followed, then turned and helped her two children down the steps. A man followed her children, a gray-haired man almost as old as Arch, dressed in range clothes so rumpled it looked as though he had slept in them for a week.

Johnny switched his glance to the second coach. A young woman got off, a pretty woman whose clothes told Johnny instantly that she was a saloon girl. An elderly Mexican woman followed her. And behind the older Mexican woman came a man who had to be Slade.

He was not a big man. He was not as tall as Johnny, nor was he as broad. He was dressed in a black suit, the coat of which was unbuttoned to allow free access to the holstered gun which sagged low against his right side. He wore a narrow-brimmed black hat.

Two things caught and held Johnny's attention instantly. One was the way Slade Teplin moved, with an almost feline grace. His feet came down softly, almost stealthily as he walked, and Johnny got the feeling that no matter what he did, or how he moved, he would never be off balance for a single instant.

The second thing that held Johnny's attention was his face. His eyes seemed almost black. And they came as close to being expressionless as any pair of eyes Johnny had ever seen.

Studying the man's face, he realized that not only the eyes created the impression of expressionlessness. The whole face contributed.

Teplin paused half a dozen steps from the coach. He carried a small valise in his left hand. His glance swept over the crowd, which was frozen and silent, and came to rest on Johnny. He held Johnny's eyes for a moment, then looked briefly at the star on Johnny's shirt. His glance fell away and touched Arch Schilling before it went on to Barney Teplin, standing just beyond Johnny and the sheriff.

Ignoring the crowd, he walked toward Barney. Johnny felt his muscles tense as Slade approached. He saw, out of the corner of his eye, the way the crowd faded away behind Slade. He could hear them moving away from behind him, and his mouth twisted almost imperceptibly. They were getting out of the line of fire. They still thought Slade might shoot it out with Johnny, right here and now.

Johnny knew Slade was aware of him as the man went past. He could feel it, sense it. He also knew Slade would do nothing now.

Slade stopped immediately in front of his father. Johnny turned to watch. He could not see Slade's face, but he could see Barney's. It was almost gray and it shone with perspiration. It mirrored so many conflicting emotions that it would have been hard for Johnny to say which of them was strongest, uppermost.

There was anger in Barney Teplin's face. There was a kind of forlorn joy at seeing his son again. There was shame, because of what his son was, what he had become, and because he knew a large part of blame for it lay with him. And there was puzzlement, because he could not guess why his son had now come back.

Slade looked beyond his father's face at the town. His voice was flat, almost as expressionless as his face. "It looks the same. It hasn't changed a bit."

"No." Barney seemed to have no words. The two stood facing each other in awkward silence for a long, long time. At last Barney said, "Come on. I've got the morning off."

He turned and Slade paced beside him, across the street and up Main on the shady side of the street. The crowd made a low murmur of disappointment that increased in volume as men began talking to each other in low, almost resentful tones. Johnny turned his head and grinned at Arch. "He disappointed 'em. They thought there was going to be some excitement."

Arch muttered, "The hell with 'em." He walked to the end of the station platform and stepped off into the dusty street. Johnny kept pace with him.

Halfway to the jail Arch asked, "What do you think of him?"

Johnny didn't reply. He was still trying to sort his impressions within his own thoughts. Slade Teplin knew about Molly and him. That impression had been very plain and clear. Yet he had sensed no particular anger in the man over it.

It followed, therefore, that the town had been wrong. Slade's pride had not brought him to Cottonwood Springs to kill.

Then what had brought him back? Assuming this was not simply a brief visit, what was here strong enough to draw Slade Teplin back?

Only one answer to that. Molly. She had to be the reason for Slade's return.

An even more sinister bit of reasoning followed. Slade would use Johnny to get her back. Knowing she might well refuse after five years, he would threaten to kill Johnny unless she did come back to him.

Johnny cursed softly under his breath. Arch said, "Yeah. I saw the way he looked at you. He knows about you and Molly, but he didn't come back to get rid of you or he'd have done it on the station platform a few minutes ago. He came back for Molly and he'll use you to get her to come back to him."

"Or else he just plain doesn't give a damn."

Arch nodded.

Johnny asked, "What's he going to do for a living, Arch? Maybe he's got a little money, but it won't last forever. He'll have to do something and he sure as hell won't be getting a job through Barney at the bank."

"No. John McCracken wouldn't have him around. There's only one thing he's fitted for, Johnny, and you know what it is as well as me."

"Law enforcement, huh?"

"Yep. And since I'm elected, that just leaves your job. You're in his way in more ways than one."

Johnny was silent until they reached the jail. Then he turned his head and looked at Arch. "You're the sheriff. You do the hiring and firing of your deputies. You going to give my job to him?"

Arch grinned. "No sir. You don't need to worry about that."

Arch went into the office, but Johnny stayed out on the walk in front. Slade Teplin and his father had disappeared, having turned the corner and headed for Barney's house. The crowd that had been at the railroad station was dispersing, streaming up the street past the jail, headed for the two saloons. The girl who had been on the train was carrying her valise in the same direction.

She stopped when she reached Johnny. She looked at the star on his shirt and smiled in a way that was both placating and defiant. She asked, "How many saloons in town? Just those two?"

Johnny nodded. She was pretty, he saw, and perhaps a year or two younger than he. But there was a quality in her that was older than her years. She asked, "You got laws in this town against a girl working in a saloon?"

Johnny shook his head. He said, "Try the Emporia."

"Thanks, I will." She seemed relieved. She hesitated a moment more, as though trying to think of something light to say. Then she gave up, shrugged wearily, and went on up the street.

Cal Reeder stopped, not looking at Johnny but at the girl's hips as she walked. "Nice, huh?"

Johnny nodded. He studied Cal neutrally. He didn't really dislike Cal, but he couldn't say he liked him either. Cal wore a gun much the way Slade Teplin wore his, low against his side in an open holster. The grips were smooth and shiny with use. Cal fancied himself a gunman, but he'd never drawn his gun against a man and he probably never would.

He was a tall young man, about twenty-three, Johnny guessed. His hair was black. His jaws showed a faint shadow of black stubble. His eyes were brown, his face narrow. His father had a ranch not far from Arch Schilling's ranch, but Cal stayed in town most of the time. He only went home when he went broke.

Cal watched the girl, his eyes bright, until she disappeared into the Emporia. Then he turned his head and looked at Johnny's face. "What did *you* think of him?"

"Slade? I don't know. I guess I haven't decided what I think of him."

"You think he's as fast as they say?"

"You don't kill sixteen men by being slow."

"Yeah, but maybe none of them was fast—really fast I mean."

Johnny looked at him wearily. He knew what Cal was leading up to. He also knew Cal wouldn't be the only young buck in Cottonwood County with the same idea. He said, "Forget it. He could put a hole in you before you got the hammer back."

"Maybe. Maybe not. I'm pretty good." Cal pivoted suddenly to face the railroad station. He crouched slightly as he turned and his hand shot to the grip of his gun. He brought it out, leveled it, but he did not thumb the hammer back. He holstered the gun and looked at Johnny's face.

Johnny shook his head again. "Forget it, Cal. Even if you beat him, which you wouldn't, what would it get you in the end? You know how a man like Slade lives? He goes from town to town and in every one he's invited to move on. Every place he goes, there's someone who wants to try him out. Most of the sixteen he's killed were men like that. Young bucks like you who figure he made his reputation by killing cripples and old men."

"I didn't say that."

Johnny grinned at him. "You as much as said it. You said maybe none of the sixteen was really fast."

"You talk like a damned old man yourself." There was resentment in Cal's eyes. "Maybe you'll end up number seventeen. As soon as Slade finds out you been foolin' around with his wife."

Johnny's voice was suddenly like a whip. "Doing what?"

A dull flush crept into Cal's narrow face. "You know what I mean. Seeing her. Goin' with her. What are you so damned ringy about?"

Johnny didn't reply. He was still angry, but he

was also aware Cal had meant no slur. He said,
"All right. All right."

Cal walked on up the street, heading toward the
Emporia. Johnny saw him go inside.

He suddenly wanted a drink himself, but he
didn't want to go into either of the saloons. He'd
had enough for now of the townsmen's speculating
looks. Besides, he knew they would be placing bets
in both saloons. Even money Slade would call on
Johnny before a week was out. Two to one, probably, that he'd kill Johnny when he did.

Filled with sour anger, he went into the office.
How long was he supposed to wait for Slade to
make up his mind what he was going to do? How
long?

Arch was thumbing through wanted posters. He
had an inch thick pile of them on his desk. He
looked up. "He ain't in here."

"You didn't think he would be, did you?"

"Nope. Just thought I'd look."

Johnny began to pace nervously back and forth,
like a caged mountain lion. Arch said, "Ease off.
The first move is up to him and you know it is."

Johnny stopped pacing and glared at him. He
said fiercely, "I'm sick of him. The son-of-a-bitch
hasn't been here an hour and I'm sick of him. Why
the hell can't we just tell him to move on—to get
out of town? Other towns do and they get away
with it."

"This one's different. Because this is his home.
Ease off, Johnny. That didn't sound like you at
all."

Johnny forced a sour grin. "Maybe not. But I
feel so damned helpless! Molly's even considering
it—going back with him. She says its because she's
his wife, but it isn't that at all. She's afraid I'll

fight with him. And she's afraid that if I do, I'll be killed." He paced back and forth a while longer, then whirled and faced the sheriff angrily. "Maybe I'll just hunt him up and order him out of town. Maybe I'll do the forcing for a change."

"He'd kill you, Johnny. You'd just be committing suicide. And he'd still be alive."

"Maybe not. Maybe if I worked it right I could take him along with me."

Arch got out of the swivel chair. He put a hand on Johnny's shoulder. "Go easy, son. Go easy. You don't even know he's going to stay."

Johnny shook off his hand and went to the window. He stared out angrily. The sun still shone brightly in the street. But to Johnny it seemed as though a cloud had drifted across the face of the sun. The town was in shadow since Slade Teplin had come home. And the shadow wouldn't be gone until Slade was gone—or until he was dead.

Chapter 4

It was a relief to Barney Teplin when he and Slade turned off Main Street and he could no longer feel the curious stares of those at the railroad station.

He felt ill-at-ease with Slade, and a couple of times turned his head to look at his son's impassive face. It was cold and impersonal, without visible feeling of any kind.

Barney wondered briefly if Slade knew about Johnny Yoder and Molly. He supposed he did. It was probably the reason for Slade's return. Yet Slade had showed no animosity toward Johnny at the station. He had glanced at him, true, but there had been no expression on his face.

Not that that meant anything, he thought. Slade's face just didn't show expression. It didn't now and it hadn't then.

He asked, "How long are you going to stay?"

Slade didn't reply. Barney looked at him and Slade, feeling his father's regard, shrugged.

Barney began to feel anger stirring in his mind. He asked suddenly, "Why *did* you come back? The way you hate this town, I'd think you'd *want* to stay away."

Slade looked at him mildly. "You forget. This is my home. You're here and so is my wife."

"Wife! You haven't seen her or written her for almost five years. You've only written me once, a couple of weeks ago."

He kept his glance steadily on his son's face, trying to fathom from it what was in Slade's mind, knowing Slade wouldn't tell him in words. He surprised in Slade's eyes, suddenly, a burning flash of hatred so strong it seemed to shrivel him. He said, "You hate me. You hate this town. I think you even hate your wife."

The revealing gleam was gone almost instantly. Slade looked at him indulgently. "You're imagining things. Your conscience bothers you and you imagine things."

Barney felt baffled, ineffectual. A couple of twelve-year-olds, their eyes wide with awe, came from behind a lilac bush and began to follow them. One of them was Tommy Schilling, the sheriff's grandson. Tommy said shrilly, "It's him all right. He wouldn't be with Mr. Teplin if he wasn't Slade."

The boys stayed a discreet hundred feet behind. Barney smiled wryly to himself, thinking that if

Slade turned his head they would probably run like scared rabbits. They must have sneaked away from school during recess.

Slade asked suddenly, "What's she doing these days?"

"Teaching school. Even Slade Teplin's wife has to eat, you know. And God knows you never sent her anything."

Slade stopped suddenly. Barney, a step beyond, stopped too and turned to face his son. Again that burning hatred was in Slade's eyes. And again it seemed to shrivel Barney's soul.

Slade said, "Don't talk to me about obligations, old man. You had one to me after my mother died. But you wanted to hide in a bottle and you didn't give a good goddamn about me. I lived like a stray dog."

Barney opened his mouth to justify himself, then closed it as suddenly as he'd opened it. Words would not undo the damage that had been done. Besides, Barney wasn't so sure there *was* justification for what he'd done.

Yet when he thought back, whenever he thought of Mary . . . the pain still came, so sharp and bitter it was almost unbearable. That pain had driven him to drink. That and the feeling that there was nothing left in the world for him with Mary gone.

Only liquor had been able to dull his pain. Without liquor he would probably have shot himself.

Yet he knew Slade was also right. A boy shouldn't have to grow up alone. He shouldn't have to shift for himself and live like a stray dog in an unfriendly world. Barney said softly, "I'm sorry, Slade. If I could undo the things I did to you . . ."

"I've done all right in spite of it. I'm the town's most famous citizen."

A crawling uneasiness touched Barney's heart. His chest felt tight. For an instant he saw unrelieved evil in Slade.

He shook that feeling off by sheer force of will, studying his son's face, searching desperately for something else.

He found it to his own inexpressible relief. It was a kind of hurt, little boy quality far back in the depths of Slade's dark eyes. It was the look you see in the eyes of a child just before they flood with tears. Then, as quickly as it had come, it was gone. And Slade was grinning a twisted, sardonic grin. "Come on. Let's get on home. Before those damned kids ask if they can hold my gun."

Barney resumed his steady pacing at his son's side. They reached the small, one-story house Barney occupied, and Barney held the gate for Slade.

The fence was neat, a picket fence painted white. The lawn was beginning to get a little dry, but it was neatly cut. The house had recently been painted. Barney had done the work himself, evenings and Saturday afternoons.

It was the house Barney had rented so many years before, after Slade's first killing jolted him out of his grief. He owned it now, having bought it, over a period of time, out of his earnings at the bank.

Slade asked, as they climbed the two steps to the porch, "You live here alone?"

Barney nodded. He realized suddenly that he had never considered anything else. True, there had been times when he had needed a woman and at times the hunger for one had been almost unbearable. Yet he had always felt so guilty and disloyal because of it that he had never sought one out. And marriage was out of the question for him. He did not even want a housekeeper. Her presence in his house would have seemed like a blasphemy.

Orville Newcomb, the town preacher, had told him many times he ought to get married again. He had told him prolonged grief twisted and warped a man. He had emphasized the fact that Mary was dead and gone and that Barney was still alive, with a life of his own to live. He had tried to convince Barney that Mary would have wanted him to remarry and be content once more.

But Mary still lived in Barney's heart. She would never die, he knew, as long as he kept her there.

He opened the front door and Slade went inside. He looked around the room, his face like carved stone. There were things in this room he remembered from his boyhood, Barney realized. There were some of Mary's things. Slade said suddenly, "I want a drink."

Barney went into the kitchen and got a dusty bottle of whisky from a cupboard. He took it, with a glass, to his son.

Slade said, "Do I have to drink alone? On my first day home?"

Barney said, "I haven't touched it for over ten years. I don't even want it any more. You go ahead."

Slade said, "Pa . . ."

Barney suddenly felt a burning behind his eyes. He hadn't been much of a father to Slade. Slade had gone a long way, but he was not yet thirty now. A lot of his life lay ahead of him. He could change.

He could spend the rest of his life making up for all that had gone before. But if his own father refused to help . . .

Barney said suddenly, "I'll get another glass. We'll drink to your coming home."

He went to the kitchen and took down another glass. He brought it into the parlor and Slade poured it about half full. Slade filled his own glass similarly.

Slade raised it. "To my coming home."

Barney raised his glass. The odor of the whisky was strong, acrid, biting in his nostrils. For some reason, the odor reminded him of waking up on a cold winter morning in the alley behind the Emporia. It reminded him of another smell, the smell of his own body and reeking clothes after a week-long drunk. It reminded him of how hard it had been to think, those days, because liquor had drugged and dulled his mind.

But Slade was watching him, waiting to drink until his father drank. He put the glass to his lips and suddenly gulped the stuff.

It burned. It gagged him and made him cough. But suddenly he realized how much he had missed that taste, how much he had missed the warm burn of whisky coursing down his throat, lying like a comforting warmth in his stomach afterward.

He held out his glass and Slade re-filled it. Slade was sipping his own drink. He was smiling at Barney and Barney realized this was the first time he had seen Slade really smile. Yet there was a quality about Slade's smile that troubled him. He studied his son's face, trying to isolate that quality in his thoughts.

Slade's face seemed blurry and far away. Barney's head felt light. After more than ten years, he thought, it didn't take much to set a man off. In the old days, half a glass of whisky had been just a starter.

He gulped about half of the whisky in his glass. Again it burned all the way down, and lay like hot coals in his stomach. Again the taste brought back memories.

Through the curtain whisky had lowered across his mind, he peered at his son's face. It was still smiling, but the smile was strained. And once more he had the vague impression he was looking at something unbelievably evil. He whispered hoarsely, "Why did you come back?"

Slade chuckled softly. Barney blinked, trying to see his son's face more clearly through the thickening haze. He wanted to lie down now and sleep. He lifted the glass to his mouth and finished it.

Anger came to him suddenly, and it was white-hot when it came. He shouted thickly, "Why? Damn you, why did you come back?"

"You'll know soon enough. Here. You'd just as well finish this." Slade extended the bottle.

Barney swung blindly. His hand struck the bottle and knocked it halfway across the room. It didn't break, but he could hear its contents gurgling as they ran out on the rug.

And he knew, suddenly, why Slade had come back. Not for peace. Not for Molly. Not for an end to the challenges that a gunfighter's fame draws to him like iron filings are drawn to a magnet. Not for any of these things. Not for anything good.

Hatred had spawned the speed in Slade Teplin's hand. Hatred had made his gun belch death sixteen different times. And hatred had brought him here. Hatred for Barney, his father. Hatred for the town. Hatred for all mankind.

Death would walk the streets of Cottonwood Springs before Slade Teplin was gone again. Unless he was killed, now, like a rabid dog.

Barney got up unsteadily. He mumbled something about being back. He left the room and went into the bedroom where he slept. Carefully, he got his shotgun from the closet, the one he used sometimes for hunting prairie chickens or quail. He loaded it with fingers that trembled almost uncontrollably. He snapped the action shut.

He turned, hearing the door behind him. He tried desperately to bring the gun to bear.

Slade was too quick for him. He took one swift step and yanked the shotgun out of Barney's hands.

His face was white and terrible. His eyes seemed to Barney as though they glowed like coals. He broke the action of the gun and ejected the two shells Barney had loaded it with.

Deliberately he turned his back on Barney. He returned to the parlor. Barney staggered to the bedroom door.

For an instant he thought Slade had gone completely mad. He held the gun by its double barrel and he swung it like a club. He smashed everything he could, vases, lamps, mirrors, furniture. The gunstock broke but he went on smashing, with just the barrel now.

His eyes blazed crazily. His face was white. Sweat streamed from his face. His breath came in short, exhausted gasps.

The room began to whirl eerily before Barney Teplin's eyes. He felt himself falling, felt the impact of the floor. Then he was unconscious and mercifully knew no more.

Chapter 5

The Cottonwood Springs school sat at the very edge of town, with the endless prairie its backyard.

It was a single-story frame building, containing two rooms and a cloakroom. Out back there were two outhouses, one labeled, *Boys,* the other, *Girls.* Beyond that was a huge cottonwood tree. Beneath the tree there was a wooden rail to which were tied the saddle horses some of the children rode to school. Molly Teplin's buggy sat nearby, its shafts resting on the ground.

On the schoolhouse roof there was a small bell cupola. And on the south side of the school there were several swings.

A low buzz of voices came from the open windows of the school. Inside, Molly Teplin left her younger class and stepped into the room that held the older children, those from the fifth grade on up.

These were the most restless ones, she thought, and their restlessness, normal this time of year, had not been helped by Slade Teplin's arrival in Cottonwood Springs.

She had missed Tommy Schilling and Tony Sanchez earlier, immediately after first recess. Now, she made a mental count of the others. All were here. But she was sure more would be missing after lunch.

Thinking of Slade, back again, stirred conflicting feelings in her. She could not help remembering the first few months of their marriage. And now, with so many years between the present and those first months, she realized something she had never realized before. She had not married Slade because she was in love with him. She had felt sorry for him and had mistaken the feeling of pity for love. She had believed him when he'd told her he had been forced into using his gun as a way of life. She had believed him when he said he had never used the gun for pay, nor killed except in self defense.

She did not believe it now. She'd had five years to think about it, to remember, to see Slade as he really was, not as her young idealism had made him seem. She knew he was a killer and she knew he would always be just that. She knew as well that some core of evil must lie within his mind, or he would not be what he was.

This morning, facing her class with hands that trembled in spite of herself, she admitted something else. She was afraid of Slade. She was afraid of what he would do to Johnny Yoder if he found out Johnny had been seeing her. She was even afraid of what Slade might do to her.

He was here, now, in Cottonwood Springs. He was here, after five long years. The morning might pass without him seeking her out. But at lunch time . . . she knew she'd see him then.

She put her hands behind her to hide their trembling. She said, "I want all of you to spend the next half hour writing a composition. The subject will be up to you. And I want no talking. Do you understand?"

Their faces were young and eager, and she had the vague impression that they were more respectful than usual today. *And why not,* she thought bitterly. *They know I am Slade Teplin's wife. They admire him—think he's some kind of hero for what he's done. Part of the luster has rubbed off on me simply because I am his wife.*

His wife. The word implied many things, all of which seemed unbearable to Molly. The intimacy of living together in the same house, sharing the same bed at night. She felt her face grow pale. She should have listened to Johnny months ago. She should have divorced Slade then. But even then, she realized, she had feared him. She had feared what he might do when he got the news.

Johnny. Her face softened as she thought of him, as she pictured him in her mind. He was all the things Slade would never be. A man who was not dependent upon reputation and skill with a gun for confidence in his own manhood. A man who was not afraid, even of Slade, even of Slade's appalling speed with his gun.

Johnny would face Slade without a qualm. She felt, suddenly, as cold as ice. It must not happen. She must not permit it to happen. Because if it did, Johnny would be killed.

Again she tortured herself with the question, "Why did he come back?"

She turned and left the room. She went outside onto the narrow porch. The sun beating against her felt good but it failed to thaw the ice that seemed to lie like a chunk within her chest. Had Slade come back for her? Was it as simple as that?

It was possible, of course. But she did not believe it. Why should he come back for her now? Why, after five long years? He had not even written her. He had sent no money for her support. He seemed to have forgotten her.

But if he had not come back for her, then why had he returned? Was it possible he had changed?

Was it possible he was weary of the kind of life he led? Was he seeking peace and a normal life?

That too was possible, she thought. Slade had been warped and twisted by his early life. He had learned to hate the town. But the years can cool even the most burning hatred. Time can ease even the most painful of wounds.

She stared toward the town, half expecting to see him walking along the street toward the school.

Impatient with herself, she turned and re-entered the building. She passed down the aisle in the room containing the older children, collecting their papers. She glanced at the titles as she did. More than half of them had titles like, "Slade Teplin, My Teacher's Husband," or "Our Town's Hero."

She wanted to tell them that Slade was no hero, that no one is who takes sixteen lives in personal duels that have no sense or reason to justify them. She wanted to remind them of the Lord's commandment, "Thou shall not kill." She wanted to tell them what Slade really was, a man filled with hatred for humanity who fed his hatred on human life.

But she knew she could not, because it would be a contradiction they would not understand. She was Mrs. Slade Teplin. She had married him.

No. She couldn't tell them about Slade. But perhaps their parents could.

She was tempted, suddenly, to dismiss school for the day. She didn't want the children to be here when Slade came. She didn't want them to see her with him.

She resisted the idea almost frantically. Letting the children out would simply be giving them permission to hang around on Main Street or wherever

Slade was for the rest of the day. If there was trouble, one or more of the children might possibly be in the line of fire and be hurt or killed.

Trouble. The only two in town who might have trouble would be Slade and Johnny. And it would be trouble over her.

Letting school out was impossible, she thought. But so was staying here, tortured by her thoughts, unconsciously listening for the sound of gunfire in the town.

What would she do if she did hear guns, she asked herself. And she knew the answer almost immediately. She'd run. She'd run as though the devil pursued her straight toward the sounds. She wouldn't stop running until she knew . . . if Johnny was hurt . . . if Johnny had been killed.

A hand was up in the back of the room but it was several moments before she saw it. When she did see it, she said, "Karl. What is it?"

"You reckon he'll kill Johnny Yoder, Mrs. Teplin? You reckon that's what he come back for?"

"Came back for," she corrected automatically. Then she said quickly, "Of course not, Karl. Whatever gave you that idea?"

"It's what my pa said was goin' to happen. As sure as God made little green apples."

"Your father's wrong this time, Karl. Nothing of the sort is going to happen. Now sit down. I'm going to write some problems on the blackboard. I want them done before the bell rings for lunch."

She turned her back and went to the board. She wrote out several arithmatic problems with the chalk.

She had to force herself to concentrate. All the time she was writing she was hearing the guns, seeing Johnny Yoder fall, seeing him limp and lifeless on the ground afterward.

When she turned away from the board, her mind was made up. No longer did she hesitate. She would go back to Slade. If he wanted her, she would go back.

She heard the smaller children chattering and went out onto the porch. Her heart seemed to stand still. What would she say to him? What could she say, after all these years?

But it was not Slade. It was Johnny Yoder, riding up on his brown gelding.

Molly felt the tension drain out of her. She felt almost weak. She made a tremulous smile and stepped down off the porch. Johnny dismounted.

His face was grave and filled with concern. He said, "You ought to dismiss school and go on home."

"I'm all right, Johnny."

"You don't look all right. Don't let him upset you this way." He peered at her closely. "You haven't seen him, have you?"

She shook her head wordlessly. How, she wondered with desperation, could she make Johnny understand what she meant to do? She wouldn't, she realized, unless she could convince him that she loved Slade and wanted to go back to him. It wouldn't be easy, because Johnny had known her for a year. But a man has pride, she thought. She would attack and destroy Johnny's pride.

She looked away from him, suddenly no longer able to meet his eyes. Destroy his pride or let him lose his life. It wasn't much of a choice, she thought bitterly.

She whispered, "You'll have to go now. The children are hard enough to manage this morning as it is. Besides, he might come and I don't want him to find you here."

"Why not? Maybe it'd be a good thing all around if we just had this thing out now, once and for all."

Molly glanced up at him. It was difficult to meet his eyes, but she held them steadily by sheer force of will. "Please, Johnny. Please. Not now. Not here. Not ever."

Johnny said fiercely, "I won't let him have you!"

"Maybe he doesn't even want me, Johnny. Maybe it's just a short visit. He might not try to see me at all."

"He'll see you. And you'd better be thinking about what you're going to say to him." Johnny's face was flushed with anger and his eyes snapped with it. But it was gone almost as quickly as it had been born. He said softly, "I'm sorry. This is as hard on you as it is on me. I just want to help."

"Then go now, Johnny. I'll stop by the sheriff's office on my way home from school."

He glanced at the windows of the school and she knew he wanted to kiss her but would not in front of all the children. He grinned. "They don't miss much, do they?"

"They don't miss anything."

He mounted his horse, sat there looking at her worriedly for a moment, then turned the horse and rode away. She watched him until he turned the corner onto Main and disappeared from sight.

Wearily she turned and went back inside the school. There was a great scramble as the younger children returned hurriedly to their seats.

Time dragged endlessly. Half a dozen times before noon, Molly went to the door and stared out. But at last the hands of the clock pointed to twelve and she rang the noon bell. The children streamed out, some carrying lard-pail lunch buckets, some to mount their horses and head for home, some to walk toward home. In five minutes the schoolyard was virtually deserted except for half-a-dozen children sitting beneath the huge cottonwood.

And then Molly saw him, standing beside a cottonwood in the yard nearest the school, about a hundred yards away.

She walked toward him, no welcome in her eyes, no welcome in her heart, but preferring to talk to him well out of the children's hearing.

He was dressed in black and wore a narrow-brimmed black hat. The holstered gun, hanging at his side, looked bigger than it ever had before. She fixed her eyes on it with a kind of fascination, thinking that this gun, in this man's hand, had killed sixteen men and would kill more.

There was no more welcome in Slade's eyes than there was in hers. There was a mocking, unpleasant smile on his mouth. He said, "Well. If it isn't my devoted wife."

She raised her eyes from his gun and met his glance. She felt her face flushing and it angered her. She wanted to be ice-cold with him, composed and self assured. Yet before his mocking smile her composure evaporated like dew in the morning sun. She said lifelessly, "Hello, Slade."

"What kind of welcome is that, after five long years?"

"It's more than you deserve."

"Why? Because you've found another man?"

"That has nothing to do with it. You've been gone five years. You deserted me. You haven't written in all that time."

"But you're still my wife."

"Yes, Slade, I'm still your wife."

He stood there staring down at her for a long, long time. Molly somehow felt unclean under his scrutiny. At last, unable to stand his silent staring any longer, she cried, "Why did you have to come back? Why? What is it you want?"

"What's comin' to me, maybe. Maybe that's what I came home to get."

"What is coming to you, Slade?"

He stood there silently, refusing to answer her. Then, without a word, he turned and stalked down the street toward town.

She watched him go, her face bloodless. She still didn't know what he meant to do. She had a feeling she wouldn't know until it was too late.

Chapter 6

After leaving Molly at the school, Johnny Yoder rode back toward the sheriff's office. He was furious and there was a murderous scowl on his face. But there was something cold within his chest, something he recognized as fear.

He turned the corner onto Main. Suddenly he found it hard to believe that Slade Teplin had been in Cottonwood Springs for only three hours. It seemed as though the man had been here for days.

This was Wednesday, but Main Street looked like a busy Saturday. Rigs were drawn up before the stores all along the street. Ranchers that Johnny seldom saw except on Saturday nodded and spoke to him as he rode down the street.

In front of the Ace High and the Emporia,

horses were racked solidly. From both saloons came the steady buzz of voices.

Johnny halted in front of the Emporia. He crowded his horse in at the already crowded rack and looped the reins around the rail. He went inside.

He didn't really want a drink. It was too early in the day for him. But he sometimes had a beer just before dinner. Besides, he wanted to be seen. He didn't want tongues wagging any more than they already were.

The place was packed. Johnny heard Slade's name half a dozen times as he pushed patiently toward the bar. He reached it and crowded in. "Gimme a beer, Sam."

"Sure, Johnny." Sam Riordan filled a heavy mug and slid it along the bar. Johnny put a nickel down. Sam wiped his forehead with a sleeve and came to stand in front of him. "I wish there'd be a Slade Teplin come to town every day. I ain't done so much on a weekday since the trail drives stopped coming years ago."

"Then it's not all bad, is it, Sam?"

"Nope." Sam leaned across the bar, lowering his voice. "I'd keep an eye on Cal Reeder if I was you. He's makin' some pretty strong fight talk."

"About trying Slade? He was talking that way this morning, but I thought it was only talk. You think he'd really do it?"

"I don't know. Maybe he'll shut up when Slade comes in but I wouldn't count on it. He's been drinking. And the more he drinks the wilder he talks."

"Where is he?"

"Over there."

Johnny followed Sam's pointing finger with his

eyes. He saw Cal Reeder, surrounded by about a dozen men, over in a corner of the place. Cal was talking. His face was flushed. Johnny nodded, finished his beer and pushed patiently through the crowd.

He reached the group in time to hear Cal Reeder say, "It don't make sense, that's all. Every one of them sixteen men sure as hell wasn't a gunfighter. Maybe he even shot some of 'em in the back."

"You better not say that to Slade, Cal. In fact you'd better not say it at all."

"Why not? I ain't afraid of him."

Johnny pushed to a place in front of him. "You'd ought to be even if you're not. I can tell you what several of those sixteen men were. Kids just like you with more guts than sense. Now finish your drink and go on home."

"Go home hell! I ain't leavin' here. This is the biggest thing that's happened in this town in years."

Johnny looked at him sourly. "It'll be bigger if you don't shut that big mouth of yours."

Cal laughed nastily. "You might be scared of him, Johnny, but I sure ain't. He's only a man, ain't he?"

"Yeah. He's only a man. But he's alive and the sixteen who faced him are dead. You think on that."

He stared at Cal's face, fixing Cal's eyes with his own steady glance. Cal started to say something but Johnny said harshly, "Shut up! You've said too much already. Go on home if you want to stay alive."

He turned his back and pushed toward the door. There was silence behind him for a moment, then he heard Cal say loudly, "I still say I'm right. Just because Slade's killed sixteen men don't mean he's some kind of a god. He's only a man."

Johnny heard another voice behind him, and recognized it as Phil Regan's voice, "Why don't you prove that, Cal? Why don't you take him on?"

Disgust and exasperation washed over Johnny. Phil Regan was all Cal Reeder needed. With Phil to egg him on he just might be fool enough. . . .

But there was nothing Johnny could do about it. He couldn't *make* Cal go home. He couldn't jail him either. He wasn't drunk and he wasn't disturbing the peace.

He reached the door and stepped outside. He almost collided with John McCracken on the walk. McCracken stopped. "Hello, Johnny."

"Hello, Mr. McCracken."

Everyone in town called McCracken mister. Johnny thought wryly that his wife probably did too. McCracken was that kind of man.

He was tall, as tall as Johnny was. He was heavier, a bulky, powerful kind of heaviness. His hair was gray and he wore a trimmed beard and mustache.

He was dressed in a dark business suit. A gold chain stretched across his vest from pocket to pocket.

McCracken made a small, frosty smile. "You ever see anything like this, Johnny?"

Johnny shook his head. McCracken snorted disgustedly, "A damned Roman holiday. I hope he doesn't stay here long."

Johnny said, "This'll wear off, even if he does." He wanted to mention Barney, but he did not. He wanted to ask how Slade's return was going to affect Barney's job with the bank. Barney needed that job. He needed the respect that went along with it.

McCracken snorted disgustedly and moved on down the street toward the bank.

Johnny fished the Bull Durham sack from his pocket and made a cigarette. He lighted it. Glancing up, he saw Slade Teplin walking down Main from the direction of the school. Behind Slade by perhaps a hundred feet, came two boys he recognized as Tommy Schilling and Tony Sanchez.

Again he could not help noticing the way Slade Teplin moved—like a cat, stalking a bird. That was the impression, yet it was not as plain as that.

He had intended returning to the sheriff's office, but he knew he couldn't now. Not until Slade had reached the Emporia, if that was where he was headed. If he left right now it would look as if he were avoiding Slade.

So he waited, tension and dislike building in him, and kept his glance steadily on Slade as the man approached.

How good Slade was, he couldn't guess. Perhaps, in a sense, Cal Reeder was right. All of the sixteen Slade had killed probably had not been particularly fast. But Johnny was also sure, in his own mind, that Slade had not hand-picked them because they weren't fast. Slade, he was certain, took them as they came.

Slade saw Johnny and stared at him steadily as he approached. Johnny didn't speak or even nod. He returned the stare impassively, but he knew the anger he felt was showing in his eyes.

Slade stopped immediately in front of him. "You must be the deputy—the one who's been seeing my wife." His voice was flat, almost as expressionless as his face.

Johnny said coldly, "I'm the one." He knew, even as he said it, that his tone conveyed the defiant, unspoken question, "What are you going to do about it?"

Slade stared at him fixedly for several more moments. Then he said, "We'll talk on that, deputy, but not right now."

Johnny said, "Any time."

Slade went into the saloon. Johnny's whole body was tense. He had half expected Slade to challenge him, he realized. He felt himself relax and suddenly felt almost weak.

Behind him, as Slade entered the Emporia, the noise quieted instantly. A moment before a steady buzz of voices had emanated from the place. Now the silence was complete.

He turned his head and glanced over the swinging doors. Slade was crossing the room toward the bar. A path had opened for him almost magically. There were no friendly greetings. There was nothing but silent awe.

In spite of his anger, his resentment toward the man, Johnny suddenly felt sorry for him. Slade Teplin lived in a lonely, solitary world. He had no friends. He was not a part of the strange but sometimes wonderful mixture of humanity.

Slade ordered a drink and Sam Riordan served him silently. Johnny wondered where Barney was. He glanced down toward the bank and searched the street with his glance but he did not see Barney anywhere.

The Ace-High was emptying and those who had been there were streaming down the street toward the Emporia. Johnny moved aside to let them in. They crowded past him and into the saloon. They filled the doorway and packed the area immediately in front of the swinging doors.

Suddenly, loud and plain in the silence, came a shout from inside the saloon. "Hey! You! Slade Teplin!"

There was a moment's silence. No one seemed to breathe. Recognizing that voice, Johnny slammed into the crowd in front of the Emporia and fought his way toward the door.

It was like fighting a yielding wall. He could only push so far and then his progress stopped. Using his hands, he began frantically to shove men aside. He yelled, "God damn it, let me through!"

He still had not reached the doors, still could not see inside when he heard the voice again, "I hear you've killed sixteen men. How many of the sixteen did you shoot in the back?"

Now there was sound inside the Emporia, but it was not the sound of voices. It was the sound of pushing, crowding. It was the sound of men frantically trying to get out of the line of fire.

Johnny heard Slade's voice, just as he reached the doors. "Go on home boy and forget it."

"Forget it hell! Unless you're too damned yellow to fight."

Johnny was fighting frantically. He roared, "Cal! Shut your goddamn mouth!"

Cal shouted, "Go on, gunfighter! Draw and let's see how fast you really are!"

Johnny was pushed back bodily from the door, pushed by a solid wall of frantic humanity, men trying to get out of the Emporia before the guns came out. He kept on fighting, flinging men aside so violently that some of them fell. But for every one he flung away, another crowded out to take his place. He heard Slade's flat, expressionless voice, "All right, sonny. Any time you're ready you just go ahead."

Johnny knew he'd never get inside—not in time to stop what was happening. Cal didn't have a chance. He roared, "Cal! Listen to me! Don't touch your gun!"

He reached the doors and got a glimpse of the pair over the heads of those still trying to crowd out of the saloon. There was an open space between Teplin and Cal. Behind Cal there was another open space in which no men stood.

He didn't see Sam Riordan at all and guessed Riordan had ducked down behind the bar. And then he saw Cal move.

His eyes, so briefly on Cal, missed Slade Teplin's movements altogether, so fast were they. But he saw the flash of Teplin's gun and he heard its obscene roar. He saw the cloud of powdersmoke that billowed out in front of it.

Cal's gun never fired at all, but it was in his hand, raising, as Slade's bullet took him in the chest.

He was driven back by the terrible force of the heavy slug. He slammed against a table and it overturned. He tripped on it, still staggering back, and sprawled over the overturned table, hanging there like a grotesque, broken doll. A red stain began to spread across his white shirt-front.

Slade Teplin holstered his gun. He looked at Johnny's face over the heads of the crowd, and his eyes held a strange glow, a fixed intensity. He said, "You saw that, deputy. He drew before I did."

Now, too late, the crowd parted to let Johnny through. He ignored Teplin and walked to where Cal lay, still draped across the overturned table.

Cal was dead. His face was relaxed, peaceful. His eyes were open but they were expressionless.

He looked like a boy—like he was maybe sixteen or seventeen.

Johnny turned angrily. He glared at Slade for a moment, wanting to say so many things, knowing how useless it would be. Nothing he could say would bring Cal Reeder back. Nothing he could say would have any effect on Slade.

He stalked to the door and went outside. The noonday sun beat down hotly into the street. In spite of it, Johnny's body felt as cold as ice.

He heard a scream, and glanced up the street. He saw Molly, running, holding up her skirts so that she would not trip on them.

He ran toward her, and half a block from the Emporia reached her and caught her in his arms.

She was sobbing uncontrollably. Her body trembled violently.

Johnny held her close for a long, long time, until her trembling lessened, until her sobs stopped. She drew back her head and looked up at him, face white, tears streaming down her cheeks. Her voice was almost hysterical, "I was listening . . . I heard a shot and I thought it was you! Oh my God, Johnny, I thought it was you!"

She pulled away from him suddenly, her glance fixed on something behind him. She whispered, "Who was it, Johnny? Who?"

Johnny turned his head. Slade Teplin was standing on the walk in front of the Emporia. He was staring at them. Suddenly he turned and went back into the saloon.

Johnny said, "Cal Reeder, Molly. It was Cal."

Molly said in a strained, tight voice, "I wish he was dead. God forgive me, Johnny, I wish Slade was in his grave!"

Chapter 7

There was a lot of confusion back there at the Emporia. Arch Schilling came striding along the street from the jail. He went into the Emporia. Johnny looked down at Molly's tearful face. "I'll walk you back to the school."

She shook her head. "No. I'm all right now." Turning, she glimpsed Tommy Schilling and Tony Sanchez peering out from a narrow passageway between two stores. She called, "Tommy, Tony! Come here this minute!"

They hesitated a moment between obeying and running away. Then, sheepishly, the pair shuffled across the dusty street. Molly said, "Get back to school this instant! Both of you!"

The boys were no longer in the grip of hero worship. Both of them were thoroughly scared. They ducked their heads and shuffled away toward the school. Molly glanced at Johnny. Her eyes were still red from weeping and they were filled with fear. "Johnny. Don't let him . . . don't get into a fight with him."

"All right, Molly. Now stop worrying."

She smiled wanly. She looked at his face lingeringly, her smile fading. Then without a word she turned and walked back in the direction of the school.

Johnny returned to the Emporia. He reached it as a couple of men carried Cal outside.

There was shock in the faces of the onlookers. In some there was outrage, or anger. One man said, as Arch Schilling came out, "This is terrible, Sheriff. It's a damned disgrace. What are you going to do about it?"

Arch didn't bother to reply. The two men carried the body down the street toward Jim Hawkins' Furniture and Undertaking Parlor.

Johnny looked around for Slade, but Slade had disappeared. Arch glanced at him and said, "Somebody's got to do it, Johnny. It might as well be you."

"Do what?"

"Ride out to Reeder's place. Tell Ward what's happened to Cal."

Johnny stared at him, hesitating. He didn't want to ride out to Reeder's place. It would take him three hours, going and coming, even if he hurried all the way. A lot could happen here in three hours.

He said, "Arch, you know how that's going to look. Like I was running away from him."

Arch's face showed sudden anger. "Who the hell cares how it looks? Somebody's got to do it."

"Then get someone else. I want to stay right here."

Arch opened his mouth to speak, then closed it with a snap. His glance went beyond Johnny and Johnny turned his head to follow. He saw Barney Teplin coming along Main from the direction of his house.

Barney was drunk. He was weaving, staggering. He banged up against a storefront and nearly fell. Recovering, he came diagonally across the street. Arch said under his breath, "For Christ's sake! I was afraid of this."

Leaving Johnny, he crossed the street, intercepting Barney in the middle. Johnny followed him. Arch took one of Barney's arms and Johnny took the other. Barney protested drunkenly but the two of them turned him and headed him back toward home again. Arch said, "You don't want any more, Barney. Come on. We'll walk you home."

As he turned, Johnny got a glimpse of John McCracken watching from the doorway of the bank. He suddenly felt a little sick to his stomach.

Slade had been here only a little more than three hours. Already he had killed a man. He had, somehow, caused his father to fall off the wagon he'd been on almost ten years. He had jeopardized his father's job and his self-respect.

Barney walked between them unprotestingly until they reached his house. At the front gate, he pulled away from them violently. He mumbled, "I'm all right. Lemme alone."

Arch caught his arm. "We'll help you in."

Barney flung his arm off so violently that he staggered and fell in a heap. "No! You can't come in. I'm all right, dammit. Now lemme alone!"

Arch looked at Johnny helplessly. Then his jaw firmed out. "I'll be damned if I'm going to leave him out here. Come on, we'll take him inside."

They hauled Barney to his feet, still protesting violently. As they approached the porch, Barney began to fight but now they had him firmly between them. They dragged him up onto the porch and through the front door.

Once inside, Barney suddenly ceased to fight. He began to weep brokenly, drunkenly.

Johnny stared around at the wreckage of the room. He stared at the broken shotgun lying in the middle of the floor.

Arch's voice was soft, but it was just like ice. "Who did this, Barney? Slade?"

"No! I did it. You know how I am when I get drunk."

"Yeah. I know how you are, Barney. You wouldn't hurt a fly."

Johnny didn't miss the bottle lying unbroken in a corner of the room. There was still a little whisky in the bottle. He also saw the two glasses lying near to it. One had been broken but the other was whole.

Barney stood swaying in the center of the room. Tears streamed unheeded down his cheeks. Arch said, very softly, very gently, "Go to bed, Barney."

Barney turned, as meekly as a child. He went into his bedroom off the parlor and Johnny heard the bedsprings creak as he fell limply across the bed.

Arch looked helplessly around the room a moment, then turned and went outside. Johnny crossed to the bedroom door and peered in at Barney. Barney was already asleep, his mouth open, his cheek still wet with tears.

Johnny went out, closing the door softly behind him. He walked along silently with Arch, not speaking until they were half a block away. Then he breathed, "The son-of-a-bitch! The dirty son-of-a-bitch!"

"Yeah. Now get your horse and ride out to Ward Reeder's place. And don't give me any back-talk."

"What are you going to do about Slade?"

Arch was silent for several moments. At last he said, "Do? What the hell can I do? Barney won't sign a complaint. There are twenty or thirty witnesses to the shooting and they all say Cal started it and drew first."

Johnny's mind was clicking rapidly. School let out at three-thirty. It couldn't be much later than twelve-thirty now. If he hurried, he could at least be back from Reeder's place by the time school let out. He'd even have a little extra leeway because Molly never left the school building until four.

And maybe Arch was right. Maybe he should get out of town this afternoon. His own anger, his own outrage was growing steadily. He was rapidly approaching the point where he'd do something about Slade himself.

They reached Main Street. Arch said, "I'm going to talk to John McCracken for a minute. You get your horse and go."

Johnny untied his horse from the rail in front of the Emporia. The place was still crowded. The conversation was excited—about the shooting that had taken place such a short time before.

Johnny mounted and turned downstreet. Then, changing his mind, he reversed directions and touched his horse's sides with his heels. The animal broke into a lope.

Johnny wheeled around the corner and headed for the school. No use letting Molly worry about him all afternoon uselessly, he thought. If she knew he wasn't even in town, she wouldn't be so likely to make any rash decisions out of concern for him.

There was a small group of children playing on the swings. Tommy and Tony sat on the porch steps, talking in subdued tones. Molly heard him and came out, to stand with a hand raised to shield her eyes from the glare of the sun.

Johnny didn't dismount. He said, "I'm going out to Ward Reeder's place and tell him about Cal. I'll be back before school lets out."

The relief that came into her eyes made him feel warm inside. He said firmly, "It will be all right, Molly. It will be all right."

She nodded, but she didn't speak. He turned and

rode away, circling the town instead of riding through it.

The sun was hot on his back. The sky was still a flawless blue, but now a few fluffy clouds floated in it like puffs of smoke. He let his horse slow to a steady trot, an uncomfortable gait for a man but an easy one for the horse and one that covered the miles fast.

He dreaded the errand that lay ahead of him. He dreaded telling Ward Reeder that his only son was dead. But it was like Arch had said. Someone had to do it and it might as well be him.

He came abreast of the butte, several miles to his left, and passed on beyond it. He was heading almost directly north.

He continued his horse's steady gait for a little more than an hour before he saw the distant cluster of buildings ahead of him. He rode for yet another twenty minutes before he reached the place.

Ward Reeder's ranch was one of the biggest around Cottonwood Springs. Reeder ran almost a thousand cattle. He had seven sections of deeded land. He hired two men and kept them busy from dawn until dark.

Johnny halted his horse in the yard between the house and barn. He dismounted reluctantly. He hoped Ward was here. He didn't want to take time to ride all over the countryside looking for him.

He breathed a soft sigh of relief as Ward emerged from the barn and yelled, "Hey, Johnny! Here I am. What the hell brings you 'way out here?"

Johnny led his horse toward the man. Ward Reeder was about fifty, he guessed. He was stocky, broad and powerful, almost the exact opposite in build and temperament as Cal had been.

Reeder asked, "Did Slade Teplin come in on the train?"

Johnny nodded.

"How's he look?"

Johnny said, "I didn't know him before. He looks . . . well, like I'd have expected him to I guess."

Reeder's glance sharpened suddenly. "What'd you come out here for? What the hell's the matter with you?"

Johnny swallowed hard. He said, "It's Cal. He—"

"What about Cal? Damn you, what about Cal?"

"He's dead."

For an instant Ward Reeder was silent. Then he grabbed Johnny by both arms and shook him. "You're a liar! You're a goddamn liar!"

Johnny didn't resist. He shook his head silently.

Reeder roared, "Quit lyin' to me! Quit it! Why'd you really come out?"

"To tell you Cal was dead. Arch sent me out."

Reeder released him. He stepped back, breathing hard. He stared at the ground for a moment. His big, broad hands were trembling. So were his thick, solid knees. He looked up. "Who did it? How'd it happen?"

"Slade. Cal forced a fight with him."

"You see it?" Ward's voice was lifeless.

Johnny nodded. "I saw it. I was trying to get through the crowd. I yelled at Cal not to touch his gun but he wouldn't listen to me. He tried, but . . . well, he never even fired."

"Where is he? I mean where's his . . ." Ward swallowed and said in a voice that almost choked, "Where's his body at?"

"Jim Hawkins' place. Arch had a couple of men

take him there." Johnny stared at him silently for a moment. He said, "I'm sorry, Ward."

"Sure, Johnny. Sure." Ward stood there uncertainly for several moments. Then he muttered, "That goddamn kid! That goddamn stupid kid! I told him. I told him a thousand times . . ."

Johnny said softly, "Can I get your horse for you, Ward? I'll ride in with you."

"No. I'll get him, Johnny. You go on ahead. I'll catch up."

Johnny mounted and turned his horse toward town. He rode out at a walk. He had gone no more than a quarter mile when he heard Reeder coming along behind.

Reeder wore a six-shooter. There was a rifle jammed into his saddle boot. His face was grim and cold.

Johnny knew the thoughts that were going through Reeder's head. He knew what Reeder meant to do.

He'd face Slade Teplin over the killing of his son. And he'd be killed himself. He'd be number eighteen on Slade Teplin's list.

Someone had to do something, he thought miserably to himself. Someone had to stop the inevitable, tightening circle of death.

The miles passed beneath their horses' hoofs. Johnny's anger mounted steadily. There was nothing he could do. There was nothing anyone could do.

Chapter 8

It was exactly three-fifteen when Johnny and Ward Reeder thundered across the plank bridge spanning Cottonwood Creek. Arch Schilling must have been watching for them from the jail because no sooner had they entered Main at the lower end than Johnny saw Arch coming down the street on foot.

Arch stopped and stood in the center of the street in front of Regan's Livery Barn. Johnny drew his horse to a halt. For a moment he thought Ward would ride past, but something about Arch's hard old eyes stopped him. Ward glowered down at the sheriff. "Save your breath, Arch. He killed my boy."

"And he'll kill you too if you give him half a chance."

Ward's heavy face held more bitterness than Johnny had ever seen in it. "What would *you* do, Arch? Let him get away with it? Cal never had a chance against him and you damn well know he didn't."

"Think you'll have a better one?"

Ward's eyes blazed. His mouth was a slash in his anger-reddened face. He said, "Sheriff, there's something dirty wrong with this. Slade murdered Cal. You know it and I know it. Now you tell me I'll have to let it go or die myself. Well maybe I won't do either one. Maybe I'll get Slade some other way."

"It'll be murder if you do. I'll have to arrest you for it."

Johnny studied Arch's face. It was filled with

anger at the injustice of what he had just said. It was filled with helpless outrage at a situation where Slade could kill but Ward could not. Arch said, "Ward, I know it isn't right, but I can't change it and neither can you. It's a hold-over from the dueling code and until the laws are changed, it'll stay that way. But some day the Slade Teplins are going to have to answer for every man they kill, self-defense or not."

Ward glowered for several moments, finally grumbling, "That's a big help to me right now!"

Arch didn't reply. Ward said, "I want to see my boy."

"He's at Jim Hawkins' place."

Ward touched his horse's sides with his heels and moved on past. Johnny held his horse motionless. Arch stood spread-legged in the street and watched as Ward rode angrily away. He turned his head and looked helplessly up at Johnny.

Johnny asked, "Where's Slade now?"

"He took a room at the hotel. He's been there all afternoon."

Johnny glanced past him up the street. There were fewer rigs tied along the street and less than half as many saddle horses as there had been earlier. He said, "Looks like the crowd's thinned out."

"Yeah. A lot of 'em went home. The streets get empty when there's a mad dog loose."

Johnny dismounted and walked toward the jail, pacing Arch. He asked, "Isn't there *anything* we can do?"

"Not one goddamn thing. Unless we can get Barney to sign a complaint."

"Think he'd be sober now?"

"Might. Why don't you ride over there and see?"

Johnny nodded. He pulled his heavy silver watch from his pocket and glanced at it. It was almost three-thirty, but he could spare fifteen minutes to talk to Barney and still get to the school before Molly left.

He swung to the back of his horse. He glanced at the hotel as he went past. The usual number of loafers were there on the porch. They watched him go by almost furtively. None of them spoke.

Johnny turned the corner and headed for Barney's place, hurrying, thinking of Molly now, and anxious to be done with this.

Ward Reeder dismounted in front of Jim Hawkins' store. He looped his horse's reins around the rail with hands that trembled violently.

He felt stunned, unbelieving yet. It didn't seem possible that Cal was dead. Heavily he crossed the worn boardwalk and went inside.

The front part of the store was filled with furniture. There was a distinctive smell of wood and cloth about the place. Jim Hawkins, an elderly man with snow-white hair, came from the back room to see who had come in.

He called, "Back here, Ward."

Ward walked down the aisle. Hawkins' gaunt, lined face was sympathetic. "I'm sorry, Ward. It's a terrible thing."

Ward grunted noncommittally. He shouldered past Hawkins into the small room at the rear.

It was a barren room. Over at one side there was a bed. Cal's body lay on it, a sheet drawn over his head. Nearby there were two straight-backed chairs.

Ward crossed the room. He knew his face was bloodless. There was a feeling of nausea in his stomach. His hand shook almost uncontrollably as he lifted the sheet and pulled it away from Cal's face. It was white, pasty-colored. Cal's eyes were closed.

Ward dropped the sheet. He stumbled to one of the straight-backed chairs and sank into it. He whispered, "God! Oh Holy God!"

Hawkins was silent for a long, long time. At last he asked, "What do you want to do about funeral arrangements, Ward? Shall I get Orville Newcomb? Do you want the funeral in the church?"

Ward stared at him numbly, and Hawkins repeated his questions gently. Ward nodded finally, and Hawkins asked, "Is tomorrow all right? About ten?"

Ward nodded again. Almost as though speaking to himself, he said, "He wasn't a bad kid, Jim. Wild is all. Ranching never interested him. Not enough excitement, I guess. But I thought it would wear out. I thought he'd get enough of drinkin' and hellin' around and packin' that damned gun."

"He would have, Ward. If . . ." Hawkins stopped suddenly.

Ward Reeder finished the sentence for him. "If he'd lived. If that damn Slade Teplin had stayed away."

He sat there for several moments more, staring blankly at the floor between his feet. Hawkins silently withdrew, closing the door softly behind him.

As the door closed, a tremor shook Reeder's stocky frame. A single, gusty sob escaped his lips.

He straightened then. He brushed impatiently at his eyes with the back of one work-roughened hand. He stood up.

Maybe he couldn't kill Slade Teplin, he thought. He couldn't outdraw the man and if he killed him any other way he'd have to stand trial for it. But there was something he could do. He could make Slade Teplin wish he'd never come back here. He could make him wish he'd never seen Cal.

He crossed the room and opened the door. Hawkins was waiting silently outside of it. Ward asked heavily, "Jim, will you take care of things? The grave and all?"

Hawkins nodded. Ward went past him to the front of the store.

He stood there, inside the door for a moment, studying the sheriff's office and jail across the street. He did not see Arch.

He went out, untied his horse and mounted quickly. He turned the horse toward the Emporia up the street.

Reaching it, he dismounted and tied the horse. He went in.

The place was far from full, but there were maybe fifteen or twenty men. Ward went to the bar. Sam Riordan came to stand in front of him, his face soberly sympathetic. He said, "Ward, I'm sorry. I . . ."

Ward asked harshly, "Where is he now?"

"Cal? Over at Jim Hawkins' place."

"I mean Slade. Where is he?"

"Ward, don't do it. Don't be a fool. He'll kill you too."

Ward reached suddenly across the bar. He seized Sam by the shirtfront and yanked him close against the bar. His voice was savage. "Where is he? Damn you!"

Sam said, "He took a room at the hotel. He's been there all afternoon."

Ward released him. He turned, as though to leave, then suddenly swung around again. Deliberately, he reached down and unbuckled his gun and belt. He laid it on the bar. "Keep this for me. I'll be back for it."

Relief washed across Sam Riordan's scared face. He breathed, "That's smart, Ward. For a minute there I . . ."

Ward stalked out of the saloon. Half a dozen of the men got up and followed him. He walked toward the hotel, the six following a dozen yards behind. A moment later another man came out of the Emporia and hurried toward the jail.

Ward reached the hotel and went inside. He crossed the huge, cool lobby to the desk. Alf Holloway started to speak, but Ward cut him short. "Which room's he in?"

"I can't . . . I'm not . . ." Alf's young eyes were terrified.

"Which room, damn you?" Reeder roared.

"I . . ." Alf tried to hold Reeder's glance and failed. He mumbled, "Seventeen, Mr. Reeder. But . . ."

Ward turned and strode across the lobby to the stairs. He took them two at a time. At the head of the stairs, he turned right and hurried along the hall. He stopped in front of seventeen.

Here, he stood for a moment, letting anger rise in him, letting it grow to an almost intolerable pitch. Then he hammered on the door.

He heard the creak of bedsprings inside the room. He heard footsteps coming toward the door. It opened and Slade Teplin stood there looking at him, his gun in his hand and pointing straight at Ward Reeder's chest.

Ward felt the muscles in his arms twitching. His chest felt tight. There was a lightness in his brain.

He growled, "You son-of-a-bitch! You dirty son-of-a-bitch! You killed my boy!"

Slade's eyes were glazed with sudden awakening. Ward bawled, "You bastard! You can kill a man and then come here and go to sleep? What kind of stinkin' animal are you anyway?"

"Get out of here before I blow your head off."

"Go ahead. You just go ahead. You'll hang for it because I haven't got a gun. Take a look. I haven't got a gun. I left it at the Emporia."

A shadow of doubt crossed Slade Teplin's face. Ward said softly, "Put it away or shoot it. Make up your mind and make it up right now."

Slade lowered the gun. As he did, Ward plunged through the door, striking him with his shoulder and knocking him halfway across the room. Slade tripped on a chair and fell on his back. The gun left his hand and skidded under the bed. He rolled like a cat, coming to hands and knees as Ward reached him. Ward dived at him blindly, grappling, and the two rolled against the wall.

Ward's hands closed around Slade's throat. They tightened down, while Slade's body thrashed like that of a turkey whose head has just been severed by an axe.

Slade's face congested darkly with blood, turning slowly blue. Ward released his throat and systematically began smashing fists into the gunfighter's face. Slade's nose seemed to burst. With each blow, his head slammed against the floor.

There was a haze of fury over Ward Reeder's eyes. He lost track of time. Slade's face was splotched with blood from his streaming nose.

Dimly Reeder heard footsteps running along the hall. Hands pulled at him but he fought them off. He fought them off as long as he could but at last they yanked him away from Slade by sheer brute strength.

He was sobbing, partly with fury, partly from shortness of breath. At the door, someone said, "Why don't you let him go? Let him finish it."

And Arch Schilling's flat, hard voice, "Shut up! Come on, drag him out of there."

Ward was literally dragged across the room. He was cursing steadily with balked fury. He caught the doorjamb as they dragged him through and clung to it desperately, glaring at Arch Schilling's face. Arch said furiously, "I told you . . . damn it, I told you if you killed him you'd hang."

"I didn't kill him," Ward panted, "but I wish I had."

Arch's glance went beyond him into the room. "You didn't miss it far," he growled. "If Sam hadn't sent someone for me . . ."

A man asked, "What do you want us to do with Ward, Arch?"

"Take him down to the jail and lock him up."

Ward's grip on the doorjamb was broken and they dragged him down the hall. Arch heard him yelling all the way down the stairs, through the lobby and out into the street.

He looked across the room at Slade. The man was groaning and trying to turn over onto his stomach. His nose was still streaming blood. One of his eyes was turning puffy and discoloring.

Arch waited, watching coldly as Slade turned over and came to his hands and knees. After a while, Slade fought to his feet, staggered across the room and sat down on the bed.

He glared at Arch murderously, but Arch's old eyes didn't flinch. He said harshly, "If I was you,

I'd stay in this room the rest of the day. I'd get on the morning train and get out of town."

"You can go straight to hell."

Arch said disgustedly, "I should have given Ward a little more time with you. But he's too good a man to hang for killin' the likes of you."

Slade's eyes held Arch's malevolently. "I'll kill him, sheriff. I'll kill him for what he did to me."

Arch shrugged. "Not tonight, you won't, because he's in jail." He turned and left the room without bothering to close the door. Before he reached the stairs, he heard it slam viciously.

Going down the stairs he scowled. It wouldn't be hard for Slade to taunt Ward into a gunfight after this. It wouldn't be hard at all. The only way he'd prevent it was by keeping Ward locked up.

But you couldn't keep a man locked up while his son's funeral was going on. He'd have to release Ward tomorrow.

He crossed the lobby and stepped out into the street. He wondered bleakly what would happen next. Slade was like a tormented rattlesnake right now, and there was no telling where he'd strike.

Chapter 9

Johnny Yoder dismounted in front of Barney Teplin's house. He tied his horse to the hitching post, the top of which was a cast-iron lion with a ring in its mouth.

He was worried about Ward Reeder. He knew how Ward must feel. Ward's fury might make him seek Slade out and if he did, he'd get killed too.

He shrugged lightly as he went up the walk. Arch wouldn't let that happen. Arch was as aware of the danger as he was himself.

He knocked lightly on the door. There was a vast discouragement in him as he stood there waiting for Barney to answer it. Sometimes it seemed as though the laws had been deliberately designed to protect men like Slade. They could kill with impunity, time after time. They developed a skill with a gun no other man could match. They could afford to let the other man draw first.

He heard sounds within Barney's house, and a moment later, Barney opened the door.

His eyes were red and his mouth was slack. He was squinting as though he had a monstrous headache. The light seemed to hurt his eyes. Johnny asked softly, "Hello, Barney. Can I come in?"

Barney hesitated, then stood aside. "Sure. Come on in."

Johnny went in. He noticed that the whisky bottle was no longer lying on the floor. It was sitting on a table that had been righted, and it was empty now. Otherwise, the room was unchanged, a shambles of senseless destruction.

Barney peered at Johnny, wincing once as a particularly painful throb went through his head. "Whadda ya want, Johnny?"

"Did you know Slade killed Cal Reeder?"

Shock touched Barney's face and turned it almost gray. He staggered across the room and collapsed into a chair. He put his head down into his hands and sat that way for a long, long time. At last, without raising his head, he asked, "Where is he now?"

"He took a room at the hotel. What's he going to do, Barney? Is he going to stay?"

"Hell, I don't know. He didn't say. I thought maybe . . . I thought he'd come home because he was tired of the way he was living, because he wanted to change."

"That was before he wrecked this room, wasn't it?"

Barney raised his head. "He didn't wreck this room. I did."

"And I suppose you dug the bottle out and had a drink just because you wanted one."

Barney didn't answer him. Johnny could imagine how it had been, with Slade home for the first time in more than five years. Slade had probably asked for a drink. He had probably urged Barney to drink with him and Barney, glad for any closeness between himself and his son, had accepted. One drink was all it took to start a man like Barney off. Johnny was willing to bet Slade knew that and did it deliberately—as deliberately as he had wrecked this room.

He said, "I'll help you clean this up."

Barney shook his head, wincing as he did. "Let it go. I'll do it later, myself."

Johnny said, "Arch wants you to sign a complaint. He wants an excuse to throw Slade in jail."

Barney glanced at him, fear showing in his eyes. "Slade wouldn't go to jail. He'd kill Arch first."

"You let Arch and me worry about that. Will you sign the complaint?"

Barney shook his head. He stared at the floor. "I can't. He didn't do it. I did it myself."

Johnny said, "Barney, think! Cal isn't going to be the only one. As long as Slade's loose with that gun of his . . ."

Barney stared at Johnny warily, a growing suspicion showing in his eyes. Johnny knew instantly what he was thinking—that Johnny wanted Slade locked up for personal reasons.

Johnny said, "You're wrong, Barney. This isn't my idea. It's Arch's."

Barney didn't reply, and after a moment Johnny said, "But you're right about one thing. He and I are going to tangle if he tries to get Molly back."

A spasm of something like pain crossed Barney's face. He buried his face in his hands again. "I can't think! Oh God, I can't think straight! I need a drink."

Johnny said patiently, "That's the last thing you need. What you need is to admit what Slade is— what he's turned into since he left here five years ago. He's a killer, Barney. He's a mad dog killer. He's so full of hate he's sick with it. He couldn't stand to see you with a decent job and a decent place to live. In less than a day he's wrecked everything you worked so hard to get."

Barney didn't bother to deny it. Johnny went on, "Do you think he's finished with you? Do you think his hate is satisfied? You know damn well it's not. Sign that complaint, Barney. Let Arch and me put Slade in jail."

Barney said bitterly, without raising his head, "And how long could you keep him there?"

"Maybe long enough to figure something out."

Barney snorted disgustedly. "A week. A week at the most. And then he'd be out again."

"A week's better than nothing at all. Maybe . . ."

Barney asked, "How did he get into a fight with Cal?"

"Cal started it," Johnny said reluctantly. "He drew first."

"Did Slade—did Slade try to stop him?"

Again Johnny nodded reluctantly. "But he didn't try hard enough. He could have turned his back. He could have just refused. I was right outside the saloon but I couldn't get through the crowd. If I'd had a couple of minutes more, I'd have had Cal. I'd have gotten to him and been able to stop it before he drew his gun."

Barney sat silently, his head down in his hands. He was still so long, Johnny thought he had gone to sleep. He got up.

But Barney was not asleep. He spoke softly, hoarsely, "I can't sign a complaint against Slade. You can see why, can't you? I let him down when he was a boy. I went on the bottle after his mother died and I'm to blame for whatever he is now. As long as there's a chance he came home to try and change . . ." He glanced up, suddenly, and Johnny was startled to see tears streaming down his cheeks. Barney's voice was almost a cry. "He's my son. He's . . . his mother's son too. I've got to give him a chance to change because I think that's why he's home."

Johnny could see Barney didn't believe what he had said. He didn't believe that Slade had come home to try and change. He believed, as Johnny did, that Slade had come home to satisfy his hatred of the town.

But he knew he'd never persuade Barney to sign the complaint Arch wanted. He shrugged and said gently, "All right, Barney. But stay off the whisky or he won't get the chance you think he wants."

He went out, closing the door softly behind him. Standing uncertainly on the porch, he pulled out his watch and looked at it. It was three-forty-five.

He hurried to the street, mounted and whirled his horse. He headed toward the school.

He passed perhaps half a dozen children walking home. He breathed a soft sigh of relief when he saw Molly's buggy still sitting with its shafts resting on the ground. He dismounted and tied his horse.

Tommy Schilling and Tony Sanchez were staying after school, punishment, he supposed, for playing truant earlier. As he came into the schoolroom, Molly said, "Tommy, you and Tony can go now. You go straight home. If I hear that you've been hanging around in town . . ."

The pair got up and shuffled from the room. The door slammed behind them.

Molly looked at Johnny. Her face was pale and drawn. Fear was strong in her eyes. "Johnny, please go away. Please."

He stared at her with exasperation. "Listen to me. You're not going back to him. Do you know what he did to Barney—to his own father?"

She shook her head numbly.

"He got Barney drunk and Barney hasn't had a drink for years. He took a shotgun like a club and deliberately wrecked the parlor of Barney's house. I won't let him near you, Molly. No matter what you say."

She turned her back on him and walked to the window. Johnny said, "He didn't come home to change. He came home because hatred for this town has been smoldering in him all these years. He came home to hurt everybody in town just as much as he possibly could."

She remained at the window, not speaking. Johnny shouted angrily, "And that includes you too. He'll hurt you all he can and then throw you away again."

When she turned to face him, her face was white,

her lips compressed. She cried, "You're a fool, Johnny Yoder! Can't you get it through your stupid head that I *want* him back! Why do you think I married him? Why do you think I've waited all these years?"

Johnny said, "That won't work, Molly. So give it up."

She began to cry, softly, almost silently. She turned to face the window again. Her shoulders shook with her weeping.

Johnny crossed the room. Gently he put his hands on her shoulders. He said, "Part of loving someone is believing in them. You've got to believe in me. I'm not going to play Slade's game. Killing me is going to be a lot harder for him than killing Cal."

She turned and buried her face in his chest. He held her tightly for a long, long time, until her weeping quieted. Then he said, "I'll hitch up your buggy and take you home."

She nodded and he released her. He went to the door and out into the schoolyard. The sun was dropping toward the horizon, but it was still hot.

He untied her horse and led him to the buggy. He backed him between the shafts and hitched him up.

Molly came out of the school and crossed the yard. He helped her into the buggy, then got his own horse and tied him on behind. He'd done this every afternoon for months, until it had become routine.

He climbed into the buggy beside her and picked up the reins. He drove out of the schoolyard and down the street toward Main.

Turning into Main, he saw several men dragging a shouting Ward Reeder down the street toward the jail. As he came abreast of the hotel, Arch came out of the door and stepped off the porch.

Johnny drew the buggy to a halt. He looked at Arch questioningly.

Arch stared at him. He said grimly, "Ward just beat Slade Teplin up."

Beside Johnny, Molly gasped. Arch said, "I'm giving you two weeks off. You take Molly and go somewhere. Go a long ways off. Drive all night if you have to, but get out of Cottonwood County and get out fast."

Arch glanced up at the hotel. Then he turned and headed toward the jail. Johnny looked that way and saw Ward Reeder being forcibly dragged inside.

He slapped the back of the buggy horse with the reins. The animal trotted down the dusty street.

Johnny resisted the compulsion to look around at the windows of the hotel. He had the feeling that if he did, he would meet Slade Teplin's eyes. He could almost feel them on him, burning, searing with their intensity.

Molly sat huddled on the seat beside him, staring straight ahead. He wondered what her reaction to Arch's suggestion was.

Whatever it was, he knew he couldn't go. He couldn't abandon Arch to handle Slade by himself. And furthermore, he knew it would do no good to run from Slade. Slade would follow. He'd find them no matter where they went.

If they ran and if Slade followed them— everything would favor Slade and all the disadvantage would be on Johnny's side. If he was with Molly any abuse of her would force him to fight no matter how much he wanted to avoid a showdown with Slade.

But if he stayed here . . . at least he had a chance. Not much of one, but at least a chance.

He frowned worriedly as the buggy horse clattered across the bridge.

Chapter 10

Slade Teplin slammed the door savagely behind the sheriff. He raised a hand and swiped at his bleeding nose.

He stood there beside the door, trembling, for a long moment. Then he drew back a foot and kicked the door with sheer frustrated fury.

He turned and crossed the room to the washstand. He bent over the basin and splashed water into his face. It stung as it touched the abrasions on his face.

He picked up the towel and mopped at his bleeding, dripping face. His whole body seemed to be trembling, from his hands down to his knees. His face worked with helpless rage. He'd kill Ward Reeder. Just as soon as the sheriff released the man from jail.

Slade was not a brawler. He was a finely tuned instrument, trained for one thing and one thing alone. He could draw and shoot his gun faster than any man alive. He could hit a four-inch target at fifty feet nine times out of ten. Not for nearly ten years had he been mauled and beaten the way Ward Reeder had beaten him.

He walked to the window and stared down into the street. He saw Arch Schilling step into sight from the hotel porch. He saw a buggy draw to a halt in front of him.

The buggy top hid the occupants, except for their knees and feet. But he knew who they were. That deputy, Yoder. And Molly, his wife.

His face twisted and his eyes narrowed murderously. He stared down at the buggy top as though he could penetrate it with the intensity of his glance.

The sheriff glanced up at the hotel, then walked on down the street. The buggy clattered after him. As it moved away downstreet he could see Molly and a moment later, the deputy. Neither looked around.

He stared after the buggy until it bounced across the railroad tracks. Then he turned, crossed the room and got down on his hands and knees beside the bed to retrieve his gun.

It lay against the wall and he had to crawl under the bed to reach it. Doing so improved his disposition not at all. He got up again and dropped the gun into its holster at his side.

He walked back to the window and stared broodingly into the street. Everything about this stinking town held memories for him, he thought. And the memories were not pleasant ones.

Up the street from the hotel was Silverstein's Mercantile, but it had been Zachary's then. He'd worked there from five in the morning until six at night for fifty cents a day. Even now he could remember the way his muscles had ached at night. Sometimes they'd ached so bad he'd just laid in bed and wept because he couldn't go to sleep.

He muttered a savage, obscene curse. If he hated this town it was because this town had taught him hate.

He turned his head and glanced downstreet at the Emporia. It was out in front of the Emporia that he'd killed his first man. He stared into the sun-washed, dusty street, and for a moment it seemed as if that day had returned. He was standing in the street, so scared his mouth was dry and his chest had turned to ice. He could hear himself —cursing—pouring out on that drifter all the bitter hatred he felt for the town, for his father and for humanity. He could feel the cold grips of the gun in his hand and could feel his hand trembling.

He'd have fired, he realized now, whether the drifter had drawn his gun or not. But the drifter *had* drawn his gun and his doing so had given the encounter the appearance of a fight.

Slade admitted to himself that the town had given him a break in acquitting him. But he did not give them credit for their motives in doing so. They had acquitted him because they were ashamed, not because they liked him. Not a single person in town had liked him. They hadn't then and they didn't now. What he did not admit was that he'd never given anyone a chance to like him. He'd been too angry to be likable. He was still angry. He had been angry all his life.

But he had come back at last. He had come back to cleanse himself of hate. He had come back to exact revenge for what the town had done to him, for what they had made of him.

He began to pace back and forth restlessly. The room was hot and his body felt like ice. His head ached savagely from the pounding Reeder had given him.

He found himself remembering other things. The taunting he had taken at school because his clothes were ragged and dirty, because his hair was shaggy and uncut, because his father was what he was. He remembered his shame whenever he found his father lying in an alley, reeking of liquor, snoring like a hog in a mud wallow.

The drifter had been the first. Until today, that drifter had been the only victim of Slade's gun here in Cottonwood Springs. But there had been other victims, in other places. Seventeen, including Cal Reeder. He sat down on the edge of the bed, finding obscure satisfaction in remembering each one of them.

From a world filled with endless weariness, shame and poverty he had worked himself into a world of awe and fear. Men looked at him nowadays with respect. They called him Mister Teplin and they did so respectfully. Some of them were ingratiating, wanting to buy him drinks, wanting to be seen in his company.

There were others, too, and without these, living would have still been hard for Slade. These were the ones who wanted to hire him to kill someone who was in their way and whom they had not the guts or skill to kill for themselves.

Slade could come into a community and kill with impunity. All he had to do was pick a quarrel with the victim and taunt him into drawing first. Then he could collect his fee and leave. It was ironic that the law protected him and others of his kind and this was a hold-over from an ancient dueling code, a code that permitted men to settle their differences for themselves as long as they adhered to certain rules.

Slade's rewards varied, of course. He had killed for as little as fifty dollars. He had received as much as a thousand. Sometimes he didn't even have to kill to collect his pay. His appearance in a particular locality occasionally was enough to make his employer's enemies capitulate.

He got up from the side of the bed and walked to the washstand again. There was a brownish stain of blood in the water. Slade stared into the mirror at his face.

His nose had stopped bleeding. So had the abrasions on his face. His lower lip was puffy, though. And one of his eyes was likely to turn black.

He'd have to show himself like this. He'd have to show the whole town what Ward Reeder's fists had done to him. But he'd also show them something else. As soon as Reeder got out of jail, he'd show them what happened to a man who laid a hand on him.

He bent his head and again washed his face. He dampened his hair and ran a comb through it. He took off his blood-spotted shirt and got a clean one from his valise. He knotted his tie carefully and put on his coat.

He slipped his gun from its holster and checked it. He punched out the empty and re-filled the cylinder from his cartridge belt. Right now he wanted a couple of drinks. Later, he'd have supper in the hotel dining room. Then he'd get a horse at the livery barn and ride out to Molly's place. Maybe he'd spend the night out there. Hell, she was his wife, wasn't she? And besides, he needed a woman tonight.

He opened the door and stepped out into the hall. As he went down the stairs, he found himself thinking of that deputy. Yoder was smart, he realized. He was probably smart enough not to let himself be sucked into a gunfight with Slade Teplin. But there were ways of getting around him, Teplin thought. If he went out and spent the night with Molly . . . that would stir Yoder up enough to make him fight.

He permitted himself a thin smile at the thought. As he crossed the lobby, the desk clerk called, "Evenin', Mr. Teplin."

He turned his head and looked at the young man, who could not steadily meet his eyes. This pleased him too, the way men almost always looked away from him.

He went outside. He made a little bet with himself that no one would mention the way his face looked. He turned toward the Emporia, after first looking the street over carefully in a leisurely, deliberate way.

It was the one thing he feared—that someone who had not the courage to face him would shoot him in the back. That was a gunfighter's nightmare.

He passed the Ace-High, pacing along deliberately, and heard someone say, "There he is! There's Slade Teplin!"

He didn't turn his head. He reached the Emporia and went inside.

Almost instantly, he felt every eye on him. It was a familiar feeling and one he enjoyed. He crossed to the bar and liked, too, the way men moved aside to make a place for him.

The bartender came toward him immediately and Slade said softly, "Whisky." He stared into the backbar mirror critically as the man moved away to get a bottle and glass.

But he wasn't looking at himself. He was looking behind him. He could always tell when someone was thinking of trying him out. There were several signs that gave it away—wide eyes, the dilated pupils of those eyes, the facial pallor, and sometimes trembling hands or hands so clammy

their owner continually wiped their palms against
his pants.

The bartender brought his drink. The man next
to Slade said, "Let me buy that drink for you, Mr.
Teplin. I'm Phil Regan."

Slade turned his cold eyes on the man. He didn't
protest and the man shoved some money across the
bar. Regan said almost breathlessly, "This town
ain't had so much excitement in years—not since
King Fisher passed through."

Slade stared at him until Regan looked uneasily
away. Slade picked up his drink and sipped it
thoughtfully.

He felt nothing but contempt for Phil Regan's
kind. And he remembered Regan, too, from years
ago. Regan had once threatened to horsewhip him
for following his daughter, Sarah, home from
school. His mouth twisted bitterly. He remembered having a crush on Sarah because she was so
pretty and so clean. But he'd never gotten closer to
her than a hundred yards.

His thoughts wandered, though his ears heard
the subdued talk going on around him. Most of it
was about him, but he didn't listen consciously. He
was thinking that he never stood in a saloon without wondering when it would happen and from
what quarter it would come. That unexpected shot,
with no warning. Or a hastily shouted, "Slade Teplin! Draw, damn you!" with the gun roaring before
the words were decently out of the shooter's
mouth.

It was true that a gunfighter enjoyed a certain
immunity from prosecution for his acts. But it was
also true that the law afforded him less protection
than it did other citizens. He was fair game and it

was up to him to see that no one got a chance to shoot him in the back.

Regan said, "Have another one, Mr. Teplin. On me."

Slade turned his head and looked at him. "Did you buy that bottle, Mr. Regan?"

Regan nodded. Slade picked up the bottle. He turned it upside down and watched the contents gurgle out at Phil Regan's feet. He glanced up at Regan's face as the last of the whisky dribbled out of the bottle.

There was the briefest flash of pure fury in Regan's eyes. It faded almost instantly to be replaced by fear. Regan dropped his glance. He licked his lips. Then he turned and hurried from the saloon.

Slade shoved the bottle across the bar. "Another one, bartender. I'll pay for this one myself."

The bartender didn't reply. But he brought the bottle and set it down on the bar with a crash.

Slade said softly, "Something the matter with you, bartender?"

The man's face flushed. He would not look at Slade. He mumbled, "Matter with me? Why should there be anything the matter with me?"

Slade smiled thinly. Down the bar a big, graying man said, "Come on, Luke. We'll have our drink at the Ace-High."

Slade glanced at him, recognizing him immediately. It was John McCracken, who owned the bank. Slade said, "Just a minute, Mr. McCracken."

McCracken paused as he passed Slade on the way to the door. Slade said quietly, "Know where your teller is?"

"Barney?"

"Yeah. Barney. He's passed out on the floor at home. Drunker than a hog on sour mash."

McCracken said evenly, "Maybe he's got that coming to him, Slade. Any farther with a son like you . . ." McCracken met Slade's glance steadily, without fear, with only loathing and contempt. Then he turned and walked on out the door.

Slade's eyes were furious. He poured himself another drink and gulped it down. It had been years since anyone had looked at him that way or spoken to him that way. God damn McCracken anyway! But he'd get to McCracken before he left.

For an instant . . . for the first time since his arrival, the faintest shadow of doubt touched his mind. The trouble was, he realized, that he had grown up here. Too many people remembered him as a boy. . . .

Then the doubt was gone. He wasn't going to stay here long. When he did go . . . after he was gone . . . they'd have another memory of him in Cottonwood Springs. This town would remember him until it turned to prairie dust.

Chapter 11

Johnny Yoder drove silently as he left the town and skirted Cottonwood Creek on the way to Molly's house. Molly sat as silently beside him, staring straight ahead.

Johnny was thinking of the coming night, because he knew what was going to happen as soon as it got dark. Slade would be riding out to Molly's place. He was still Molly's husband. He had come back because he hated the town and because he wanted revenge for what he believed the town had done to him and he wouldn't miss a chance like this. He'd assert his rights as a husband, knowing Johnny would fight him, on any terms, if he did.

And he *would* fight Slade, Johnny thought. The man was sure as hell right about that. He also knew that, in Slade's kind of fight, he would have no chance. He was better than most men with his gun, but he was far from a match for Slade.

Arch had probably been right in urging him to take Molly and leave. The trouble was, Johnny had his own pride too. If he let Slade drive him away, if he let Slade make him run . . . he'd be less of a man afterward. Besides, it would do no good. Slade would follow them. Trailing a buggy would be ridiculously easy by daylight tomorrow. Then Johnny would have to face him anyway.

Molly turned her pale, scared face to look at him. "Johnny, what are we going to do?"

He covered her hand with his big, calloused one and squeezed gently. "Let me worry about that, Molly. I'll figure something out."

"But what, Johnny? What? You can't face him —you can't fight him on his terms."

"There are still almost four hours left before it gets dark. A lot can happen in four hours."

She sat in frozen silence for a long, long time. At last she said with quiet desperation, "I've been afraid he would come back for five long years, Johnny. Until I met you, I didn't dare even think of marrying again. I knew what Slade might do when he heard." She was silent for a moment and when she spoke again, her voice was an anguished cry. "I couldn't help myself when you came along! I couldn't! I fooled myself into thinking I had been wrong about Slade—that he didn't care—that he wouldn't come back. Now I know I was wrong. And unless we run away, Slade will . . . he'll kill you, Johnny. Like he did Cal Reeder this afternoon."

Johnny said softly, "Running wouldn't help, Molly. Slade can follow a trail. He'd find us no matter where we went. We'd just be putting it off. And maybe I've got a better chance if I have it out with him right here."

"Chance?" she said bitterly. "Johnny, you have no chance! You've got to admit that and not let him goad you into a fight. I may be his wife, but he's not going to force me into anything!"

Johnny said, "Then we've got nothing to worry about."

He drew the buggy to a halt in front of her tiny house. He helped her down, then climbed back up and drove the buggy across the yard. He unhitched, led the horse to the stable and took the harness off. He led the horse to the creek and let him drink. Then he returned him to the stable and threw him several forks full of hay from a loose pile in one corner.

He returned to the house, leaving his saddle horse tied to the buggy. He went into the kitchen.

Molly had a fire going in the stove. She pulled the graniteware coffee pot forward so that it would heat. He noticed that her hands were trembling.

He crossed the room and put his arms around her. He kissed her cheek.

She turned and threw her arms around him desperately. She clung to him fiercely, as though she would never let him go.

He held her this way for a long, long time. Then

her body went limp. She dropped her arms and stood listlessly, as though she had lost all hope.

Johnny said, "I've got to get back. But I'll see you again before it gets dark. He won't come out here before dark."

She nodded, avoiding his eyes.

He studied her suspiciously. He said, "You've got something going in that pretty head of yours. What is it?"

She refused to raise her glance. He took her shoulders in his hands and forced her to look at him. What he saw in her eyes was determination, quiet and fearful but implacable. He asked, "You wouldn't be thinking of shooting him yourself, would you?"

"What if I am?"

"Molly, don't be a fool! You'd go to prison for it."

"Not if I said it was self-defense."

"Who'd believe it, Molly? Everybody in town knows I've been seeing you. Everybody knows I want to marry you."

"They also know Slade. They know how violent he is."

"They know how damned careful he is too. They know he wouldn't dare hurt you. Too many people are just waiting for him to make one mistake."

He released her. He crossed the room and picked up the rifle from a corner of the room. He said, "I'll take this with me, just in case. And you stop worrying. I'll handle Slade somehow."

At the door he turned and glanced back at her. Tears of helplessness were overflowing from her eyes. He didn't want to leave but knew he must. He felt her eyes on him all the way across the yard.

He untied his horse and mounted. He smiled at

her, trying to make his smile show a confidence he did not feel. Then he rode out toward town.

He felt a rising irritability as he rode. He was beginning, already, to get sick of Slade Teplin and the problems he had raised. And while he knew feeling thus was dangerous, he still could not help himself.

It was twenty minutes of five when he halted his horse in front of the jail. He looped the reins around the rail and went inside.

After the heat of the afternoon sun outside, the office seemed cool. Arch was sitting in his swivel chair, feet on the desk, pipe in his mouth. He wore a faint frown.

Johnny asked, "Ward all right?"

"Uh-huh. But I'm scared to let him out. He wouldn't last thirty minutes if I did." He stared at Johnny irritably. "I thought I told you to keep going."

"What good would it do? Slade can follow buggy tracks. He'd catch up with us tomorrow."

"Maybe not. Maybe he wouldn't even try."

"You don't believe that. And neither do I."

There was a clatter of hoofbeats in the street and two plunging horses pulled up in front of the jail. Glancing out, Johnny saw Ward Reeder's two hired men, Les Isaacs and Willy Hogg. They tied their horses and came in.

Les was a tall, gangling man, all elbows and knees and feet. He had an unruly shock of yellow hair and a two-day growth of whiskers. Willy was of medium height and slightly overweight. He looked soft, but Johnny knew that was deceptive. No one who worked as hard as Willy did could be soft.

Les asked in a soft, southern drawl, "You know

where Ward is, Arch? He left a note for us—said Cal had been killed. Is that true?"

Arch nodded. He gestured with his head toward the jail cells at the rear. "He's out there in a cell. Go talk to him if you want."

Les stared puzzledly at him, then at Johnny. With a faint shrug he said, "Come on, Willy."

The two crossed the office and opened the door leading to the cells. Johnny heard them say hello to Ward. Then the door closed and after that he could only hear the murmur of voices behind it.

He asked, "Think he'll put them up to something, Arch?"

"Mebbe. I know he'll try. I'll talk to them before they leave." Arch studied Johnny carefully. "What I want to know is what *you* are going to do. Suppose Slade goes out to Molly's place tonight?"

"I'll stop him. One way or another, I'll stop him before he gets there."

"He has a right . . ."

"Right hell! He's got no rights at all. He doesn't give a damn about her, or he wouldn't have stayed away from her this long. The only reason he'd go out there would be to start something. With me. He can't stand for this town to know Molly prefers me to him."

"Maybe I ought to just order him to leave town."

"You can't make it stick."

"I can try."

"There's no train out until nine-thirty tomorrow morning. By then, it'll probably be too late."

Les and Willy came out of the door leading to the cells. Arch said, "I don't know what Ward said to you two, but take my advice and don't do anything stupid. You work for Ward, but it ain't part of your job to get killed for him."

Les gave him a slow grin. "Don't worry, Arch. We ain't about to choose Slade, if that's what you're driving at."

"Fine. Cal's body is across the street at Jim Hawkins' place, if you want to see it."

"That's what Ward said. I reckon we'll just mosey over there and see Cal. You're gonna let Ward out in time for the funeral in the mornin', ain't you?"

Arch nodded.

Les made a slow, deliberate smile. "So long, Arch."

Arch grunted sourly. Les and Willy went out and started across the street. Arch said, "Ward's put them two up to something, sure as hell. You watch, Johnny. When they come out of Hawkins' store, follow 'em. Keep an eye on 'em for a while."

Johnny nodded. Arch got up ponderously and went back to talk to Ward. Johnny doubted if he'd get anything out of Ward Reeder, but it wouldn't hurt to try. Arch closed the door and again Johnny heard the murmur of voices behind it.

Les and Willy disappeared into the furniture store. A buckboard passed the jail, heading out of town. A few minutes later, two men on saddle horses entered town and passed, heading toward the hotel. Johnny didn't recognize them. From the looks of them, they were just drifting through.

Les and Willy emerged across the street. They came across to the jail, untied their horses and mounted. They rode up the street and stopped in front of the Emporia where they talked for a minute. Then Willy rode on up the street and turned the corner. Les dismounted, tied his horse and went into the Emporia.

Johnny grabbed his hat and went outside. There

were long shadows now in the street. The air was hot and still. Johnny smelled woodsmoke in it, and the smell of frying meat.

It was a little after five. He hurried along the street, but he didn't believe Les would be fool enough to start anything with Slade. Certainly not all by himself. Still, rangeland loyalties were strong, and he could not be sure.

He went into the Emporia and paused for an instant just inside the doors. Les was at the near end of the bar. Farther along, Johnny saw Slade Teplin, a bottle and glass in front of him. There was a strong odor of whisky in the place, as though some had been spilled.

Slade's head turned as he came in. His face was cold and expressionless. One of his eyes was turning black and his mouth was puffy. There were several noticeable abrasions on his face. His eyes, staring so steadily at Johnny, were malevolent.

Les turned his head and grinned at Johnny as he approached. "Arch tell you to check up on me?"

Johnny returned his grin, liking Les. He nodded. "He just wants to be sure you don't dig your grave with that big mouth of yours."

"Don't worry. I ain't that stupid."

Sam Riordan called, "What'll you two have?"

Les yelled, "Couple of beers, Sam!" He glanced at Johnny. "That all right with you?"

Johnny nodded. Sam brought two thick mugs of beer and Les slid a dime across the bar. Johnny sipped the beer. He could feel Slade's eyes on him. It made him both angry and nervous, wondering what the man was thinking, what he intended to do. Les murmured softly, "He's sure watching you, Johnny. He sure as hell is."

Johnny shrugged, but he did not glance toward

Slade. Suddenly, Les gulped his beer. He said hastily, "See you, Johnny," and ducked away from the bar, heading toward the door.

Arch needn't have worried about Les taking Slade on, Johnny thought. He acted like he was scared to death.

The incongruity of it struck him suddenly. Les wasn't a scary man. And Johnny was willing to bet he wasn't really scared of Slade. Not enough to run just because the man approached.

He turned his head. Slade came up beside him, carrying his bottle and glass. He put the glass down and dumped some whisky into it. He said, without looking at Johnny, "I want to talk to you."

Johnny's body was suddenly as tight-drawn as a fiddlestring. His heart felt as though it was trying to beat a hole in his chest. He waited a moment before he answered, and when he did his voice was steady and indifferent. "All right," he said, "talk away."

Chapter 12

Slade turned his head. He looked straight into Johnny's eyes and said, "You're a dirty, back-alley, wife-stealing son-of-a-bitch."

So unexpectedly did the words come, and in such an unemotional tone of voice, that for an instant Johnny was stunned, almost unbelieving. Words like that should be spoken in fury, not the way Slade had spoken them.

But an instant later he understood. There was no passion in Slade. He didn't love his wife, didn't even want her, really. He was just looking for a fight.

The instant comprehension struck him, Johnny felt his wild, sudden anger begin to fade. He said in an equally unemotional voice, "And you're a murdering, mad-dog killer that wouldn't know a fair fight if it hit you in the face."

Slade stepped away from the bar. Johnny knew what was coming. Slade would back slowly away until ten or fifteen feet separated them. Then he'd begin cursing Johnny and if that didn't work, he'd bring Molly into it, defiling her with his words until Johnny could stand no more.

Johnny's hand went out suddenly. He grabbed Slade by his shirt-front and yanked him close. Simultaneously his knee came up, catching Slade in the crotch.

Slade's gun was already in his hand. Johnny batted his hand as the gun came up, deflecting the muzzle, deflecting the bullet that roared out on a searing lance of flame and smoke.

Releasing Slade's shirt front with his right hand, he seized the man's wrist with it. With his left hand he twisted Slade's gun away and flung it savagely across the room.

Slade was sick. His face was almost green with the pain of Johnny's knee. Johnny knew he'd never get another chance like this. Slade was disarmed and sick. He'd created a disturbance and for that Johnny could throw him into jail.

Deftly he seized Slade's left arm, twisted it until it was behind the gunman's back. He raised it until Slade winced with pain. He said with soft breathlessness, "All right, gunfighter, you can cool off tonight in jail."

He pushed Slade, unresisting, toward the door.

He heard the collective sigh that seemed to come simultaneously from every man in the room. He reached the door as Les Isaacs settled in his saddle in the street and realized with a shock that everything that had taken place had happened in the time Les had needed to walk out of the Emporia, untie and mount his horse.

Slade had found his voice and was now cursing Johnny in words that were unbelievably obscene. Johnny said harshly, "Shut up, or by God we'll leave a trail of your teeth all the way from here to the jail."

Slade's cursing continued, unabated. He finished with Johnny and started cursing Molly. Johnny released his arm and gave him a push. Slade turned in time to catch Johnny's clenched fist squarely in the mouth. He staggered back, with Johnny following murderously.

Chopping rights and lefts smashed into Slade's face. He retreated, staggering, down the street toward the jail. Back in front of the Emporia a man yelled, "Kill him, Johnny! Kill the son-of-a-bitch!"

Johnny suddenly dropped his hands. He said savagely, "Git! Get on down to the jail before I do kill you!"

Slade glared at him murderously for a moment, then turned and shuffled toward the jail. Following him, Johnny wondered for the first time whether what he'd done was right. He hadn't really had much choice. It had been this or facing Slade on Slade's own terms.

He saw Arch come out of the jail and glance toward him. Arch stood there staring unbelievingly, but as Slade drew close, a grin spread slowly across Arch's face. He held the door for Slade with mock ceremony and Slade went in, scowling fiercely. Johnny followed.

Inside the office, Slade made a rush for the gunrack. He seized one of the shotguns and whirled—

Johnny drew his gun and fired. His bullet tore into the floor a couple of inches from Slade's foot. Slade dropped the shotgun as though it was too hot to hold.

Johnny stood there glaring at him challengingly, waiting. Slade turned and shuffled toward the door leading to the cells. He opened it and meekly went into one of the cells. Johnny slammed the barred door and turned the key in the lock. He withdrew the key.

Ward Reeder got up and came to the bars of his cell, grasping them with both his hands. He didn't speak, but his knuckles were white. He glowered at Slade for a long time before he said between clenched teeth, "You ain't turnin' out to be such a big man after all, are you, killer?"

Slade spat toward him viciously, then sat down on the bunk. Johnny went back to the office and closed the door.

Arch asked, "What happened?"

"He started cussin' me out in the saloon. He began to back away so he could start a gunfight but I grabbed him and roughed him up before he could. I guess we could charge him with creating a disturbance, couldn't we?"

"Sure. We can hold him until morning that way. Unless we decide to file a formal charge. If we do, we might make it last a week."

"Let's see what happens between now and tomorrow. Somehow or other, I don't think Slade is going to be in jail very long."

"What the hell are you talking about?"

"The town's beginning to get mad. Someone hollered at me to kill the son-of-a-bitch a while ago."

Arch frowned, but he didn't speak. Johnny rolled a cigarette with fingers that trembled slightly. He licked it and stuck it into his mouth. He lighted it, then sank down on the office cot.

The showdown had been postponed at least, he thought. Molly would be safe tonight. He got up suddenly. "I'd like to ride out to Molly's place and tell her Slade's in jail. She's probably worried sick."

"Sure, go ahead."

Johnny went out, untied his horse and mounted. He whirled the horse and galloped out of town, only slowing for the plank bridge that spanned the creek.

He held the horse to a steady lope all the way to Molly's place. He saw her come out and stand, her hand upraised to shield her eyes from the late afternoon sun. He pounded into the yard and swung, grinning, from his horse. "Slade's in jail. You can quit worrying, at least for tonight."

She stood there, frozen, staring at him almost uncomprehendingly. Then she lowered her hand and ran toward him.

He caught her in his arms. She was laughing and crying at the same time. He squeezed her, hard, then held her away, grinning.

"How did that happen, Johnny? What did he do?"

He told her swiftly all that had happened. As he did, a cloud seemed to cross her face. "How long can you keep him in jail?"

"Overnight."

"Then come out for supper, Johnny. I'll fix something special."

He nodded, studying her face, his own expression sober. Her thoughts were the same as his own in one respect, he realized. She knew, as he did, that he had only postponed the inevitable. And yet, he had given himself a respite by throwing Slade in jail. He had given her a respite too.

He said, "I'll go and stay at the jail until Arch has had supper. Then I'll come back."

She nodded. "I'll have it ready about seven."

He bent his head and kissed her thoroughly. He felt his blood begin to pound crazily. If she didn't marry him soon . . .

Her face was flushed as he released her and swung to the back of his horse. She met his glance, then glanced away.

He knew what was in Molly's mind, and suddenly he loved her more than he ever had before. She was going to let him stay out here with her tonight. She was afraid that tomorrow . . . that there might not be another night for them. Tonight was going to have to take the place of the lifetime together that they had planned.

The realization stirred wild excitement in him, and made him temporarily forget Slade Teplin altogether. But he did not forget him long. The town came into sight and he crossed the plank bridge below the railroad tracks. Suddenly Slade became an insoluble problem once more.

He dismounted in front of the jail and went inside. Slade and Ward Reeder were yelling at each other behind the closed door leading to the cells. He glanced at Arch. "How long has this been going on?"

"Ever since you left."

"Molly asked me for supper, Arch. Why don't you go ahead and eat? She said it wouldn't be ready until about seven."

Arch nodded. Johnny opened his mouth to ask Arch if he could have the rest of the evening off but he closed it without saying anything. He was suddenly embarrassed, knowing Arch would realize why he asked, would know exactly what was in the wind.

This was, actually, his night off anyway. He'd spent last night here at the jail. Last night had been his night to put the town to bed.

Arch took his hat off the coat-tree and went out. The shouting in the cells had stopped. Probably both Slade and Ward were out of breath, Johnny thought.

He sat down in Arch's swivel chair, frowning to himself. He couldn't rid himself of a strange uneasiness, a feeling that something was going to happen. He scoffed at the feeling. He didn't see what could happen now. Ward was in jail and so was Slade.

He got up and went to the window. The sun was low on the horizon and the whole street was shady from the buildings on the west side of Main, from the cottonwood trees beyond. A light breeze had sprung up and little puffs of cotton from the trees drifted lazily across the street.

Activity in the street was almost normal now. He wondered how Barney was. He wondered if Barney would be able to throw off the setback he'd had this morning. He knew that once a reformed drunk had a drink, he was usually back on the stuff again. He hoped it wouldn't be true of Barney. Barney had had enough trouble as it was.

He saw the two strangers he'd noticed earlier

come out of the Emporia and stand talking on the walk in front of it. Both of them were looking at the jail. After several moments they untied their horses and mounted. They rode down the street past the jail not looking at it until they drew abreast. Their stares were steady and appraising, but when they saw Johnny they looked away. They continued down the street to Regan's livery and turned in.

Johnny frowned. They were going to stay the night, he thought, and wondered why.

Disgustedly he turned away from the window. He was getting to be a regular old woman. Sure they'd stared at the jail. They'd been told Slade Teplin was here, and they were curious. Just like everybody else in town.

And why the hell shouldn't they stay the night if they wanted to? Drifters came through all the time, especially in the spring and fall, looking for work on the ranches that surrounded Cottonwood Springs for fifty miles in all directions.

These two didn't seem any different from the others that had come and gone over the past month or so. They certainly didn't look like Slade Teplin's kind, even though they did wear guns.

He returned to the window in time to see the pair come from Regan's and walk back up the street. They walked on the far side, and this time they only glanced disinterestedly at the jail. He watched them until they turned in at the hotel.

He turned away from the window, surprised at his own nervousness. He crossed the office, opened the door leading to the cells and glanced inside. Ward Reeder was sitting on his cot and so was Slade. Both of them looked at him, Ward resentfully, Slade with quiet virulence. Neither spoke.

For some reason, Johnny glanced at both cell windows, and wondered why he did. He closed the door and began to pace restlessly back and forth.

Hell, he was being stupid and ridiculous. Both cell windows were securely barred. The bars were set in stone. They'd have to be sawed through before either prisoner could escape.

He rolled another cigarette and forced himself to stand still while he smoked it. But he couldn't quiet his uneasiness. He couldn't calm his jumping nerves no matter how he tried.

Chapter 13

It was still not quite six o'clock. Johnny saw Arch go into the hotel. A few moments later, he saw John McCracken come out of the bank. McCracken locked the door and strode away toward home.

Tonight, the street seemed ordinary, neither busier nor less busy than usual. With Slade Teplin in jail, most of the curiosity seekers had disappeared.

Johnny turned away from the window, frowning faintly to himself. He couldn't entirely get rid of his uneasiness. Jailing Slade had been too easy, he supposed, to seem believable.

He crossed the room and picked up the shotgun Slade had dropped. He returned it to the rack. He headed for Arch's swivel chair, catching movement out of the corner of his eye as he did.

Two riders were passing the jail, coming from

the north end of town. He stared at them, his frown deepening.

Two more drifters, looking much like the first two had. And suddenly Johnny didn't believe in the coincidence of two pairs of them arriving by chance today.

He walked to the window and studied them carefully. One was about forty, he guessed, and the other was probably around twenty-five. Both were dressed in range clothes, dusty from the trail. Their shirts were rimmed with sweat at the armpits and down the back, its salt showing white against the dark blue of the shirts. Both had several days' growth of whiskers on their faces.

They passed, dismounted before the Emporia and disappeared inside.

Johnny got up quietly and crossed to the door at the rear of the office. He flung it open.

Slade was standing at the window of his cell, looking out. Ward Reeder was sitting on the edge of his bunk, staring disconsolately at the floor at his feet.

Johnny frowned, thinking of the two drifters that had just now passed and of the other two.

All four, he realized, were so ordinary, so average he would have difficulty in describing them. What the hell was he worrying about?

He closed the door, returned to the window and stared into the street. It was deserted now. Everyone had gone home for supper, or had gone into the hotel to eat.

Suddenly, from the direction of the deserted livery stable across from Regan's he heard a volley of shots. He burst through the door and stopped, listening, on the walk.

Another volley of shots racketed down there. Johnny began to run toward the sounds.

Halfway to the place he stopped and glanced back uneasily at the jail. He shouldn't leave with Slade locked up. . . .

He hesitated there in the middle of the street. Men were running out of the hotel and out of both saloons. They made an uncertain cluster in the street, their faces white and all turned this way.

Johnny thought he heard a shout back at the jail. He whirled and began to run.

He burst in through the open door, crossed the office and yanked open the door leading to the cells. He stopped instantly.

Ward Reeder was gone. The bars at his window had been literally torn out, as though by a giant hand.

Slade Teplin yelled, "You goddam stupid fool! Where were you? They hitched a team to those bars and just yanked 'em out. They . . ."

Johnny's gun was in his hand. He ran back, plunged through the door and rounded the corner at full speed. The team was still standing just below the window of the cell Reeder had occupied. But Ward was gone and so was the man who had brought the team.

Johnny cursed softly, disgustedly to himself. They'd had to draw him away from the jail so he wouldn't hear Slade's shouts or the noise of the bars breaking loose. One of Reeder's men had fired a couple of volleys over behind the deserted livery barn. As soon as Johnny ran that way, the other had hooked a chain to the bars. The whole thing hadn't taken more than two or three minutes at most.

He returned to the front of the jail. Arch was

coming down the street, his napkin still in his hand. Johnny said angrily, "They took me in like a damn schoolboy. A few shots over there to draw me away from the jail. And while I was gone, one of 'em hitched that team to the bars and yanked 'em out."

"And now Ward's loose."

"I'm sorry, Arch."

"For what? I'd have done exactly what you did. We're both on edge. Besides, I'd have turned Ward loose tomorrow anyway." He eyed Johnny a moment as though trying to evaluate his frame of mind. Then he said, "My supper's getting cold," turned and walked back toward the hotel.

Johnny went into the jail. He felt foolish for allowing Ward to escape. But he knew why Ward had escaped and what he would try to do. He'd kill Slade if he could, in any way he could, even by shooting him through the bars of his cell.

He paced back and forth, scowling to himself, puzzled at his growing uneasiness. It was as though he sensed something that was not readily apparent yet.

Slade was yelling for him, so he opened the door and looked through at the man. Slade said, "Do something, damn you. I'm a sitting duck in here. Reeder will be along any minute and shoot me through the window. That's why he had 'em break him out."

Johnny stared at him bleakly. "What would you suggest I do? Turn you loose so you can kill Reeder before he gets to you?"

"I don't care what you do."

Johnny shrugged. "Maybe you shouldn't have come back. Maybe I'd be doing the town a favor if I let Reeder kill you."

He slammed the door angrily. Supper with

Molly was out of the question now. So was taking the night off. He'd have to stay here all night.

He went outside into the street. He made a circle of the jail.

It stood by itself, surrounded by weed-grown vacant lots. The nearest building was twenty-five feet away. He wondered how and when Reeder would strike.

He returned to the front of the jail. It was ironic that he should be trying to keep Slade Teplin alive when more than anything else in the world, he wanted him dead.

Arch was coming toward him from the direction of the hotel. He was carrying a tray. Johnny held the door for him and Arch went inside. Johnny opened the cell door and Arch took the tray in to Slade. He came back out and Johnny re-locked the door. Arch said, "Go ahead and eat. I'll bring a chair back here. If Ward shows up at one of those windows he's going to get his head blown off."

"I can eat in town. I don't have to go out to Molly's place."

"Go ahead. Ward ain't a fool. And he knows we ain't fools."

Slade glanced up from his food. "Eat a hearty meal, deputy. It's the last of my wife's cookin' *you'll* ever eat."

Johnny glanced at him disgustedly. He wondered if he should tell Arch about the drifters. He decided not to say anything, for now at least. Chances were he was worrying unnecessarily. He guessed it had been just too easy, getting Slade in jail. He hadn't believed it would be that simple and he was worrying now to compensate.

Ward Reeder constituted no real threat. He wasn't going to fight either Johnny or Arch in order to kill Slade. He'd try getting to Slade, of course, but if they remained on guard . . .

And the four drifters were probably exactly what they seemed to be. He went outside and untied his horse. He mounted and rode around to the side of the jail. He picked up the team's halter ropes and led them toward Regan's Livery Barn.

Regan was sitting on a bench out front. Johnny asked, "These yours?"

Regan nodded, got up and took the halter ropes from Johnny's hand. "I didn't know—I didn't know what Ward was goin' to use 'em for."

"You're a liar, Phil. You knew damn well what he wanted 'em for." He stared coldly down at the man. "I wonder if Ward knows who it was that egged Cal on today."

Phil's face lost color. "I didn't . . . Ward wouldn't . . ."

"Don't count on it. If I were you, I'd stay out of sight tonight."

Phil looked physically sick. Johnny left him and rode past the railroad station.

He was thinking that Slade had been in Cottonwood Springs less than one whole day. He was thinking, too, that the day wasn't over yet.

As he clattered over the bridge, he thought of Barney, and wondered how he was. Then he kicked his horse into a lope and thundered toward Molly's place.

The sun was going down. It dipped its rim below the butte west of town, flaming pure gold and throwing visible golden rays upward into the sky. Johnny watched it sink. By the time he reached Molly's house it was beneath the horizon and the clouds above were flaming with its afterglow.

Molly came to the door and watched him approach. She had changed her dress. Her hair caught the gold color from the clouds.

Johnny dismounted. He grinned. "You're the prettiest thing I've seen today."

Her skin, already flushed from the stove inside, flushed even darker now. Johnny said, "I was going to clean up, but I didn't have time. Ward's two men broke him out of jail by hitching a team to the window bars."

Her face clouded and Johnny nodded unwillingly. "I'll have to eat and run. Arch and I will both have to stick around tonight."

"Why don't you just let Ward . . . ?" She didn't finish but Johnny knew what she had been going to say. She said, "I didn't mean that, I guess. I don't know."

He took her in his arms and kissed her on the mouth. The kiss, which he meant to have been light, grew long and when Johnny let her go he was all stirred up. He said, "Damn Ward anyway."

She smiled, but it was a wan smile that soon faded from her face. She said, "Come in, Johnny, and wash. I'll have it ready right away."

He went in, got some hot water from a teakettle on the stove and poured it into the washpan. He washed and dried his face and hands. He sat down at the table and watched her move around the kitchen.

But his thoughts were back in town. Several things puzzled him.

Slade's return was one of them. Plainly Slade hated the town bitterly and wanted to hurt it as much as he could. His action in getting his father drunk and then wrecking things at Barney's house gave substance to that theory. Cal had been an accident, Johnny supposed. Slade couldn't have planned or anticipated Cal's challenge earlier to-day.

Next, he had tried to pick a fight with Johnny himself. If he'd succeeded, he would have hurt Molly by killing Johnny off. Thus, he would have hurt the two closest to him as much as they could be hurt.

But what about the rest of the town? How did he plan to go about hurting all the rest of the people he hated here? How could one man hurt a whole town anyway? How could Slade ruin Cottonwood Springs the way he had ruined Barney, the way he would have ruined Molly if he'd succeeded in killing Johnny a while ago?

That was what puzzled him, because he didn't know. A man could burn a town, he supposed, but it wouldn't be easy to do. Cottonwood Springs was a good-sized place. There were close to four hundred people here.

And there were the four drifters. Where did they fit in? Or didn't they fit in at all?

Molly began to put food on the table. Fried chicken and cream gravy. Mashed potatoes, and a dish of early garden vegetables. He could smell an apple pie as she took it out and put it aside to cool.

He put thought of the town, of Slade and Ward, of the four strangers out of his mind. He smiled at Molly, across the table from him.

But a core of uneasiness lingered in his mind, and he unconsciously ate faster than was necessary.

Chapter 14

When Johnny left, Arch picked up a straight-backed chair and carried it through the door leading to the cells. He set it down next to the wall, then returned to the office for his pipe.

Returning, he sat down in the chair and tilted it comfortably against the wall. He glanced at Ward's window, and at Slade's, absently making sure he had a clear shot from here at both of them. Then he began to pack his pipe.

His movements were slow and deliberate. Slade glared at him. He finished packing the pipe and lighted it carefully. A cloud of smoke lifted into the upper half of the room.

Arch was thinking that what he'd told Johnny wasn't strictly accurate—not in its implications at least. True, Ward Reeder wasn't a fool. And he knew neither Arch nor Johnny was. But that didn't mean he wasn't going to try getting Slade, and Arch had implied it did.

Ward would come. Maybe he wasn't fool enough to try killing Slade through one of the jail windows but he'd figure something out.

Slade paced nervously back and forth. He kept glancing at the windows, one after the other. Once he said irritably, "Goddamn it, do we have to just sit here and wait?"

"What's the matter, you scared? Maybe if you get good and scared you'll know how all the men you've killed felt just before they died."

"They all had an even break."

"Oh sure. Like the one out in front of the Emporia years ago. The first one, in case you've forgotten him. You had your gun in your hand and he had to draw. You call that an even break?"

"That was different. That was the first one and I was just a kid."

Arch said conversationally, "I'm curious about something. What do you do when you get into an argument with someone you know is just as good as you, or maybe better?"

"We don't—" Slade stopped suddenly.

Arch smiled lazily. "Go ahead. Finish. You don't shoot it out with men like that, do you? Seems to me I can't ever remember two real fast gunmen shootin' it out with each other. Maybe they don't like the odds of taking on someone just as good as they are."

Slade was silent, frowning, obviously trying to recall one example of a gunfighter shooting it out with another of his kind.

Arch watched him speculatively for a long time. Slade's scowl deepened. Arch said finally, "So that makes it murder, doesn't it? It's just like a rigged poker game where you know you're going to win because you've stacked the cards."

"I always let the other guy draw first."

"Sure. Sure you do. You can afford to. Besides, it's smart. It gives you immunity from prosecution. But you know, every time who it is that's going to die. Like with Cal Reeder earlier today." An expression of disgust crossed Arch's hard old face. "Hell, I'd ought to let Ward Reeder have you. And I would if it wasn't for the fact that I'd have to arrest him for it."

"Watch the windows, old man, and stop shooting off your mouth."

"Yeah. Maybe I should at that. I wouldn't want anything to happen to you. You ain't through with us here in Cottonwood Springs yet. You've got your pa to drinking again and you've wrecked his place, but you haven't finished with Molly, have you? Or with Johnny Yoder for wanting to marry her. Who else did you come back to get, Slade?"

He stared steadily at Slade. Slade's eyes were murderous but he didn't reply.

Arch persisted, "Who? What's the matter, can't you talk?"

"Maybe you, old blabbermouth. Maybe you."

"I suppose you hate me because you had to carry supplies out of the store for me when you were a boy."

"Why not? There you'd sit, like you thought you was God, up on your wagon seat while I sweated gettin' your goddamn stuff loaded up. You're no different from the rest of the bastards in this town."

Arch peered at him. Slade's eyes were alive with hate. His face was twisted with it. Arch said mildly, "You think you're hurting us. But you're the one that's sufferin'. I wouldn't be you for all the money in the world."

Slade whirled and strode to the window. With his back to Arch, he stared angrily outside.

The sun was down, now, and cool shadow had crept across the town. A few high clouds, watching the sun's rays and reflecting it, threw a warm, red-gold light upon the town. It would be a hot summer, Arch thought. Probably a dry one too.

For some reason he did not himself understand, he began to think of his own early years. He'd come up from Texas with a trail herd immediately after the war. He'd like it here and so had stayed. He'd taken up a quarter section a dozen miles north of town and, over the years, had managed to acquire, by purchase, forty or fifty more from settlers who had thought they could raise farm crops on this land. The farm crops all dried up and the buffalo grass took over once again.

Those had been good years. The juices of youth had been strong in him. He wished, though, that he'd been able to have a son. But he'd had his wife; he'd had Faith, and she had been all any man could ask. Once, he remembered, he'd even considered taking Slade to raise. But he hadn't, and right now he couldn't remember what it had been that had made him decide against doing it.

Johnny Yoder was more like the son he would have wanted, he mused. And a sudden realization struck him. He thought of Johnny almost as if Johnny had been his son. He worried every time Johnny went out after someone and it wasn't the professional worry of a sheriff for his deputy.

He chuckled deep in his throat at his own blindness. He was an old fool, he guessed. He was a damned old fool.

And yet, he told himself, he hadn't tried to spare Johnny from any of the hazards of the job. He had only worried.

He heard the street door open, pushed his chair away from the wall and stood up. He drew his gun and with it in his hand, opened the door leading to the office. He went through it, closing it behind him.

Les Isaacs and Willy Hogg were standing by the outside door. Both looked a little scared, but there was something determined about them too. Arch asked, "What do you two want?"

He had an uneasy feeling, suddenly, and knew

he had to get rid of this pair quickly so that he could return to the cells and guard Slade.

Neither of the two answered him immediately and he barked, "Damn it, what do you want?"

They split, one going to the right, the other to the left. They moved casually, making it seem as though one was heading for the office couch, the other for a chair.

Arch took a backward step. Suddenly both Les and Willy had guns in their hands. Les's voice was sharper than Arch had ever heard it be. "Stick it in the holster, Arch, and sit down someplace."

Arch experienced a sudden feeling of relief, one he was ashamed of instantly. It would be so easy to let them hold him here. He would have a perfect alibi. Soon he'd hear a shot out back, or two or three, and after waiting a couple of minutes Les and Willy would go. He'd go back to the cells and Slade Teplin would be dead.

Johnny would be safe from Teplin's deadly gun. He'd be free to marry Molly. Barney would quit the liquor again and the town would go on as it had before. All Arch Schilling had to do was let Les and Willy hold him here. For two or three minutes at most.

No one would blame him, he thought. In fact everyone would probably be relieved.

Everyone except Ward, he thought suddenly. Ward would be the one who paid. Ward would go to trial and while no jury here would hang him, he'd at least spend a good long time in prison.

He still had his gun in his hand. He lowered it but he did not holster it. He said, "I'm going to turn my back and go through that door. I don't figure either one of you has got the stomach to shoot me in the back. But if you do, just go ahead."

Les said sharply, "Arch, goddamn it . . . !"

Arch looked at him. Les said, "He's a dirty, stinking killer, Arch! Why the hell are you so set on protecting him?"

"Slade?" Arch looked at Les in amazement. "I ain't protecting Slade. I'm thinkin' about Ward right now. Ward will get ten years for this at the very least."

He turned his back deliberately, careful to make no sudden movements that might be misconstrued. His back, at one spot in the center of it, ached suddenly. He reached out a hand for the doorknob.

Les barked, "Arch, damn you, I'll shoot!"

Arch grasped the knob. He opened the door and stepped on through.

He glanced first at Slade's window, then at the other from which the bars had been torn earlier. Then he leaned back against the door.

He felt weak. His knees trembled and he was sweating heavily. His chest felt as though there was a cake of ice in it.

He said, "Slade, get over under the window and lie down against the wall."

Slade looked at him, then suddenly dived for the window. He flopped on the floor and rolled against the wall.

Arch smiled grimly. Slade was no different from others of his kind. He could kill with icy calm as long as he knew what the outcome was going to be. But let him face death unarmed and that icy calm evaporated like dew before the rays of the morning sun.

Arch kept switching his glance back and forth, from one window to the other. Chances were, he thought, that Ward would appear at the window of what had formerly been his cell. There would be no bars there. And it commanded a good view of Slade's cell.

Arch yelled, "Ward! Don't do it because I'm waiting for you!"

There was only silence outside. Arch glanced at Slade and said contemptuously, "How does it feel, killer?"

Slade growled, "If I had a gun . . ."

"But you don't. And neither did Cal, really. He'd just as well have grabbed his tobacco for all the good it did him."

Slade didn't reply. Arch said, "I'm going to turn you loose tomorrow morning, Slade. I'm going to escort you down to the railroad station and put you on the train—without your gun. If you come back, I'm warning you, it's open season. I'll shoot you on sight and so will my deputy."

"You can't . . . I haven't broken any of your goddamn laws."

"Get an injunction then. But until you do, stay out of Cottonwood Springs."

He heard a movement in the weeds outside the window of the cell Ward Reeder had occupied. He yelled, "Ward! Don't!"

He saw Reeder's face at the window, saw the blue barrel of Ward's gun. He fired instantly, not at Ward but at the wall beside Ward's face. The bullet rang against the stone wall like a blacksmith's hammer against an anvil. Almost instantaneously it rang again, against one of the bars on the other side of the room.

Ward swung his glance from Slade to Arch. His gun swung too. Arch yelled, "Ward! Damn it . . . !"

The gun belched flame and smoke. Something hit Arch in the chest, driving him back like the angry kick of a mule. He slammed into the chair he had just left, overturned it and fell on top of it.

Ward Reeder's face disappeared. Arch felt a numbness in his chest. He brought up a hand and felt the warmth and stickiness of blood.

He'd been shot before, but never this bad, he realized. And to get it defending a son-of-a-bitch like Slade. . . .

He tried to get up, but he could not. Still holding his gun, he crawled toward the door.

He'd closed it a few moments before, he remembered now. Somehow he had to reach high enough to turn the knob. . . .

He pulled himself as close to the door as he could. His head was reeling and clouds were forming before his eyes.

Straining, grunting softly with exertion, he reached up and turned the knob. He fell back down and moved aside enough to pull the door open. Laboriously, he crawled on through.

He crawled, inch by inch toward the outside door. Pain came now to his chest, pain worse than anything he had ever known before.

He supposed that this was it, for him. He was going to die. Damn few men made it with a bullet in the chest.

But he hung on angrily, waiting for someone to come. He couldn't give up now. Not while Slade Teplin was alive. Not until he knew for sure that Johnny Yoder was safe from him.

Chapter 15

Johnny reached the outskirts of town in the last, cool light of dusk. He had not been gone very long, he realized. He had practically bolted his food.

He could see the length of Main and the crowd spread out in front of the Ace-High and the Emporia. He muttered, "Good God, what now?"

The crowd was static, silent. It was a fearful crowd, he thought, and all faces were turned in his direction.

As he went past Regan's livery, Phil Regan called, "There were some shots in the jail a few minutes ago, Johnny. I don't know . . ."

Johnny didn't hear the last few words. He touched heels to his horse's sides, forcing him to gallop, and swung to the ground in front of the jail.

The horse stopped and stood, reins dragging on the ground, while Johnny crossed the walk at a run.

Gun in hand, he burst in through the door. The first thing he saw was Arch Schilling, lying on the floor, and the second was the blood, drenching Arch's shirt-front and pooling beneath his chest.

He ran to the rear door and flung it open. He plunged through, gun ready, hammer back.

Slade was lying on the floor against the wall staring at the window from which the bars had been yanked earlier. Johnny whirled, holstering his gun. He returned to the office, crossed to Arch and knelt at his side.

His throat felt closed and tight and it was hard for him to breathe. He said, "Arch . . ."

Arch groaned slightly and stirred, but he did not open his eyes.

Johnny got up, crossed to the open front door and stepped outside. He stared toward the crowd up in front of the town's two saloons and roared, "Get Doc Allen, someone, and get him fast! It's Arch!"

He waited until he saw one man run toward Doc's office, another toward his house. Then he went back inside.

He crossed to the door leading to the rear and removed the hinge pins from it. He carried it to Arch and laid it down beside him. Arch would have to be moved, either to Doc's house or to his office, and the safest way to move a badly wounded man was on a door.

Now he paced back and forth helplessly. He had no experience with serious wounds and he didn't know what to do. He kept going to the front door and looking out and finally, as the last gray light of dusk faded from the sky, he saw Doc running toward him, carrying his bag, paced by one of the men who had gone to fetch him earlier.

He hurriedly lighted both lamps and set them on a table so that their light would shine on Arch. Doc came in and the other man followed, to stop and stand beside the door, eyes wide, face white. Doc knelt beside Arch and cut away his shirt-front to expose the wound. He studied it for a moment or two.

Doc was a short man, thick-set and growing heavier in his advancing years. His face was incredibly ugly, Johnny thought as he watched it in the faint lamplight, but it had neither coldness nor hardness in it. It was as soft as a woman's face if

you could manage to look past its ugliness. Now
Doc turned his ponderous head and looked up.

"You two lift him carefully onto that door.
Bring him to my house."

With Doc's help and that of the other man,
Johnny got Arch Shilling's body onto the door.
Then, Johnny and the other man lifted it and carried it out the door. Johnny heard Slade yelling
something as he went out, but paid no attention to
it.

It was obvious to him that Slade was scared.
And if Slade was scared, it meant he didn't have a
gun with which to defend himself. If he was still
unarmed, then someone else had to have shot Arch.
That someone could only be Ward Reeder or one
of his two men.

Doc's house was three blocks from the jail. As
they moved along the street, other men came from
the shadows and helped to carry the door. By the
time they reached Doc's place, seven men were
carrying it.

Doc supervised them as they carried it inside. He
had Arch placed on his big dining-room table. A
couple of men carried out the door, on which there
was a pool of blood.

Doc curtly directed his wife to light all the lamps
she could find. He turned and looked at Johnny
irritably, yet with compassion too. "Get out of
here and do your job. I'll do mine."

"Will he . . . ? When . . . ?"

"I'll send someone to tell you how he is when I
get through with him. Now git!"

Johnny went out. He stood on the porch of Doc's
house for several moments, long enough to roll and
light a cigarette. If he hadn't gone out to Molly's
for supper tonight . . .

He shook his head angrily. He couldn't have anticipated that Ward would be fool enough to shoot Arch. And Arch had told him to go. Even if he'd only gone to the hotel, it wouldn't have changed anything.

Slade! He'd been in town a single day and already one man was dead, another near to death, another facing a stiff term in prison if he was caught. And Slade sat it out in the jail, charged with nothing, free to leave town tomorrow if he chose.

The other men who had helped carry Arch stood in the darkness of Doc's lawn silently. There was a fragrance in the air—from blossoming lilacs somewhere nearby. One of the men asked, "Is he . . . ? Will Arch be all right?"

Johnny swung around irritably. "How the hell should I know? He's shot in the chest and damn few men . . ." He stopped suddenly. In a softer tone he said, "I'm sorry."

"Hell, forget it. We all know how you feel about Arch."

Johnny stepped down on the porch and walked away into the darkness. Behind him, he could hear them talking in lowered tones.

He felt like kicking something and he was scared. Scared that when Doc did send someone, it would be to tell him Arch was dead.

He reached Main. Lights glowed in the windows of both saloons and in the hotel. The rest of the street was dark.

He went into the Emporia and looked around. He didn't see Ward Reeder, or Willy or Les. He stopped just inside the door and yelled, "Did anybody see anything down at the jail just before you heard the shots?"

The buzz of talk quieted. There were a couple of men who seemed to be avoiding Johnny's eyes. Johnny crossed to them and said, "You two. What did you see?"

"It might not mean anything——"

"Damn you, what?"

"Well, we saw Les and Willy go in the jail before we heard the shots."

Johnny nodded. "Thanks." He turned and went back outside. Frowning, he walked toward the jail.

No one else would have reason for shooting Arch, he thought. No one else but Ward. If someone had tried breaking Slade out, Slade would have had a gun. Or he'd have been free. Only Ward Reeder would have panicked after shooting Arch. Only Ward would have panicked enough to run away.

He reached the jail and went inside. The two lamps were still burning on the table. From out back, Slade yelled. "That you, deputy?"

"Uh-huh." It occurred to Johnny that Slade must have been an eyewitness to Arch's shooting. He called, "You see the man that shot Arch?"

"Sure. It was Reeder. He was tryin' to get me."

A couple of men came in, carrying the door. The bloodstain had been wiped up but it still showed plainly. Johnny took the door from them, hung it and replaced the hinge pins in it. He closed it, leaving Slade in darkness. Slade was reasonably safe, he knew, as long as it was dark back there. The two men went away, subdued and silent.

Johnny sat down in the swivel chair and rolled a cigarette. He was alone now. Arch, even if he lived, would be laid up for weeks.

He thought of the four drifters again. He hadn't

seen them in the crowd that had collected down here when they carried Arch out. He hadn't seen them in the Emporia or on the street. Not that their absence meant anything. Yet it bothered him, making a small stir of uneasiness in the back of his mind.

He finished his cigarette and threw the stub into the spittoon. He got up and paced uneasily back and forth. He kept thinking of Arch, how strong, how solid, how durable and tough the old man was. It seemed incredible to him that Arch now lay, pale and weak and unconscious, on Doc's dining-room table.

He walked back and opened the door leading to the cells. "I'm going out. I'll lock up. You'll be all right."

"With Reeder still loose? He can get in that window just as easy as he got out. He can shoot until he gets me."

Johnny said, "Right now I don't give a damn whether he does or not. I'm going to go see how Arch is getting along."

He slammed the door. He picked up the cell keys from the desk and put them in his pocket. He went out, locking the outside door behind him.

For a moment he stood there, his back to the door, feeling the cool night air stirring against his face. Even here, where the smells were of stable and saloon, the air still held a hint of lilac. The damn things must be blooming all over town.

The lilac made him think of Molly and thinking of her made him realize that nothing had been solved. Slade would still go free tomorrow. He would have to face Slade then, on the killer's own terms. He didn't see how that could be avoided.

He found himself wishing that Ward *would* get

to Slade while he was gone. Maybe that was why he was leaving, he thought sourly. Maybe he was, unconsciously or deliberately, giving Ward his chance.

He almost turned back. Then, shrugging, he walked quickly toward Doc's house.

The lamps were burning brightly in Doc's dining room. Johnny walked around to the side of the house and stared in the window.

Arch's body was still stretched out on the table. Doc's wife was holding a lamp high while Doc bent over Arch's chest. There was blood on Doc's hands and on the instrument he held in one of them. As Johnny watched he turned and released the bullet to fall upon the floor.

He left the room, apparently to wash his hands because in a couple of minutes he returned, his hands now clean. He put a thick, folded compress on Arch's chest, then began to bandage him while his wife helped.

Johnny went around to the front of the house. He knocked, then went inside. "Can I help you move him to a bed?"

"I thought you'd gone."

"I came back. How is he, Doc? Is he going to make it all right?"

"He's got a chance. The bullet missed his lungs and heart. And he's pretty tough for a man his age."

"How soon . . . ?"

"Will I know?" Doc peered up at Johnny wearily. "A couple of hours will tell how he took the shock of getting the bullet out. If he gets over that all right, and if nothing unexpected comes up, then he'll probably live."

Johnny helped Doc Allen carry Arch to a bedroom and settle him in a bed. Leaving, he said, "I'll come back after a while."

"Yeah, Johnny. Do that. I'll stay with him until I'm sure he's going to make it through the night."

Johnny walked slowly toward the jail. Ward had probably ridden back out to his ranch, he thought, but he'd check until he had made sure.

Suddenly, in spite of himself, in spite of what Ward Reeder had done to Arch, he felt sorry for the man. Ward had lost his son and now had committed a felony. And the man who had killed Ward's son was still alive.

Chapter 16

Johnny walked back to Main and, quickly, along the near side of the jail. He crossed the street and unlocked the door. He lighted a lamp then walked to the rear door, opened it and called, "You all right?"

Slade only grunted sourly.

Johnny closed the door. Had his prisoner been anyone but Slade, he would probably have felt sorry for him. Slade was certainly a sitting duck, vulnerable to Ward's attempts to kill him, yet unable to defend himself.

He took time to roll a cigarette and light it. He frowned to himself. He hated to leave the jail again, to leave Slade unguarded, but he didn't see that he had much choice. Ward had shot Arch and if the sheriff died would have to stand trial for killing him. Furthermore, Ward Reeder was dangerous. He was desperate; he was tortured now by two things, guilt over the fact that he had shot Arch and the unavenged death of his son. There was no predicting what he might do next. The safest place for Ward was in jail. Only this time he'd go into one of the cells at the far rear of the jail, the ones that had no windows in them.

He blew out the lamp and went outside. He locked the door, then walked uptown toward the Emporia.

There was a crowd in the Emporia, but it was a shocked and subdued crowd. Johnny paused for a moment just inside the doors, looking the room over for Ward Reeder or either of his men. Then he crossed to the bar.

Sam drew a beer and brought it to him. Johnny asked, "Seen Ward, or Les, or Willy?"

"Not since Arch was shot. How is he, Johnny? Somebody said he'd been shot in the chest. Is he going to . . . ?"

"Doc can't tell yet. He got the bullet out, but Arch lost a lot of blood. Doc won't know anything for a couple of hours. He said by then he'd know how Arch took the shock of getting the bullet out."

Sam nodded. Johnny gulped the beer. He saw the girl who had come in on the train with Slade talking to a couple of men at a corner table. "You hire her?"

Sam nodded.

"Think she knows Slade?"

Sam shrugged. "I didn't ask her that."

Johnny finished his beer and crossed the room. He said, "I see you got a job."

The girl smiled. The two with her, cowhands from a ranch twenty miles south of town, looked up at Johnny neutrally.

He pulled out a chair and straddled it, leaning

his arms on the back. He watched the girl's face closely as he asked, "Do you know Slade Teplin?"

She shook her head, but did not meet his eyes and he knew that she had lied. He asked, "What's your name?"

She was a little paler now, and her eyes were scared. "Rose. Rose Malloy."

Johnny said, "I'm glad you don't know Slade. Knowing him could be dangerous."

She didn't reply. The two cowhands were staring at Johnny impatiently. He rose, nodded briefly and walked away. He went out and turned up the street toward the Ace-High. He stared into the darkness of the passageway between the two saloons as he passed it, but he saw nothing there.

He went into the Ace-High, stopping just inside the doors as he had at the Emporia. He turned and left when he failed to find Ward or either of his men.

He started toward the hotel, but stopped when a voice called out, "Johnny! Wait a minute. I want to talk to you."

He turned and waited. John McCracken had come out of the Ace-High and was now hurrying along the walk toward him.

McCracken stopped. "How's Arch?"

"He was shot in the chest. Doc got the bullet out and Arch is still alive. That's all I know for now."

"He should have let Ward kill the son-of-a-bitch."

"You don't mean that. Ward would have gone to prison for it. That's what Arch was trying to prevent."

"Maybe I didn't mean that. I guess I didn't. But it seems to me there ought to be something . . . I mean it doesn't seem right that a killer like Slade can come here and wreck people's lives the way he has."

Johnny asked, "Have you seen Barney lately?"

McCracken shook his head.

Johnny said, "Why don't you go see him then? Along about now I'd bet he could use some shoring up. Are you going to fire him for getting drunk?"

McCracken hesitated, then said almost reluctantly, "I don't suppose so, as long as he doesn't get like he used to be."

"Then why not go tell him so?"

"Maybe I will. By God, maybe I will. It's a good idea." He turned and crossed the street. Halfway across he called back, "Thanks, Johnny."

Johnny turned in at the hotel. He crossed the whitetile lobby floor to the desk. Alf Holloway asked him about Arch, and Johnny gave him the same reply he'd given McCracken a few minutes before. Then he asked, "Which room has Ward Reeder got?"

"Seven. But he ain't—"

"Give me the key."

Alf shoved the key across the desk. Johnny took it and headed for the stairs.

In front of number seven he stopped. Carefully, he put his ear against the door panel. Then he knocked loudly.

He heard no sound inside—no sound at all. He inserted the key, turned it, then flung the door open with his left hand while with his right he drew his gun and thumbed the hammer back.

The room was dark. Johnny stepped inside, struck a match and looked around. The room was empty, but the bed was mussed as though someone had laid on it.

He went back out and re-locked the door. Down in the lobby, he returned the key to Holloway. "If he comes in, you send someone to let me know. Understand?"

Alf nodded. Johnny crossed to the door and went outside again. He had looked all the obvious places for Ward. Alone, he couldn't comb the town. The best plan would be to wait for Ward down at the jail. Either Reeder had been so shocked after shooting Arch that he'd gone home to his ranch or else he'd try for Slade again.

He walked slowly along the street toward the jail. He couldn't help thinking of Molly and wondering how she was taking the suspense. He doubted if she'd stay out on Cottonwood Creek all night. She'd probably come in and stay with friends in town. Or take a room at the hotel.

On impulse, he whirled and returned to the hotel. He crossed the lobby to the desk. "I saw four strangers in town today. Dirfters. Cowhands maybe. Did they take rooms here?"

Holloway shook his head. "I got no strangers registered."

Johnny nodded, turned and went back outside. He was frowning as he walked hurriedly toward the jail. There was a connection, he told himself, between Slade Teplin and the four strangers who had ridden in today. There was a connection someplace if he could only figure out what it was.

He reached the jail, unlocked the door and went inside. He lighted a lamp and trimmed the wick. He opened the door leading to the cells.

The shot was almost deafening. A shower of splinters flew from the doorjamb beside Johnny's

head. Half a dozen of them penetrated the skin of
his face and one narrowly missed his eye. He flung
himself back instantly, slamming the door as he
did.

A second shot, muffled by the closed door, came
closely on the heels of the first. This bullet tore a
hole in the door-panel, chest high.

Ruefully, Johnny raised a hand and began to remove the splinters from his face. Slade Teplin had
a gun. Or else Ward had returned and was now inside the cell he had formerly occupied.

Johnny yelled, "Slade?"

"Yeah. It's me, deputy. Who did you think it was?"

Someone had gotten a gun to him. The girl, Rose
Malloy, knew him but she was with those two cowhands up at the Emporia. It had to have been one
of the four drifters, Johnny thought. No one who
lived in town would give Slade Teplin the time of
day.

He stared uneasily into the darkness outside the
office window. He resisted an impulse to go blow out
the lamp. He suddenly wished that Arch was here.
Because Slade Teplin was not alone in town. At least
two of those drifters knew him and quite possibly
all four of them did.

He ought to swear in some deputies, he thought.
But he knew he'd have a hard time getting them.

In the first place, no one would serve as a deputy in order to protect Slade's life from Ward. Nor
would their willingness to serve be increased by the
knowledge that Slade had a gun.

But there was another cause for his reluctance,
another reason even better than those two. He didn't
want the town to think he couldn't handle the situation by himself. He didn't want anyone saying he
was afraid of Slade.

And that was exactly what they would say if he asked for help. He had no proof the four drifters had any connection with Slade. He had no proof that Slade intended to break out of jail. Phil Regan might have slipped that gun to him simply because Phil was a troublemaker. Phil had egged Cal on earlier today. He wasn't above slipping a gun to Slade tonight.

He rolled a cigarette, sat down and put his feet up on the desk. He tried to relax his muscles but they remained tight-drawn and tense as a fiddle-string. If Ward came after Slade tonight, then Ward would get himself killed.

He got up and walked to the window. He began to pace nervously back and forth. On impulse, he blew out the lamp and opened the outside door.

Instantly a gun flared across the street. The glass beside Johnny shattered as the bullet struck.

He ducked back inside, slamming and locking the door. He stared across the street, trying to see the man who had shot at him.

Either the man was a damn poor shot or else he hadn't even tried to score a hit. Johnny was inclined to believe the latter theory.

They wanted him pinned down in here. They had him fixed so he could neither go outside nor go back to the cells where Slade was confined.

But why? What did they hope to accomplish? Until a few moments before, Slade had been confined only on a simple disturbance charge.

One thing seemed fairly sure. Slade wanted him dead but he wanted to do the killing himself. Else the man across the street would have killed him a minute or two before. There had been enough light in the street for that and he must have been silhouetted against the door.

It was a stand-off, then, for now. Johnny crossed the dark office and took a double-barreled ten gauge down from the rack. He loaded it, and took a handful of ten-gauge shells loaded with buckshot from a drawer of the desk.

He sat down on the office couch. The initiative belonged to Slade and all he could do was wait.

Slade's friends could do one of two things. They could get a team from the stable and yank the bars of Slade's cell out, the way Ward's two hired men had done. Or they could come through here, kill him and get the keys from him.

But why? For God's sake why? Slade would have been released tomorrow. Johnny scowled angrily in the darkness. He'd know what Slade's plan was before very long. If they didn't get him first.

Chapter 17

Molly stood at the kitchen doorway and watched Johnny ride away. She remained there, staring into the darkness long after he had gone, long after the sounds of his horse's hoofs had died away.

Turning, she began to pick up the dishes from the table. Her hands trembled violently and twice she almost dropped a stack of dishes. At last she gave up and sat down in one of the kitchen chairs. Tears filled her eyes and ran silently across her cheeks.

She had been wrong, she realized now. She should have divorced Slade long ago, when Johnny first asked her to marry him. Perhaps if she had . . .

Then she realized it would have changed nothing even if she had. Slade would still have returned eventually. He would have killed Johnny. Things would have been no different than they were right now.

Except for one thing. She would have been married to Johnny for a while. They would have had each other for that time, at least.

She got up hurriedly, washed the dishes and put them away. She got a light coat and put it on. She picked up a lantern, set it on the table and lighted it. She turned toward the door. She wasn't going to spend the night out here. She was going to town, where at least she would be near Johnny and know what was happening to him.

She heard a horse's hoofs approaching rapidly. She went to the door, expecting to see Johnny returning.

But it was not Johnny. It was a man she had never seen before. He dismounted in front of the kitchen door and asked, "Are you Molly Teplin, ma'am?"

"Yes. What is it?"

"I . . . I'm afraid I've got bad news for you."

Something cold, like an icy hand, closed around Molly's heart.

She forced herself to be calm. She asked, "What bad news? What's happened?"

"It's that deputy—Yoder, ma'am. He's been shot. The saloon-keeper asked me to ride out and tell you that."

"Shot . . . ! How bad . . . ?"

"I don't know, ma'am. I left right after it happened. Want me to help you hitch up your buggy horse?"

"Yes, please . . . if you would." She picked

up the lantern, blew out the lamp and hurried out the door. She ran across the yard, the man striding along behind her, leading his horse.

She held the lantern while he led out the buggy horse and harnessed him. It seemed to take an eternity. The coldness inside her body had spread until she was cold all over. Johnny was dead, her mind kept telling her. It was over, because Johnny was dead. Slade had shot him and Slade never missed.

Numbly she climbed into the buggy. Numbly she handed the reins to the man, who had tied his saddle horse on behind. She said, "Hurry! Please hurry!"

He yelled at the buggy horse and slapped his back with the reins. The horse trotted away. The man kept yelling at him until he broke into a rocking lope.

Molly turned her head. "How did it happen? Who shot him?"

"I don't know who it was, ma'am. I didn't see it."

"Where did it happen?"

"In front of the saloon. I just rode up and the saloon-keeper yelled at me to ride out here. Maybe he's all right, ma'am. Maybe he ain't hurt bad at all."

Molly's lips formed the words of a prayer—that Johnny was alive—that he was not badly hurt. She cried, "Can't we go faster?"

"This horse, he won't go much faster, ma'am."

Shivering, Molly huddled in the corner of the buggy. She saw the town's lights, and heard the thunder of the horse's hoofs crossing the plank bridge. They rattled across the railroad tracks, then turned abruptly west. She screamed, "Where are we going? The saloons are on Main Street!"

"You never mind, ma'am. I know what I'm doing."

She tried to wrest the reins from him but he shoved her back into the corner of the buggy. She tried to jump out, but he caught her arm in a powerful hand and held it. His fingers bit into her flesh cruelly.

For an instant she sat there frozen, overcome with a wild and sudden joy. He was not taking her to the saloon where he said Johnny had been shot. He was taking her someplace else, perhaps to Slade, and if part of his story was a lie, perhaps the rest of it was also a lie. Johnny might not have been shot at all.

Almost immediately, however, she was touched with fear. Wherever he was taking her, Slade would be waiting. And if Slade had ordered her brought to him it could only be for one reason. She was to be the bait in Slade's trap. Johnny was still alive, but she was to be the means by which Slade killed him.

The buggy drew to a halt in front of a small one-room shack. There was a rotting picket fence around the place and the yard was overgrown with weeds. No one had lived here for a couple of years, she knew. The house was deserted, its windows broken, its doors hanging open.

The man got out of the buggy without releasing her arm. He dragged her from the buggy after him. He said, "Come on, ma'am. Don't make no trouble now."

Molly opened her mouth to scream. The man's hand clamped over it, stifling the scream. She bit his hand savagely.

He yanked his hand away with an angry curse. He cuffed her on the side of the head, hard enough to make her senses reel. He dragged her into the house and kicked the door shut behind him.

She struggled violently, scratching, kicking, biting. He hit her again, this time with his fist.

She slumped, only half conscious, and he dragged her to a chair. He tied her to it with a coarse, rough-feeling lariat. He tied a bandanna around her mouth. By the time her senses had fully returned she was helpless, unable to cry out, unable to move.

The man rolled a cigarette and lighted it. He said, "Now we'll wait. We'll just relax and wait for Slade."

Occasionally, Johnny went to the window and stared across the street. His eyes were now accustomed to the darkness and he could make out the shadowy form of a man at the corner of a store building over there. He debated trying to shoot the man but gave up the idea because he knew he would be unable to see his sights.

He paced back and forth disgustedly. They certainly had him in a bind, he thought. He could go out, of course, and take a chance that the man would miss. But what could he do, even if he did get out? There were four of them.

No, he thought, his best chance lay in staying here, in forcing them to come to him. If they came in, he'd have a slight advantage over them. They'd be visible in the faint starlight in the street; he'd be hidden in the darkness here.

He heard voices from the cell block at the rear. A moment later he heard the sound of metal clanging against metal.

He charged toward the door and flung it open. He fired at the window of Slade's cell and heard the bullet ricochet and whine away into the night.

Instantly, a gun there in the cell opened up. A bullet clanged against one of the bars. A second buzzed past Johnny's ear like an angry bee.

He flung himself aside. He heard a man shout outside the jail and heard the rending sounds as the bars tore loose.

He poked his head around the doorjamb and fired again, ducking back to avoid the instant barrage that followed. He was glad this wall was brick. At least the bullets couldn't penetrate.

The air was now choked with powdersmoke. Bullets clanged regularly against the bars, or buzzed through the door, shattering the windows in the front of the office, thudding into the furniture, floor and walls.

And then, suddenly, all was quiet. Johnny leaped through the door, gun in hand, hammer back.

The cells were empty. Slade Teplin was gone.

Johnny unlocked Slade's cell and went inside. He stared out the high window.

He could see the team standing there, their tugs still hitched to the chain that had been secured to the bars. But he saw nothing else.

Frowning, he returned to the office, went to the window and stared across the street. The shadowy figure was gone.

What in the hell did Slade have in mind, he wondered sourly. What was he up to now?

His immediate inclination was to leave the jail, round up some townsmen and arm them, then search the town for Slade. He did not understand his own reluctance to do so. Instead, he continued his pacing, scowling, trying to make sense out of this seemingly senseless jail break.

Slade hadn't had to get himself broken out of jail. He'd have been released in the morning anyway. It followed, therefore, that Slade had something he wanted to do tonight—something that wouldn't wait for tomorrow.

He crossed to the door and slowly, silently opened it. He retreated to the rear wall and stood there, the loaded ten gauge in his hands.

He didn't know how he knew, but he did. They would come to him. He was part of their plans, whatever those plans might be. Slade was crazy with hatred and the thirst for revenge. And Johnny was now number one on Slade's list because he was the one who had taken Slade's wife away from him.

The minutes dragged endlessly. Faintly, Johnny could hear the excited talk uptown. They had heard the shots, he realized. But they wouldn't help. They'd figure this was his job. None of the townsmen were fighting men. They just simply didn't know what to do.

And it was his job. Now that Arch had been shot, it was Johnny's job.

He wondered how Arch was. Doc ought to know by now whether Arch was going to make it or not. He wished he could leave and go to Doc's house. He wished he could find out.

He heard a scuffing sound outside at the corner of the jail. He held his breath for a moment and froze exactly where he was. He stared through the shattered windows into the starlit street.

"Deputy." It was a voice he had never heard before, calling softly from the corner of the building outside. He did not reply.

"Hey, deputy. I got something to tell you."

Still Johnny did not reply. His breathing was slow, quiet, controlled, but his hands were shaking as they gripped the shotgun stock.

He saw the man's head as he peered into the window. He saw the man's form cautiously emerge from concealment and approach the door.

He laid the shotgun down carefully on the floor. The man would be coming in through the door in another minute. He could shoot him, but he wanted him alive. He wanted to know exactly what Slade was planning now.

The man came through the door. He had a gun in his hand and he tried to peer into the corners of the room, tried to pierce the darkness with his glance. He came as far as the center of the room and whispered, "Deputy? You here?"

Johnny's muscles were tense. He was crouched, silent, ready. The man turned back toward the door.

And Johnny launched himself. He plunged across the room like a great, silent beast of prey.

Chapter 18

At the first sound from behind, the man whirled. Before he could line his gun, before he could fire, Johnny struck him with the point of his shoulder in the chest.

He was flung back helplessly. He crashed into the unbroken window on the left side of the door, shattering it.

Johnny was on him like a wolf, grappling for his throat. The man rolled among the broken shards of glass from the window, and brought up a savage knee that caught Johnny in the groin.

Johnny's hands closed around his throat. Both hands and throat were bloody from glass cuts and it was like trying to clutch a greased pig. The man thrashed violently. Johnny released his throat and smashed his fist into the stranger's face.

He straddled the man, trying to ignore the fiery pain in his groin and lower abdomen. His fists smashed methodically into the man's face.

The man still held his gun. He rammed it against Johnny's side.

Johnny groped for it frantically. His hand closed over the cylinder just as the hammer fell.

It fell on the loose skin between his thumb and forefinger, cutting through, causing such a sharp pain that Johnny grunted involuntarily. But the gun did not fire. Johnny wrenched it away and batted the man on the side of the head with it.

It struck only a glancing blow. The man arched his body convulsively, flinging Johnny off and to one side. He scrambled to his feet and staggered toward the door.

Johnny plunged after him, the gun still hanging from his hand. He caught the man's ankles in a flying dive and brought him crashing down, inches short of the door. The man brought both legs up close to him and kicked out violently with both feet.

One foot caught Johnny squarely in the face. The heel took him on the chin, the sole squarely on the nose. He could feel the warmth of blood spurting from it.

The kick stunned him briefly, but he groped until he had regained his grip. The man sat up and began to flail Johnny with his fists. Johnny released his ankles and swung wildly with the hand in which the gun still hung.

He missed and the gunhammer tore through the flesh of his hand. The gun skidded across the room. The man turned and scrambled after it.

Johnny plunged after him. He landed on the man's back while his hand was still inches short of the gun. He seized the man's hair and began to slam his head methodically against the glass-strewn floor. But his hands were so bloody and slick that he lost his grip.

He fought with a single-minded concentration that excluded all else from his consciousness. He had been all but helpless since Slade Teplin had come in on the train. Now his frustration was coming out. He was hurt and bloody and had little to gain from this. But he was enjoying it as he had enjoyed nothing since he had jumped Slade earlier in the Emporia. He was revenging Arch, who would not have been shot had it not been for Slade. He was revenging Molly for the anguish she had felt all day. And he was revenging himself.

The stranger broke away, got up and plunged toward the door once more. Johnny, charging across the room after him like a maddened bull, struck him and bowled him bodily aside, into the desk, over its top, to fall on the opposite side in the wreckage of the kerosene lamp that had been sitting on the desk.

Johnny followed him over the desk-top and landed once more on top of him. The man was fighting with a silent desperation now, fighting for his life. Each blow he struck had a sodden, smacking sound because both his fists and Johnny's face were wet with blood. And he was tough. He was wiry and strong and no stranger to this kind of fight.

But he lacked one thing, one thing that Johnny had—anger, righteous indignation and outraged fury. Johnny had these things in quantity. For every blow the stranger struck, Johnny retaliated with another, harder one.

The man was weakening. They rolled across the glass-strewn floor to the window and back again. And at last Johnny felt the man go limp.

He stumbled to his feet and for a long, long time stood there, head hanging, lungs working like a gigantic bellows. His belly still hurt from the kick he had received early in the fight. His nose still bled. His hands were two masses of glass cuts and the pain from the mangled flesh, torn by the gunhammer, was excruciating still.

He glanced toward the door uneasily. It didn't seem logical that the man had come alone but Johnny was relieved that no one else appeared. He was in no condition to fight anyone else right now.

When he could breathe again with some normality, he stopped and grasped the man beneath his shoulders. He dragged him through the door into the cell corridor. He dragged him into one of the cells at the far rear, those with no windows in them.

Weakly, nearly exhausted by the exertion, he sat down on the bunk. He still didn't know what the man had come here to tell him. What he did know was that he had cut down the odds. Instead of being five to one, they were now only four to one.

On the stone floor, the man stirred, and groaned. Johnny stared at him apathetically. It was almost completely dark in here, but there was enough light to see the man's dark-lumped shape lying on the floor. The man groaned again.

Johnny said softly, "You're going to talk, you son-of-a-bitch, or I'm going to kick your head in. You understand what I said?"

The man raised his head groggily. On hands and knees he tried to scramble out the open cell door into the corridor.

Johnny got up, circled him and took a position in front of the door. The man stopped crawling. Johnny said, "You got just one more chance."

The man tried to get up. Johnny kicked him deliberately. He had no real stomach for what he was doing, but he had to know what was in the air. Four drifters and Slade. They added up to real trouble for the town. They added up to more than Slade's personal revenge against two or three individuals.

The man laid still for a long, long time. Johnny said softly, "You may not be able to talk by the time I get through with you. But you'll be able to write if you have to write on the floor with your own damn blood."

The man made it to his hands and knees. Johnny moved to one side and kicked him in the stomach. The man collapsed again.

Twice more the man got to his hands and knees. Twice more Johnny kicked him down. At last the man groaned softly, "All right. All right. To hell with Slade anyway."

"What's going on? What's he planning to do?"

"He's got his wife in a shack down on the edge of town. He told me to tell you the old Montoya place. He figured you'd come down there and he could kill you in front of her."

Johnny felt his fury growing. Slade had Molly. If he'd hurt her . . .

He said harshly, "What else?"

"That's all."

Johnny drew back his foot angrily. The man yelled, "Wait!"

"All right, you son-of-a-bitch! What else?"

"It's the bank. They're going to clean it out, and burn what's left, papers, records and everything. He wants more than the money. He wants to break the town."

Johnny crossed the cell and went out into the corridor. He closed the cell door, locked it and dropped the keys into his pocket. He felt automatically for his gun but his hand encountered only an empty holster.

He returned to the shambles the fight had made of the office and searched around until he found his gun. Crossing the room, he picked up the loaded ten gauge from the floor.

He went to the door and peered outside. There was still a knot of men up in front of the two saloons, but it had thinned out some. Johnny knew he ought to go up there. He ought to alert the townsmen to the danger. They could scatter, arm themselves and be back in ten minutes at the most.

Hesitating, he stood in front of the jail, wiping his bleeding hands on the sides of his pants. He thought of Molly, with Slade. It would please Slade to assert his rights as Molly's husband. Even if he had to do it on the dirty floor of a deserted shack.

He couldn't afford ten minutes. He couldn't afford any time at all. To hell with the bank. Molly was more important now.

Turning, he hurried along the street toward the lower end of town.

The shotgun was slick with blood in his hand. Twice, he shifted it to the other hand and wiped the one it had been in on his trouser leg. Three strangers and Slade. He wondered how many of the strangers were there with Slade.

How had they gotten Molly to town, to the old Montoya place? Probably by telling her he'd been hurt, he thought. Damn them. Damn them!

He turned the corner just short of the railroad station. He followed the tracks for half a block, then turned right again. The old Montoya house loomed up in the darkness ahead.

A soft breeze blew toward him from the creek. He could hear the sound of the water, and the rustling of the cottonwoods.

He stopped and stared at the dilapidated house. He could make out nothing, no shadows, no movements that might have been made by men. There was only one way to do this, he decided. Let them know that he was here. Force them to take the initiative.

He raised the shotgun and let go one barrel at the house. The roar of the gun was deep and sonorous, echoing and re-echoing through the town. The shot rattled against the walls and roof.

Temporarily blinded by the flash, Johnny flung himself to the ground. In the window of the Montoya place a revolver flashed, then again and again. Johnny got up and sprinted up the street, beyond the house, to fall prone again.

The revolver barked twice as he sprinted past the house. He could hear the bullets tearing into the building wall behind him.

But he had learned one thing. He knew with reasonable certainty that only one man was in the house. By staying here an instant more he would find out if any others were waiting for him outside the house.

He held his breathing quiet and reloaded the empty shotgun barrel. The gun made a click as he snapped the action shut.

He crouched there, searching the shadows with his glance. Then, suddenly, he got up and ran directly across the street, weaving and zig-zagging as he ran.

Again the revolver barked. Johnny felt a sharp pain in his right shoulder and realized he had been hit. He flung himself over the sagging fence and rolled to a halt in the high, thick weeds, only a dozen yards from the door.

He heard Slade Teplin yell, "Molly! He's out here! Yell out and tell him who you want to be married to!"

Johnny called softly, "I've got a ten gauge, Slade. Two barrels loaded with buck. And I'm close enough to cut you in two."

There was no answer from the house. Johnny called, "I'm going to stand up. I'm coming in. You shoot, Slade, and I'll have a target to put this buckshot in."

"Molly's here!"

"Is she? All I've got is your word for that."

"Damn you, woman, sing out!"

Johnny heard a cry of pain. Molly was there all right. He would have known her voice anywhere. He froze where he was, knowing he didn't dare spray that flimsy house with buckshot now.

He called, "I'm going to the bank, Slade. Your man spilled everything he knew. If you want to kill me, you'll have to come up there."

He began to crawl forward through the weeds. Slade emptied his gun again, yelling as he did,

"God damn you, deputy, if you go now you'll find Molly dead when you come back!"

Johnny crawled until he reached the corner of the house. He leaped to his feet and ran to a side window.

He had only the briefest glance as he rammed the shotgun through the window, the briefest kind of glance into a pitch-dark room. He saw three squares of light and nothing else. Two windows and a door. He could make them out because of the starlight beyond in the street.

He didn't see Molly; he didn't see anything in the room. But then he saw a shadow silhouetted dimly against the door, a shadow that could only be Slade.

Slade was diving frantically, falling even as Johnny fired the left barrel of the gun. The roar, the flash, filled the room with sound and light. In this light he saw Molly, bound to a chair, and he saw Slade rolling on the ground outside.

He scrambled through the window frantically. At least, he thought fleetingly, he had separated Slade from Molly. He had put himself between the two.

He tripped and fell as he plunged across the room toward the door. He recovered and plunged on. At the doorway he stopped, raised the gun and fired at the dimly seen, running shape.

Slade, halfway across the street, staggered and nearly fell. Then he disappeared behind the building across the street.

Johnny reloaded the gun. He turned, fumbling for his pocket knife. He whispered, "Molly, are you hurt?"

"No. I'm . . ." She was trembling violently and close to hysteria.

Johnny said, "I'm all right, too. Now listen. Will you do what I tell you to?"

"Johnny, please . . ."

His voice turned sharp. "Molly! Listen! It's important that you do exactly what I tell you to."

He finished cutting her loose. Careful not to touch her with his bloody hands, he kissed her lightly on the cheek. She whispered, "I'll do whatever you say, Johnny."

"Good. Leave here by the back door. Head for the creek. When you reach it, follow it south and stay out of sight. At the footbridge, leave it and head for the school. Wait for me there."

"All right." Her voice still trembled on the brink of hysteria. "Be careful, Johnny. Please."

"I will. Now hurry."

He heard the floorboards creak as she left the room, went through the kitchen and out onto the back porch. He heard the rustling of the weeds out back. Then, with a soft sigh of relief, he headed for the door. He'd hit Slade a moment or so before. He'd hit him hard enough to make him stagger and nearly fall. Maybe he'd find him over by that building wall.

He crossed the street cautiously. He reached the building across the street and moved carefully to the corner of it where Slade had disappeared. But Slade was gone.

He headed toward the bank, staying in the alley, walking carefully. He still had four of them to face, but it was better than five. At least Molly was safe. He was in a better position than before. Even if there wasn't much chance that he would win.

Chapter 19

To Slade Teplin, there was nothing quite so terrifying as a shotgun. He had seen what a shotgun could do to a man. He had seen men with their heads literally blown off by a shotgun charge.

He ran along the building wall through the high-grown weeds, limping from a pellet that had penetrated his leg. He cursed softly, savagely to himself.

Nothing had gone right for him since he'd arrived on the train this morning. Almost everything had gone wrong. This town was a goddamn jinx. Or so it seemed. Yet he had to concede that it hadn't all been bad. He'd gotten Barney drunk, and that had been part of his plan. Before he left town tonight he'd loot and burn the bank. The only thing he had failed to do was get that deputy and he'd still have another chance at him.

He turned up the alley toward the bank. He knew this town as well as any of its inhabitants. He'd grown up here.

Russ and Joe had gone after Barney. Del was supposed to be waiting at the back door of the bank. The fourth man, Brothers, had gone to the jail to bring Yoder to the old Montoya house. He didn't know where Brothers was now. Yoder might have killed him—or thrown him in jail.

Del was waiting for him at the back door of the bank. Slade whispered, "How's the street out front? Any people there?"

"What's the matter with you? You're limping."

"Shotgun pellet. Don't worry about it."

"The street's pretty near deserted now. A lot of men came out of the saloons when the ruckus started at the jail and later when you and Yoder shot it out. They've gone back in."

"All right, come on. Russ and Joe ought to be along with Barney pretty soon."

He had told them to bring Barney even if they had to carry him. He wanted more than Barney's keys. He wanted Barney himself. He wanted to leave his father in the bank so the whole town would know how he'd gotten in. Let Barney live that down. Let him try living in a town whose inhabitants blamed him for ruining them.

He walked silently along the passageway between the bank and the building next to it. He reached the street and peered out carefully.

He saw Russ and Joe coming down the street from the direction of Barney's house, supporting him between them. He was drunk, all right, but he was not passed out.

They reached the passageway. Barney's head lolled drunkenly. He said thickly, "So itsh you! I mighta knowed!"

Slade said, "Shut up."

Russ said, "The banker was there with him. Joe rapped him on the head."

"You got Barney's keys?"

"Yeah." Russ handed the keys to him. Slade said, "Wait here out of sight. If he tries to yell, stuff something in his mouth."

He glanced up and down the street. Seeing no one, he went to the door of the bank, inserted the key and opened it. He beckoned and the others came in, dragging Barney along.

Slade said, "You got all the horses?"

"They're tied a couple of doors up the street. In front of the Emporia so they wouldn't draw attention."

"Then let's get busy. Russ, you stay here at the door."

Del and Joe dragged Barney through the waist-high gate and back toward the safe at the rear of the bank, following Slade. Slade knelt in front of it and struck a match.

"You know the combination?" Del asked.

Slade said contemptuously, "Don't have to. They never spin the knob. They turn it right to ten and all I have to do is turn it back until it clicks."

He turned the knob slowly, carefully. He stopped, and swung the safe door open. He glanced around and up. "Got the kerosene?"

"It's outside in that little passageway."

"Get it."

Del left. Slade began to remove canvas money sacks from the safe. He placed them in a small pile beside him on the floor. Then he began to rake papers out. They made a good-sized pile next to the money sacks. Notes, abstracts, mortgages. He laid the bank's record books on top of the pile. Then he gathered up the money sacks.

Barney was mumbling drunkenly, but his words were not understandable. Slade said, "Drag him up front and hit him with your fist. I want him here, but I don't want him to burn to death."

Joe began to drag Barney toward the front of the bank. Slade picked up the money sacks and carried them after him. He handed them to Russ, waiting at the door. Joe's fist, hitting Barney's jaw, made a sharp crack. Barney slumped and Joe laid him down at one side of the door.

Del came back with a can of kerosene. Slade

took it from him and carried it back to the safe. He poured it over the bank's books and papers. He reached in his pocket for a match.

Slade struck the match and flung it on the pile. It caught immediately, blazing up halfway to the ceiling. Drawing his gun he ran for the front door.

A gun began to bark steadily in the street. Del staggered out the door and fell on the boardwalk. Joe was driven back and also fell, twisting and writhing with agony on the floor. Russ, down below window level, shouted furiously, "That fire! It made targets out of us and we can't see a goddamn thing!"

He got up and sprinted out the door, carrying the money sacks. He didn't get ten steps. He doubled, ran another two steps that way, then fell on his face and laid still, the money sacks scattered in front of him.

Slade stared for an instant in unbelief. Only one gun was firing out there and it had momentarily stopped, probably while the shooter reloaded it.

He turned and ran for the rear door of the bank, raging inwardly. He hadn't realized the fire would make targets of everyone inside the bank. God damn this town to hell! God damn that deputy . . . !

The rear door had a padlock on it. Slade fired and the lock sprung open. He snatched it out of the hasp and flung open the door. He plunged blindly into the dark alley and began to run.

When Johnny Yoder reached the rear door of the bank, Slade and his two companions had already gone. Johnny halted for a moment, hesitating. Then he returned the way he had come until he reached another passageway. He ran along it to the street, avoiding tin cans and debris.

He reached the street and without slackening his pace, turned left and headed toward the bank, angling out into the street as he did. On the far side of the street, directly across from the bank, he stopped.

This range was too great for the shotgun, he judged, and laid it aside. He drew his revolver, checked the loads absently, then thumbed the hammer back. If they went out the back door, he would lose them. But he could see that the front door of the bank was open, and he suspected that their horses were among those tied in front of the Emporia. They'd probably come out this way.

He saw a shadow leave the door and enter the passageway. A moment later, the shadow returned and disappeared into the open door of the bank.

The waiting seemed endless. Johnny realized he was foolish for trying to handle this all by himself. But he also knew there wasn't time to alert anyone else now. He had no choice but to handle it himself.

If only it wasn't so dark! If he could only see better, so that when the time for it came, he could shoot.

He waited, his hands shaking noticeably. It was quiet, over there. The only sounds in the street were the muffled sounds of voices in the two saloons. He hoped nothing would bring men crowding out into the street. He didn't want any bystander casualties if it could be helped.

Suddenly the whole front window of the bank lighted up. Johnny could see flame in the rear of the bank, leaping high, nearly to the ceiling. And he could see the men . . . three of them.

He fired instantly. One of the men staggered out the door and crumpled on the walk. Another was driven back into the bank. He also fell and Johnny lost sight of him.

He held his fire momentarily, punching out empties, punching in fresh shells. He saw Slade run toward the front of the bank. He drew a bead but did not squeeze the trigger because Slade ducked down out of sight.

Suddenly another man leaped to his feet and plunged out the door. This one was loaded with canvas money sacks. Johnny followed him with his gun, the sights showing plainly against the reddish light caused by the fire. He fired.

The man seemed to stumble. Crouched, he ran a couple of more steps before he fell. Switching his glance back to the bank door, Johnny saw Slade running toward the rear. Before he could get his sights on the man, Slade disappeared.

Johnny snatched up the shotgun, ramming the revolver into its holster as he did. He sprinted across the street.

Men were pouring out of the the two saloons. Johnny bawled, "The bank! There's a fire in there! Get after it!"

He plunged into the passageway next to the bank, and ran along it recklessly. He reached the alley and skidded to a halt, swinging the shotgun toward the rear door of the bank.

It was open. Slade was gone. He hesitated a moment, glancing up and down the alley. It was almost completely dark, except for the small amount of light shed by the stars. Holding himself completely still, Johnny listened. From his left he heard the scuffing sounds of a man's running feet.

Instantly he turned and plunged after them. He was out of breath, both from running and from excitement, but he realized that he would never have a better chance at Slade than he had right now. Three of Slade's companions were either wounded or dead. Another was in jail. Slade was all alone and furthermore, his chance of forcing Johnny into a duel of speed and accuracy was gone. This was a hunt and while Slade was armed and dangerous, his greatest advantage was gone.

Slade reached the street, briefly visible. Then he plunged out of sight to the right. Johnny followed recklessly, well aware that Slade was probably waiting for him, waiting to fire until he would run out of the alley into the open.

He reached the street and raced out into it, not turning until he reached the middle.

Swinging around, he saw that Slade had stopped. Slade was waiting beside a high board fence, facing Johnny, his gun in his hand.

In that split second, Johnny saw something else. He saw three more men up at the corner of Main and knew instantly who they were. Ward Reeder, and Les and Willy, his hired men.

He flung himself aside, falling, trying to bring the shotgun to bear. Slade's gun spat wickedly and the bullet grazed his thigh, burning like a hot iron.

The light was bad for shooting, but Johnny didn't need light if he could only bring the shotgun to bear before Slade could shoot again. Rolling, he swung it around and thumbed one hammer back.

Up at the corner, three more guns opened up, laying a concentrated fire against the fence. Johnny could hear the bullets tearing through the boards.

Slade hesitated between shooting at Johnny and defending himself against the other three. He hesitated for the smallest part of a second but it was enough. Johnny squeezed the shotgun's trigger and felt it buck against his hands.

Shot rattled against the fence like hail. Slade's
gun fired, but it was pointed at the sky. Johnny
got up and ran toward him, thumbing the second
hammer back. He heard the sounds of other running feet.

He reached Slade, who was motionless on the
ground. He stirred Slade with his boot.

Ward and his two men charged up. Johnny
swung the shotgun. "Easy, damn you. Drop those
guns or I'll cut you in two."

The guns thudded to the ground. Johnny said,
"Ward, you and Les pick him up. Take him down
in front of the bank."

Meekly, Reeder picked up Slade's head and
shoulders. Les picked up his feet. Willy supported
his sagging body in the middle. They shuffled silently toward Main, turned the corner and headed
for the bank.

Johnny felt weak. He felt as though he might be
going to fall. He gritted his teeth and shook his
head savagely against the mounting dizziness in it.

Men were coming toward him. Down in front
of the bank there were forty or fifty men, forming
a bucket brigade, running in and out of the bank.
Slade's companions had been dragged out of the
way and now lay in a neat row, side by side. On
the chest of the middle one were piled the canvas
money sacks.

Followed by half a dozen men, Johnny herded
his prisoners to the bank. He said, "Lay him down.
Ward, you see if he's dead."

They laid Slade down and Ward picked up his
wrist. He turned and looked up at Johnny. "He's
dead. The son-of-a-bitch is dead."

"All right. Head for the jail."

He followed them down the street to the jail. He

herded them in, watched while they threaded through the office wreckage and meekly entered the other cell at the far rear. He fumbled in his pocket until he found the key. He locked the door.

Only now did he break the shotgun and take the live shell out. He returned to the office, closing the door behind him.

A crowd of more than a dozen men were waiting in front of the jail. Johnny went out, leaving the shotgun behind. The wounds in his thigh and shoulder had begun to burn fiercely.

He said, "A couple of you stay here and watch this place. Get hold of Ern Powers and have him come down and clean things up."

Limping slightly, he turned and walked slowly toward the bank. He was thinking of Molly, thinking that nothing now stood in their way. He was heading toward the school when he suddenly saw her pass the bank, holding up her skirt so that she wouldn't trip, running like a frightened deer.

She reached him and flung herself into his arms, sobbing hysterically. "You're hurt!"

"Nothing serious." He held her close, feeling her trembling, feeling her softness and her warmth. He bent his head and kissed her, and felt the wetness of tears on her soft, smooth cheek.

The specter of death, which had hovered all day over Cottonwood Springs, was gone. Tomorrow it would be the same sleepy, pleasant town it had been yesterday. Johnny said, "Let's walk over to Doc's and see how Arch is getting along."

Limping, with Molly supporting him, he crossed the street and headed for Doc Allen's house. He was thinking that they weren't going to wait any longer. They were going to get married tomorrow. The waiting was at an end.

Lewis B. Patten wrote more than ninety Western novels in thirty years and three of them won Golden Spur Awards from the Western Writers of America and the author himself the Golden Saddleman Award. Indeed, this points up the most remarkable aspect of his work: not that there is so much of it, but that so much of it is so fine. Patten was born in Denver, Colorado, and served in the U.S. Navy from 1933-1937. He was educated at the University of Denver during the war years and became an auditor for the Colorado Department of Revenue during the 1940s. It was in this period that he began writing Western fiction that was from the beginning fresh and unique and revealed Patten's lifelong concern with the sociological and psychological effects of group psychology on the frontier. He became a professional writer at the time of his first novel, *Massacre At White River* (1952). The dominant theme in much of his fiction is the notion of justice and its opposite, injustice. In his first novel it has to do with exploitation of the Ute Indians, but as he matured as a writer he explored this theme with significant and poignant detail in small towns throughout the early West. Crimes, such as rape or lynching, were often at the center of his stories. When the values embodied in these small towns are examined closely, they are found to be wanting. Conformity is always easier than taking a stand. Yet, in Patten's view of the American West, there is usually a man or a woman who refuses to conform. Among his finest titles, always a difficult choice, surely are *A Killing At Kiowa* (1972), *Ride A Crooked Trail* (1976), and his many fine contributions to Doubleday's Double D series, including *Villa's Rifles* (1977), *The Law In Cottonwood* (1978), and *Death Rides A Black Horse* (1978).

WILL COOK

NELSON NYE

Two Classic Westerns
In One Rip-Roaring Volume!

"His Westerns are in a class by themselves!"
—*Los Angeles Times*

Trigger Talk. With a draw as fast as lightning and a face as mean as hell, Misery Jones is hired as a ramrod the minute he rides into Galeyville. Soon everyone will learn the hard way that not even the most ruthless crook uses Misery Jones and lives to see another sunrise.

And in the same action-packed volume...
The Wolf That Rode. After six long years on the trail, Brett Fasken returns home and finds himself battling his own sister for control of a cattle empire. But Brett believes that blood is thicker than water, and with bullets flying he is determined to prove his point.
_3479-4 $4.50

Shotgun Law. When the toughest owlhooter in the territory kidnaps a wealthy banker's daughter, lawman Girt Sasabe has to ride straight back into a rattler's nest where he almost lost his life once before.

And in the same low-priced volume...
Hellbound for Ballarat. Everyone in the Arizona Territory wants to make life miserable for Jack McCann, and he has no choice but to let his Peacemaker Colt prove that a man can only be pushed so far....
_3397-6 $4.50

LEISURE BOOKS
ATTN: Order Department
276 5th Avenue, New York, NY 10001

Please add $1.50 for shipping and handling for the first book and $.35 for each book thereafter. PA., N.Y.S. and N.Y.C. residents, please add appropriate sales tax. No cash, stamps, or C.O.D.s. All orders shipped within 6 weeks via postal service book rate. Canadian orders require $2.00 extra postage and must be paid in U.S. dollars through a U.S. banking facility.

Name _____
Address _____
City _____ State _____ Zip _____
I have enclosed $_____in payment for the checked book(s).
Payment <u>must</u> accompany all orders.□ Please send a free catalog.